The Hoffmann Plague

The Hoffmann Plague

By

Tony Littlejohns

THE HOFFMANN PLAGUE

ISBN-13: 9781090131768

First published in paperback in Great Britain 2019

Dedicated to the memory of my dear mother, Marjorie.

With huge thanks to my family and friends for their enthusiasm and help; who spurred me on through the difficult times in the writing and editing process.

One

He wondered if he might see the woman again, or if she was even still alive. If she'd survived this long there was a good chance that she would be, or so he hoped. That had been nearly three weeks ago; she'd been the first living person he'd seen in over two months.

The glare from the morning sun off the sea and the wet sand hurt his eyes, exacerbating his headache and making it difficult to concentrate. He turned around and headed west instead, which made it a little easier. He should have brought his sunglasses with him but he'd forgotten them and kicked himself. There were many things he needed to be more mindful of, and should be doing or planning; he knew that.

It was a beautiful April morning but he didn't appreciate it as he would have done in happier times. He was hungry; the reason for the headache. His last meal the evening before had been a meagre affair of red lentils cooked with a stock cube, some dried onion flakes and half a tin of carrots. *Nothing to write home about*, he thought. *Not that there's any home left to write to... Or postal service to deliver it!* He smiled grimly to himself.

There was no fresh produce left anywhere, not for a long while, so he was living on tinned, dried and pickled food. He'd been eking-out his meals in recent weeks, but his stock of food in the flat was getting low; hence that morning's forage for shellfish along the beach. He still had a small supply of canned meats and other high calorie food, but wanted to save them for desperate times ahead. He knew they wouldn't last much longer if he relied solely on them – as he had been doing until now - which was why he'd been going out to forage. Desperate times weren't far off, seemingly.

He'd already found some small mussels and limpets amongst the rocks, enough for some much-needed protein with his other food. He was hoping to find some razor clams, which would be a great bonus. So far, though, he was unsuccessful, and the reason he was concentrating so hard to find their holes at low-tide. He knew there were razor clams in the area as he'd seen their shells occasionally when walking on the beach, though he'd never tried collecting them before. Most of Bexhill beach was pebbles and shingle, but at low tide large areas of sand became exposed, especially on the eastern side.

He thought again of the woman; who she was, where she lived and how she'd survived. When he'd seen her before, he was just coming out of the sea after going down to bathe for the first time in weeks. She had been less than a hundred yards away down the beach and hadn't seen him while he was in the water. When he'd emerged from the sea he had seen her to his left and had shouted and waved. He'd been naked, of course, and she had turned and run away beyond the promenade. By the time he'd put on his clothes and boots and ran after her, she was long gone. He'd sat on the promenade and cried with frustration, grief and loneliness, cursing and swearing. The pandemic had killed his family, his friends and, seemingly, almost the entire population of Bexhill.

From the corner of his eye he saw a spurt of water from a small hole in the sand. Amazed, he moved quickly but softly over to it. He poured some salt into the hole from the small tub he'd brought with him and waited, then saw the top of a razor-clam's shell appear. He grabbed hold of it between his fingers but didn't pull; just held on. After a while the clam relinquished its grip and he was able to pull it out. He laughed for the first time in months and put it in his bucket. In the next ten minutes he got two more, which was enough for a meal with the other shellfish, so he headed home feeling rather pleased with himself.

Walking back along Sackville Road, there were uncollected refuse bags torn open by seagulls, their contents scattered across the pavement and road. Cars still lined the street, a couple of them parked at odd angles- abandoned by their owners in haste. In one car on the other side of the road a corpse sat rotting in the driver's seat. The town was utterly silent apart from the screeching of gulls.

Thankfully, there had been relatively few corpses on the streets. He'd seen some- often smelling them beforehand- and given them a wide berth, but the week before he'd come across a body on the beach that had made him vomit. It was a homeless guy with a Big Issue bag next to him, in the advanced stages of decomposition. There wasn't much left of him after the seagulls and other creatures had had their fill.

He looked at each shop, making a mental note of which ones might be worth breaking into to see if he could find anything useful. The fishing tackle shop was a priority. With a rod and reel and some lures or beach-casting tackle he could start fishing. *Wow! Fresh fish would be great.* He'd been motiveless for long enough and it was time to get organised.

He stopped walking as he thought of something: Bexhill Sea Angling Club by Galley Hill, at the promenade's eastern end. There were many boats on the beach there: with a small boat and a pair of oars he could get out on the sea, which would increase his chances of catching fish dramatically. He felt sure he'd find a pair of oars there somewhere. He didn't know anything about boats, but how hard could it be? He carried on walking, lost in thoughts of his new plans and feeling energised by them.

If he'd turned around at that moment he might have seen a person silhouetted on the skyline. From the rooftop of the De La Warr Heights building the woman was watching him through a pair of binoculars. Crossing over into Terminus Road he noticed a window open in a house, and as he walked past he could smell decomposing bodies. He put his head down and walked faster.

Back home, he cooked the shellfish on his Coleman

camping stove, which ran on petrol. Over the last week he'd managed to get enough fuel for his needs from the cars in his road; he didn't want to use his own stock until he had to. There had been no electricity or gas for weeks; or was it months? He'd lost track of time. He still had a few jars of pickled eggs, so he sliced one and added it to the pan, along with some gherkins and half a tin of potatoes. While it simmered he made himself a coffee. He had many packets of coffee beans, which he ground on a manual grinder; it was a personal luxury he would sorely miss when it was gone.

He ate the food with relish and it seemed like a feast to him with the fresh shellfish. Afterwards, he sat down on the old sofa in the lounge and rolled a cigarette to have with his coffee. He knew that he needed to be more proactive, and to start planning ahead and doing more to ensure his survival, including raiding all the surrounding houses to see what food he could find. He couldn't bring himself to do it yet as all the houses would have rotting corpses in them. He'd existed in a scared, depressed and apathetic state for too long, despite his initial foresight and good sense in stockpiling food and supplies when it had started around four months ago.

As he sat there he made notes, writing down ideas as they came to him. Clearly, he wasn't the only person to have survived; there was the woman he'd seen and he assumed there must be others around, too. He wasn't sure how he felt about that: on the one hand, company would be good and they could help each other; on the other hand, in the lawless state that now existed, it would be survival of the fittest and Darwinian law would rule. If he had things that others needed, they might fight or kill to get them. He'd never been a violent man and the thought worried him, but he realised he needed to prepare himself, both mentally and physically, for such eventualities. He'd worked in engineering, landscaping and handyman-type jobs most of his life so had a good collection of tools. He looked through them and found his gardening machete and scabbard, a claw hammer and a sheath knife. He also picked out a small wrecking bar, which would be useful for breaking into places, and resolved to carry them with him whenever he went out.

By then it was mid-morning and he sat there thinking about what to do next. His apathy and depression over the last month or two was fading, and his brain was working overtime to come up with new plans and what to do for the best. He felt the first stirrings of positivity since the world had turned to hell several months ago, and that he might, actually, be able to survive. And then the thought hit him: *Survive for what? There's nothing left!* Oh, well; he'd just do what he could to muddle through and stay alive, and see what transpired. His favourite verse from *A Shropshire Lad* by A.E. Housman came to him, which he thought was rather apt under the circumstances:

Into my heart an air that kills
*   From yon far country blows:*
What are those blue remembered hills,
*   What spires, what farms are those?*

That is the land of lost content,
*   I see it shining plain,*
The happy highways where I went
*   And cannot come again.*

He'd always had a love of survival and bushcraft programmes and books, so he knew the Rule of Threes: under normal or favourable conditions a human being could survive for three minutes without air, three days without water and three weeks without food.

He hadn't given it any thought after waking from the coma, but he wondered now how he'd survived for six days without fluids. He kind of knew that in a coma a person's body more or less shut down and its needs were minimal, so he guessed that was it. He liked knowing things, though, and had the electricity and the internet still been working, he would have Googled it. Had he done so, he would have found documented cases of earthquake victims surviving after being buried for eight days or more.

Well, air definitely wasn't a problem and water shouldn't

be an issue for him, he thought. Egerton Park was only a five minute walk away, where there was an ornamental lake. He knew that as long as he followed basic survival rules of filtering and/or boiling the water, there should be no problem. Added to that he still had several packs of bottled water, along with whatever rainwater he could collect, but he wanted to save his supplies for difficult times and make use of what was around him. He studied an Ordnance Survey map; if it came to it and he was desperate there was a stream just beyond Sidley, about one-and-a-half miles away, and there was also a large network of ancient waterways in the marshland beyond Cooden; two to three miles away. He didn't relish the thought of having to walk there for water and carrying it back on a regular basis: a litre of water weighed one kilo.

His car still worked and he had run it several times to charge the battery, but he knew he mustn't rely on it, and should only use it in emergencies or when he needed to make longer trips. He had a thought: his bicycle was in good shape and he had spare parts for it, along with puncture-proof tyres. There was also a bike shop close-by where he could get spares. If he got some paniers and a rack for it he was sure he could adapt them for carrying water containers and other things. Okay, then: he needed to go to Halfords on the Ravenside Retail Park two miles away, to see what he could find. Water was his highest priority and he wanted to cover all eventualities, so wrote it down at the top of his list.

Food was, seemingly, a more difficult issue than water. He could raid all the houses in the area to find tinned produce, but that wasn't a good long-term solution, and he shuddered at the thought of going into all those houses filled with decomposing corpses. He needed fresh food, and apart from needing it he craved it. He'd always been a keen cook and hated using convenience food and tinned produce. He needed protein, fat, carbohydrates, fresh fruit and vegetables. He was fairly confident about catching fish from the sea. He wrote on his list to visit the angling shop in Sackville Road and the sea angling club by Galley Hill. He could also lay snares for rabbits, birds and other animals if he needed to, he imagined.

There were plenty of green spaces around Bexhill, as well as the railway line, so he was pretty sure that finding rabbits wouldn't be an issue.

Vegetables and carbohydrate staples were going to be more difficult to source. He knew there was an abundance of fruit trees in the area, so apples, pears and even cherries wouldn't be hard to gather; although it would take time to find suitable locations and they would only be available for a short time each year. He added it to his list. He thought about vegetables, then glanced down to the floor and saw the stack of books lying there. During that first busy week of stockpiling supplies and equipment, he'd gone to several bookshops in Bexhill and Hastings and bought books on subjects that he knew little about, and which he thought might be useful for the future. There were books on growing fruit and vegetables, farming, survival, domestic skills such as repairing and making clothes, along with other essential craftwork books.

Looking at those books, he realised he couldn't stay in his flat for much longer and needed to find somewhere else to live if he was to survive. His flat didn't have a chimney, so he couldn't light a fire for warmth or for cooking indoors. After the gas and electricity had failed he had been very cold and had put several more blankets on his bed. He needed somewhere with an open fire or, preferably, a log-burning stove, and a good-sized garden where he could grow vegetables, fruits and herbs. His small courtyard was paved over and had no soil areas for growing things.

He felt this was a priority and resolved to start looking for somewhere suitable in the coming days. He looked out the window and also at his watch: there were still eight or nine hours of daylight left, so he decided to walk to the retail park and then get his bike fitted with a rack and paniers. That would make getting about much easier and quicker- not that time was an issue- and would mean he could roam further during daylight hours when he needed to.

He made ready to go out, strapping the machete and knife to his belt. He put the hammer and the small wrecking bar in his rucksack, along with a water bottle, a torch and a packet of flapjack. He donned his coat and hat and left the flat. He decided to walk along the sea road and over Galley Hill to get to the retail park; that way he could stop by the angling club and check out boats and oars, etc. It was a slightly longer walk, but far more pleasant than the main road and he needed to visit the angling club anyway.

Walking down Sackville and past the angling shop, he looked at the metal grille over the door, but saw that the windows were unprotected, so he could smash the glass to get in when he needed to. It made him think, though, that he might need something more than just a wrecking bar to break into other places, so he decided to visit B&Q while he was at the retail park and get some bolt cutters. They would be a big and heavy item to carry around, but with a pair he could cut off padlocks when he needed to.

As he turned from Sackville into Marina, the woman watched him from her apartment. She'd come home only ten minutes earlier from a foraging trip and was glad she hadn't been a bit later and met him; at least not yet. She wasn't sure if she was ready for that, or how she felt. She'd seen him a few times over the last month and he probably lived fairly close by. He seemed to be coping and surviving, like her, and there might be items or knowledge they could trade. Despite being a strong and determined woman, though, she was wary and still a little scared of meeting any male survivors.

A few months earlier, when there were still some people on the streets, she'd been attacked in an alley by a man who had tried to force himself on her. He'd clearly been infected and she knew that was how she had contracted the plague, even though she'd been wearing a mask. She'd managed to fight him off and run away by kneeing him in the crotch and slashing his face with her keys, but it had shaken her terribly. Her symptoms had started within a few days and she had slipped into a coma, but had woken up after five days, weak and dehydrated.

Obviously, she didn't know anything about the man-in-the-hat (as she called him) or his situation, but she hadn't been nearly as prepared as he had been. She had stored some provisions in her apartment, but the majority of her food had been obtained in the weeks following her recovery. She had broken into the apartment opposite hers, which she knew to be empty as the owners had gone to London three months before. They hadn't returned, so she assumed they must be dead, and had used their apartment as a storage area for everything that she collected. Where she had been organised, though, was in water collection. She'd gained access to the building's roof and had many containers there collecting rainwater. She had also been cooking up there on a barbeque, always after dark and when the weather allowed, but didn't have a shelter there, which irked her. She thought she would need to find somewhere else to live very soon.

Two

Back on the seafront, the man had stopped first at Bexhill Sailing Club to examine the boats on the beach there to see if they could be of use to him. He didn't know the technical names, but they were small sailing dinghies of various sizes. The cables on the masts twanged and sang in the breeze. Some had no masts and were small enough for his needs, but none appeared to have rowlocks fitted for oars, though he felt sure he could improvise something. He jotted some things down in his notebook: he never went anywhere without it, as it was important to write down locations of things he saw that he intended to go back to, or ideas that came to him.

Now, he was kneeling by the beach huts on De La Warr Parade, looking at a clump of plants growing from the pebbles. It looked like a large sort of cabbage, but more open. He'd always seen them along the coast above the high-tide mark, but hadn't paid much attention to them in the past. He figured it was time to start paying attention to lots of plants that he came across. There were many varieties growing along that stretch of coastline that he'd often noticed; some of them with succulent stems and leaves. He needed to find out which were edible as they could be an important source of vitamins, minerals and carbohydrates. He decided to cut some samples on his way back and try to identify them from his books.

At the angling club a bit further on, he didn't have much trouble breaking in with his wrecking bar and hammer. As he opened the door he recoiled in shock; there was a badly decomposed corpse slumped on a chair. He withdrew and tied a bandana around his nose and mouth before going back in, but at least he didn't vomit this time. He assumed that since he'd had the disease and recovered he was now immune to it, and he also knew that bacteria couldn't survive in the open for long, so it would be okay to touch things. He wondered if the guy had locked himself in there to avoid infecting others, or maybe he'd just had nowhere else to go.

A quick search revealed some useful items. He found two pairs of oars leaning against the wall; they were far too cumbersome to carry back once he had his bike rack and paniers, but at least he knew they were there and could come back another time. There were a couple of lockers containing fishing rods, reels and tackle- fab! There was also a cupboard filled with old junk that people had chucked in there, thinking it might be useful one day; the sort of thing every bloke had in his garage. Rummaging through it, he found a pair of hefty brass rowlocks, complete with nuts and washers attached. That was great news; with his hand-brace he could drill holes in the gunwale of a suitable boat and attach the rowlocks, enabling him to fit the oars and get out on the sea whenever it was calm enough. On a cork notice-board he saw a book of tide-tables for the year, which he took and put it in his rucksack. That would be useful for knowing the times of high and low tides, and could save him wasted trips. It occurred to him that in future years- if he survived that long- he wouldn't have that information; obviously, no one was going to be printing tide-tables again in the foreseeable future. He assumed there must be a formula or something for calculating tide-times, so he wrote in his notebook to look into it from the books he had.

He was pleased with his findings and made ready to leave. He looked at the body and hesitated; he didn't like leaving it there for when he came back, so he looked around for a way of disposing of it. There was a shovel, a broom, a mop and other cleaning supplies in another cupboard, so he went outside and cut off a tarp from a boat. He laid it on the floor in front of the corpse and hesitated, cringing. 'Sorry mate, but you've got to go. Rest in peace.' He used the shovel to tilt the chair up until the body fell off and landed on the tarp, then dragged it outside and left it ten yards from the building. There was an old paraffin lamp hanging by the door so he took it down, went back to the body and poured the contents over it. He lit a piece of rag and tossed it on top; the fuel caught immediately and he turned his back and walked away.

He walked up Galley Hill, stopping at the top. It wasn't much of a hill, but it was the highest point on the coast between Hastings to the east and Eastbourne to the west, having good views along the coastline. He gazed towards Hastings, which was much bigger than Bexhill, and wondered how many had survived there. He thought that, surely, there must be more people left alive here in Bexhill than just him and the woman he'd seen? There was a low concrete plinth there, with an inlaid metal surface inscribed in the form of a compass, pointing to various places in the world and their distances. He looked down and read some of them: New York- USA- 3,508 miles; Gibraltar- 1,056 miles; Rome- Italy- 841 miles; Sydney- Australia- 10,556 miles. He wondered what was happening in those places, and if it was the same there.

As he moved to leave, a memory came back to him of happier times: his brother and him, sitting in his car eating fish and chips on that spot, just over a year before. He burst into tears and sat down on a bench, overcome with grief for his family; cursing what had happened and cursing that he should be left alive in this God-forsaken place. He looked at the cliff-edge and thought, just for a second, of throwing himself off it, but the logical part of his brain told him it was too low, and he'd probably just break his legs and lie there in agony for three days before dying. He smiled grimly to himself, pulled himself together and got up from the bench.

He walked down the hill and then turned left through the underpass for the railway and onwards into the retail park. As he passed Marks and Spencer a smile crossed his face; *maybe I'll pop in there on the way back and get some of their nice ready-meals, to save cooking tonight!* The car park was fairly empty, with a few cars parked randomly at odd angles, including a burnt-out wreck. As he passed it he saw the charred remains of two corpses inside.

He reached B&Q and the doors were open, so he walked in. It was dim inside so he turned on his torch and played it around. It was a mess; stuff was strewn everywhere, from crazed people panic-buying or looting. He walked to where the tools were and found some bolt cutters, took a pair and went to leave.

As he approached the checkouts, a man stepped out from the aisle to his left and barred his way, giving him the fright of his life. He was perhaps forty, but it was hard to tell; he was in a terrible state and none too steady on his feet.

'Give me the bag,' he said. There was a knife in his right hand, the blade glinting in the light from the doors.

He dropped the bolt cutters from his left hand and pulled out his machete with his right. 'Tough shit- mine's bigger than yours!' he replied, with far more conviction than he felt.

The guy paused for a second as if trying to take it all in, then spun around and ran for the exit. In his haste and poor state of health, he tripped and fell headlong into the plate glass. It didn't shatter as it was safety glass, but his head snapped back at an acute angle and he crumpled to the floor, his neck broken. He lay there twitching for a few seconds, then became still.

He picked up his bolt cutters, stepped carefully around the guy and out the door. As he walked away he cursed himself for being so careless; just because he hadn't seen other people didn't mean there weren't some around. Also, there wasn't anything in the rucksack worth dying for and he could have handed it over. *The hell with that!* he thought. *No one's going to take what's mine.* The fact that he'd nearly had to use the machete on a person shook him up, and then a line from some old film came to mind: *Get busy living, or get busy dying.*

He hurried onwards to Halfords, keeping the bolt cutters in his left hand rather than putting them in his rucksack. They were heavy and could slow him down in a fight-or-flight situation, and that way he could just drop them if need be. He looked at Tesco and wondered about going in for a look around, but now wasn't the time; he just wanted to get home.

Halfords' doors were open and he walked in with more caution than he'd shown at B&Q. He went upstairs to the bike section and soon found what he wanted; a universal bike rack and paniers to fit it. Downstairs in the camping section he found some collapsible water containers in various sizes, which would be perfect for putting inside the paniers. As he was leaving he noticed some small petrol and diesel-powered generators on a shelf; the kind people used with caravans, etc. That made him think; *electricity- light- heat*. He paused for a second, took his notebook out of his coat pocket and scrawled *genny!* Putting the notebook back in his pocket, he found a screwed-up £10 note in there. As he passed the checkouts he put the note by the till in payment for his goods and smiled to himself.

He was happy to get back on the coastal path and stopped briefly at the bottom of Galley Hill, just long enough for a drink of water and a few flapjacks. Instead of going back over the hill, he skirted it and walked along the beach path at its foot, looking at plants. He collected a few likely-looking samples, and some more on the way back along the seafront.

Feeling pleased to get home, he made some coffee and a late lunch. For the remaining afternoon he worked on fitting the rack and paniers to his bike and adapting it to his needs. He made a wooden platform, as large as was practical, and fixed it securely to the rack with bolts, brackets and wingnuts. He incorporated mounting points for bungees or straps so he could tie things securely onto it, and was pleased with the end result. A small trailer would be of more use probably, but he thought it unlikely that he would find one; maybe that was something to build at a later time.

That evening after his supper, he sipped a whisky while reading by gas-lamp through books on plants and survival, and was delighted to discover that two of the specimens he'd collected were edible, which was great news. He was unsure about the others; their pictures were ambiguous, so he decided to leave them for now. Unless he could make a positive identification he couldn't risk eating them and maybe getting sick. The large cabbage-like plant he identified as sea kale, and found that the whole plant was edible, including the roots, which could even be eaten raw. The other was sea beet, the leaves of which could be eaten like spinach, and also the root. Interestingly, he found that sea beet was the genetic ancestor of modern beetroot, sugar beet, chards and spinach; all of which had been grown from selective cultivation over the years. Looking through the books, he was also reminded that common plants such as dandelion leaves and nettles were also abundant, nutrient-rich and easily gathered.

On the rooftop of her building, the woman stood by the parapet wrapped in a blanket, staring out over the sea after eating a rather cheerless meal. She longed for fresh food and living conditions that were more suitable. Her flat was secure enough, and the rooftop had good views along the coast, but climbing the stairs laden with things was becoming a burden. Added to which, she needed somewhere suitable for lighting fires for cooking and warmth, and also for growing food. She decided it was time to look for somewhere else to live.

She had seen the smoke earlier in the day, when the man had burnt the corpse at the angling club, and had wondered what it meant. Although the man-in-the-hat had been going that way, she had no way of knowing whether it was anything to do with him. She went to bed worrying about things and couldn't sleep.

He put the books down and sat there fretting for a while. The encounter with the man in B&Q had shaken him and he wondered if that would be the norm with any other survivors he might meet. He felt scared and anxious about his situation, as was to be expected. He had been wondering for weeks whether he should make trips into Hastings and Eastbourne, to see what the situation was in those towns and if there were others he could make contact with. From TV and radio broadcasts before the services had failed, things were likely to be the same as Bexhill; with the rest of the UK probably the same, too. He didn't feel inclined to go to those places, risking potentially dangerous encounters, armed only with a machete and a hammer. Guns of some sort would be useful and comforting to have, but he had no idea where he might find any. He felt rather pleased with his day for the first time in ages and went to bed happy with his achievements, though he lay awake for a while thinking about things, unable to shut down.

Three

The shock, the horror, and the speed at which it had happened had been difficult enough to deal with, but on top of that he'd had the deaths of his mother, his brother and sister and their families, too. As for the rest of his extended family, he had no idea if any were still alive up north. The pandemic had spread in no time and society, communications and infrastructure had broken down rapidly. In a relatively short space of time after the first cases, the utilities were becoming intermittent as staff levels fell due to the disease. All systems were automated, of course, and some lasted longer than others, but eventually they had all collapsed, and far sooner than he would have thought possible.

The first cases had appeared in Glasgow and had spread at an alarming rate. It was thought to have come from eastern Asia or maybe Africa, though they didn't know for sure. At first it was reported, incorrectly, as a new strain of influenza; some type of avian flu maybe. They soon discovered they were wrong and that it was a bacterium rather than a virus. A German doctor named Dirk Hoffmann, who worked at Glasgow's Queen Elizabeth University Hospital, was the first to discover what the disease was.

It was a new strain of pneumonic plague; a mutation of the *Yersinia pestis* bacterium that had caused the Black Death of the fourteenth century, with continued outbreaks for around four hundred years. Most people didn't know that, far from being extinct, plague bacteria had produced small, irregular outbreaks of bubonic or pneumonic plague around the world throughout the twentieth century and into the twenty-first, even in North America. If caught early enough it could usually be treated with antibiotics, which drastically reduced the likelihood of death. Pneumonic plague was the rarer of the two, and usually developed as a result of bubonic plague. Antibiotics and modern standards of hygiene had stopped those small outbreaks from spreading and becoming epidemics or pandemics. A few new strains had been discovered in recent years, though, that showed resistance to some antibiotics.

This new variant, however, was pneumonic, with no initial bubonic stage. It started in the respiratory system and was airborne from the outset, spreading rapidly. It was a mutation unlike anything they'd seen before and proved completely resistant to all available antibiotics. The medical community was at a complete loss to know what to do about it; though, of course, they didn't make that public. The mortality rate was virtually a hundred percent and death occurred within thirty-six to forty-eight hours after symptoms developed. Those who looked at first like they might fight it and survive soon slipped into a coma, from which few recovered. There had been much written in recent years about the growing ineffectiveness of antibiotics, and how so many bacteria were becoming resistant to them.

Information got leaked to the press and by the second week one of the tabloids had labelled it "The Hoffmann Plague". Before they fully realised the implications and seriousness there were lurid headlines like "HOFFMANN PLAGUE: THE NEW BLACK DEATH!", "PLAGUE IN THE UK!", and other similar things.

Initially they estimated its R_0 ("R- nought") figure- the basic reproductive number- to be between one-point-three and two-point-five, using previous models for pneumonic plague; for which there wasn't a huge amount of data. But infections and deaths were occurring so quickly in so many different locations that it was obviously much higher than that. They soon had to revise their figure and estimated that it was higher than smallpox, which was six or seven, but it was difficult to give an accurate number. That meant that a contagious person was likely to infect another six or seven people- or even more if their estimate was low. It depended on several factors; how strong people were, their movements and contact with others, and their ability to get around before they succumbed to the disease.

What was strange was that the incubation period seemed to vary from person to person before the main symptoms developed; anywhere between two and seven days. That meant that a person could be contagious and not realise they'd contracted it. People touch their faces many times an hour, then transfer those bacteria onto any surface they touch, ready for the next person to pick up the bacteria and become infected. People would also be sneezing and coughing from colds and other viruses as well as from the plague, spreading the bacteria to all in their vicinity.

It soon became obvious that this wasn't just scaremongering or sensationalist reporting by the tabloids about bird flu or Ebola that had occurred in recent years. This was real; it was happening here and now in the UK and was spreading incredibly quickly around the country. He'd spoken to a friend in Scotland towards the end of the second week, who had told him the emergency services and hospitals were already struggling to deal with the number of cases and all the bodies. By then, many hundreds of deaths had also occurred in London, Manchester, Birmingham, Leeds and Sheffield, with thousands more showing symptoms.

At the end of that phone call he'd made a decision: he knew that Bexhill-on-Sea wasn't exactly a thriving metropolis or a major hub for nationwide travel, but it was only two hours' drive from London and the plague would surely reach there soon. He'd sat down and made a list of all the things he might need for survival in the short and long-term, and withdrew all his money from the bank. Over the next week he made numerous visits to all the supermarkets, food stores, pharmacies, hardware and camping shops in the area. He bought as much canned and dried food as he could fit in his car at each visit, along with all the bottled water he could get, earning him some strange looks from people at the supermarkets. He didn't care; he'd rather be safe than sorry. He also couldn't believe that more people weren't doing the same as him yet. He had the conversation with his brother, but his opinion was that they'd soon develop a vaccine and it would blow over.

He bought extra torches and large quantities of batteries, all the candles that he could find, and many water filters and purification tablets. He bought extra containers to store rainwater in- dark ones to prohibit the growth of mould and fungus- and jerrycans of petrol for his camping stove and lantern, along with tins of butane gas and a couple of camping stoves. He even remembered to get another bow saw and extra blades for cutting wood. He thought that gas and electricity might not last long, so he had to have means of cooking and boiling water. The chimenea on the patio of his small courtyard would serve as a usable barbeque and he could easily rig up a tarp for protection from the rain. He already had enough general tools to get by. As an afterthought he also bought a large quantity of disposable plates, bowls and cutlery as he didn't want to waste precious water for washing dishes. By the end of that week his flat was almost full; the long hallway was stacked floor-to-ceiling with everything he'd bought. He went over his lists again to see if he'd forgotten anything.

In the following weeks he'd stayed indoors the whole time, having made sure all the windows and doors were closed properly and locked. And then it came. Gradually at first, but rapidly increasing in frequency, he heard the effects of the plague as it spread like wildfire through the town, causing terror and chaos: muted somewhat by his double-glazed windows but frighteningly apparent. Frequently he would hear the chilling screams of people in pain or anguish from nearby houses and sometimes out in the streets. The cries of children were hardest to bear and he was often in tears. Police and ambulance sirens were a constant occurrence. Often there was the sound of people running down the road, of shouting, or of breaking glass. Once there was the frantic ringing of his doorbell and banging on his door; he didn't dare to go to the door, but stayed in the kitchen with the rolling-pin in his hand.

All he could do was try to close his ears to it all and sit there terrified. He felt horrified at the suffering going on around him, and also a bit guilty: unable to help anyone or do anything. It seemed to go on for ever before gradually becoming quieter in the following weeks.

Occasionally he thought of things he'd neglected to get, which he wrote down, thinking to go out when it might be safer. He had a stock of disposable dust masks to put on for when he did need to go out; that had been the medical advice that was broadcast on the news. The problem, though, was that the masks soon became damp from exhalation, especially in the cold weather, quickly rendering them ineffective. The medical broadcasts didn't mention this, but there was nothing else they could do. The general advice was to stay indoors and have no interaction with other people, but how could that work in the real world?

He had trouble remembering the exact timescale now, but his last phone-call had been with his brother, who'd lived just over a mile away in Sidley, on the northern edge of Bexhill. Dave had rung him in tears to say that his son and daughter had died in Eastbourne, and that he and his wife now had the symptoms as well. His brother had implored him to keep away and to stay indoors, even though he had wanted to go round to see him. Their mother and sister in London had already died two weeks earlier and he was still reeling from the shock and grief of that, along with the deaths of his nieces on his sister's side. It had been a relatively short conversation, filled with tears. There wasn't much to be said, really. What can you say to someone who will be dead in a day or two, apart from that you love them? He'd come off the phone and broken down, sobbing uncontrollably and cursing. He couldn't even go to see his brother one last time to hug him and tell him that he loved him.

When he'd stopped crying, he turned on the TV to see if there was any news. Most stations were already off-air. The

BBC still had some broadcasts, but even they were breaking down rapidly. There was some pre-recorded newsreel footage of looting, mayhem and terror all around the country, and then the broadcasts had stopped abruptly. He'd tried the local radio stations and it was the same with them.

Although Bexhill Hospital didn't have an A&E unit it was swamped nonetheless. Hundreds died there before it shut down; overwhelmed by the number of infected and many of the staff dead or dying. Most people died at home, either by themselves or with loved-ones, and many were too weak to go out again once the infection took hold. A certain percentage, inevitably, avoided the plague's clutches due to being housebound by old age, illness or disability. Once the utilities had failed, though, and unable to fend for themselves effectively, they soon perished from a combination of dehydration, starvation and weakness. The vast majority were just completely caught out by the rapid escalation of events, the high rate of infection and the incredulity of it all, with not enough time to prepare adequately.

Ten days or so after his last conversation with his brother he had become sick himself. The streets had become eerily quiet, with hardly any sounds of people or vehicles. The only regular sounds were the plaintive cries of seagulls, as always, and he'd thought it should be safe to go out wearing a mask. The streets were empty, and the two people he saw while on his way to the supermarket were in a great hurry and looked desperate. Aldi was deserted; the doors were wedged open and the aisles strewn with trampled produce from people panic-buying. There were no staff members anywhere in the shop and most shelves were bare. He managed to find a few bottles of cooking oil and some other items, including- miraculously-two bottles of whisky lying on their sides on the top shelf. He then walked down to Sainsbury's and it was the same story there. He found a few useful items, along with some tobacco and cigarettes, and put them in his rucksack. As he was leaving, a woman turned the corner and ran into him, dislodging his mask. She was red in the face and breathing heavily, her hair matted with sweat. She didn't stop or say anything, but ran off, coughing.

By evening of the third day he was sweating profusely and sneezing. He had a terrible headache, was aching all over and his breathing was laboured. It felt like someone was kneeling on his chest. He coughed in the bathroom and saw blood on the wall, and then vomited. *Shit!* This was it. He didn't know what to do and panicked, before realising there was nothing he could do, so he got a bottle and a glass from the drinks cupboard and sank down onto the sofa in despair. He had an air of resignation to it as there was no one he could go to for help or to talk with about it. He picked up his mobile phone and tried some numbers but there was an automated message every time saying it had not been possible to connect his call and to try again later. He didn't even bother cooking an evening meal, but drank a lot of whisky and spent the evening thinking back over his forty-two years, frequently in tears. He remembered things he'd done, friends and family, women he'd loved but never got to be with. Around midnight he passed out and collapsed on the sofa.

When he'd awoken it was light, and he assumed it was the following day. He was amazed that he'd woken at all and was still alive. He tried to get up, but was so weak that he fell back down again. His head hurt and there was vomit on the floor next to the sofa, mixed with blood. He struggled to the bathroom and was sick again, then went into the kitchen, leaning heavily on the surfaces for support. He was desperately thirsty and opened the taps, but only a trickle came out. He opened a bottle of water and drank a pint straight down, then made up two sachets of Dioralyte rehydration powder and drank them. After that he made some strong coffee with lots of sugar and some salt. He had terrible hunger pangs, but didn't feel like eating anything yet.

He sat on the stool and looked at his watch: he didn't know why- what did it matter what the time was? He noticed the date window, but couldn't focus properly to read it, so he found his reading glasses and looked again. He did a classic double-take. *What the hell?* It was six days since he'd passed out, as far as he could recall. He'd lost six whole days! No wonder he was weak. He guessed he'd slipped into some kind of coma... He had no idea what had happened, but he was alive. He didn't know whether he had a natural immunity to the plague bacterium, or whether he just had a great immune system that had fought the disease. They'd said the mortality rate was approaching a hundred percent, which meant there was a small chance that a few people might survive.

It took over a month to regain his health properly, during which he ate as healthily as his food supply allowed, resting frequently and also taking vitamin supplements. As he felt vigour returning he exercised to regain strength. Meanwhile, in turn, all services and utilities had failed completely. There was no sound at all from the surrounding streets.

When he felt strong enough he worked outside in his small courtyard. His cordless drill's batteries still had full charge, so he rigged-up a shelter to enable him to cook outside with wood that he would collect, thus saving valuable fuel. The containers he'd put out to collect rainwater were full, so he put lids on them. In the third week of his recuperation he found an envelope stuck through his letterbox that he'd missed. It was a letter from the guy upstairs, saying that he and his partner were infected and were going to his mum's to spend their remaining time with her. There was a key to their house and he told him to help himself to anything useful. He ended with the lines *Ain't life a bitch! Good luck.* Curious, he went upstairs and let himself in. He found that Paul had also stockpiled supplies and, importantly, there were multiple packs of bottled water, plus numerous boxes of dried and canned food.

For the next few weeks he became aimless and depressed, unwilling and scared to go out and face things; but eventually he'd snapped out of it and ventured out as his food supply diminished.

Four

The next morning, during breakfast, he was undecided on his next course of action. He wanted to go back to the angling club to pick up the oars and fishing tackle, then find a suitable boat for fixing the rowlocks to so he could get out on the sea to fish. While that would be good start to becoming self-sufficient in terms of fresh food- especially protein- he realised that he needed to get *properly* organised. There was no point fetching and arranging things for his future survival without first finding himself somewhere more suitable to live. There was no more room in the flat, anyway.

He also wanted to try out his bike with the new paniers, as he needed to start collecting water instead of using up any more of his precious bottled supply. But the same consideration applied to that, too: until he found a new home he didn't really need the bike for water collection, as he could walk to Egerton Park for it, which wouldn't be much of a problem. He could forage for shellfish for protein while he was still in his flat, and maybe fish from the beach if he needed to. And, with his new-found knowledge from the plants he'd identified, he could have fresh greens. Therefore, the most important thing, in his mind, was to find a new place to live first, and then start organising things for his future. These were important concepts for survival, and who would have thought that, in the twenty-first century, he would have to think of such things?

He decided to begin searching at the western end of Bexhill towards Cooden, which was just over a mile away. He knew there were many large properties in that area, with large gardens to match. He thought of South Cliff; the houses there backed onto the promenade and beach and had direct access from the gardens. While they would be nice and convenient, he also thought they might not be conducive to growing vegetables and other produce, being at the mercy of strong sea winds that battered the coast regularly. He thought maybe he should be looking one or two roads back from the coast, to give some protection from the winds. He wanted a south-facing property, if possible, to get maximum sunlight for growing things, a large garage to use as a workshop, a conservatory that would double as a greenhouse for growing tomatoes and other plants, and open fires or wood-burning stoves.

He decided to go by bike; the area he intended to cover wasn't that big, but getting there and back would be far quicker by bike. He packed what he would need in his rucksack, including food, water and a few tools. The bolt-cutters he strapped onto the bike rack; they might prove useful, even though they were heavy.

It proved to be a slow process and far more time-consuming than he had imagined, as well as being very harrowing. A house might look suitable from the front, but when he looked round the back he was disappointed. And sometimes it was difficult to gain access to the back gardens, involving climbing walls, fences or gates- often to be disappointed. Some places were suitable in some respects but not in others. He looked through windows and broke into several places- in some cases the doors were unlocked- to see if there were open fires or log-burners and to get a general feel for the suitability of a property. Death was present almost everywhere he went; people alone, couples, entire families- sometimes in bedrooms and sometimes all together in the lounge. In one house he found the bodies of a couple lying on the floor in the lounge in front of a cross on the wall.

By late afternoon he was frustrated, exhausted and sick to

his stomach by the stench of death. He hadn't found anywhere that ticked all the boxes on his list in the roads one or two rows back from the sea. He thought, though, that he had the answer to something that had been bothering him: why weren't there more dogs around? He had wondered about it and found it strange; he'd imagined there would be packs of them roaming the streets. It seemed, though, that most had died indoors with their owners; whether from the plague or from dehydration he didn't know. He had heard some dogs barking over the last months, but relatively few.

He did, however, have one lucky find: he gained entry to one house he thought might be suitable, only to find that the rear garden was mostly paved over. *Damn!* In the master bedroom, a couple rotted in their bed; on the bedside table were an empty bottle of whisky and two empty pill bottles. They'd obviously taken a less painful death, rather than waiting for the plague to finish them. *Good for you. Rest in peace.* In the next bedroom, which had been turned into a study, there was a gun case on the wall containing three shotguns, all twelve-bores: one side by side and two over and unders. He smiled to himself; *Yeah, baby, come to Papa!* On the walls were various photographs of the owner at clay pigeon shooting competitions, at clubs, and out in the countryside shooting game. He used the bolt cutters to cut off the lock and removed the guns.

Underneath was a locked cupboard that he broke into, containing boxes of cartridges in varying shot sizes. He knew from his old fishing days about sizes of lead shot- the higher the number, the smaller the size, and it was the same for shotgun cartridges. The boxes varied from No.9 down to No.4, which was fairly large shot. Each lead ball in the cartridge was over 3mm diameter and they would pack a hell of a punch. There was also a boxed kit for gun maintenance and cleaning, service manuals and two shoulder bags for carrying them. On a bookshelf were a number of books on shotguns, shooting and hunting. He knew nothing about guns apart from what he'd seen in films or read in novels, so he picked two that covered gun maintenance, shooting and hunting techniques and put them in his rucksack, along with all the boxes of cartridges and the cleaning kit; it was bloody heavy!

Outside, he strapped the shotguns to the bike rack and cycled home slowly due to the extra weight; a little frustrated at not finding a suitable house, but at the same time elated with finding the guns. He hoped he'd never have to use them on people, but was aware of the possibility with the way things were now, and he felt a lot safer having them for self-defence as well as for hunting.

That evening he drank a bottle of red wine and listened to music on his MP3 player; he had two solar-powered chargers for various sizes of batteries and also for his MP3. The track *Sovereign Light Café* by *Keane* was very nostalgic as he'd often gone to that café on the seafront before the plague, and it brought back memories of how life used to be; he got upset and turned off the music.

He felt lonely: he'd always been comfortable with his own company and had lived alone since his divorce many years earlier, but the new status quo changed everything. Before, if he'd felt the need to be among people, he had only to visit one of the umpteen cafes in town; that ability was now gone, obviously. Bexhill had become a ghost-town and walking the silent streets was creepy and infinitely depressing. The prospect of never again hearing a child's laughter brought tears to his eyes whenever he thought of it.

He wrote a few lines in his diary; he'd tried keeping a log of events since it had started, but had often lapsed. On a whim, he scrolled back through the diary to a point where the pandemic had begun; he couldn't remember exact dates, so just chose the beginning of the year. He decided that there should be a new calendar system of year-classification to replace B.C. and A.D. as they seemed somehow irrelevant now. On the 31st December he wrote B.P. (Before Plague), and on the 1st January he wrote A.P. (After Plague, or even Anno Peste; year of the plague). So he was now living in the year 1AP; if the human race ever recovered, he wondered if his system would be adopted and gave a little smile. He then read sections from the shooting books and practised stripping the guns down for cleaning and maintenance before going to bed.

The next morning was wet and cold. He awoke early, feeling strangely refreshed and clear-headed, and sat on the stool in the kitchen with a cup of coffee and a cigarette, remembering his last thought before he'd fallen asleep. He now had three shotguns: the two over and under guns he decided to leave as they were as they were easier to aim when hunting. The side-by-side, however, he decided to cut down and turn into a sawn-off: that way, it would be about two feet shorter and would fit into his rucksack, making it far easier to carry around and turning it into an effective self-defence weapon, should he need it. It didn't take too long to cut the barrels off with his hacksaw, and he filed and sanded the ends smooth to remove all burrs. He felt like a gangster in some East-End film getting ready to rob a bank and smiled!

Afterwards, he took it down to the beach, along with one of the other shotguns, and fired off some practice shots at signs and at one of the groynes to get a feel for handling the guns. Satisfied, he went back to prepare some food.

During breakfast he decided to look at the houses along South Cliff after all, despite his previous thought that they would be unsuitable as they backed onto the seafront and would be too windy. He packed everything he might need into his rucksack, including the sawn-off shotgun, loaded with No.4 shot, and spare cartridges in his pockets and rucksack. He decided to walk this time as he hated cycling in the rain, so he left the bolt-cutters behind as they would be cumbersome.

He walked along Terminus Road, looking up at the sky as he headed west. The rain clouds were hastening eastwards and the sky ahead was getting brighter and clearer, which was good news. He turned left after the surgery and into the pedestrian underpass for the railway. In the middle of the tunnel, against the wall, was a corpse that had been picked at by birds or foxes: it had no face left but was wearing a distinctive coat with a patch that looked familiar. He realised it was a guy he'd known from the pub across the road. They hadn't been friends as such, but he was shocked nonetheless as they had often talked together over a pint. He shook his head and carried on in a sombre mood, exiting the underpass and then across Wickham Avenue and down Brockley Road to West Parade, coming out at the Sovereign Light Café on the seafront. Heading west on the promenade, he looked at the beach as he went, noting patches of sea kale and sea beet that he would soon start harvesting. He reached South Cliff and began searching for his new home.

He stuck mainly to the houses on the southern side, as the houses opposite would all have north-facing gardens, which he didn't want, though he did try some. It was the same as yesterday's search, with death nearly everywhere he looked. In the houses that didn't contain corpses, he guessed that they had either been taken into hospital, to die there, or had left to be with loved-ones. Maybe some were second homes or weekend retreats for rich people who had lived elsewhere during the week for their jobs.

He had the same problems as the day before in having to climb fences, walls and gates to gain access to the rear of the properties. At one house that he broke into to take a closer look, an alarm bell went off, shattering the silence; it obviously had a battery-operated back-up system. He stepped back, looked up and saw the alarm box with its flashing light high up on the wall. He pulled out the shotgun, took aim and blew the alarm box off the wall, then removed the spent cartridge and loaded a fresh one; the house, unfortunately, proved unsuitable.

Half a mile away the woman heard the alarm followed by the shotgun report. Without the noises of modern urban life sound carried a long way in the silence that now surrounded the town. Earlier on, from her apartment, she'd also heard some distant reports that sounded like a shotgun, as the man had practised on the beach. She fingered the hammer that was attached to her belt by a loop, feeling inadequately armed; the thought of meeting a male survivor armed with a shotgun was worrying to her and she resolved to be extra-vigilant while walking around. She, too, was scouting for somewhere new to live and, like the man, had so far been unsuccessful. She carried on with her search, keeping to the rear gardens and avoiding the road as much as possible.

The man was standing outside another house looking at a long-wheelbase Land Rover pickup truck on the drive, with a metal roof over the load-bed. He thought it would be a useful vehicle to have, and much more practical than his hatchback. He could use it for moving all his stuff into the new property when he found it, and it had off-road capability, too, which could be handy. It even had a winch with metal cable on the front. He decided to return later and break into the house to find the keys, then "borrow" it for an indeterminate period of time!

By lunchtime he thought he had found the perfect property. There was a bungalow that looked promising, so he climbed over a high wall with a gate, on the building's right side, and walked down to the back. The wall enclosed the whole garden and at the rear was a sturdy gate, which led to a flight of steps descending maybe twenty feet to the promenade and the beach. The wall would give good protection from the sea winds and, being a bungalow, roof and gutter maintenance would be easier, too. The mature garden contained several small fruit trees along the western side towards the rear; maybe apple, pear or cherry- he didn't know which. There were herbaceous borders, a vegetable patch and a good-sized pond with a solar-powered water pump that was still working. He could see koi carp swimming lazily around; *Lunch,* he thought!

The property had a large conservatory across the back and the windows were all of conventional type, rather than double-glazed, making it easier for him to gain access through a rear window. He was becoming rather a dab-hand at breaking-and-entering and grinned, shaking his head!

Once inside, he got a little excited and his pulse quickened. The large kitchen, which opened into the conservatory and looked onto the garden, had a Rayburn solid-fuel cooker that burned coal or wood. There was an alcove beside it for storing fuel, containing smokeless coal and seasoned logs. He had a suspicion that it might also provide hot water and maybe even central heating. An inglenook fireplace alongside it contained a wood-burning stove. There was no way the kitchen would need both for heating, so he guessed that the log-burner had been there first as it looked older, and they'd fitted the Rayburn later but hadn't wanted to get rid of the stove; good news for him.

There was no smell of death in the place and as he walked around the property he found it to be empty. There was another wood-burning stove in the lounge with a decorative fire-screen in front of it, for when the doors were open. On the chimney-breast were photos of a nice-looking middle-aged couple, taken in several countries around the world; there were no photos of children that might have been theirs, so he guessed they had been childless. Maybe they had been among the first victims and had died in hospital. In the hall was a traditional telephone table and chair, in which he found spare keys to the doors, windows and garage. The property had three bedrooms and a study, along with the kitchen, bathroom and a large lounge. He opened the front door and went outside; the driveway had parking for at least two or three cars and there was a double-garage to the left side, which could also be accessed from a door in the hallway. He thought it would suit his needs perfectly and felt relieved at finding it. He went into the garage through the hallway door and found a well-equipped workshop; there were work-benches with metal and wood-working vices, tools arranged neatly on racks on the walls, and a pair of small gas bottles with welding equipment. *Perfect!*

Five

The rain had passed and the sky was now clearer, with periods of sunshine between the clouds. He went out to the garden and ate his lunch on the patio; some homemade drop-scones, with tinned fish and curried lentils. While he ate, his head was filled with plans for his new home. He loved the fact that he would have direct access to the beach for washing, fishing and foraging. He would dig up the lawn and create more vegetable-growing areas. The pond would be filled continually by rain and was also aerated by the solar-powered pump, so he would have fresh water that he could filter or boil for drinking; there was also a rain-water butt collecting run-off from the roof that he could use.

He thought about digging a pit and building a shelter around it for a composting toilet, but then realised that he wouldn't need to: being by the sea, he could fetch buckets of sea water for flushing the toilet. That was another problem with being in his flat- having to use collected rainwater for flushing the loo, and it wasn't pleasant when there hadn't been much rain for a while.

He was eager to start moving his possessions from his flat into this place, so he packed his things away and left by the front door. He walked back down the road to where the Land Rover was and climbed over the fence to look around the property. He managed to gain access through a rear window and the smell of decomposition hit him immediately. He held his breath and hurried through the house; in the hall, on hooks next to the telephone, he found two sets of keys to the Land Rover. He left by the front door, unlocked the vehicle and climbed into the cab. It took a while to start as it had been sitting for a few months and the battery was running down fast as he turned it over. He thought it wouldn't make it, but then it fired into life; the fuel gauge showed nearly a full tank of diesel.

He drove a circuitous route home to give it a bit of a run and then left it idling outside his flat for half an hour to charge the battery. He decided to move the less important items first and thought about what to take. He didn't need to take things like bedding and towels as there were plenty at the new place, and the same for cutlery and cooking equipment; though he did pack his favourite items, which he'd had for years and was attached to. He managed to make two trips in the afternoon and would finish the job the following day.

There was still some light remaining before sundown, so he put a hip flask filled with brandy in his coat pocket, slung the sawn-off over his shoulder and walked down Sackville to the seafront. There was a fabulous sunset and he sat on a bench on the promenade listening to the waves, sipping brandy and watching the sun go down beyond Beachy Head. His head was filled with thoughts of life in his new home. It wasn't going to be easy, he knew that full-well: growing his own food and foraging to be self-sufficient would be incredibly hard and he would be at the mercy of nature and the elements- just as the whole of mankind had been since time immemorial.

He would be living a life that combined the hunter-gatherer existence of the old world and the settled, farming existence of the new: two completely different stages of human evolution spanning countless millennia. In his favour was the fact that he was by the sea, and therefore had a bountiful source of protein in the form of fish and shellfish. At least he wouldn't have to go out hunting animals with a bow and arrow! He had the shotguns and a good supply of ammunition, but what about when that ran out? That was something for the future, so he took out his notebook and wrote it down; maybe there were gunsmiths in the area, or farms that he could visit. He felt sure that farmers would have shotguns and ammo.

The biggest problem, as he saw it, was that modern people, individually, lacked the necessary skills to survive in a world without the technologies and service industries that we had relied on. Our ancient ancestors, by comparison, had passed down their knowledge from generation to generation and people had grown up with the necessary knowledge and skills to survive: from hunting and finding food, to making clothes, building shelters... the list was endless. He was pretty sure, though, that he wouldn't have to resort to making animal-skin clothing and footwear!

The vast majority of people in the UK had led an easy life in terms of survival- relatively speaking. Their food had come from supermarkets, with all kinds of fruits and vegetables available all year from all around the world. Their meat had come pre-packed and shrink-wrapped in trays, ready to cook. Having to grow their own food, or to hunt, kill and skin it before being able to eat was something unknown to most people because of modern life and civilisation. He knew he had a lot to learn and it was daunting, but he felt he should be able to do it.

The woman saw him from her apartment as he walked down beside the De La Warr Pavilion to the promenade. She'd had a gruesome and unsuccessful day looking for a new home and had walked home feeling sick and frustrated. She got her binoculars and watched him sitting there on a bench overlooking the beach, looking at the sunset and drinking from what looked like a hip flask. In her mind men fell into two groups; either good or bad, basically. And to her way of thinking, bad men weren't usually the type to sit by a beach at sunset watching the sun go down: not very rational, maybe, but it had usually worked for her. She had the feeling he was lonely and part of her wanted to go down and talk to him, but the other part was still too cautious to do so. She felt lonely herself: lonely, scared and worried about the future. As the light faded, she saw him get up and walk back along Sackville.

By evening of the following day, Sunday, he had completed his move into the bungalow. He'd left behind many things that seemed to have no place in his future life, such as financial records and the like, but had taken with him personal possessions and photographs of family and friends; all now dead, he assumed. He went upstairs to Paul's place and gathered the remaining supplies of tinned food, dried produce and bottled water, took a last look at his flat then locked the door and drove off. If there was anything he needed to go back for, it wasn't far away. He parked the Land Rover in the bungalow's garage and felt worn out, so he had a quick meal and went to bed not long after. It felt strange not being in his own bed, but it was nice to hear the sea and he fell asleep to the sound of waves crashing on the beach.

Over the next week he organised his new home; familiarising himself with where things were and arranging it more to his liking. He started on some improvements and collected buckets of sea water for the bathroom to flush the toilet.

On Monday morning he looked into using the Rayburn cooker and found it could provide hot water, which pleased him greatly. It appeared to be a gravity-fed system via a hot-water cylinder in the loft, and thus down to the taps. Heating the radiators, however, relied on an electric pump, so that was unavailable. And then it hit him: *There's no bloody water supply, you idiot!* He felt foolish, as he'd wasted half an hour reading the manual for it; there was no way to fill the cylinder and header tank with a continual supply of water. He wasted a bit more time dreaming up an elaborate system for diverting rain-water from the gutters into the header tank, but soon realised it was futile and gave up. The thought of having hot water had got the better of him.

At least he would have the Rayburn for cooking on, and its two ovens would be great for baking and roasting. The wood-burning stoves in the kitchen and lounge would heat the place adequately, he thought; especially if all the doors in the place were left open. In colder months he had the option of sleeping in the lounge rather than the bedroom, which would have no heating of its own.

He made two useful discoveries on that first day; the first being a small wine cellar under the study floor. He hadn't paid much attention to the study, seeing it only as a useful storage area; but while carrying a box in he nearly tripped on the corner of a rug, which rucked-up, revealing a trap-door. Lifting it, he found a short flight of wooden steps into a space about two metres square, lined with bottle racks. He could see by the available light that it was a wine cellar, but got his torch for a better look and climbed down into it. It wasn't deep enough to stand up straight and he had to crouch. There were only a dozen bottles in there; ten reds and two whites, for which he was grateful, and it was a useful thing to have.

The second discovery was in the kitchen; he found various jars of homemade jams, pickles and chutneys in the larder that would be a welcome addition to his diet. There were also various items of preserving equipment in another cupboard, including more preserving jars in various sizes.

That set in motion a train of thought he hadn't addressed before: *How am I going to keep fresh food?* Without a fridge or freezer, food- and especially meat- would soon spoil. He'd been so accustomed, like everyone, to buying food and storing it in the fridge or freezer in his old life. In recent months he'd been living off tinned and dried food and hadn't given thought to the problems of storing fresh produce. He'd been excited recently at the prospect of catching fish and foraging coastal vegetables, but how was he going to store and preserve them?

Until he grew vegetables that he could harvest on a daily basis- which would take a long time- he would have to forage for fresh food. What if he caught four fish, maybe, or shot several rabbits; how would he keep them for future meals? If he picked surplus vegetables or fruits, the same applied. And what about bread? He had a good store of flour and he might be able to get more from the supermarkets if there was any left, but what of the future? Any remaining stocks of flour would surely go off within a year, and he had neither the space nor the knowledge to grow and harvest such things- or the equipment to do so.

It wouldn't be practicable or efficient to go out every day to catch a fish or shoot a rabbit and pick some vegetables for his next meal; he would probably burn more calories doing so than he could replace with each meal, which would be stupid! And what if the weather precluded going fishing for a while- would he go hungry? He needed to think about not just his next meal, but start planning for days, weeks and months ahead if he was to survive! When locally-available fruit and vegetables were abundant from summer to autumn he would need to gather as many as possible and have ways of storing or preserving them for the lean winter months, when little would be available.

His initial jubilance disappeared. He realised he'd been naïve before, in thinking that everything would be okay just because he had a nice house with a garden and would soon be out on the sea catching fish and picking or growing vegetables. The reality of his situation and the practicalities necessary for self-sufficiency and survival dawned on him, and he felt suddenly daunted by what would be involved and the tasks ahead. Furthermore, he was on his own! How would he manage to do it all by himself? And if he got injured or became sick and couldn't go out to fish or to forage, what would he do?

As the enormity of it all came crashing down on him he had a panic attack. He poured a large brandy, rolled a cigarette with shaking hands then went outside to sit at the patio table; he felt scared and overwhelmed and his heart was thumping. After several minutes he started to calm down as the logical and practical parts of his brain kicked-in with possible solutions.

Mankind had survived for millennia before electricity, fridges or freezers: those inventions were a mere blink of the eye relative to our existence. There were numerous ways of storing and preserving food; he had a grasp of the basics from his general knowledge and love of food and cooking. He felt that with further research from his books, and with practice, he could master it. He had a book on preserving by Oded

Schwartz somewhere in his belongings, which he hadn't looked at for a long time: years before, he'd intended to do some preserving but had never got around to it.

He knew that meat and fish could be preserved by air-drying, like jerky or biltong; by salting or smoking; or by a combination of all three methods. It could be potted, like pâté, rillettes or confit; where the meat was cooked slowly in fat until tender and then put into dishes or jars and sealed with more fat on top, he seemed to remember. Fish, in particular, could be pickled in vinegar, like rollmops. Fruit and vegetables could be preserved in various ways; using salt, sugar, vinegar, oil or alcohol. They could be salted and preserved in brine by lacto-fermentation, such as sauerkraut; turned into jams and chutneys; pickled in vinegar; stored in oil; air-dried (mainly fruit, he thought); or a combination of these methods. He knew the principles and would need to do more research.

Many fruits and vegetables would also keep in their natural state for far longer than people thought, if they were stored in the correct way. Most people had been accustomed to putting these foods in the fridge, or in a basket in a cupboard, often wrapped in plastic bags; consequently, food would go off quickly due to bruising, condensation or lack of air-flow. If they were hung up, or wrapped in soft, breathable material to prevent bruising in a cool, well-ventilated area, then most foods would keep well for several weeks, or months in some cases.

From his childhood he remembered his mother wrapping apples and pears- and maybe carrots and other vegetables-individually in newspaper and storing them in wooden or polystyrene boxes in the garage all through autumn and winter. She would also hang up bunches of onions tied together, or placed in old pairs of nylon tights. He thought the wine cellar should have a cool, fairly constant temperature all year-round, and with minor modifications could be turned into an excellent larder.

He made some coffee then fetched his notebook and wrote down some ideas, followed by the materials he would need and a list of places where he might find them. He needed to visit builders' merchants; there were a couple close to his flat that should have the things he wanted. If not, he would have to try B&Q and Wickes on the retail park- he planned to go there anyway to visit Tesco to see what was left. He needed to go to Sainsbury's as well; he wanted to get as much salt, sugar, vinegar and oil as he could for preserving food, and while there he would visit Warburtons, the small garden and pet supplies shop nearby. He put a few tools into the Land Rover and the sawn-off into his rucksack then reversed from the garage, closing it after him. *Right- time to go shopping!*

His first visit was to the two builders' merchants in Beeching Road, which were close to each other. He managed to break into them with some difficulty, collected what he wanted then carried it all back to the vehicle. He got two galvanised steel dustbins, a large rain-water butt, lengths of guttering and drainpipe with fittings, sheets of thick corrugated plastic, a roll of sturdy wire mesh and various lengths and sizes of treated timber. He also collected various items of hardware such as brackets, steel rebar, screws, hooks, etc. Between the two places he found everything he thought he would need; if there were extra fittings or other small things he needed, he could always cycle back another time.

He was about to drive off when he had an idea; the batteries for his drill at home wouldn't last long and he had no way to recharge them. He made two more trips to both places and collected several cordless power tools: a sabre saw, a jigsaw, a circular saw, a more powerful drill than he had, and an angle grinder. He chose tools of the same make so the batteries would be inter-changeable, plus a few extra batteries. He *could* do the work using hand tools, but it would be a lot quicker and easier with power tools. Once the batteries were spent he would just have to throw them away.

Before going to Sainsbury's he decided to drive to the retail park and have a look in Tesco's to see what was left there, so he headed off up Beeching Road to the traffic lights and turned onto King Offa Way. He was there in a few minutes and parked by the entrance. Climbing from the cab, he slung the sawn-off over his shoulder and walked into the store, listening. The place was a mess, like the other stores he'd been in, and there was a faint smell of decayed fruit and vegetables from produce trampled on the floor. As he walked past the tills towards the second aisle he heard a squeaking noise that sounded familiar and then a man appeared suddenly out of aisle three, pushing a trolley laden with goods. He was in his mid-thirties probably and had a shotgun on his shoulder. There was a tense moment of surprise and indecisiveness from both men, and then both started reaching for their shotguns.

'Hold on!' said Jamie, sharply.

The guy stopped, hesitating, then Jamie lifted his hands, palm outwards in a peace gesture.

'No need for either of us to get hurt,' he said, his heart pounding.

The man looked nervous and unfriendly. 'Keep away from me,' he said, glaring at him. 'I don't want trouble, but stay away; you hear?'

'Okay, but I'm not sick. My name's Jamie. Where are you from?'

'None of your business, and I don't care what your name is.'

'But there's no-one left! We might be able to help each other, surely?'

'I don't need your help. I've got a family to look after and we're doing okay. Walk away and come back after I've gone: that way we won't have any trouble.'

'Bloody hell! This is stupid; can't you see that? Everyone's dead! We could help each other.'

'I don't care! Just leave me alone and piss off, mate, otherwise there'll be trouble!'

Jamie shook his head incredulously. 'Okay, pal, have it your own way.'

He backed away a few steps then turned and walked away, glancing over his shoulder at the man to keep an eye on him. He left the store, got back in the truck and pulled away. Just then, a Nissan 4x4 drove up behind him. In the mirror he saw a woman get out and look at him, then go to meet the man coming out of the store with his trolley. He drove away;

shaking his head at what he thought was utter stupidity.

His next stop was Sainsbury's; he hadn't been there since he'd caught the plague months before and had a sense of déjà vu. The encounter with the man was still on his mind as he walked around and it had upset him. He went along the aisles with a trolley and found some things that others hadn't thought to buy or loot. Most people had concentrated on the fresh produce first, followed by the tinned and dried food. He found lots of vinegar, salt, sugar and vegetable oil, and jars of pickling spices and herbs- things he hadn't thought to look for on his last visit. On a whim, he thought he'd have a look in the warehouse behind the shopping area to see if anything was left in there. The doors were locked, so he went out to the truck and got a large wrecking-bar; bigger than the one he usually carried in his pack.

He managed to force the doors and stepped inside. *Oh my God!* It was like Aladdin's Cave. The shelves and racks were by no means full, but there were still loads of products everywhere he looked. He shone his torch around and had a quick walk along the aisles, noting where things were. He thought they probably hadn't had the time or the staff to put everything out in the store before the shit had hit the fan. He went back for his trolley and loaded cases of salt, oil, sugar and vinegar into it, along with a case of baked beans and some boxes of pancetta: he figured that as the meat was cured and vacuum-packed it should keep well without refrigerating. He also took a case of single-malt whisky and two cases of cheap vodka. The whisky was for sipping and the vodka was for preserving things like soft fruits; and after the fruit was eaten he would have nice fruit-flavoured vodka to drink!

He thought that would do for now, so he left and loaded the truck; knowing that all of this was here, he would return again soon. He didn't need to go to Tesco's on the retail park now, but wondered if he might find a similar situation there, with a warehouse full of goods. Before leaving, he walked through the short alley to the garden and pet supplies shop on the street front. The window was smashed and the door open, so he went in and looked at the selection of seeds, taking several packets of all the common vegetables, fruits, herbs and salads. Salads would be a real boon as they were quick to grow and were "cut-and-come-again", so would provide a huge crop from each plant, well into the winter. He also picked up several bags of potting compost and a few bags of compressed wood cat litter.

He drove home feeling pleased with his trip. Back at the bungalow he reversed into the garage, then closed the door and unloaded some things, but the rest could wait until tomorrow. He'd had enough for one day as it was now late afternoon and he was hungry. He decided to get the wood-burner going in the fireplace and cook on that, rather than using up his gas or petrol on the camping stoves. His thoughts on the Rayburn were that he should use it only during the coldest months, or when he needed to bake or roast food at other times, as it would probably use a lot of fuel to heat it. During the winter it would be great for cooking and would also heat the kitchen and much of the house. While the stove heated up he opened a pack of pancetta and prepared other stuff to make a risotto.

He went out to the patio, filled a glass from the water butt and held it up to the light; it looked pretty clear but he decided to filter it. He didn't think it would be suitable to drink without boiling or treating first as it had been standing for some time and could contain harmful bacteria. He drew off some more, poured it into his water filter and let it drip through. He got the key to the padlock on the back gate and a pair of scissors then walked through the garden to the rear. Unlocking the gate, he walked down a few steps and looked around; just a few yards away was a patch of sea beet so he cut a handful of outer leaves and went back to the house. He felt ridiculously excited at the prospect of fresh greens for the first time in months and smiled!

When the stove was hot enough he cooked his risotto on it, along with the sea beet, and it was the best meal he'd had in a long time. The kitchen and conservatory were now warm and cosy, lit by a couple of flickering candles, so after his meal he poured a large single malt whisky and sat on the sofa in the conservatory. He drew plans and made notes for the construction projects he had in mind, which he would begin the next day.

After a couple of hours he went to bed, feeling the happiest he had felt in months, despite his breakdown that morning and the encounter with the man. There was so much to do and to learn, but he had made positive steps today. He was a bit more realistic about what would be involved in self-sufficiency and the difficulties it posed, and tomorrow would start putting his ideas into action.

Six

Over the next three days he worked solidly on his projects and the weather was favourable to him; overcast and chilly, but at least the rain held off, which was all that mattered. He started early every day and worked until dusk, eager to get things finished. He was conscious that it was spring and that he needed to sow vegetables and fruits soon if he was to see any results by summer, so he worked with a will. Once these initial projects were finished he would work on the garden.

His first task was to build a covered porch area outside the back door, between the conservatory and the garden wall. He needed an area protected from rain where he could air-dry and smoke meats, work on things, or just sit outside without getting wet. The space was nearly five metres wide and four metres deep.

Five metres was a long span of wood, so he decided to put in a central support: he broke a hole through the patio and drove in a metal fence—post spike to hold an upright member. He constructed a framework using pressure-treated timber that would resist rotting, fixing it securely to the conservatory, the brickwork of the house, the upright post and the garden wall. For the roof he used the corrugated clear plastic panels he'd got from the builders' merchants. It began below the existing roofline and guttering, sloping down at the same angle as the conservatory roof. Along the front edge he fitted new guttering, which went into a drainpipe, which in turn fed into the new water-butt. It was awkward work on his own and he had to improvise some props held in the jaws of his portable workbench to allow him to fix the framework in place.

His secondary aim with the new porch was to create a source of drinking water that wouldn't need filtering or treating before being potable, which would be used up quickly, rather than standing for a long time. The existing water-butt took all the run-off from the roof, which was covered in seagull droppings and other organic matter, and needed filtering and then treating or boiling before being drinkable. The way he had constructed it, the water being collected in the new water-butt would be rainfall that had only come into contact with the new plastic roofing and guttering. He knew it wasn't ideal; the seagulls could still poop on the new roof, but there was no way around that. He figured that at least the plastic was clear and he could see when it needed cleaning. The water flow into the butt could be diverted by means of a simple valve, for maintenance purposes. A thought crossed his mind and he chuckled: *What the hell! I survived the plague, so what's a little seagull crap in my water?* Overall, he was pleased with the result; it maybe wasn't the most elegant thing, but it was functional and sturdy.

The next task was to make two home-smokers from the galvanised steel rubbish bins. At this point he was working almost blind. His books contained no detailed instructions on how one could be built; only references. He knew that the purpose of smoking was not to cook the meat, as such, but to semi-dry it; and the act of smoking prevented microbial growth in the meat, increasing its useful life and improving its flavour. But smoked meat still had to be used fairly quickly, he thought. That wasn't quite what he wanted, though: he needed to be able to dry meats to preserve them for long periods; or maybe a combination of both.

He remembered watching a Ray Mears programme the previous year, showing how Native American peoples would air-dry, or "jerk", their meat, hence the name "jerky"; though the actual word derived from an ancient Quechua term meaning "dried meat". The raw meat was sliced thinly, sprinkled with salt and hung on racks to dry: the salt drew out moisture as well as helping to preserve and flavour it. A smoky fire was then lit underneath to keep insects away while the meat dried, and also to impart flavour. He realised it might take some experimentation, revisions and practice to get it right.

He cut a hole at the base of one of the bins for a fire and a circle of wire mesh to fit inside as a smoking rack. He used lengths of thin steel rebar for supports, which could be set at three different positions to alter the height of the smoking rack. The rack needed to be high enough above the fire that the meat wouldn't cook, but would just dry in a warm atmosphere and be protected from insects. He then drilled holes in the lid and sides of the bin for airflow and to let smoke escape, thinking to try it with and without the lid to see which worked best. He stood back, looking at the finished product: it seemed good to him, but he wouldn't know if it would work as intended until he tried it; and for that he would need fresh meat or fish.

His next project was to build two drying racks to hang from the conservatory roof; like the old-fashioned airers you might see in older houses, which people used these days as trendy items in their kitchens to hang pots and pans from. His aim was to have a means of drying herbs, fruit and maybe some vegetables. The conservatory, being all-glass and south-facing, would get very warm when the sun was out, even on fairly cold days, and he hoped to exploit that fact for this purpose. He wasn't sure whether it would work or if it was the right way to do it, but he had nothing to lose by trying.

He made two lightweight wooden frameworks, with thin doweling for the middle struts, and cut some wire mesh to cover them. He screwed hook-eyes into the four corners and suspended them by rope hung onto hooks screwed into the rafters. They were high enough that he wouldn't knock his head on them, but within easy reach for putting things up onto. After they were finished he modified the wine racks in the cellar for storing vegetables on: all they needed was wire mesh cutting to size and fixing to the top surface of each shelf, enabling vegetables to be stored on them without falling through the gaps. He would need to look out for some sort of soft, breathable material for wrapping the vegetables in, like sacking, maybe… Or hay? He thought of Warburtons near Sainsbury's, where he'd got the seeds from; they had bags of hay there for rabbit hutches.

By Thursday afternoon of his first week in the bungalow his initial projects were finished and he felt pleased with his achievements. He ate a late lunch and then decided it was time to go and fetch the oars from the angling club by Galley Hill, along with the fishing rods and tackle. He would also look for something suitable to fit the rowlocks to, giving him a rowing-boat that he could fish from. He was eager to start catching fish; for fresh meat and also to experiment with drying and smoking them in the apparatus he had made.

He drove to East Parade and stopped briefly at the sailing club to have another look at the dinghies there. Although some of them were small enough for his needs, they also looked a bit shallow for his liking and he wouldn't feel comfortable being in one, so he carried on to the angling club and parked outside. It was just the same as he'd last seen it and he avoided looking at the remains of the body he'd burned. He collected the oars, fishing rods and tackle then loaded them into the truck. He also found a tackle box filled with assorted lures, weights and hooks that he'd missed before.

Outside, he looked at all the boats to see which might be suitable, but they were all too big and cumbersome to use as a rowing-boat. He then came across a smaller shape covered by a tarp, which he removed: clearly, it wasn't designed as a rowing-boat as it had fittings for an outboard motor at the back, but he felt it was small enough and would do the job. The hull was fibreglass, which would be much lighter than a wooden boat and easier to handle. He examined the gunwale and saw that it would be thick enough to drill and mount the rowlocks onto.

It was sitting on its trailer and chained to a ring set into the concrete at the edge of the beach. He used the bolt-cutters on the light chain then dragged it along the beach to a sloping concrete ramp and back to the Land Rover, hitching it onto the towing hook. He drove off, stopping at the pet supplies shop first for some bags of hay. When he got to the end of West Parade, where it joined South Cliff, he stopped at the entrance to the promenade. The barrier was closed and had a padlock fitted, which he cut off with the bolt-cutters and then drove along the promenade to a space in the railings for taking boats through. Unhitching the boat, he dragged it onto the beach and back to the bungalow, which was hard work across the pebbles. He tied it to the railings with a length of nylon rope then drove home and parked in the garage.

There was still some daylight left, so he got the rowlocks, his hand-brace and a few other tools, then walked through the garden, down the steps and onto the beach. It was a fairly simple task to bore holes in the gunwale: the carpenter's hand-brace had been his father's; it was at least forty years old, but he had maintained it well and it worked perfectly. He fitted the rowlocks and tightened the nuts with a spanner. Satisfied, he covered the hull with the tarp and secured it well to keep the rain out. Before going in, he picked some sea beet leaves from another clump to have with his meal.

Back inside, he poured a whisky and then lit a fire in the kitchen stove to warm the place up and to cook on later. He looked at the bags of coal and wood in the alcove; there was still a reasonable supply, but he would have to start making trips to locate and fetch more wood soon. Collington Wood, just over the railway line off Westcourt Drive, was less than half a mile away and he could get plenty there, but it would be a lengthy process. He thought it unlikely that he would find enough dead wood there to sustain him over the years, which would mean cutting down trees, bringing the wood back and storing it for months before it was usable. *Not a good idea,* he thought.

No, what he needed was a supply of ready-seasoned logs. *Where did the previous owners get theirs from?* He had an idea and went out to the hall. In a drawer in the telephone table he found an address book and flipped through to the "L" section. Sure enough, there was a handwritten heading- "*Logs*"- and underneath it an advert cut from the Yellow Pages stuck in with tape. The listing was for a farm near Hooe, about four miles away. He found that it was marked on the Ordnance survey map, and also that there were several other farms in the vicinity of Hooe and Gotham.

He decided to take a trip over there sometime soon and load up with logs. It also occurred to him that any farm would surely have its own supply of red diesel for tractors and other farm machinery. That would be great; he could fill up the truck when it was getting low and also fill some jerrycans to have at the bungalow. Red diesel was a low-tax fuel used for agricultural and other non-road-going vehicles, and for heating and generators. It was the same as regular diesel but had a red dye mixed in to make it easily detectable by the authorities, and had been half the price.

He was aware of his predicament regarding fuel and using the Land Rover. Any supplies that he found would have a finite life before they were all used up- once they were gone there would be no more. Although it was a diesel, the Land Rover was a heavy vehicle and wasn't as economical as a car would be. He needed to restrict its use to when he needed either its load-carrying or its off-road abilities. Despite the plans that he was putting into action for survival and self-sufficiency, he knew there would still be occasions when he would need a vehicle; whether for transporting things that he couldn't carry, or for scouting missions further afield.

He thought it might be a good idea to find a small, economical diesel car to use, for those times when he didn't need the truck. He wrote it down in his notebook, and while flipping back through previous pages he saw the word "*genny*" scrawled down quickly. He remembered the portable generators he'd seen at Halfords: with a good supply of diesel he could run a generator when he needed electricity. He would collect a couple on his next trip out, along with some more fuel containers.

After cooking and eating his meal he read through some of his books on survival, crafts and growing vegetables, making notes on a few things as he read. An interesting piece in one book told how you could make a long-burning survival candle using vegetable fat- the sort normally sold in solid blocks or tubs and used in baking. He was aware that his candles would be a short-lived commodity and that it would be difficult to find more, so this was useful to know. He was tired after all his work over the last few days, but it felt good to be getting things done, so he went to bed early.

Three miles away in a pub on the Pevensey Levels, three men- two brothers and a cousin- decided between them that in the morning they would leave the pub for the first time in about three months. They hadn't heard any vehicles go past for at least six weeks and it was time to see what was happening in the world outside, and to see what they could find. Their food was nearly gone, they were stir-crazy, and they had drunk every last drop of all alcoholic beverages in the pub, its storehouse and its cellar.

The Star Inn, on Sluice Lane at Normans Bay, was an ancient building dating back to 1402, although it wasn't used as an inn until the mid-sixteenth century. Until the mid-nineteenth century it had been a well-known meeting place and hide-out for smugglers; in particular the notorious Little Common Gang. The Pevensey Levels was a large area of ancient marshland between Eastbourne and Bexhill, with a vast network of streams and drainage channels, and now a National Nature Reserve and Site of Special Scientific Interest. The pub had been a popular place for families to visit, especially in the summer months or when the weather was good, though there hadn't been any visitors except the three men since the pandemic began.

When the plague hit Eastbourne, Bexhill and the surrounding areas they had fled their homes in Eastbourne and decided to hole up at The Star Inn until it had all blown over or was safe, as they thought. The pub was fairly isolated in the countryside away from urban areas, so they had thought it would be a good place. They had filled two vans and a pickup truck with all the food they could get, by purchasing, looting or threatening behaviour; taking advantage of the chaos and panic that was sweeping everywhere to get what they needed.

All three men were thugs and brutal characters, with a string of criminal convictions between them. Adjacent to the pub was a small development of twelve chalets and they checked these first to see if anyone was around; looking through windows they saw that all were either uninhabited or had been vacated. They had knocked at the pub's door, pretending to be nice, concerned citizens from Normans Bay, and asking if they were okay or needed anything. Their act only lasted long enough for them to ascertain that the owners weren't infected and then they had killed them with a shotgun and buried their bodies out back.

Once inside they had boarded up the downstairs windows and locked the doors. They painted signs that said "CLOSED. PLAGUE. KEEP AWAY" and fixed them to doors and walls that could be read from the road. After that they had settled in, made themselves at home and stayed there for three months, doing little except drink. They weren't particularly bright, but they'd had the sense to use all the food in the fridges and freezers before the power failed, and there was a stream beside the building that supplied them with water.

But now they had run out of nearly everything and it was time to venture out. Being where they were, and with no media to inform them, they didn't know what the situation was. They decided to go to Bexhill in the morning to see what they could find in the way of food and drink.

The elder brother with the beer-belly was the dominant one; he looked at his brother and cousin. 'You never know- we might even find some women left alive to have some fun with!' The other two just nodded and grinned.

Seven

When Jamie got up in the morning the overcast sky had gone and the sun was shining. The conservatory was already warming up nicely, so he sat in there with a cup of coffee, thinking on what to do next. While there he checked on the progress of his seawater evaporation experiment. Three days earlier he had put some seawater into a shallow dish on the window-ledge to let it evaporate and collect the salt that would be left behind. Although he had a good store at the moment he wanted to test this out as a way of obtaining salt in the future. As it had been overcast recently it was taking a long time to evaporate, but he could see salt crystals forming around the edge already. He smiled to himself; now the sun was out it wouldn't take much longer to finish evaporating and then he would taste it.

He decided his first act of the day would be a bathe in the sea as he was feeling rather grubby. While unpacking after moving into the bungalow, he had found the box of liquid travel soap he'd bought months earlier. It was supposed to lather in salt water, which normal soap wouldn't do, so he thought he'd try it. He got undressed and put on his dressing gown and a pair of sandals to walk down in.

The sea was cold- only eleven or twelve degrees Celsius- and he sucked in breath sharply as the waves broke on his legs. Undeterred, he dived in and swam around for a while before fetching the bottle of soap. It didn't lather as well as normal soap in fresh water, but it was okay and did the job. He climbed out and put his gown back on, feeling cold but refreshed, and walked back to the house. After drying himself and putting on warm clothes he got some food ready for a breakfast of pancetta and baked beans with some flatbread.

He'd taken to using the wood-gas camping stove and the Kelly Kettle for cooking and boiling water during the day, as he wanted to save the petrol and butane gas for when he was low on logs for the stove. Both were extremely efficient, requiring only a few handfuls of twigs from the garden, which he collected and stored under the porch to keep them dry. The wood-burner in the kitchen he wanted to use only in the evenings to warm the place up and to cook on.

He went into the hall to put on some shoes as the floor was cold and stopped suddenly, listening; he thought he'd heard a vehicle. Yes, there was definitely a vehicle in the road, coming from the west. He went into the lounge and peered through a gap in the curtains; a Toyota pickup came into view, moving slowly. There were three men in it; two in the cab and one standing in the load area riding shotgun- literally. He could see the gun in his right hand while he held onto a roof bar with his left, and didn't like the look of them at all.

He heard them shout something and then the truck suddenly revved and lurched forward, moving out of his line of sight. In a few seconds there was a squeal of brakes and tyres as it came to a sudden stop and then a shotgun blast, followed immediately by a woman's scream. He ran out to the hall and picked up a shotgun, checking it was loaded, then grabbed a handful of cartridges, put them in his pocket and went out the front door.

The woman had been unsuccessful so far in finding a suitable place to move to. Nothing she'd seen had matched the criteria on her list of things she wanted or needed in a place, so over the last two days she had widened her search area and today was looking at houses along South Cliff. She emerged from a house on the north side of the road and stepped out onto the pavement. Immediately, she heard a shout and an engine revving and spun to her right, seeing a truck bearing down on her. She turned and ran the other way as fast as she could. Just as she was about to turn off the road into a large garden the truck stopped sharply behind her. There was a loud blast followed immediately by agonising pain down her right leg. She staggered, wavered and limped away as fast as she was able. It was supposed to have been a warning shot, but the idiot hadn't counted on the spread of shot and several pellets had struck her leg.

The truck came closer and stopped; she heard the doors open and close and looked back to see two men approaching. There was no way to outrun them so she turned and stood facing them, a large claw hammer in her right hand, held down by her side. The men stopped two yards from her.

'Drop the hammer, bitch,' said the older guy with the beer-belly. She just stood there defiantly, glaring at them.

'If you don't drop the hammer, my cousin up there will blow your foot off.' She didn't have much choice, so dropped the hammer.

'That's better! How are we supposed to have some fun when you've got a dirty great hammer in your hand?' His brother next to him laughed. She knew exactly what sort of fun they had in mind, and was damned if she'd let it happen; she'd rather die first.

She groaned and leaned forward, reaching her right hand behind and under her jacket to the small of her back. Her hand came to rest on the long wooden handle of a small hammer in her back pocket, which she always carried with her. Beer-belly took a step towards her, reaching out. She stood up straight and raised her left hand, distracting him. His eyes moved to her left hand and with lightning speed she whipped out the hammer with her right and swung it at his head, delivering a staggering blow. It was only a lightweight 4oz ball-pein hammer, and some people might have laughed at it as an effective weapon, but the effect was like being shot in the head with a .50 calibre bullet. It punched a big hole right through his skull and he dropped like a stone; dead before he hit the ground.

'You bitch!' screamed his brother, and lunged at her. She spun around and tried to run away but her injured leg hampered her. Before she had gone four paces he was on her, punching her to the ground and kicking her. She curled into a ball to protect herself. At that moment there was another blast from a shotgun, and the cousin in the back of the pickup tumbled over the cab, bounced off the bonnet and landed on the ground in front of it, a huge bloody hole between his shoulder-blades.

Jamie came out of his door and peered cautiously over next-door's hedge to see what was happening. The truck was stopped fifty yards or so down the road. A short distance ahead of the truck was the woman he'd seen on the beach a month or so before; she was holding her right leg and he could see blood on her fingers. The two men from the cab were walking towards her, while the third stood in the back of the truck pointing the shotgun at her.

He didn't want the woman to see him and give him away inadvertently, so when she looked down he moved quickly into the middle of the road to put the truck between them and advanced quietly down the road towards the scene. The guy in the back of the truck was too intent on what was happening in front to pay any attention to his rear. He reached the back of the truck and halted, raising the shotgun to his shoulder, undecided what to do and with his heart pounding. *Shit, shit, shit!* He could see what was happening through the Toyota's rear and front screens.

When the man lunged for the woman he saw her lash out with a hammer and the guy fall to the ground. He heard the other man scream "*You bitch!*" and saw him launch into her with his fists and feet, and the woman falling to the ground. He aimed between the shoulder-blades of the guy in the back of the truck and pulled the trigger. He felt the kick of the stock against his shoulder and saw the man tumble over the cab. He stepped a few paces to the right and forward, to see the other guy looking down at his cousin, confused, and then turn to look at him. He saw the guy's hand move to his pocket and

56

pulled the trigger to fire the second barrel. The shot hit him in the centre of his chest and he flew back over the woman lying on the ground, landing just beyond her.

He broke open the shotgun and the two spent cartridges ejected with a puff of smoke. He pulled two more from his pocket, inserted them into the breach and closed the weapon, then moved cautiously forward. The woman sat up, looking at him; she had tears in her eyes and the pain was evident in her face. He checked all three guys; they were dead as dodos.

Adrenaline was coursing through him and he was shaking. He was just a normal guy; he'd never even fired a gun before- apart from at the alarm-box the other week- let alone shoot someone. And yet he felt no remorse for the men; as far as he was concerned they were scum and deserved what they got.

The woman gave him a weak smile and then her face clouded over with anger and she turned away slightly. 'Bastards! Fucking low-life scumbags! I mean… Jesus!' She shook her head, wincing in pain, and then looked at him again. 'I'd have been in deep shit if you hadn't turned up! I can't even bear thinking about it… Thank you.'

'You're welcome. I'm so sorry, and I'm just so glad I got here in time.'

He knew exactly what they'd had in mind and felt disgusted. He was embarrassed and didn't know what to say and just stood there looking at her. She looked to be in her late thirties; she had short brown hair and a nice face, with a wide mouth and laughter lines around her eyes.

In an effort to take her mind off what had just happened and get her thinking of something else, he coughed and said 'Um… D'you like coffee? Only, I was just about to make some when I was interrupted. I've got Kenyan, Columbian or some nice strong Javan.'

She gave another weak smile and kind of snorted. 'I haven't had a good coffee in months; I'd love some.'

He swung the shotgun by its strap onto his shoulder, reached down and helped her to her feet; she was around 5'6" with a curvy figure. She staggered a bit and then got her balance. As they passed the body of the guy she'd hit with the hammer, she said 'Scum!' and kicked it with her good leg, then looked at him and nodded. With his left arm around her waist and her right arm around his shoulder they walked up the road.

'Don't worry,' he said, 'it's not far and you'll be okay. We'll soon have you patched up.' She just grunted in response.

They continued on towards his place and he could feel the adrenaline wearing off. 'I'm James; or Jamie, if you like.'

'I'm Jane; pleased to meet you.'

'Likewise.'

They reached the bungalow and he helped her inside, through the hall and into the kitchen. She sat down on a chair at the table and he took the shotgun off his shoulder, propping it against the wall by the door.

'Would you like a shot of something stronger before your coffee?'

'Oh God; yes please!'

He took a bottle of whisky off a shelf, got a glass and poured her a stiff measure. She downed it in one and he poured her another, which she drank half of.

'We need to take a look at that leg of yours. We've got to remove the pellets as soon as possible and wash the area and treat it, to stop infection.'

'Yes, I suppose you're right,' she replied, with no great enthusiasm.

'If you go into the bathroom and take your jeans off, there's a bathrobe on the door. I'll put some water on to heat.'

She nodded and he helped her to stand up, then she limped to the bathroom. She took her jeans off, wincing in pain, and suddenly felt a bit self-conscious of her hairy legs. She hadn't really thought about it in the months on her own, but no man had ever seen her with hairy legs before. She shrugged and thought *Don't be stupid, Jane!*

He busied himself with the stove and kettle, then got his first-aid kit from a cupboard and took it into the conservatory, putting it onto a low table next to the sofa. When he came back into the kitchen she was standing there in his robe.

'Where do you want me, doctor?' she smiled nervously. The initial shock was wearing off and she was lightening-up a bit.

'I think the conservatory's best,' he replied. 'It's warm in there and you can lie on the sofa. This is going to hurt like hell, and I'm afraid I haven't got any anaesthetic, apart from the old-fashioned kind,' he said, pointing at the Scotch.

She nodded. He poured her another good measure, which she picked up and drank, before moving through into the conservatory and lying face-down on the sofa. He occupied himself in the kitchen for a few minutes; she could see him in there checking the water and looked at him. He was around six feet tall, with a medium build and looked in good shape. He had longish dark hair flecked with grey and a beard to match, with friendly blue eyes and an open face.

'You're not the man-in-the-hat any more,' she said.

'Eh? I'm not with you,' he replied, turning towards her.

'Well, I've seen you several times over the last month or more, though you've only seen me the once; that time on the beach when I ran off. In my mind I called you the man-in-the-hat.' She giggled; the whisky had gone straight to her head and she was feeling slightly tipsy already. He smiled in understanding and she continued: 'And now you're not: the man-in-the-hat, I mean. You're just Jamie.'

He came in carrying a bowl of hot water. 'Well, I've been called worse things in my life, so man-in-the-hat's not bad,' he smiled. 'Right, let's take a look at the damage.'

He put on a pair of latex gloves, knelt down and examined her leg. It was smeared with blood, which he washed off with hot water to get a better look. There were six puncture wounds in a small group, between the top of her calf and the back of her knee. He pressed gently next to one; she winced and blood oozed out. There were also several large red areas from where the man had kicked her.

'You're lucky they were only loaded with small bird-shot. If it had been bigger shot, like BB for instance, you'd have been in real trouble. I'm going to have to root around with some forceps to get the pellets out. Tweezers are smaller, but I'm worried they won't grip the pellets enough for me to pull them out, so it's *really* going to hurt. Do you want something to bite on?'

She shook her head. 'No thanks; just get on with it and let's get it over with.'

He dipped the forceps' jaws first into surgical spirit, then put his fingers either side of the first wound, stretching the skin to widen the hole. She squirmed and then held her leg as still as she could, gritting her teeth while he probed with the forceps. He felt the pellet, maybe half an inch below the surface, and opened the jaws wide enough to go around it. He got a firm hold on the piece of lead and pulled it out, examining it. He was relieved to see that it was intact, as he'd been worried that some might have broken off, especially if it had been from a ricochet off the ground.

He wiped the blood away, then put a jeweller's loupe into his eye and bent down for a closer look. He opened the wound as wide as he could and examined it closely. Just inside, he could see some fibres from her jeans that had been punched into the wound, which he pulled out with tweezers. He then put a few drops of iodine tincture from an eye-dropper into and around the wound, and she jumped and winced, then relaxed and let out a deep breath.

'One down; five to go!' he said.

She reached for her whisky and took a long gulp. 'Bugger me, that hurt!'

It took him over forty minutes to remove all six pellets and more fibres from the wounds. He was as sure as he could be that there was nothing left in any of them, and all the pellets had been intact. He cleaned the remaining blood from her leg, dried it with cotton wool and put plasters over the wounds, before helping her to sit up. By now, Jane was feeling rather groggy from the pain and the whisky, so he went into the kitchen to make some coffee.

'Thank you, Jamie. I don't know what I would have done without you.'

'Don't mention it. I don't think they need bandaging, so I've just put plasters on them to stop the bleeding. We can have a look later to see if any need changing. You've got some nasty bruises forming as well. Have you checked the rest of your body for more?'

'No, not yet, but it hurts in several places. Have you done anything like this before?'

'Never: you're my first, and I hope my last, surgical patient!' he smiled. 'Why don't you go into the bathroom and check yourself, and put some of this on them.' He handed her a bottle of witch hazel and some cotton wool balls. 'It will help with the bruises.'

'Okay, thanks,' she said, getting up stiffly and making her way to the bathroom.

Meanwhile, he got a fire going in the log-burner to warm up the kitchen for her and poured some coffee for them both. She came out smelling of witch hazel, still in his bath robe, and sat at the table to drink her coffee.

'Oh God, that tastes good! I've missed real coffee; thanks.'

He smiled at her and she smiled back over the rim of her mug.

'I was just about to make some breakfast earlier, but I seem to have got distracted! Do you want some? I'm cooking pancetta with baked beans and some flatbread I made. I've also got one carton of orange juice left. It's a bit past its use-by date, but it'll be fine.'

'I'd love some, but do you mind if I have it later? I'm feeling a bit groggy and think I need to lie down for a while.'

'Of course you can; no problem.'

He helped her through into the conservatory, where she lay down again on the sofa. He walked through to the lounge to fetch a blanket for her and by the time he came back she was fast asleep. He laid the blanket gently over her and then went back to the kitchen to make breakfast, feeling pleased to have her there and also relieved that things had turned out as they had; it could have been a lot worse.

Eight

He was about to start cooking breakfast when he realised there was something that needed doing: out in the street were three bodies, an abandoned truck and a shotgun. Whilst he knew that the police wouldn't be coming to call anytime soon, he felt he had to dispose of the bodies and the truck, rather than just leaving them where they were. He sighed and put down the saucepan that was in his hand. As he walked to the hall, the bathroom door was open and he saw Jane's blood-stained jeans on the floor, so he picked them up and went outside. With a bucket of seawater, a scrubbing-brush and some detergent he cleaned off as much blood as he could. He went back inside and hung them next to the log-burner to dry.

He put a few things into his rucksack, along with the sawn-off, put on his hat and coat and prepared to leave. He turned at the door and went back into the conservatory; Jane was still sleeping soundly. He didn't want her waking up to find him gone, so he wrote on a piece of paper; *Just popped out to dispose of the bodies. Back soon. Help yourself to anything you fancy. Jamie.* He propped it on the coffee table by the sofa and then left, taking with him two large water containers to fill while he was out.

He walked down the road to the scene of the carnage and stood there, shaking his head in disbelief. Never in his life had he imagined that this might happen to him. He sighed and dragged the three bodies to the Toyota's rear, then opened the tail-gate. Something niggled at the back of his mind and then he remembered what it was; the second guy he'd shot reaching for his pocket. He turned him over and looked in his jacket pocket, to find a revolver. It was large, old and well-worn, with a blued-steel finish and chequered walnut grip. The barrel was about four inches long and on the left side it said *Smith and Wesson*. He turned it over and on the other side it said *.357 Highway Patrolman*.

He didn't know it, but it was a Model 28; made by Smith and Wesson for around thirty years until the late '80s. It was a stripped-down and cheaper version of a previous model, produced especially for law-enforcement officers and manufactured in huge quantities. It had also been the first revolver designed to fire the .357 Magnum round. He took a deep breath and let it out slowly; if the guy had been carrying this in his hand when he'd shot the first man, then things might not have worked out as well for him and Jane as they had done. He smiled, shrugged and put it in his rucksack.

He decided to have a look around the truck. In the load area was a tarp covering some items and he pulled it off them. There was a jerrycan filled with diesel for the Toyota and another filled with petrol, presumably for another vehicle of theirs. There was also a toolbox, a socket set, a felling axe, a small hatchet and various other assorted tools and hardware. He climbed down and went round to the cab, which had discarded food wrappers littering the floor. In the glove-box he found an almost-full box of cartridges for the shotgun, plus a box of fifty shells for the revolver, labelled ".38 Special", with six rounds missing. This confused him, as the gun was clearly stamped with ".357". His limited knowledge of guns came only from films, TV and novels, and he obviously had heard of .357 and .44 Magnums.

He took the gun from his rucksack, opened the cylinder and removed one of the six shells; it matched those in the box. It obviously must work with them, so he shrugged again and put the revolver and the bullets in his pack. If he'd had more interest in guns- or access to the internet- he would have discovered that a revolver chambered for the .357 Magnum round could also fire the .38 Special round (which was much cheaper and more widely available), but not vice versa.

He went to the back of the truck and, with some difficulty, managed to lift them all into the load-bed and closed the tailgate. He found the shotgun in the road on the far side of the vehicle, picked it up and put it in the cab then looked around; there was a lot of blood on the road, which he couldn't do much about, so he left.

He drove to the industrial area on Beeching Road, which wasn't far away, looking for something specific. It didn't take long to find what he wanted: in a yard next to an industrial unit he saw a skip and drove up to it to look inside. It was nearly empty; perfect. He reversed the truck up to the skip and it was almost at the same level as the load-bed. Looking around, he saw several discarded wooden pallets, so he dragged four over to the skip. He put two in the bottom, then climbed up and pushed the bodies in on top of them. He then threw the other two pallets on top and sloshed some petrol from the jerrycan over them.

After moving the truck away a few yards, he picked up a stone and wrapped some food wrappers from the cab around it, to give them some weight. He stood back several yards, lit the wrappers and tossed the bundle into the skip. The petrol ignited with a *wumph* sound and he felt the air displacement from where he stood. He got back into the cab and drove the short distance to Egerton Park at the Wickham Avenue entrance, where he filled the two water containers from the ornamental lake. After putting them in the truck, an idea occurred to him.

He got the revolver from his rucksack and a plastic bag- he always carried a few for collecting plant samples- and went back into the park. There were numerous ducks on the lake or by the side of it and they were used to being close to humans and being fed by them. He selected a nice fat mallard on the bank and moved slowly to within a few yards of it. Crouching down, he cocked the hammer, took careful aim and pulled the trigger, blowing the duck's head off. The rest of the birds erupted into the air and flew off. He picked up the duck, put it into the plastic bag and walked back to the truck. *Roast duck tonight- nice!*

While he was out in the truck, he decided to go to Halfords on the retail park and pick up two of the portable generators he'd seen when he was last there. It was only two miles away and didn't take long to get there on the empty roads. Driving well over the speed limit, straight through dead traffic lights and junctions without even slowing, he felt reckless and had a slight feeling of euphoria as if he'd taken some kind of drug; a reaction to shooting the thugs, rescuing Jane and surviving unscathed. Despite the awful events that had happened and the terrible situation that he and the country were in, he was living an adventure and felt more alive than he had ever done before.

The retail park was just as he had last seen it, although there was a Ford estate car there that he didn't remember seeing before. Maybe his memory was wrong, but he didn't want to take any chances; he'd learned already that he needed to be cautious. He took the sawn-off from his pack, checked it was loaded and put a few extra cartridges in his left pocket. After a second's thought he also took out the revolver, replaced the spent round with a new one from the box and put it into his coat pocket, then got out of the truck. He stood outside the door to Halfords listening for a minute, looking around the parking area and at the other stores. He heard nothing to alert him so he went in, walked straight to the shelf and picked up two generators- one diesel and one petrol- then took them out to the truck. Walking past the till he saw that his £10 note was still there next to it. As he drove home, he decided that he liked the Toyota and would keep it. He didn't see the point in abandoning it when it was a perfectly good vehicle and seemed to be well-maintained. Two vehicles were better than one! Besides, it could be something for Jane to drive if she wanted to.

Back at the bungalow, he parked on the drive and went inside. Jane was up and heard him enter; she came to the kitchen door, walking stiffly and looking concerned.

'I heard a shot some time ago; was that you? Are you okay?'

'Yes, it was me and I'm fine.' He held up the plastic bag and smiled. 'Roast duck for dinner tonight! Ever prepared a fresh one?'

She smiled in return. 'Oh, wow! That would be great. And yes, I have. My dad showed me how when I was young, bless him. He was a country man and was always bringing something back for the pot.'

'That's good news, because I've never done it, though I'm okay with cutting up joints of meat.'

'I've not long been up. I was just preparing a late breakfast as it was obvious you hadn't eaten before you went out. I got your note.'

'Yes; I thought I'd better get rid of the bodies first.'

'What did you do with them?'

'I put them in a skip along Beeching Road and burned them.'

Her face clouded over slightly. 'Thank you for that... again.'

'Don't mention it; no problem. Well, I'll just get the truck unloaded while you carry on with breakfast.'

He turned and walked back outside and brought the things in. He carried the water containers through to the porch out back, then the tools and jerrycans into the garage, and the shotgun he brought indoors and left in the hall. He emptied his rucksack onto the worktop and held up the Smith and Wesson.

'Look what else I found on one of them.'

Her eyes widened. 'Bloody hell!'

'That's just what I thought! We were lucky he didn't have it in his hand when I came along, rather than in his pocket. I guess he thought Butthead with the shotgun had it covered.'

'I suppose so. Where did you get your shotgun- or did you always have it?'

'No, I found them last week in a house down the road, while I was looking for this place.'

'Oh- so you've just moved in here? I did wonder. I had a quick look around after I woke up and it looks like you've been busy on some improvements.'

'Yes. I'll show you after we've eaten and tell you my thoughts.' He picked up his sawn-off and showed her. 'This was one of the three I found. I cut the barrels down to make a sawn-off, so it would be easier to carry around for protection. I'll leave the two over and unders as they are as they'll be better for hunting. That makes four shotguns and a revolver I now have; I'm getting quite a collection!'

She gave a wry smile. 'You're becoming a regular Rambo!'

He gave a short laugh. 'Well, that's funny, because before last week I'd never even held a gun before! How does the leg feel, and the bruises?'

'The leg feels painful and kind of stiff, and the bruises are very sore.'

'They will be for a few days, I'm sure. Maybe you should keep moving around as much as possible.' She agreed with him.

By then, the food was ready so they sat at the table to eat. They were both hungry and ate in silence until they had finished. It was nearer lunch than breakfast, so he opened a tin of peaches and a small tin of custard as well.

'Wow, that was fab- thanks,' said Jane afterwards, wiping her mouth. 'And thanks also for washing my jeans.'

'No problem. Coffee?'

'Yes, please.'

He ground some beans and put the kettle on, then washed the dishes in a bowl of seawater with some detergent and dried them. 'I find that if I wash up as soon as I've eaten, the seawater and detergent works well enough; then I use the dirty water to flush the loo.'

He made coffee and they went outside, where he showed her the new porch area with the water butt, and the two smokers he'd made from the rubbish bins. He pointed inside the conservatory at the drying racks hanging from the rafters and said they were for drying fruit and herbs.

She was impressed. 'You've done all this since Monday?' He nodded. 'You've done really well; great work, Jamie.' He blushed slightly and said 'Thanks.'

He crooked a finger at her, saying 'Follow me,' then

walked off down the garden. He let her follow at her own pace and didn't offer to help her. He was conscious of not wanting to crowd her or seem over-protective, as men can sometimes be towards women. She was obviously a strong woman; she'd showed that in the way she'd stood up to the thugs that morning. When she caught up he opened the back gate and started down the steps. She hesitated and looked at them with uncertainty, so he asked if she wanted a hand coming down, to which she agreed. He came back up and gave her his arm to negotiate the steps, then pointed to the boat; she leaned on the railing while he climbed down and removed the tarp to show her the new rowlocks and oars.

'I got it from the angling club by Galley Hill, along with some fishing tackle, then brought it back here and fitted the rowlocks. It seemed a bit of a priority to me to start catching fish for protein. Once I've caught some I can experiment with smoking and drying them in the bins I modified.'

'Sounds good, Jamie. You've obviously given a lot of thought to certain things recently.'

As they made their way back to the house he told her of his panic attack and breakdown on Monday, when he realised the enormity of his situation and the realities of survival and self-sufficiency- especially being on his own. They sat down in the conservatory.

'Oh, God, tell me about it! The number of nights and days I've sat at home crying my eyes out, wondering what to do,' she admitted.

'I was a bit naïve at first,' he said, 'but after the reality hit me on Monday I sat down and did a lot of thinking and writing down ideas and plans. We're not going to survive by living and eating on a day-to-day basis; we've got to plan weeks and months ahead, especially for the winter. That's what got me thinking about ways of storing and preserving food.'

'I agree. I'd come to similar conclusions as you, but hadn't yet got around to thinking about how I was going to do it. I think I've been too focussed on finding somewhere else to live and planting vegetables and fruit.'

'I know- I was just the same!'

They talked all afternoon. He showed her the cellar with the modified wine racks for storing fruit and veg' and spoke of his plans for preserving foods by drying, pickling, salting, smoking, or storing in oil, and to collect as much salt, vinegar and oil as possible. He then told her about finding Sainsbury's warehouse stacked with food of all sorts. She listened with great interest, adding her own thoughts and suggestions, and they threw ideas back and forth between them. She had some experience of growing fruit and vegetables from previous places she'd lived, when she'd had gardens.

Their talk gradually moved on to more personal things and experiences; the plague, how they'd survived, the loss of family and friends and the awful realisation that there were almost no other survivors. He related the incident in B&Q when the man had threatened him, and the encounter with the other man in Tesco. Jane had lost her mother and both sisters in the weeks before she had become infected. He told her of his awful last conversation with his brother, and how Dave had begged him not to come round. They both got a bit tearful at that point, so he got up to make some coffee. He poured a generous slug of whisky into each mug and handed her one; she smiled in appreciation and raised her mug to him.

'Listen', he said, 'you're welcome to stay the night here and rest here tomorrow as well, or until you're feeling better. But… given what's happened, I'm well-aware that you might not feel comfortable doing that and want to be in your own home. We have, after all, only just met. If you'd rather go back to your place tonight I can drive you back after we've eaten.'

She smiled at his understanding, but shook her head. 'No, it's alright, really. I feel totally comfortable with you and yes, I'd love to stay the night, thanks. The thought of going back to my flat and being on my own tonight wasn't a happy one, but I didn't want to ask or impose.' She hesitated for a second; 'To be honest, Jamie, now that I've met you I feel a bit guilty for running away that time and for not approaching you on the other occasions I've seen you. I was scared, though, and couldn't bring myself to do it.'

'Don't even think of it; I understand completely.' He

smiled at her. 'Good. You can have the third bedroom; there's a single bed in there. The largest bedroom, as you saw, I've turned into a store-room along with the study, and I've got the second bedroom. I plan to build some more shelves for the other rooms for storing jars of preserves.'

The afternoon had flown by with their conversation and it was now early evening, so they agreed it was time to prepare a meal. She went outside to pluck the duck while he built the stove up. There were still plenty of glowing embers so it didn't take long to get going again. After Jane had prepared the duck he took her back down to the promenade, telling her of his discovery about sea beet and sea kale. She was fascinated by this and he showed her how to identify the sea beet with its glossy green leaves; the sea kale was pretty obvious. They picked a few handfuls of sea beet leaves from different plants, along with some new leaves and young stems of sea kale, and then went back to start cooking.

The duck went into a small cast-iron casserole pan with some seasoning, which he placed in the stove to roast. He prepared a casserole with the sea vegetables and some tinned potatoes and carrots. There was a bit of pancetta left from that morning, which he threw in for extra flavour, along with some parsley he'd found in the garden, which was mature and a bit overgrown around the borders. He made a mental note to have a good look around sometime soon, to see what other herbs might be lurking in the undergrowth.

While it cooked, he went into the cellar to fetch a bottle of wine as he hadn't had any from there yet, and now seemed like a good time. It was a mature Chilean Cabernet Sauvignon and they said *Cheers*, clinked glasses and took a mouthful.

'Oh, wow! That tastes good,' she said. 'I haven't had any wine in months and have missed it!'

'I've had a small supply, but it was getting low; I found eleven more bottles in the cellar. I'm hoping there will be a lot more in the warehouse at Sainsbury's. We'll need to visit there and make an inventory of the food and drink that's left,' to which she agreed. She made a face and reached down to touch the back of her right leg.

'Jamie, would you mind having a look at my leg again? I think some of the wounds are weeping.' She turned around on the chair and stretched her leg out and he bent down to have a look.

'Yes; three of them need new plasters and probably a swab.'

He fetched the first-aid kit and a bottle of surgical spirit then removed the plasters. After cleaning the wounds he dried them and put on new plasters. There were yellow-purple bruises developing around all the wounds, adding to the orange staining from the iodine, so he dabbed them with witch hazel as well. She thanked him and they sat back around the table. He toyed with his glass for a few seconds, took a mouthful of wine and cleared his throat.

'Jane, I've been thinking today; well, not just today, obviously, but especially today since we met. I've realised this week what a daunting and difficult task it's going to be to survive and become self-sufficient, and damn-near impossible on my own; there's just so much to do! In fact, I don't mind admitting that I'm terrified at the prospect. My biggest fear is of getting injured or becoming ill and not being able to fend for myself. All it would take is a twisted ankle, for God's sake, and I could be stuffed for days, maybe; unable to gather food, or fish, etc.

There are so many skills that we need to learn- skills that we haven't really needed in the modern world until now; things that our ancestors took for granted because they'd grown up being taught them. What are you- late thirties?'

'I'm thirty-eight.'

'Okay; well, I'm forty-two. We have no way of knowing what the situation is in the rest of the country; but, based on what we've seen so far, it doesn't look good, to put it mildly! I've only seen seven living people so far in Bexhill, including you, in over two months. From the news reports on TV and radio before the services failed it seemed to be the same everywhere in the UK; I don't recall hearing of anywhere that was unaffected. There's no infrastructure left and no utilities. There are bound to be other survivors somewhere, but we're faced with the probability that it won't get any better than this.

If we live that long, we may have another thirty or forty years of things being this way! In a matter of months we have- virtually- been taken back to the Stone Age, or at least the Middle Ages: apart from cars and some other stuff, but you know what I mean. We've relied on technology and service industries for so long that, as individuals, we've lost the basic skills necessary for survival and for making things. We've taken everything for granted up until now because they've always been available; but how many people know how to produce or make even simple things like vinegar, salt, candles, or fire?

… And what about more complicated things like metal for tools, etc.? How many people left alive will know how to locate and mine metal ore, build a furnace to extract the metal, and then forge it into knives and other tools? It's mind-boggling when you think of the implications!

We have no electricity and will have to live without it, pretty much, for the foreseeable future. I know I've picked up two generators, but the fuel I can gather for them will only be used for essential stuff, when it's needed.' He paused.

She was looking at him intently. 'Go on.'

'What I'm getting to is… Well, what do you think about teaming-up and becoming kind of partners; to work together and to help and support each other in the future? Based on today, we seem to get on well, and I think we're going to need each other. Now, don't get me wrong; I'm not talking about moving in together and playing happy families and all that crap! I don't know if I want that or am even ready for something like that; but what about, maybe, moving in next door, or at least a house nearby? What are your thoughts?'

She looked at him for a few seconds and then looked down. She was silent for a while and then her bottom lip quivered and she wiped tears from her eyes. She drank some wine and looked at him again, a tearful smile on her face.

'I can't tell you how pleased I am to hear you say that! Today started out as the shittiest day of my life: being shot and then knowing I was going to be gang-raped… I've never been so terrified. And then you came along, and it turned into the best day I've had in months, since this whole fucking thing began! I don't just mean about you saving me; it's more than that. I've thought about some of the things you've just spoken of and, like you, I've been terrified at the prospect of trying to survive on my own.

Hearing you talk today about planning for the future and what we need to do has highlighted to me that I hadn't given nearly enough thought to what would be involved, and that made it even more scary for me. I'd maybe assumed that you were just being a good and decent man in helping me today, and that afterwards we'd go back to our own lives. I'm relieved that's not the case, though, because I like you. So, yes, I'd really like for us to become friends and partners in survival!'

She got up, came around the table and gave him a quick hug. They both felt a little embarrassed, while also feeling very relieved. She sat down again and he raised his wine glass.

'To new friendship and new beginnings!'

'New friendship and new beginnings!' she repeated.

They clinked glasses and drained their wine, then he refilled them. The food smelled like it was ready, so he removed the duck from the stove and took the casserole off the top. He carved some meat and served up the food then they tucked into it, chatting all the while. It was delicious and just what they had needed at the end of a hard day. Afterwards, he opened another bottle of wine and they sat in the conservatory with a few candles lit, talking for several hours before retiring. Tomorrow they would find her a place to live nearby.

Nine

The following morning Jamie awoke early, feeling the effects of the two bottles of red wine they'd consumed between them, plus some brandies. Jane was still sleeping. He made a large pot of coffee and took a mug outside to wander around the garden. He went first to the vegetable patch and was delighted to see shoots at regular intervals along several lines. He was no expert, but to him they looked like onions or garlic, or possibly both; it was hard to tell at this stage. The previous owners must have sowed them last autumn. That was great news and a good start to having fresh vegetables, ahead of his proposed planting.

Walking around, looking in the rather overgrown borders, he identified a large patch of chives, a rosemary bush and a spreading bay tree around four feet high. There was also a plant he was pretty sure was lovage, which Jane confirmed later. He was pleased, as he loved herbs and they would be welcome additions to his diet for extra flavouring, along with vitamins and minerals. He stepped across the border to the wall and scrambled up it to take a look at the house on the right, on the western side. He was looking around the garden and at the house when he heard the back door open and looked round. Jane was standing there looking rather bleary-eyed.

'Morning!' he said, smiling.

'Morning,' she replied, with rather less enthusiasm. He

jumped down, walked back up the garden and followed her into the kitchen.

'Bloody hell, that wine was strong! I haven't drunk much at all in recent months; I've turned into a lightweight!' she said sheepishly. He smiled and gave a small laugh.

'A few cups of this Java will sort you out!' He poured her a large mug. 'How does the leg feel? Any better?'

'Yes, a little better, thanks. It's not as stiff, and the bruises are coming out. It was probably good that I kept moving on it yesterday, and I think the witch hazel has helped, though they're still pretty sore. At least the wounds aren't bleeding or weeping any more.'

'That's good. As long as they stay that way today, maybe you should take the plasters off tonight to let them dry out and get some air to them,' to which she agreed.

He told her about finding the herbs in the garden, and the onions or garlic that were shooting. 'That's good news. Hopefully we can find a place for me today, and as soon as I've moved in we can start planting. There's a lot of stuff that should have gone in already, I think.'

'Well, fingers crossed, but we might not have to look far. The house next door looks promising, from the outside at any rate. The garden is slightly bigger than this one, I think, and there are beds and borders that can be dug up for planting, along with areas of lawn. There's no conservatory, but the French doors open onto a patio. What *is* good news is that there must be open fires, log-burners or a range of some sort, as there's a wood store outside, against the far fence. It looks like just a shed with the door removed. There's a lot of wood stacked up in there and it has a new felt roof. The downside is that it's a house, rather than a bungalow, which means roof and gutter maintenance will be harder, but we've got ladders here in the garage, so it shouldn't be a deal-breaker.'

Jane grinned. 'It would be great being next door. It would make working on the gardens so much easier for us, and for coming-and-going.'

'Yes it would. Anyway, let's not get our hopes up too much, yet. We'll have some breakfast first and then go and take a look. There's an upstairs window ajar, so we can take the ladder round and get in from up there.'

'Okay.'

'I've just realised that after I found this place I stopped looking and didn't go any further along the road. This looked like it would suit my needs, so it never even occurred to me that there might be a *better* place further down!'

Between them they made some Scotch pancakes with sultanas, covered in honey, and he fried some pancetta to go with them. While they worked they said what a shame it was that there was no butter or eggs, but at least he had some powdered milk.

He took the pan off the heat and Jane said 'You know, if we took a drive around the surrounding countryside sometime, we might even find a farm with some chickens roaming around. If we could catch some and bring them back we could have fresh eggs regularly. It wouldn't take much to knock-up a pen from fencing wire and a hutch for them; or is it a coop? In fact, why would we even need a pen? This place has a high wall all around it, anyway.'

'That's a good idea. Wouldn't it be cool to have our own supply of eggs? I really miss them. I've still got a jar or two of pickled eggs left, but it's not the same as being able to make omelettes and other things with fresh ones.' A thought occurred to him. 'I found out the other day where the previous owners got their logs from; it's a farm out near Hooe that used to deliver to here. I'd already decided to take a trip out there soon and get a supply of logs for the range and the stoves. There is a possibility that there'll be chickens there, or maybe somewhere nearby. Once we get you moved in somewhere we can take a trip out there.'

'That sounds like a plan! It will be nice to get out of town for a while, too.'

They had breakfast and cleared up, and then Jamie went back outside with a step-ladder and climbed over the wall to next door. He walked down the far side of the house to the front, where he withdrew the bolts on the side gate and opened it, then went across the two driveways to his garage.

76

Between them they carried the big ladder across the front and then down the side to the back garden. Jane stood on the bottom rung while he climbed up and peered inside; it wasn't a pretty sight. He looked down at Jane with a grimace.

'Two corpses in the bed.'

She made a sour face and then shrugged resignedly. 'Well, we had to half-expect it, and it's not like it's anything new to us by now, is it?'

He used the large wrecking bar to force open the window, passed it down to her and then climbed inside. After a quick search he came downstairs and opened the back door for her. 'There's another one in the smallest bedroom; a young girl. She's still holding a teddy-bear, bless her. Fucking hell!'

Jane looked sad and shook her head. 'Ah; poor thing.'

Jamie shook his head to brush the thought away and then gave her a small smile. 'But I think this place is going to suit you well. Come in and have a look.'

He stepped back and she followed him into the kitchen, which was bigger than the bungalow's. There was a large farmhouse-style table and chairs and on the right-hand wall was a large fireplace and chimney-breast with a range cooker in it. They bent down to examine it; it said *Esse*, but neither had heard of the make. He opened the doors to look inside; the left-hand door for the fire was glass with an ash-collection door under it, and an oven to the right. On top were two hotplates with hinged covers. They stood up.

'This is wood-fired and just does cooking and heating, like a stove,' said Jamie. 'There are no controls for a boiler or central heating.' Jane agreed with him. To the right of the fireplace, in the run of worktop, was a conventional gas cooker and oven; obviously for use during warmer months when the range wouldn't be needed. A large ceramic butler sink and wooden drainer were against the rear wall, overlooking the garden. The kitchen had three doors; one out to the hall, another into the lounge to the left, and the third led into a utility room. In there was another butler sink and wooden drainer, with a washing machine, tumble-dryer and dish-washer; not that they'd be of any use. The huge lounge ran the whole length of the house, with a large open fire in the centre.

'It's a shame there isn't a log-burner in here, rather than a fire,' he said. 'They're far more efficient with fuel. Trouble with an open fire is that most of the heat is lost up the chimney.'

'Still, a girl can't have everything she wants! On balance, I think the fact that it's next door to you outweighs that.'

'I agree. And it could be a possible project for the future to install one; who knows?'

They went out through another door into the hall. Opposite was a dining room behind the kitchen, a small study to the front, and a cloakroom with toilet between them.

'There are four bedrooms upstairs,' Jamie said, 'and a large bathroom, with an en-suite to the rear bedroom. There's not much point going up, unless you want to.'

She shook her head. 'Not right now, anyway.'

They went outside and carried the ladder back to the garage, then went inside to make some tea. While making it he turned to Jane. 'Well, what do you think?'

'I think it will do fine. It's not perfect, from a purely survivalist point of view, but it's got a wood-fired range and an open fire, which are the most important aspects. Strange, isn't it, how our viewpoints have changed, and everything we look at now is from a utilitarian perspective?'

'I know what you mean. It's a big house, though, and it'll be difficult to heat in the winter.'

'I thought of that, too, while we were looking round. One solution would be to bring a bed downstairs into the lounge in winter, or I could sleep on the sofas. If the doors to the hall were kept closed it would prevent heat from being lost upstairs. With just the door between the kitchen and lounge open, and between the range and the fireplace, I'm sure it will be warm enough.'

'Yes, I agree; that might be the best thing to do. So, is that a thumbs-up for your new home?'

She smiled. 'Definitely! The pros easily outweigh the cons.'

Jamie smiled back. 'Good. We'll get started straight away in removing the bodies.'

He gave her a cup of tea then took his outside for a smoke

and sat in the porch. She came out to join him and said 'What shall we do with them?'

He shrugged. 'I'm not sure; any thoughts?'

She thought for a few seconds. 'Well, I saw a stack of old tarps in the garage. We could make some body-bags from them, put them in the Toyota and take them to the skip where you dumped the others and burn them.'

'That's a good idea. It would save us having to drag them through the garden and down the steps to the beach.' After a while, he added 'Something's bothering me, Jane. I'm not a scientist or a doctor, and I don't know whether we're now immune from the plague because we caught it and survived, or if we can catch it again. I know with some viruses you can build up immunity, but the plague isn't a virus, it's a bacterium, and I don't know if the same thing applies.'

'Oh God! I never thought of that. I just kind of assumed that I couldn't catch it again; but now you mention it, I'm not sure.'

'I know bacteria can't survive out in the open for more than a few hours, so touching things and surfaces isn't a problem. But those bodies might still contain the plague bacteria. Or would they? Do the bacteria need a living organism to survive in and die off at the same time as the host body?'

Jane shook her head. 'I haven't the faintest idea, but we can't take the chance, can we?

'No, we can't. I think when we remove the bodies we should be booted and suited, with rubber gloves, masks and visors, just to be sure. Then we'll burn everything afterwards. We can go to Screwfix to get boiler suits and the rest of the stuff. It's in Beeching Road, not far from the skip, and just around the corner from my flat.'

At that, he had a thought and groaned. 'God, I'm stupid!'

'What is it?'

'Well, I've been driving the Land Rover around for the last week, and now the Toyota as well, and it didn't occur to me that my car is still sitting outside my flat with about three-quarters of a tank of petrol in it! It's a Seat Ibiza 1.4, and much more economical than the trucks. If there are trips we have to make where we don't need to carry big loads, we can use that. It's got to be good for around four hundred miles.'

Jane tutted then grinned. 'You're not the only one who's stupid! My car's still sitting round the back of my block and the same thing applies. I haven't used it since before I got infected, and forgot about it!'

'Ha-ha! Okay, I'll walk back to my flat and get my car, then go round to Beeching Road to get the stuff we need and drive back here. I should be about forty-five minutes.'

'In the meantime, I'll make three body-bags from those tarps. There are rolls of duct tape in the garage, and plenty of twine. Would you pick up some more tarps while you're there in case we don't have enough?'

'Okay, no problem,' he replied.

Jamie got his rucksack and put the sawn-off in it, along with a hammer and a wrecking bar, and found his car keys. His knife in its sheath had become a permanent fixture on his belt, as had his Leatherman multi-tool. He put on his coat and hat and just before leaving remembered to check Jane's shoe-size.

He walked to the end of the road and turned left into Richmond Avenue, then crossed Cooden Drive and under the railway. He turned right into Terminus Avenue, walking at a steady pace. As he went, he saw blossom on some fruit trees along the way, which was a good sign. Hopefully, by the end of summer they would be laden with apples, pears and cherries for them to pick, store and preserve.

Arriving outside his flat, he was tempted to go inside but decided not to. That was his old life, and he had everything he needed from it anyway. His new life lay ahead, at the bungalow and with Jane. He unlocked his car, got in and turned the key in the ignition. The engine turned over slower due to the battery being run-down, but it caught after a while and fired into life. He patted the dashboard and smiled, then drove round to Screwfix on Beeching Road and parked outside, leaving the engine running to charge the battery a bit more.

The front door was locked, so he got the hammer and smashed the glass, reached in to turn the latch and went inside.

After searching up and down the aisles in all the racks, he found what he wanted. He got Wellington boots, disposable boiler suits, several pairs of thick rubber gloves, industrial dust masks and two face visors. He also took several packs of tarps in various sizes, rolls of duct tape, two yard brooms and two shovels. As a last thought, he picked up a few bottles of methylated spirits.

He loaded the car and after a couple of trips was ready to leave. He was back at the bungalow in less than five minutes and parked on the drive beside the Toyota. The door was open and Jane came out to help unload the car.

'Hiya; any problems?'

'No, it was pretty straightforward, really. Didn't take much to break in and I found everything we needed.'

On the driveway were three improvised body-bags made from blue tarps. They were taped all round with duct tape to seal the edges. All they had to do was to push the remains off the bed and onto the tarp, pull up the sides and ends and then seal them with more tape.

Jamie looked at them, nodding. 'Excellent- they should do the trick.'

'Right, let's get this bloody thing over and done with!' to which he agreed.

She got into the Toyota, drove into the road then reversed back onto the drive next door, stopping close to the front door. They got changed into the boiler suits, boots, gloves and face masks, then Jamie picked up a broom and the shovel, while Jane took the body-bags. They went in and up the stairs to the rear bedroom first. Although muted by the masks they could still smell the decomposing bodies.

They laid a tarp on the floor beside the bed, pulled the covers off and used the shovel and broom to push the first body onto the tarp. It was a repulsive task and they also felt sad for having to treat the remains this way, but there was no alternative. They pulled the sides and ends together, taped them up so it was sealed, then carried it down the stairs and lifted it into the truck. They repeated the process with the second body and then moved to the small bedroom and did the same with the little girl. Under their masks and visors, both had tears in their eyes.

When all three bodies were in the truck they went back up and brought down the bedding and mattresses and piled them on top of the bodies. They stripped off the protective clothing and last of all the gloves, then threw them on top, too. After putting their shoes back on, they closed the garage and house and got into the truck. Jane drove to the skip on Beeching Road and reversed up to it; the remains of the three other bodies were still smoking.

Jamie opened the tailgate, climbed in near the cab and pushed the mattresses and clothing into the skip with the clean shovel, while Jane helped from the side with the other broom. It wasn't an easy task as the mattresses were heavy, but they got it done. Both of them were silent throughout. They did the same with the body-bags, threw the broom and shovel in after them and poured the bottles of methylated spirits over the lot. He'd thought it would do the same job, but save on precious petrol.

They moved the truck away then he lit a rag wrapped around a stone and threw it into the skip. The meths ignited and they got back in the truck and drove home in silence. Jane parked on the drive then they went inside and through to the kitchen, where Jamie poured two glasses of Scotch and passed one to her. They raised their glasses in a silent toast and downed them.

'Well, thank God that's over and done with,' said Jane.

Ten

Over a late lunch they decided to go to Jane's apartment that afternoon and move her possessions into next door. She was eager to get settled-in as soon as possible, and Jamie asked her how much stuff she had to move. She thought for a minute, going over in her mind what she needed and what she wanted to bring with her to the new house.

'I think we'll get it all into two truck-loads easily. Obviously, there's a lot of crap that has no place in my new life. Apart from some personal and sentimental things it's mainly clothes, bedding, some favourite cooking equipment, some books and various other things. After that it's just food and water that I've stored. It might be an idea to bring extra water containers and a funnel as I've got a lot of rain-water collected on the roof. We can bring it back and empty it into the new water-butt.'

Jamie thought he would test her a little; with a wry smile he said 'I suppose we'll need to make a separate trip for all your shoes.'

She feigned indignation, but couldn't sustain it and burst out laughing. 'Good one! Actually, I'm more of a jeans, boots and comfortable shirt kind of girl.'

He smiled. 'I guessed that, which was why I said it.'

She looked wistful for a second. 'God; how nice it feels to laugh again- I mean, really laugh!'

'I know what you mean. I haven't done too much laughing

in recent months.' They smiled.

'You know something I find ironic? I- along with most women- used to spend a small fortune every year on "beauty" products;' she mimed inverted commas with her fingers, 'toners, cleansers, moisturisers, make-up, etc. I haven't used any of that crap in over three months, and my skin is in better shape now than it was back then. It makes me think that us women have been sold a crock of shite for most of our lives!'

Jamie laughed and nodded. 'Well, that's the power of advertising and the media for you.'

'Furthermore,' she continued, 'I haven't shaved my legs or armpits in as many months and I've stopped using deodorant, because what's the point? And I often go for days without washing. I've got used to all of that by necessity, and yet I feel more comfortable with myself than I have in years; it's bizarre! Oh- and I've also lost well over a stone from all the right places!'

Jamie mimicked an American advertising voice-over. 'Are you unhappy with your beauty regime? Tired of products that just don't deliver? Want to lose weight? Then what you need is The Hoffmann Plague to get you into shape: it's the ultimate detox!' Jane was in the process of taking a mouthful of coffee and it spurted out all over the table as she burst into laughter. She wiped her mouth with her hand and they couldn't stop laughing. After a while they composed themselves and cleared things away, smiling as they did so. It felt so nice to be able to smile and laugh again with someone, even in the face of adversity.

They decided Jane should take the Toyota to her apartment and start packing: there wasn't much Jamie could do in that respect, so he would bring the Land Rover in two hours and help carry things down and load up the trucks. Before she left, he took the Smith and Wesson from the dresser drawer and handed it to her, along with a handful of extra shells. Things turned serious again after their brief interlude of laughter.

'I don't think you should go out on your own unarmed any more, so take this for now; it should fit in your pocket.' He showed her how to open the cylinder and push the ejector rod to remove the spent shells. 'You don't even need to cock it. All modern revolvers are double-action, which means the first half of the trigger-pull cocks it and the second half releases the hammer to fire it. But you can cock it manually if you want. That looks especially good if you're pointing it at someone; it shows intent!'

He demonstrated it to her, and how to safely release the hammer again if she didn't need to fire it. He reloaded the gun and gave it to her. She had a deep inside pocket in her coat that the revolver fitted in, and the spare shells went in her left outside pocket.

'I'm going to cut down the shotgun that we got from your attackers and make another sawn-off for you to have. It'll be a good weapon to carry around with you; there's nothing better at close range and it doesn't take much aiming. And believe me; *no one's* going to fuck with you if you're pointing a sawn-off at them! Plus, of course, if you're out and you see a rabbit or a duck, or something, you can bag it for our dinner! We'll have some practice either tonight or tomorrow.'

She gave a slightly nervous but grateful smile and, on impulse, gave him a quick hug. 'Thanks, Jamie,' she said, and then left. He heard the Toyota start up and drive off, then looked at his watch to note when he had to meet her. He picked up the shotgun, went into the garage and lit the gas lamp. He hadn't looked at it properly since picking it up from the road the day before, but it was an older design than his, with external hammers rather than the internal ones that his model had. It looked a bit short and, on inspection, he found that someone had already cut down the barrel by probably a foot.

He secured it in a vice on the work-bench and cut off the barrels with a hacksaw to a few inches in front of the fore-end, then removed the burrs and smoothed the ends with a round file and sandpaper. He made a new attachment for the sling and fitted it on the front stock, so Jane would be able to carry it on her shoulder by its strap if she wanted to. After that he reloaded it and went back into the kitchen.

He put the gun on the table then made some coffee and went outside for a smoke. As he was walking down the garden he spotted two pigeons together in a tree next door. *Don't move,* he thought. He put his cup down, rushed back to the kitchen and picked up the shotgun from the table, then came back out. They were still there and he walked slowly to within about seven yards of them. He raised the gun and took aim as best he could: with almost no barrels left it was a bit awkward, but at this range it wouldn't be a problem. He cocked both hammers then pulled the trigger for the first barrel and both pigeons fell off the branch in a flurry of feathers. He took the shotgun back inside, fetched the step-ladder and climbed over the wall to retrieve the birds.

He left them in the porch for Jane to prepare when she got back. He'd never done it before and didn't want to make a hash of it, so decided to let her show him how later. He finished his coffee and went into the conservatory to check on the seawater evaporation. All the water was gone and there was a layer of salt crystals around the dish's edge. He licked his finger, wiped it around the rim and tasted it. It had a pleasant flavour, just like the sea salt he had used in his cooking for years, and he smiled.

It was still less than the two hours they'd agreed, but he thought he might as well leave now. He got the Land Rover out of the garage, put some water containers in the back, closed the garage and drove off. Jane saw him approaching along West Parade and went down to the entrance on Sackville Road to let him in. He parked the truck behind the Toyota then went up with her. She had most things ready so they carried them down to the trucks. Jane's leg was still rather painful so Jamie did most of the work, but she insisted on helping.

When the majority was loaded, he went up to the roof with the large water containers, while Jane carried on packing the smaller items. He filled them with the funnel from her buckets, tubs and bowls, then carried them down to the trucks. He went back up for the containers that had lids but left the few remaining ones that were open. Before going down for the last time he leaned on the parapet and looked out, east and west. It was a fine view and he could see for at least ten miles; east towards Hastings and west towards Eastbourne and Beachy Head beyond.

When all the water was loaded he went up to Jane's apartment to help with the last few things. He found her sitting on the sofa crying her eyes out, clutching a framed photograph to her chest. He sat down, putting his arms around her, and she leaned into him and sobbed, her chest heaving. After a while she wiped her eyes on her sleeve and showed him the photo; it was of Jane, her mother and two sisters, standing smiling in front of the De La Warr Pavilion. They all looked so alike.

'This was taken last summer,' she said, breathing hard. 'Mum and Debs and Kate came to visit for the day. We had a lovely lunch there and then strolled arm-in-arm along the seafront for a few hours, chatting and catching up on stuff. It was a perfect day, and that was the last time we were all together.'

'I'm so sorry, Jane.' He didn't know what else to say to console her.

'Were you close to your family?' She asked.

'Yes. Not a day goes by that I don't think of them. I miss my mum terribly. Sometime last week, I think it was, I was up on Galley Hill and remembered my brother and I sitting on that spot eating fish and chips a year ago. I broke down and, just for a second, I thought of throwing myself off the cliff; I felt so alone and hopeless.'

'Aw! Well, I'm so glad you didn't, because then we wouldn't have met.' She smiled at him and gave him a hug. 'And,' she added after a second, with a cheeky grin, 'if you had done that I really would have been up Shit Creek without a paddle yesterday!' They both laughed.

'Right,' he said, 'let's get these last few bits downstairs and go home.'

'Okay.'

They carried the remaining things down to the trucks then drove home together and unloaded everything into the two houses. All of Jane's clothing, bedding and personal possessions were taken next door and left in the lounge for her to sort through. The food, water and supplies they carried into the bungalow. They decided it would be best for now if they put all the food together in his spare bedroom. They planned to make an inventory of everything they had, so kept similar foods together. All the water was poured into the new water-butt outside.

They decided it was time for a well-deserved cup of coffee, and while it was brewing Jamie showed her the new sawn-off shotgun and the pigeons he'd shot earlier.

'Excellent,' she said. 'We can make a pigeon casserole tonight, with some tinned tomatoes.'

'And we can add some rosemary, bay leaves and chives to it as well, now we know they're in the garden,' he added.

'Jamie, would you mind if I stayed here for another day or two before I move in properly next door? I want the bedroom at the back for the sea view, but it still smells of death in there. I've opened all the windows upstairs and want to let it air for a few days before moving my stuff in.'

'Of course you can; no problem.'

'That's great, thanks.'

She looked out the kitchen window; the sun was getting low in the sky as evening drew on. 'I think I'll go down to the sea for a wash while there's still some warmth in the air. I know I've got used to not washing for days, but after the events of the last two I feel the need to get clean.'

'Good idea; I think I'll join you.' He realised what he'd said and blushed. 'I didn't actually mean join you… I meant I'll do the same and go down after you.' She laughed.

'Here, take this; it lathers in salt water.' He passed her the bottle of travel wash and a cup of coffee then took his cup outside to hide his embarrassment.

'Thanks,' she replied. She gave him a minute and then followed him out. He was looking at the wall between their gardens.

'I was thinking after you left earlier; what about knocking an entrance through the wall, near the house? It would make coming-and-going much easier and be handy for when we're working together on the gardens, for wheelbarrows and stuff.'

'I think that's a great idea. I don't like the thought of us having to knock on each other's front door every day, like polite neighbours do!'

'Great. I'll get onto that tomorrow, I think. It won't be difficult. And if we need to, for whatever reason, I can always build a gate to go in there.'

Jane finished her coffee and then went next door to get some fresh clothes. She was back in a few minutes with a small bag of clothing and went into her bedroom. She came out in her bath robe and a pair of sandals, took the travel wash and a towel and headed off down the garden.

Jamie found a marker pen and walked across the patio to the wall. He shinnied up it and looked over, making sure that where he was going to mark an entrance was across both patios, then drew two lines down the wall, just under a metre apart. He reckoned that with the angle-grinder and a hammer and bolster it wouldn't be a difficult job.

Jane was back in less than fifteen minutes, puffing out her cheeks and shivering, and with a concerned look on her face. 'Jamie, there's an injured dog lying on the beach! I didn't see it at first, but when I came out of the sea I saw two seagulls pecking at something and then jumping back because it moved. I went over to look and it's a black Labrador; it looks half-dead.'

'Oh, bloody hell! I'll go and have a look.' Jane rushed off to put on some clothes and he took the revolver out of the dresser drawer, intending to put it out of its misery. He walked down the garden and through the gate, then down the steps to the promenade. He could see the dog about twenty yards away; three seagulls were pecking at it, so he shouted and they flew off. Jane caught up with him and they went across the beach and knelt down beside it. It was rather thin and its coat was matted and dirty. It wasn't moving, but they could see a weak rise and fall of its chest. There were nasty wounds on its hindquarters; herring gulls have big, strong beaks.

'Poor thing!' said Jamie, and lifted the gun to end its

suffering. It had a collar and tag with an engraved mobile phone number. Jane turned the disc round and read out loud 'Max.' On hearing its name, the dog's ears pricked up; it opened its eyes weakly and whimpered.

'Oh, God! Jamie, can't we do something? D'you think we might be able to save him?'

'Well, we've got to try. I can't bring myself to shoot him while there's a chance. Go back to the house: in the garage there's a bin filled with rags, old sheets and blankets. Put some on the floor in the kitchen and get the stove fired up. I'll carry him back.'

'Okay,' she replied and rushed off. Jamie stroked the dog's side and scratched behind his ear; he whimpered again and his eyes opened. He tried lifting his head but was too weak.

'Poor fellow! Come on, Max, let's get you home and into the warm.'

He picked it up carefully, avoiding touching the wounds on its flank, then walked to the nearest steps up to the promenade and made his way back to the house. Kicking the gate shut behind him, he went down the path and into the kitchen. Jane had put a pile of sheets and blankets on the floor and was busy getting the stove going. He laid the dog down gently onto the blankets and then got his first-aid kit, a bottle of surgical spirit and cotton wool. He swabbed the wounds made by the gulls and the dog whimpered again at the sting of the spirit. Then he went into the bathroom and got his old beard trimmer, which he hadn't used in months. The batteries were flat, so he fitted new ones and shaved the area around the wounds then put a few drops of iodine tincture onto them. He rubbed on some antiseptic cream and then stuck dressings over the wounds.

Jane had the fire going in the stove and flames were roaring away as she closed the doors. Jamie put a blanket over Max and stood up. 'I'm going to shoot down to Warburtons, by Sainsbury's, and get some dog food. There was a load in there when I went in earlier in the week for some things. Do you think he'll be able to drink anything? He must be really dehydrated.'

'I don't know. I'll put some water down by him and see if I can help him to drink. Water's probably more important than food right now.'

'Yes, you're right, but I'll still go down and get some food. If he survives the night he's going to need it. I won't be long.'

'Okay.'

He got his car keys and a couple of shopping bags from the larder and left. He was there in a few minutes and parked outside, leaving the engine running. Under the counter were several bins of loose feed; a kind of doggy "pick 'n' mix". He scooped some from each bin into one bag, then filled the other with tins of dog food from the shelves and drove home.

Jane gave him a big smile as he walked in. 'He's managed to drink some water. I sprinkled a few drops over his nose and into his mouth and he licked his lips and opened his eyes. I lifted him slightly and held his head and he was able to drink from the bowl. It took him a few minutes, but he must have drunk at least a pint!'

'Ah, well done! That's good news, and a good sign. I don't think we should give him any food just yet; what do you think?'

'No; it might harm him at the moment as he's dehydrated. If he survives the night and perks up by tomorrow, we'll give him some. Right now, water is probably enough.'

Jamie put the dog food away in the larder then knelt down next to Max and stroked his head and sides. 'Hello, mate. You hang in there. You're a survivor, just like me and Jane.' Max wagged his tail feebly in response.

Jane smiled and then went outside to prepare the pigeons for cooking. They soon had a casserole simmering on the stove, with a few herbs from the garden and some sea beet that Jamie picked, along with some lentils and rice thrown into the pot. He opened a bottle of red wine and poured them both a glass.

He raised his to Jane. 'Here's to Max; fingers crossed.'

'To Max!' she said and clinked glasses with him.

Eleven

Jamie couldn't sleep. He was worried about Max and lay in bed for over an hour, tossing and turning. He loved animals and had always wanted a dog, but had never been in a position to have one. He would be a great companion for them and also useful, both as a guard dog and as a gun-dog if they went hunting for birds or rabbits; it was, after all, what Labradors had been bred for. He hoped Max pulled through: it *would* be an added responsibility for him and Jane, in terms of feeding him as well as themselves, but he felt the benefits outweighed that. *Do dogs eat fish?* He wasn't sure. They needed to make a trip to the warehouse at Sainsbury's anyway, so they could stock up on food for Max as well while they were there. He gave up trying to sleep, lit the candle by his bed then got up, put on his dressing gown and went into the kitchen.

Max raised his head to look at him as he entered, and whined. He tried to stand, but his legs were unsteady and he only made it to a sitting position, his tail wagging. His water bowl was empty so Jamie refilled it and he had another long drink, while he knelt down and stroked him. He patted the blanket and Max lay down again and curled up, looking up at him with his big eyes. He put the blanket back over him, opened the stove doors and raked the embers then threw another log in. He poured himself a small whisky, rolled a cigarette and sat at the table for ten minutes before going back to bed and falling asleep, feeling much happier.

When he awoke in the morning and went into the kitchen Jane was there already, making coffee. Max was sitting up on his blankets looking at him and wagging his tail.

'Morning, Jane.'

'Morning, Jamie. Well, look how much better our little guest is feeling!'

Jamie bent down and stroked Max, who wagged his tail harder and whined. 'Wow! He looks so different to yesterday.'

'That might have something to do with the tin of dog food he polished off about an hour ago!'

'Really? That's great!'

'Did you get up in the night?'

'Yes, I couldn't sleep- worrying about him.'

'I thought so; I saw the whisky out.'

'He'd finished the water we put down before bed, so I refilled it.'

'Well, he'd finished that as well when I got up, so that must be getting on for three pints he's put away. He certainly needed it. I wonder how he got so dehydrated: I mean, he's thin, but not scrawny, so he's obviously been eating something.'

'Well, his back legs are much weaker than his front; more so than could be attributed to just the wounds from the gulls' beaks. It occurs to me now that the wounds were pretty deep. I didn't think of it at the time I was cleaning them.'

'You know what I think?' said Jane. 'I reckon he attacked something for food that fought back; maybe a small deer. Those wounds could have come from antlers and some deer, like muntjacs, have tusks. Could even have been from a wild boar; I believe there are large numbers in Sussex.'

'Ah! That makes more sense; you're probably right. Poor thing, but at least he's starting to perk up.' They looked down at Max, who seemed to know they were talking about him and wagged his tail.

While drinking their coffee they discussed things that needed doing for the week and made a list, which they pinned to a cork-board on the wall. They added another sheet of paper, headed *Ideas!* If either of them had a bright idea about

93

something they could jot it down when they thought of it, for the other to see. Jamie went down to the sea to bathe, having missed the opportunity the previous evening due to finding Max, while Jane prepared breakfast.

During the next week they got a lot of work done in the gardens of both properties, working long hours. There was much to do and they set to it with enthusiasm. Sometimes-weather permitting- Jamie brought his MP3 player outside, plugged into some mini speakers, so they had music while they worked and sang along to popular tracks. It made the days pass quicker and kept their spirits up, as well as increasing the friendship between them. At one point, after they'd both been singing their hearts out, Jamie said 'You can tell a lot about a person by the way they react when *Bohemian Rhapsody* comes on the air!' and they both laughed. They also picked up Jane's car, a VW Golf, from behind her flat; its battery was low so they jump-started it from the Toyota and she took it for a run to charge the battery.

On the Sunday morning after finding Max they made an inventory of all the food and supplies they had, noting things they needed to stock-up on. They took both trucks to Sainsbury's warehouse and parked in the goods yard. Jamie walked around the block to the entrance, through the store to the warehouse and opened the delivery doors at the back. Jane came inside and couldn't believe how much was in there. They walked along the aisles collecting things in trolleys and wheeling them out to the trucks. They filled the vehicles with tinned vegetables, meat, beans and fruit; dried foods like rice, pasta and pulses, and found various boxes of meats such as salami, pancetta and chorizo. These were a real bonus as they had a long shelf-life, being cured and vacuum-packed.

They also stocked-up on many less-essential items that would nourish their spirits, if not their stomachs! They loaded boxes of red wine, whisky, cognac and brandy into the trucks alongside the more mundane food items, and were lucky to find a few boxes of candles and tea-lights that would be useful. Jamie was pleased to find several boxes of his favourite tobacco, too. They drove home and unloaded everything between the two houses. Max barked enthusiastically when they entered, and Jane gave him some dog biscuits and treats from the larder. By the time they had finished all the cupboards and larders in both kitchens were full, and food was stacked up on the floor of Jane's lounge and Jamie's spare bedroom. For the rest of that day Jamie was busy putting up new shelves in the spare bedroom to store food on, and also some in Jane's lounge. He started one of the generators for the first time to charge some batteries for the power-tools.

On the Monday Jamie made an entrance through the wall between their gardens. He cut down through the brickwork with an angle-grinder and then knocked out the bricks with a hammer and bolster. He had some lengths of 3x2 timber left from his porch construction, so he fixed two pieces across the top on both sides of the wall using long coach bolts, for strengthening.

As the bungalow already had a decent-sized vegetable plot they worked on that first; turning the soil over and sowing seeds for carrots, potatoes, cabbages and parsnips. They left vacant lines between them so they could re-sow more in a few weeks, to stagger the planting. In Jane's garden large areas of the borders contained only weeds or a few flowers and shrubs, which were easy to remove, replacing them with seeds for root vegetables and various herbs in between, along with more onions. They removed the turf from other areas of both lawns and turned the soil over for sowing more vegetables. It was hard work and they were worn out by the end of each day. The first thing they sowed was salad plants in tubs on the patio and in the conservatory, as they would be quick to grow and yield a large crop all through summer and autumn. They also sowed tomatoes in tubs in the conservatory, as it would act like a greenhouse and provide much warmer conditions.

During that week the change in Max's condition was amazing and they both felt heartened by that. He always ate well and started putting on weight. His coat began to look glossier as he cleaned himself, and he began walking around the garden; slowly at first, but getting stronger every day, sniffing at everything and following them wherever they went. By Wednesday he could manage a slow trot up the garden when Jane called him, so she decided to take him for a short walk along the promenade to exercise and strengthen his muscles. He was panting by the time they got back and went under the porch to curl up on his blanket, which they'd put outside while they worked.

On the Tuesday they had a nice surprise. Jane was moving into next door, and she carried over the few things that she had at the bungalow. The house had been well aired over the last three days and she'd also lit some scented candles, so it no longer smelled of decomposing corpses. Between them they took the mattress from another double bed and put it onto the bed frame in the rear bedroom. They realised that they hadn't even looked in the garage when first checking the house on Saturday. They found the keys in the hall, along with two sets of car keys; one marked "BMW" and the other, much older, marked "Ford". They went out the front and lifted the huge door to the garage, which opened smoothly and almost silently. Jamie's mouth opened but no sound came out, and Jane looked at him with amusement.

There were two cars in there; on the left was a four-year-old BMW 3 Series estate, but it was the car on the right that had Jamie's attention. It was a V-registered Mark II Ford Escort RS2000, which made it a 1979 or 1980 model. They stopped making them in 1981, Jamie seemed to recall. It was a real classic, with its "droop-snoot" front-end, and worth a fortune.

'Blimey! I can't remember the last time I saw one of these,' said Jamie. 'I loved them when I was a kid. I mean, they'd stopped making them years before I could drive, but I always wanted one.'

'I'm sure I've seen this driving around town occasionally!' Jane smiled. 'So why don't you take it for a spin, then?'

He looked at her and grinned. 'Fancy a ride?'

'Bloody right, I do! I remember Doyle driving one of these in *The Professionals!*'

He unlocked the driver's door, got in and turned the

ignition key. The battery was low so they had to jump-start it from Jamie's Seat, and when it burst into life there was a lovely burbling sound from the sports exhaust. He revved it a little, then put it in gear and drove out onto the drive. Jane closed the garage and he unlocked the passenger door for her. She climbed into the Recaro bucket seat and fastened her seat belt.

'Where to, madam?'

'How about a blast along the seafront to Galley Hill?'

'You're on!'

He took it steady along West Parade at first, getting a feel for the car. He also tested the brakes hard; they didn't want to get to Galley Hill doing 100mph and not be able to stop! It was a completely different driving experience from modern cars: there was no power steering, it was noisy, it only had a four-speed gearbox and the ride was really hard. There were also lots of rattles and squeaks. There was a radio-cassette player in the centre console and Jane rummaged in the glove box and found a handful of tapes.

'Ah! This'll do nicely,' she said. It was an old tape of Bryan Adams' greatest hits. She put it in the stereo and found the track *Summer of '69*. Jamie stopped on the other side of the roundabout by her apartment block, facing east along Marina. He revved the engine and let out the clutch as Bryan Adams started singing;

'I got my first real six-string,
Bought it at the five-and-dime…"

The car leapt forward in a cloud of smoke and squealing rear tyres and Jamie red-lined it in each gear as he changed up through the gearbox. They had the windows open and were singing at the tops of their voices as they roared along the empty seafront for a little over a mile. They had a fantastic feeling of recklessness and excitement that was a huge release from the tensions and horrors of the past months. They topped-out along De La Warr Parade at 110mph and he took his foot off the gas as they approached Galley Hill. They slowed going up the hill and turned round at the top, where Jamie pulled over.

'Come on then; your turn!' Jane grinned at him and they

changed places, then she roared off down the hill and along the flat. When they got to the roundabout by her flats she turned onto West Parade and drove home at a more sedate pace, both of them laughing and grinning from ear-to-ear. Back at the house she parked the car in the garage then they went inside feeling elated and made some coffee. After laughing some more about their crazy ride they went back to the gardening with smiles on their faces.

Something happened on the Wednesday that Jamie had to tell Jane about when he got home from a trip to the retail park. She had prepared lunch while he was out and they sat down to eat when he returned.

'Well,' he said, 'there's at least one more person alive in the area, maybe more.'

'Why, did you see them?'

'No, but a car was gone from the park by Tesco's, which was there on Friday when I got the generators- a Ford Mondeo estate. I forgot to tell you about it at the time. I couldn't remember if it had been there on my last visit and I had a lot on my mind, but it was definitely there on Friday and now it's not.'

They talked about the implications of this, but couldn't decide if it was a good or a bad thing. Ostensibly, they should have felt pleased that others had survived, but so far two of their three encounters with other survivors had been bad ones.

'It's possible they don't even live in Bexhill,' said Jane, 'but came in from the surrounding area.'

'That's true. Oh well, there's nothing we can do about it; we'll either meet them, or we won't. We'll just have to be cautious whenever we go out, and make sure we're always armed, to be on the safe side.' Jane agreed with him.

He thought for a second. 'On that note, I think it's time we went down to the beach to give you a bit of instruction on the shotguns. You can fire off a few cartridges to get a feel for them.'

'Okay, that's a good idea.'

They finished lunch and cleared up then he brought the two sawn-offs and one over and under into the kitchen and

98

put them on the table. He broke them open, removed the cartridges and demonstrated the differences between them. Her sawn-off was the oldest and simplest design, with two external hammers that you cocked manually and a separate trigger to fire each barrel.

'I'd avoid firing both barrels together, if I were you,' he said. 'The kick would be huge and might hurt your shoulder!'

The other sawn-off and the over/under were more modern designs, with internal hammers. He explained that they cocked automatically when you broke open the barrel and closed it again, and there was a safety catch on top of the stock.

'That means that if they're loaded and closed they're always ready to fire; all you need to do is slide the safety off and you're ready to rock 'n' roll!'

He pointed out that his sawn-off had two triggers, like hers, but the two over/unders had just a single trigger which fired each barrel in turn. 'The recoil from the first shot automatically re-cocks it, ready for the next shot.'

Jane practised opening and closing, loading and handling them, then they took all three guns and the box of cartridges they'd got from the Toyota down to the beach. Max followed them down the garden, but waited on the top step and watched them go onto the beach.

They didn't go far and stopped ten yards from the nearest groyne, in line with one of the posts. Jane loaded the first sawn-off, cocked it and held it loosely up to her shoulder. Jamie stopped her immediately. 'Whatever you do, don't fire it like that! You'll hurt yourself. It's got to be snug against your shoulder to absorb the recoil. If it's loose, the recoil will drive it back into you and you'll end up with bruises. If it's tight against you, your body moves with it to absorb the shock.'

She settled it snugly into her shoulder, aimed at the post and pulled the trigger. She gave a little shriek of excitement and turned to grin at him. Max barked behind them. They turned and waved at him and he barked again as if to say *"Just checking!"* She raised the gun again and fired the second barrel, then tried Jamie's sawn-off. She broke it open, loaded it, closed

99

the barrel and slid the safety on. She raised it to her shoulder, slid the safety off with her thumb and fired each barrel in turn.

They walked up to the post and Jamie showed her the spread of shot either side of it. They walked back to the same spot and she did the same with the over and under gun. Jamie said to hold it away from her at a slight angle when she broke it open, so the automatic ejectors wouldn't throw the spent cartridges into her face. She broke it open and the cartridges ejected, followed by a trail of smoke. When they went up to the post she could see the much tighter grouping of the shot pattern because of its longer barrel. They repeated the process another ten yards further back.

'Excellent,' said Jamie. 'Feel comfortable with them?'

Jane grinned and nodded. 'Cool! I wish I'd tried this years ago.' He smiled and asked her which sawn-off she felt happier using, and that she could choose which she preferred. She said she was happy with the one she had. They walked back up the steps to Max, patting and stroking him, and Jane gave him a dog treat. After putting the guns away in the house they carried on with the gardening.

That evening they cooked and ate their meal together in his kitchen. Even though she was now sleeping next door since the previous night, it made much more sense for them to cook together, rather than both of them burning wood on a single meal each. They planned to continue doing so every day, and it was much more sociable like that, anyway.

After they'd eaten and cleared the things away they sat and talked for a couple of hours in the kitchen, with Max stretched out on his blanket in front of the stove, then Jane yawned and announced that she was ready for bed. They said goodnight and she stroked Max, then picked up her shotgun and a box of cartridges and went next door.

Jamie poured a glass of cognac and went to sit on the sofa in the conservatory, looking out at the night sky and listening to the waves break on the beach. Max heard him move and looked up; satisfied that he wasn't going far he put his head back down on the blanket. Jamie sat there for half an hour, thinking. He decided that the next day, weather permitting, he would take the boat out for the first time and attempt to catch some fish. Apart from wanting fresh food, he was eager to try the smokers he'd built to see if they worked as they were, or if they would need modifying. He finished his drink, stroked Max and said goodnight, then went to bed.

Twelve

On Thursday morning when he got up, Jane was again up before him and they greeted each other. Max was devouring a bowl of food and she was sitting at the table with a mug of coffee, reading a book. She said there was coffee in the pot so he poured himself a mug and sat down with her.

'I was thinking last night after you went to bed;' he said, 'I'd like to take the boat out to try it with the oars and see if I can catch some fish. We need to start getting fresh meat and learning to preserve it. The sooner we can stop using tinned meat, the better, as far as I'm concerned. I think we need to treat those foods more as emergency rations for when we can't get fresh stuff. Obviously, we'll have to continue using the tinned veg' and fruit until later, when we can pick fresh stuff.'

'I agree. I was looking at all the food we got before I went to bed last night and thinking similar things. I mean, it's great that we've got it, and there's still a lot more in the warehouse, but it's no substitute for fresh stuff and we can't rely on it. Also, there is still the possibility that more survivors will show up and find the warehouse, and we can't exactly claim it as ours!'

He nodded, agreeing with her. 'I'm conscious, though, that we've still got a lot to do in the gardens, and I don't want to spend loads of time out on the sea, maybe catching nothing, while you're working hard here on your own.'

'No, but you've got to try it sometime soon, anyway. I

think it's a good idea and you should do it. It's nice outside today and calm, which will make it easier with the boat. Why don't you give it an hour or two while I carry on in the garden, and see how it goes?' to which he agreed.

'Also,' she added, holding up the survival book she was reading, 'I think we should start laying snares for rabbits in various places. We don't want to rely on using the shotguns because our ammo is limited. I know we've got a good supply from what you found with the guns, but we don't know if we'll be able to replace it with more in the future.'

Jamie smiled. 'Good thinking… You're not just a pretty face!' He ducked as her hand came up to clout him and they grinned at each other.

'There's a roll of thin garden wire on the wall in the garage that should do the job,' he said.

'Okay. Where d'you think would be good places to find them? The railway line might be good.'

'Yes, it probably would. We could get to it easily from the bridge over Westcourt Drive, which is only a five-minute walk. There must be lots of burrows there.'

'… And the green space either side of Down Road, too.'

'Definitely; I've seen rabbit droppings there when I've been out walking. The hardest part will probably be finding the entrances to the burrows.'

'Okay, so why don't we each spend a few hours this morning doing that? You go out fishing and I'll go out and see if I can lay some snares, then afterwards we can spend the rest of the day together in the gardens.'

'Okay, that sounds good.'

'I'll take Max with me; he'll be great at sniffing out the burrows, I'm sure.'

'Do you think he's up to it yet?'

'Well… I know it's only a short walk to the railway, but if I take your car it will save Max's legs until we're there, and he won't have to do much apart from sniffing-out the burrows. I bet he'll love it.'

'Okay, go for it. Tell you what, though; take the RS2000 instead of my car. It's got a quarter of a tank of petrol and we may as well use it,' which Jane thought was a good idea.

They ate breakfast and washed up then Jane went into the garage to make some snares while he got the fishing tackle out. There were four rods with reels that he'd got from the angling club and each was set up with a different fishing rig. He chose one of the lighter rods with a fixed-spool reel that was set up for light lure fishing. He'd never used the multiplier reels on two of the rods before, but was familiar with fixed-spool reels from his coarse fishing days as a teenager. The tackle box contained numerous different lures and he had a landing net with a 4ft handle to bring fish into the boat... if he caught anything!

He got changed into some warm clothes and a lightweight jacket and got ready to leave. Max looked at him expectantly, wagging his tail. He reached down and stroked him. 'No, Max, you're going out with Jane today, to find some rabbits.'

Jane came out of the garage with a rucksack containing a dozen snares she'd made, with some sharpened pieces of doweling for stakes to tie the snares to.

'Right; I'm all set,' she said, putting the sawn-off into her pack along with a bottle of water and some treats for Max. 'Have fun on the sea, be careful... and catch us some fish! I'll see you later. Come on Max, let's find the rabbits!' Max barked and wagged his tail even more.

'Bye;' Jamie replied, 'you be careful, too.' She smiled at him and nodded.

He heard the Escort start up and pull away, then picked up the fishing tackle and his pack and walked out the back door. Once down on the beach he removed the tarp from the boat and tied it to the railing so it wouldn't blow away. He put everything in the boat then pulled the trailer down to the water's edge, where he unhitched the boat and slid it off the trailer into the water.

He waded in, pushing the boat out until it had enough depth to float, then jumped in and fitted the oars into the rowlocks. He felt a bit nervous as he had limited experience with boats of any kind. He grabbed the oars, bent forward and started rowing. Despite the sea being fairly calm, it was still hard work pulling against the surf and he made slow progress until he was a little way out and over the breaking waves. He could see the blue tarp tied to the railing easily, and he kept that in view as a point of reference in case he drifted too far.

He rowed until he was about fifty yards out, although from his perspective it seemed further than it actually was. He was nervous of going out too far and wondered if he should have an anchor of some sort to tether the boat in one spot. He thought he'd use a small lure first as he'd rather catch several small fish than use something that was too big and not get anything. He picked up the rod, fitted a lure and started casting out then reeling in, jigging it up and down. After five minutes he had forgotten his nervousness and was lost in the fishing. He used to do a lot of lure fishing for pike and perch as a teenager in lakes and rivers, and this was the same principle.

Every few minutes he would look up and note his position in relation to the blue tarp on the railings. After a while he could see that he was drifting slowly eastwards, although it wasn't a problem. After about half an hour he'd drifted a fair way so he rowed back to roughly where he'd started. He was getting no takes so he changed lures several times over the next half-hour, but still had no luck. He decided to row out further and try again; it was difficult to judge the distance, but he guessed he was about a hundred yards out now.

He'd been out for nearly ninety minutes and was getting a bit despondent. He'd imagined hauling in lots of fish within half an hour! He was starting to ache as well as feeling chilly, despite the sun. He drank a mouthful of whisky from his hip flask, picked up the rod and carried on casting. Suddenly he felt a tug on the rod and struck to set the hooks. He could feel a fish fighting on the end of the line and he played it carefully, not wanting to lose it. It didn't feel too heavy, so he wasn't worried about the line snapping; it was probably 15lb line on the reel, or similar. He reeled it in and then netted it with a big grin on his face.

He wasn't too well up on sea fish but thought it was a bass and it weighed probably two pounds at least: he bashed it on the gunwale and put it in a canvas bag. Within the next thirty minutes he caught another smaller one and also two good-sized mackerel that were both about half a pound. That was good enough for him for two hours so he decided to head home. He'd drifted eastwards again, so had to row back further. He made it back to the beach with aching arms and shoulders, jumped out and got the boat onto its trailer. He pulled it up the beach and tied it to the railing, removed the tackle, his pack and the fish bag, then secured the tarp over the top and went back to the house. On the way he picked some sea beet leaves and put them in his pack.

After Jane left, she drove along Westcourt Drive and under the railway bridge, turned around and parked underneath it. She got out and opened the rear door for Max, who climbed out carefully, still favouring his back legs slightly but full of beans. His tail was wagging furiously, as if he knew what they were there for. She climbed up the embankment through the bushes, looking back to check that Max was okay; he was following at his own pace and doing fine. She took some wire cutters from her pack and cut a section of fencing then peeled it back. She walked onto the railway track and a few seconds later Max joined her, panting a little.

She didn't have to go far before seeing rabbit droppings. The banks either side of the track were heavily overgrown, mainly with brambles that formed a dense carpet. Jane crouched down next to Max and pointed to the droppings, then picked some up and held them under his nose.

'Where are the rabbits, Max? Come on boy!'

Max set off slowly with his nose to the ground, following the scent. She stood there watching and just left him to it. After about ten yards he stopped and went still then looked back at Jane and she walked up to him. Just where he'd stopped there was a small opening under the mass of dense brambles, which she would probably have missed. Bending down and looking closely, she could see bits of fur stuck to some thorns and the ground beneath was smooth from the passage of many feet. She got up, patted and stroked Max, then reached into her pocket and gave him a treat.

'Good boy, Max! Good boy!' He whined quietly and wagged his tail.

Jane took off her pack and removed a snare and a stake. She pushed the stake firmly into the ground to one side of the opening, fixed the wire securely to it and laid the open noose across the hole with a few bits of grass over it. She pointed ahead and Max set off again with his nose down until he found another.

After searching around and laying eight snares Max was flagging, so she decided to head for home, praising him all the way. She watched him closely as he went back down the embankment, but he was okay. Her own leg was still sore from the shotgun wounds, although they had healed well.

Back at the house she parked in the garage and saw a remnant of thick carpet from the lounge. She thought it would be more comfortable for Max than the blanket on the kitchen's tiled floor, so she looked around and found a Stanley knife in a tool box. She cut off three pieces big enough for him and took them with her into the bungalow with Max.

Jamie wasn't back, but she realised she'd only been gone just over an hour and it was still only late morning. She took up Max's blanket from the floor and replaced it with the three pieces of carpet, which made a nice cushioned bed for him, then put the blanket on top. He flopped down gratefully onto it then she gave him a couple of biscuits and stroked him. 'Good boy, Max, you did great today!' He whined and licked her hand.

She was a bit worried about Jamie. She knew he was a competent bloke, but couldn't help being rather worried as anything could happen out on the sea. Their friendship had deepened over the last six days through spending all their time together, and far more so than would have happened back in their old life due to their circumstances. She found the binoculars and went next door and up to her bedroom. Raising the binoculars and scanning around, she saw him over to the left, quite a way out. He seemed to be okay and she breathed a sigh of relief then went back next door. She made a cup of tea then sat down on the sofa in the conservatory to rest her leg, and Max followed her in. He climbed up next to her, lying down with his head on her thigh, and within a few minutes she had dozed off.

Thirteen

That was how Jamie found them when he returned an hour or so later. Max heard the back door, looked up and barked, which woke Jane. She sat up and rubbed her eyes.

'Hiya. Blimey, I didn't intend to fall asleep! What's the time?'

'Nearly lunchtime, by my reckoning,' he smiled. Jane got up to heat some water for coffee.

'How did you get on?' she enquired.

'Not very well; all I got were these…' he said with a wry smile, as he tipped the four fish out onto the worktop. Jane's eyes lit up and she beamed at him, then gave him a big hug and kissed his cheek.

'Oh wow! Jamie, that's fantastic. Well done, you.'

'Thanks, but I think it was more by luck than judgement! Sea fishing's a complete mystery to me. I've no idea where to look or what I should be doing, really.'

'Well, you must have done something right!'

'I suppose so, but I don't know if it will always be like that. It took me two hours to get these, and I didn't start catching until I was a hundred yards out, maybe. I got all these in the last half-hour.'

'I saw you: when I got back about an hour ago I was a bit worried, but I realised you'd only been out an hour or so. I took the binoculars up to my bedroom and saw you, which relieved me, so I came back down and then fell asleep. I was a bit nervous, though.'

'You weren't the only one! To be honest, I was a bit nervous myself. I know I was only a hundred yards out, but when you're out there in a small boat it seems much further.'

Jane made coffee and they sat at the table, where Max came up to Jamie and nuzzled his leg, so he reached down and stroked his head.

'So, I got four fish from two hours' work. That's going to be... what, ten meals? We'll have a mackerel each, and the other two- I think they're bass- will make about four meals each. That's not bad for two hours' fishing.'

'It's not bad at all. But, of course, we've got to be able to keep them, somehow. If we have the two mackerel now for lunch, and half a bass between us tonight, then we've got to preserve the other one-and-a-half for later. Even in this weather we can't keep fish for several days without refrigeration.'

'No, you're right; not as they are. It's time to try the smokers I made, but the fish will have to be salted and cured overnight first. I'm guessing that if the smoking works, then they might be good for a day or two; what d'you think?'

'Sounds plausible, but I suppose, ultimately, we'll have to go by our noses; if it smells bad, then it is bad. It's all going to be trial and error, and if we're in any doubt at all then we won't eat it. We can't risk getting food poisoning.'

'Maybe I should smoke the half we have left over from tonight's meal and see how it goes, and completely dry the other one? If that works, we can then re-hydrate it for use in casseroles.'

'Okay. I'll start preparing the mackerel for lunch while you prepare the others for salting. It does make me realise, though, that despite being next to the sea, eating fresh fish is going to be a relative luxury. I mean, it's probably not going to be practical, is it, to go out every day to catch fish? And there'll also be days when you don't catch anything, or when it's too rough to go out. So we'll be limited to having fresh fish only on the days you go out and actually catch something. Anything else you catch will have to be smoked, dried, or pickled.'

'Yes, I suppose so. God! There's just so much to think about isn't there? Stuff we never gave a second's thought to in our old lives. We'll have to develop a regime using a mixture of methods for all the meat we get. If we get fresh meat or fish on a particular day then we'll have to eat some of it fresh that day, maybe smoke some of it for use within a day or two, and dry or preserve the rest for future meals.' Jane agreed with him.

'The other possibility,' he went on, 'is fishing from the beach with legered bait such as ragworm or bits of leftover fish, on days when it's too rough to take the boat out. I've seen people doing it here for years, so it must work.'

'Yes. And with rabbit and other game we can turn some of it into jerky for long-term keeping, and make terrines and other potted dishes for shorter-term use.'

'I agree about the jerky, but I'm not sure now about terrines and potting the meat; for that we'd need fat such as lard or clarified butter to seal it- I read about it weeks ago in my preserving book.'

'Okay, then maybe we can just use oil, and seal it in preserving jars, or similar? That must work, too? I mean, you always see speciality food like that on the shelves in the better supermarkets, don't you?'

'Yes, you're probably right. The purpose of the fat on top is to exclude air from the meat, to stop it going bad. Oil will do the same job I suppose, but you can't leave it exposed to air in the same way as, say, lard on top of terrines. I remember seeing it used in the book, though, for certain foods in preserving jars. Our problem will be having enough for the future, and any oil we get from the supermarkets will have a shelf life. After we've used it all, or it's expired, what are we going to do then?'

Jane thought for a second. 'Well, what did our ancestors use, like in the middle-ages? I'm guessing they boiled up the carcases of animals and rendered them down to get the fat. Plus, I suppose some would have had access to butter.'

'Yes, that's true. We could do with some ourselves! By the way, how did you get on this morning?'

'Oh, Jamie, you should have seen Max, he was fab!' Max's

ears pricked up and he looked at them. Jane rubbed his ears. 'I couldn't have done it without him. There were thick beds of brambles everywhere, and finding the entrances to the burrows was much more difficult than I'd imagined. I'd have missed most of them if it wasn't for Max. I pointed some rabbit droppings to him and picked some up to let him smell them, and off he went... He stopped at every entrance and I put snares down at each point. We got eight done, but he was getting tired so we came home.'

'That's great. Well done, Max!' He reached down and stroked Max, who whined and wagged his tail. 'And well done you, too. Well, rabbits normally come out at dusk, but I'd guess that without humans around now they'll be active all day. Maybe you should go back later this afternoon and check the snares?'

Jane grinned. 'Ahead of you, there... I'd already decided to do that!' Jamie laughed.

While Jane prepared the mackerel for lunch, he read through some of his books. He'd planned to use the bags of compressed wood cat litter for the smoking, but discovered that pine and other softwoods couldn't be used because of their resin content. At least they'd be good fuel for the Kelly Kettle and the wood-gas camping stove, though. He put the books aside and started preparing the two fish.

Jane grinned at him and he smiled back; it felt good to be productive and learning new things for their futures. He gutted the fish, removed the heads and fins, then cut one fish in half for their meal that night, and the other one-and-a-half he cut into thin fillets. He layered them in a tub with salt between each layer and covered the top with more salt, then put on the lid to store them overnight. The salting would draw out moisture and help prevent microbial growth, and after that they could be smoked or dried.

They ate the fried mackerel with sea beet, chives and flat-bread, dressed with olive oil and vinegar: it was delicious and both said they'd never eaten fish that fresh before. After clearing up they had some coffee then spent the afternoon working in the garden.

As evening drew on and the sun got low in the sky Jane set off to check the snares. Max followed her out, but she sent him back in to Jamie as she was going to walk there. It took her under ten minutes and once there she climbed up the embankment and onto the railway. She was delighted to find rabbits in two snares- one small and one average-sized- and grinned to herself. The others were empty, but three had either fallen or been knocked over. She reset all the snares, put the rabbits in her pack and headed home.

Max came to the door as soon as she walked in and followed her back to the kitchen, where Jamie was sitting at the table with a glass of wine, reading up on preserving food. He poured her a glass, which she accepted gratefully.

'Well?' he enquired with a smile.

Jane tried to play it cool but failed, and broke into a big grin.

'Two! I couldn't believe it when I saw them.' She took them from her pack and put them on the kitchen counter.

'Oh, that's brilliant, Jane, well done!' She beamed at him and they clinked glasses and toasted each other.

'Listening to my dear old dad all those years ago paid off, bless him. I never thought I'd use the knowledge, though!'

'Well, I've been reading the books on preserving, including two others I found belonging to the previous owners, and the meat can be cooked with oil, spices, vinegar and sugar, then put into preserving jars. To keep them longer than a few days you can heat-process the jars in boiling water for about twenty minutes, which causes a vacuum inside, and after that they'll keep for up to a year. Isn't that fab?'

'That's really good news. It also sounds a bit more palatable to me than jerky!' she laughed.

'We can do both. The jerky will be great for travelling food when we go out and as snacks. We can also rehydrate it in casseroles if we want to. I think we'll have to see if we can find some more preserving jars as well.'

'What about that kitchen shop on Devonshire? I'm sure there'll be some in there.'

'Yes, we'll have to pay a visit as we're going to need all we can find.'

For their evening meal Jamie steamed the remaining fish with soy sauce and chives and made some rice to go with it. They also ate some of the chutney and pickles that the previous owners had made. Afterwards, they sat on the sofa in the conservatory with a few candles lit, drinking wine and discussing plans. Max lay stretched out between them looking contented.

They spent part of Friday morning preserving the meat and the rest of the day gardening. While looking around her house after moving in Jane had found a cloth bag of potatoes under the sink that were wizened and sprouting large roots. Some had rotted, but others looked okay so they planted them.

They kept one rabbit as food for that day, while Jane prepared half of the larger one and cooked it with spices, sugar and vinegar, sealing it into three preserving jars for later use, according to the instructions in the preserving books. The other half Jamie cut into thin strips and salted for turning into jerky. He chopped up some hardwood from the wood-pile and lit a small, smoky fire in the bottom of one of the converted bins. The fish was rinsed of its salt cure and the smaller half he put on the lowest rack to smoke. The remaining fillets from the whole fish, along with the rabbit, he put on the top rack where it was coolest, to dry it completely.

Throughout the day, in between gardening, he fed small amounts of wood onto the fire to keep the smoke going. Max would stand next to him sniffing at the smell of fish, looking at him enquiringly to see if he was going to get any, though he had no reason to be hungry as he had eaten the leftovers from the rabbits.

By late evening, after maybe twelve hours, it was evident that the smoking hadn't worked as he'd hoped. The fish on the lowest rack had cooked rather than smoked, and was rather tough. Probably half that time would have done the same job, but made it nicer to eat. It wasn't a huge problem, but it meant that it wouldn't keep for long and would have to be used up soon, maybe in a casserole.

The fish and rabbit on the top rack, however, had dried

114

out nicely. The fish was hard and almost brittle once it had cooled. The rabbit jerky was leathery and splintered when bent. After letting them cool, he tasted the rabbit jerky and found it to be perfectly acceptable, if a little bland. Jane reached the same conclusion. They decided the next lot they made would be marinated first in a kind of barbeque sauce before drying, to give it more flavour. The dried fish was put into a cloth bag and hung in the cellar. They went to bed that night feeling rather pleased with their first attempts at food preserving, but they knew it would take a lot of trial and error to perfect techniques and develop a working system that suited them.

When they awoke on the Saturday morning the weather had turned. It was windy and overcast with a constant drizzle of rain. They looked out the window while drinking their coffee, then looked at each other; neither of them felt like working on the gardens in that weather. They knew that from now on they would have to work outside in all weathers because their survival depended on it, but they had achieved a lot in that week and most of the initial work was done. They had many seeds planted in the gardens and in tubs on the patios, as well as for tomatoes in the conservatory.

They were both tired and aching from the week's work, so decided to take the morning off and drive out to the farm near Hooe that used to supply the previous owners with logs. They weren't desperate by any means, but would need more logs in the near future and this seemed like a good opportunity to go while the weather was bad. They both agreed that it would also be nice to get out of Bexhill for a few hours to the countryside.

Jane took Max out for a short walk to do his business before they left, while Jamie got a few things ready in a bag for them. He packed a water bottle and some snacks, including some jerky, along with a pair of binoculars, a few tools and the bolt-cutters. When Jane returned with Max they put the Smith and Wesson revolver with extra rounds in the Land Rover's glove-box. They also took a sawn-off and an over/under shotgun, with the cartridges they'd got from the Toyota and another box of larger shot, in case they had the opportunity to bag some pheasants or rabbits.

It was still drizzling when they left and Max sat between them on the seat, looking excitedly out of the windscreen. They'd checked the location on the map beforehand, and Jane had an Ordnance Survey map open on her lap for when they got closer. They drove up Peartree Lane and then left at the crossroads into Whydown Road towards Hooe. It was a narrow, twisty country road and they weren't going fast as there was no rush. As they approached a sweeping right-hand bend Jane raised her hand suddenly and said 'Stop! Pheasant!' Jamie came to a smart stop and Jane grabbed the shotgun and got out. Sitting on the left, she had been able to see round the bend and spotted a pheasant in the road thirty yards ahead. Jamie could see it now, too; a plump male bird in the middle of the road.

Jane knelt down by the front bumper and raised the shotgun to her shoulder. She tucked it in tight as Jamie had told her, took aim, slid off the safety with her thumb and fired. The pheasant went down in a clean kill; Jamie clapped his hands and Max barked, too.

'Wooh-hooh! Bloody good shooting, Jane!'

She gave him a big grin then called Max down from the cab as she wanted to test him. Max climbed down onto the road and she pointed and said 'Fetch, Max! Fetch!' He set off at a slow trot, picked up the bird then came back and stood in front of her. She took the pheasant and patted him, saying 'Good boy, Max! Good boy,' then gave him a couple of treats from her pocket. She put the pheasant in the load area then climbed back in after Max.

They carried on and after nearly two miles there was a track on the right; a hand-written sign said "Logs." There was a makeshift barrier across the entrance, with another sign that said "PLAGUE- KEEP AWAY!" Jamie got out and moved the barrier aside, then got back in and drove onto the track. It was roughly-made, with numerous pot-holes, and went on for about three hundred yards before coming to a large concreted yard. A right fork went up a slight incline to another yard and they could see outbuildings up there.

They went forward into the main yard and stopped. On

their left by a line of trees an old, rusting Renault Master van was parked. Before them was a huge modern barn with two full-height roller-shutters and a central door that was open. On the right corner of the barn, set back slightly, was a large farmhouse with a single-storey annexe on the side, and an old mobile-home ten yards to the right of that with a small lawn in front. They got out, leaving Max inside the cab, and listened; there was no sound apart from birds.

'Seems quiet enough,' said Jane. 'Let's have a look in the barn.'

Jamie took a torch from his pocket and they walked up to the barn and in through the central door. A rich smell of sawdust and resin hit them. It was completely dark inside apart from the area by the door, and he shone the torch around. They saw huge piles of sawn logs stacked up high and ready-packed logs in different-sized bags. On the left-hand side were various machines for cutting wood. Everything was neatly arranged by size and it obviously had once been an efficiently-operated business.

'Well,' said Jamie, 'we wanted logs and it looks like we came to the right place!' Jane smiled.

They'd been inside less than a minute when Max started barking loudly. It wasn't his usual excited bark, but one of warning. They moved back to the door and stepped out into the light. To their left stood a large man with a thick beard, pointing a shotgun at them. Jamie cursed himself for leaving the guns in the truck.

Fourteen

'Stay where you are,' said the man. 'Who are you and what are you doing on my property?' Max was still barking angrily from the cab and trying to get through the half-open window.

'I'm really sorry,' Jamie replied, 'we thought the place was deserted or that everyone was dead. We don't want to cause you any trouble.'

Behind the man a girl poked her head out of the front door to the house. 'Who is it, Daddy?' The man spoke over his shoulder, keeping his eyes on them. 'Go back inside, sweetie, and stay with your mum.' The girl went back in and closed the door.

'We've come out from Bexhill. I'm Jane Roberts and this is Jamie Parker. We needed seasoned logs for our ranges and stoves and found your details in an old Yellow Pages advert, so we thought we'd drive out here. We weren't expecting to find anyone alive, to be honest. We've seen almost no other survivors in the last two months in Bexhill.

Of course,' she added with an ironic smile, 'normally we would have rung first, but my mobile doesn't appear to have a signal. Damn things; you can never rely on them!'

That broke the ice and the man suddenly smiled and chuckled, lowering his shotgun. 'Yes, I know what you mean. I'm Bill; Bill Anderson.' He held his hand out and they both shook it. 'Sorry about the frosty welcome, but you can't be too careful these days. We had an incident about six weeks ago when a couple of blokes tried to steal some of our chickens. My daughter surprised them and they threatened her with a knife. They ran off when they saw me coming with my gun and I shot one of them in the arse. Only caught him with a few pellets, but I haven't seen them since.'

'That's okay,' said Jamie, 'we understand completely. We've had our own share of nasty run-ins. Three blokes attacked Jane just over a week ago, but luckily I was able to step in and help. That was how we met. They won't be bothering anyone again.'

Bill shook his head. 'Aargh! Bad times; but good for you! Will you come in for a drink and a snack and meet the family? I'd be interested to hear your news and stories.'

They both agreed and said that would be nice. Max had stopped barking now but was still whining. Jamie went back to the truck to let him out, picked up his rucksack and slung it over his shoulder. He left the guns in the cab as there seemed no need for them and he didn't want to alarm Bill or make him wary. Max trotted up to Bill, who knelt down and offered his hand for Max to smell and then stroked him. Satisfied, Max went back and stood by Jane. Bill looked back at the house and waved; the girl came outside and ran up to him. She was around twelve with long, dark brown hair and a little shy of the strangers. She pulled her dad's arm, so he bent down while she whispered in his ear. He stood up, smiling.

'This is my youngest, Sally. She wants to know if she can stroke your dog.'

'Hello, Sally. Of course you can,' Jane replied. 'His name's Max and he's very friendly.'

The girl bent down and stroked Max, who wagged his tail in response. They walked into the house and Bill introduced them to his wife, Emma, and their son, Peter. Emma was well-built, curvy and in her mid-forties, with thick auburn hair and rosy cheeks from the cooking she'd been doing. Peter looked around seventeen and was tall and lean, with reddish hair and glasses. Bill invited them to sit at the big table in the kitchen while Emma made tea for everyone.

'Whereabouts in Bexhill are you?' Bill asked.

119

'We've taken over a house and a bungalow next to each other on South Cliff fairly recently,' said Jamie. 'We needed somewhere with good-sized gardens near the sea, as we were both in flats. The family in Jane's house were dead and my bungalow was empty; I assumed they must have died in hospital early on.'

'Does it have a Rayburn and a pond in the garden with koi carp?' asked Bill, which Jamie confirmed.

'That was Brian and Lisa. I'd been supplying them with logs for years. We were friendly and spoke now and then. You're right; they died early on, not long after it hit Bexhill. Nice couple; both wanted kids but they couldn't have them. I haven't been into town since the plague hit, but I understand it's terrible and quiet as a graveyard.'

'Like you wouldn't believe,' Jane replied. 'There's no one left; well, if there are we haven't seen them in over two months.'

'... Apart from the guy I met in B&Q and the other in Tesco's,' Jamie added, and related the story to them.

'Phil and Sophie have been in several times and said it was awful,' said Emma. 'They're a young couple who live here now with us. They worked for us when we had a business, before the plague came. Their car broke down when things were getting really bad everywhere and they got kind of stranded here. We said they could stay with us until the car was fixed, expecting it to be just a few days. By the time we got the car fixed both their families were infected and they had no homes to go back to, so they stayed on here with us. They've gone over to Wartling today to see friends of ours who've got a smallholding there. They've been to the retail park in Bexhill a few times to get clothes and supplies.'

'Do they drive an old, red Mondeo estate?' asked Jamie, and Bill confirmed that they did. 'Ah! That solves that mystery, then. I saw it when I was there getting stuff once, and it was gone the next time. I told Jane about it, but I never saw them.'

Emma brought them tea, along with a plate of fresh cheese, dried apricots and apples. Jane and Jamie looked in amazement at the cheese, and then at Bill and Emma.

Bill smiled. 'We've got three dairy cows and a bull; had them for two years now. We make our own cheese and butter. We've also got two goats, six sheep and a ram, plus lots of chickens. We're pretty much self-sufficient here, and have been for a good while. We grow our own veg' and have got a small orchard, with apples, apricots, cherries and pears. We've got solar panels on the barn roof that charge up a bank of batteries and an inverter, so we've got mains power, too. As long as we don't run too much stuff and overload it, we're okay. Our water comes from a well fed by an underground spring.'

Jane's mouth was watering. 'Oh my God, I have *so* missed cheese!'

They tucked into the cheese and dried fruits and were soon making appreciative noises. Bill and Emma watched them with amusement for a second and then joined them. Sally came back in with Max after playing with him and gave him a bowl of water. After they'd eaten Bill led them to some comfy chairs in a conservatory on the back of the house and poured them a brandy each.

'Don't tell me you make this yourself?' Jamie asked with a smile.

Bill chuckled. 'Sadly, no. This is spoils of war, as you might say.' He was keen to know how they had survived and what their plans were for the future.

'To be honest, Bill,' said Jamie, 'neither of us has a clue how we survived. We both caught the plague several months ago after it hit Bexhill, slipped into some kind of a coma and woke up days later, weak and half-dead. Things had become deathly-quiet outside and Jane said that, like me, it took her a month to recover enough to go out. It was like a ghost-town by then. Fortunately, I'd had the foresight to stockpile supplies when it started spreading so quickly up north.'

'And I didn't!' said Jane. 'I struggled for a long while to find enough stuff when I was strong enough to go out.'

'I saw it coming, too,' said Bill, shaking his head, 'and started preparing, just in case. When I was fifteen or so, my granddad told me about the Spanish Flu pandemic between 1918 and '20, and how people were dropping like flies, with mass graves being dug for all the corpses. He lost a lot of family back then. When I saw on the news about the mortality rate and how quickly it was spreading, I remembered his stories. I closed the business down and started stockpiling things here. We spent a week or two bringing in supplies and then made a makeshift barrier at the bottom of the drive with that sign about plague. After that we kind of just battened down the hatches and laid low for months. Obviously, it hit the urban areas first and then spread out to the villages. Apart from our friends at Wartling, I don't know of any other survivors around here.'

They sat talking for the rest of the morning. Jane and Jamie took turns in telling them about the things they were doing: the garden work and the seeds they had sown; fishing and snaring rabbits; learning to preserve food, and how they had rescued Max and nursed him back to health. Jamie reached into his pack and gave them some rabbit jerky to taste; they were impressed and congratulated him. Emma asked if they would stay for lunch, which they accepted gratefully. She cooked them a big plate of scrambled eggs with ham, which they devoured with gusto!

'Some neighbours we knew kept pigs and made their own hams,' explained Emma. 'After they died we decided to liberate their hams; I mean, why not? It was all very sad and traumatic, but we were alive and they weren't. We didn't really have the means or the inclination to look after their two remaining pigs, so we slaughtered them. We've got two big chest freezers full of pork and I've made hams and bacons. They're hanging up in a store-room and won't be ready for months yet. I just hope our electricity supply holds out, otherwise we'll lose a lot of meat.'

Eventually it came time for them to leave, which they were reluctant to do as it had been a wonderful surprise meeting Bill and his family. As they were preparing to leave Phil and Sophie pulled up in the Mondeo and introductions were made all round. They were both in their early twenties. Phil was fairly stocky, with a shock of blond curly hair and an open, friendly face. Sophie was short, curvy and pretty, with long dark hair that she tucked behind her ears, and a fringe. They seemed like a nice young couple and were pleased to meet them.

Bill said he would give them a few bags of logs to take back with them, for which they were very grateful. 'Well, we've got more than enough for our needs, for many years to come; the barn's pretty full and there's more out back seasoning, too.'

They reversed the Land Rover up to the roller-shutter, which Bill opened, and then he brought out enough bags to fill the load area. He also gave them a jerrycan of red diesel for their truck. Emma came out carrying a cardboard box containing a dozen eggs, a pint of milk and two fresh cheeses wrapped in waxed-paper. Jamie and Jane were moved almost to tears and thanked them several times.

'Think nothing of it,' said Bill. 'Please come out again soon. We're so happy to see some survivors like you and wish you well. We'd love to see you again and to keep in touch, to see how you're doing.' They both assured them that they would and Bill and Jamie shook hands while the women exchanged hugs.

Jamie felt guilty that they didn't have anything to offer in return, and then had a thought; 'Bill; how well-off are you for shotgun cartridges?'

'Not very good, actually; I'm down to my last box of fifty.'

Jamie walked to the cab and came back with the box he'd got from Jane's attackers and gave them to Bill, who was pleased with the gift and thanked him sincerely. The two kids came out to say goodbye and to stroke Max again, then they got in the truck and drove off down the track, waving goodbye. At the bottom, Jane got out to put the barrier back in place and they drove onto the road, heading home.

They stopped off first at the railway bridge when they got back to Bexhill, and Jane went up to check the snares, coming back with a rabbit and a big grin on her face. Jamie clapped his hands and kissed her on the cheek. They carried on driving and discussed moving the snares to another location. They wondered if the rabbits might get used to them and start avoiding the area, so they thought it best to move them for a while to somewhere else, and then put them back at a later date. They agreed to try the green space around Down Road and also Collington Wood, just past the railway, and to take Max with them to sniff out the burrows.

Their second stop was at the kitchen shop on Devonshire Road, where they came out with several boxes of preserving jars. Jamie had to break the glass with a hammer to get in, but it wasn't a problem. Back home, they hauled the bags of logs off the truck and dragged them into Jamie's garage.

They spent the remaining afternoon preparing and cooking the rabbit and pheasant for preserving. Now that they had a good supply of logs they fired up the Rayburn for the first time, so they had the two hotplates and the two ovens to cook with. Jamie played some music on his MP3 player while they were working and they chatted about Bill and Emma, saying how great it was to have met them and that there were other survivors for them to interact with. They roasted the pheasant for that evening and the next day, and cooked up the rabbit meat and sealed it in preserving jars. Max was given the leftovers, which he scoffed out in the garden.

After their evening meal of roast pheasant they sat in the conservatory with a bottle of wine and ate some of the cheese Emma had given them, savouring the taste. They talked for a long while, with Max curled up between them on the sofa, going over plans and ideas, and also resolved to go back soon to see Bill and Emma. They were more realistic by now about the hard times that lay ahead and what they needed to do. They knew that despite their efforts in the garden over the past week and in the future, they would be at the mercy of nature and the weather. They fully expected to have setbacks and failures, and that survival and self-sufficiency were going to be tough. They both agreed, though, that in the scheme of things today had been a good day.

They said goodnight and hugged, then Jane went next door. He filled Max's water bowl, stroked him and then went to bed, where he lay awake for a long time thinking about many things.

Fifteen

The inclement weather continued for another two days and got worse, peaking early on the Monday, with regular squalls of wind and rain from leaden, overcast skies. It was certainly too rough to think of taking the boat out to do more fishing. They did some more garden work on the Sunday but soon gave up as the soil was difficult to work and they just ended up covered in mud. After getting drenched they went back inside. Jane went next door to change into dry clothes then they lit the stove in the kitchen and hung up their wet things to dry.

Instead, they decided to visit the other areas that they thought might be good for laying snares. It would still mean getting wet, but there was nothing they could do about that, and at least they wouldn't be constantly scraping clods of mud off their boots, spades and forks. They took Max and visited Collington Wood just the other side of the railway and then went to the green space along Down Road, laying new snares and marking their positions clearly with Christmas ribbon so they could find them again easily. Max seemed almost impossibly jubilant, both with his new tasks and with his new family, and didn't seem bothered in the least by the weather. His back legs had healed well; he loved the work and being outside with them both, running around like a mad thing when he wasn't tracking for them.

It took the rest of the morning to locate new burrows and lay the snares, and by the time they'd finished they were drenched again. It made them realise that they needed better outdoor clothing than they currently had if they were to work outside in all weathers. They couldn't think of anywhere in Bexhill where they would find appropriate clothing as there weren't any camping or outdoor-type shops, and neither of them fancied going into bigger towns like Eastbourne or Hastings. Jane knew of a country clothing shop in Battle, so they decided to drive over there after lunch and get kitted out with some better coats and maybe trousers also. During lunch Jane mentioned an idea she'd had.

'I've been thinking since yesterday about Bill and Emma, and about what we could give them as a thank-you for their generosity and hospitality to us.'

'What did you have in mind?'

'Well, I wanted to ask what you thought, and if you had any ideas.'

Jamie thought for a few seconds, recalling what he'd seen at their house. 'I think treats would be good; they seem to be pretty well set up with the basics and the essential things. So why not get them some nice things they might be lacking? I don't suppose the kids have had much in the way of treats since this all began. What about things like sweets, crisps, snacks and sodas- stuff like that?'

'Yes, and I'm sure Emma would be grateful for some pampering things for herself, as well as feminine hygiene products.'

'That's a good idea. I'm sure Bill would like some more whisky and brandy, and he needs more shotgun cartridges. I know we've got a good supply at the moment, but we'll need to see if we can find a local supplier where we can stock up for ourselves, anyway.'

'The house where you got the shotguns from: where did they use?'

'I was just thinking the same thing myself,' he replied, smiling. 'I'll walk there and have a look around- won't be long.'

He put on his coat and boots then left, after picking up the Smith and Wesson and putting it in his pocket. He walked a few streets away to the house where he'd found the guns and went up to the study. He rooted through the desk, finding an address book containing the names of various suppliers to the shooting fraternity, along with flyers, business cards and pamphlets obtained from gun clubs and shooting competitions. He sorted through them all; some were internet-based companies but there were also details of gunsmiths and suppliers in the south. He found there was a gun and shooting-supplies store on the outskirts of St. Leonards and Hastings, on the road to Battle. *Perfect!* He took the pamphlet and went back to the bungalow.

Max greeted him like he'd been gone for hours, rather than just thirty minutes, as usual. He relayed the news to Jane and said they could stop there first on the way to Battle. They now had a small fleet of six vehicles at their disposal, depending on their requirements: their two cars, the Land Rover, the Toyota pickup, the BMW estate and the Escort RS2000. They decided to take the Land Rover as it had a covered load area, and they never knew what they might find and need to bring back with them, or where they might need to drive; its four-wheel drive could come in handy.

They packed a few things into Jamie's rucksack, along with his sawn-off, and put some tools in the back of the truck. Jane took an over and under shotgun into the cab along with a box of cartridges, then Max climbed in and she closed the door on him. She went to open the garage door but stopped for a second and turned to Jamie.

'I was just thinking; are we sure we're going to be able to get into this place? I mean, if it's a gun store then security's going to be bloody good, isn't it? Do you think a wrecking bar and bolt cutters are going to be enough?'

'Hmm… You could be right. Good thinking, Batman! I'll bring the welding gear, too.' She grinned at him. He climbed from the cab and got the small oxy-acetylene bottles on their wheeled rack then hoisted them into the back of the truck. He also picked up the welding face mask, some leather gauntlets, a leather apron and a flint striker to light the torch. Jane opened the garage door for him to drive out, closing it again after him.

Driving along the new link road they were there in less

than fifteen minutes. They had an address for the gun-supplies store on The Ridge West, but turned left initially at the roundabout and had to double back once they realised they'd gone the wrong way, before finding it. They drove onto the drive of a large house with a shop to one side and got out; Jamie sounded the horn several times but there was no one around. Security was very good; understandable given the nature of the premises. Behind the door and windows was a security roller shutter and there was little chance they could have broken through it with just the tools they had originally planned to take. Jamie got back in the truck and repositioned it with the tow-bar pointing at the middle of the door, then reversed into it. The glass in the door was obviously toughened as it didn't shatter, but the tow-bar had punched a hole through and cracked the surrounding glass.

He pulled the truck forward, got out, and then with the wrecking bar and hammer he was able to remove the glass from the door frame. He unloaded the gas bottles, put on the face mask, apron and gloves, lit the welding torch and then cut an entrance through the shutter big enough for them to get through. They put Max back in the cab because of the broken glass then went inside.

There were several racks with new and used shotguns, hunting rifles and air rifles, along with boxes of ammunition of every description on shelves. After searching for a while, Jamie located the size of cartridge suitable for their guns and they carried numerous boxes in varying shot sizes out to the truck, both for them and for Bill. He also found boxes of AAA cartridges, which was large buckshot; each pellet was around 5mm diameter and they would be very effective against large game. He selected a nice over and under shotgun to give to Bill as a second gun, broke it open and loaded it with two AAA cartridges then closed it and slid the safety catch on. They had four shotguns already, so didn't really need any more.

'What about a couple of hunting rifles with telescopic sights?' suggested Jane. 'They could be useful.'

'Good idea; you're right.' He grinned at her.

He didn't know anything about rifles and the variation in

calibres was rather bewildering: a rifle would be chambered for a specific type and calibre of round. Looking at the shelves of ammunition there were boxes of .223 Remington, 30-06 Springfield and over fifteen other calibres.

He chose a calibre that he'd heard of from films and books, which was .308 Winchester. He checked carefully to find two rifles chambered for that round and found two Howa Hunter rifles with lovely walnut stocks, which he took out to the truck, along with bags for the guns and many boxes of ammunition. He also picked out a few books from the shelf on rifles and shooting, along with manuals for the two guns, just as he had done with the shotguns; it would be worth reading up on them so they knew how to maintain them properly.

They got back in the cab, started the truck and headed off to Battle. They got there within ten minutes and drove slowly past Battle Abbey, where they saw the remains of two corpses on the pavement by the gates: a pair of crows were picking at them. They continued up the high street, looking around: almost every shop had been broken into and glass littered the pavements, along with much rubbish, leading Jamie to wonder if there were more survivors here, as it was something they hadn't encountered as much of in Bexhill.

'Doesn't necessarily follow, though;' said Jane, 'it could have been just one person did it.'

'Yes, that's true.'

They carried on slowly up the hill, turned around by Mount Street and parked outside the country clothing shop, whose door was broken and standing open. They got out, leaving Max in the cab again because of broken glass on the pavement, and entered the shop. Jane carried her shotgun by its strap on her shoulder, but Jamie left his in the cab with Max. Looking through the racks of clothing, they found Barbour waxed jackets in their sizes and tried them on. Jane put on a Barbour hat, too, and posed with her shotgun and a smile on her face.

'What d'you reckon, Jamie? D'you think I'll fit in with the Sussex hunting set?'

He grinned and chuckled. 'Oh, I think you'll do. In fact, at the moment, we probably *are* the Sussex hunting set!' They both laughed.

They picked out some comfortable moleskin trousers, various shirts, a couple of hats and some waxed over-trousers, along with two coats each and several tins of re-proofing wax. They carried them out to the truck and Jane got into the cab. Jamie was securing the tailgate when he heard movement behind him. He turned and saw four young men coming from the alley beside the shop. They were in their late teens or early twenties and all four were armed; two with baseball bats, one with a hammer and one with a machete.

They stopped a few yards from him. He knew they were trouble and weighed up the situation, thinking that his sawn-off was in his rucksack in the cab. They'd only been a few yards away while in the shop so hadn't thought to take both guns in with them. The new shotgun was loaded and within reach, but he didn't think he'd be able to spin round and pick it up in time so he waited, counting on Jane. The guy with the machete spoke first.

'Take that stuff out and put it back, mate. This is our town now and no one comes here without our say-so and takes stuff.'

Jamie tried to stall them, thinking *Come on Jane, where are you?* 'Your town?'

'Yeah, that's right,' he replied, 'this is our town now. We've taken over this place, and no one's gonna come here and…'

He stopped in mid-sentence as Jane climbed from the cab and came quickly to the back of the vehicle, with Jamie's sawn-off up to her shoulder and aimed at the guy's face. She'd been leaning over in the cab playing with Max: they hadn't seen her there and she hadn't seen them approach, but had heard them speaking. She'd reached down quickly to Jamie's pack and pulled out the sawn-off; the over/under shotgun in the cab was too long for this situation.

The guy stood there with his mouth open, staring down the barrels, before speaking again. 'Listen, lady…'

Jamie spun round and reached into the back of the truck, pulled out the new shotgun and held it at waist-level, sliding the safety off as he pointed it at them.

'No, *you* listen!' said Jane furiously. 'I've had a fucking bad time recently! I've been shot and almost raped; I've already killed one bloke and my friend here has killed another two. Frankly, I'm getting pissed-off with wankers like you who think they can behave like this towards other survivors. You know, right now I'm just really tempted to fire both barrels; from this angle I could take out all four of you little shits!'

Behind them, in the cab, Max was barking loudly. All four guys looked nervous. 'Hold on a second, lady...' the man began, but Jane interrupted him again.

'SHUT UP! We're getting in the truck and driving away with our clothes. And we'll come back whenever we want to; without your say-so. Now, if you don't FUCK OFF right now I'm going to unload in your face!'

The four guys looked nervously at each other then back at the shotguns, and especially at the scary woman with the sawn-off. They backed away, turned round and walked back to the alley. Jamie went round to the cab, jumped in and started the engine. Jane waited until they were several yards down the alley then climbed into the cab and Jamie roared off down the hill. He looked across at Jane, who was red in the face. She puffed her cheeks out, let out a big breath and then burst out laughing.

'Oh my God! That was probably the most exhilarating moment of my life! To see them looking scared of me... Wow! You were right last week when you said no one's going to fuck with me if I was pointing a sawn-off at them! How did I sound?'

'Scary- very scary! And where on earth did "*I'm going to unload in your face*" come from?'

She sniggered. 'I remembered it from *Pulp Fiction*; do you remember Tim Roth says it to Samuel Jackson in the diner near the end? I thought it sounded appropriately menacing and cold-blooded!'

'Well, it certainly did the trick!' he said, and they both laughed. Max was beside himself with excitement, bouncing across the seat between them.

They left Battle at a more sedate pace and had a steady drive back to Bexhill, stopping off first at the two new sites where they'd laid snares that morning. They found one rabbit at the Down Road location and another one at the woods by the railway. They'd hoped for more, but were delighted to have two, anyway. They drove home and unloaded their things into the bungalow after parking the truck in the garage.

Once in the kitchen Jamie poured two whiskies and gave one to Jane; she downed it in one go and stood looking at him. She was still feeling exhilarated by the encounter and threw her arms around him, kissing him forcefully on the lips. He responded in kind and then they were grappling with each other's clothes and heading for the bedroom.

Shared danger and life-threatening situations can be a great aphrodisiac, and this was certainly true in their case, but it was more than just that; they'd got to know each other well and become very close in a short space of time due to their circumstances. It was a life-affirming act: they were alive and almost everyone else was dead, and all their fear, grief, loneliness and gratitude at finding each other came out at that moment.

They lay for a long time afterwards holding each other, before getting dressed and going back to the kitchen to cook their evening meal from the left-over pheasant. Jamie opened a bottle of wine and they raised their glasses in a silent toast. Jane touched his arm affectionately and they smiled at each other.

Sixteen

Jane spent that night with Jamie in the bungalow, but in the weeks ahead would sleep mostly in her place; spending nights together whenever the mood took them. By late-morning on the Monday the bad weather was blowing over, with the sky beginning to clear from the west. While it was still raining early on, they prepared the rabbits they'd collected the previous evening and cooked one for preserving, saving the largest one for meals over the next two days. Max, as usual, was pleased to get the remains and ate them in the garden.

Jamie stripped down all four shotguns and cleaned them, more for practice than from necessity, as well as reading the manual for the hunting rifles and doing the same with them. Jane worked with him as she knew it was important that she could do the same, in the event that she was on her own and a gun jammed, for instance. When the weather cleared up they walked to the bottom of the garden and opened the gate to have some practice shots with the rifles. Jamie fetched a patio chair and an old cushion from the garage to rest on, and they selected posts on several groynes on the beach at increasing distances to shoot at.

Jamie fired the first shot and they got the shock of their lives; neither had been prepared for the loudness of a shot from a high velocity rifle, and their ears were ringing. It was far removed from the dull report of a shotgun, which itself was loud enough.

'Bugger that!' he said, and went back to the garage. He rummaged around in his tool boxes to find two pairs of ear defenders and gave a pair to Jane. Max, who had followed them, retreated after the first shot and lay down under the porch. They each fired several shots at the posts, increasing the distance each time up to about three hundred yards, and she proved to have a better eye than him. Satisfied that they knew what they were doing and could handle the rifles, they went back inside for lunch.

After they'd eaten they made ready to leave for Bill and Emma's, via Sainsbury's warehouse. They decided to take the BMW estate from Jane's garage for a run, but first had to jump-start it from one of the trucks as the battery was low. They laid flat the rear seats to give a bigger load area, put in their bags and two shotguns, then Max jumped in and they headed off. Jane drove this time and she parked in the yard by the loading bay, leaving the engine running to charge the battery. Jamie walked around to the front, through the store to the warehouse and opened the doors.

Jane walked through to the store and went along the aisles picking feminine things for Emma along with sanitary pads, tampons and other hygiene products from what remained. On reflection, she realised that Sally might well be old enough to need them too, so she picked things for her as well. Meanwhile, in the warehouse Jamie was collecting boxes of whisky and brandy, along with cartons and crates of fizzy drinks, crisps, snacks and sweets; some of it for Bill and Emma and the rest for themselves. Jane wheeled her trolley through and they loaded everything into the car. She had also picked up some nice treats for Max and gave him a couple for being so patient. There was a lot of broken glass in the aisles that could cut his feet so they'd left him in the car.

It didn't take long to get to Hooe and as they pulled into the yard they saw one of the roller shutters up and Bill working inside the barn. He didn't recognise the car and came out with his shotgun, but put it down again when he saw it was them. He waved and came to greet them.

'Well, this is a nice surprise,' he smiled. 'I didn't expect to see you again so soon.' He kissed Jane and shook hands with Jamie.

'No, well, we decided to come back with some things for you as a thank-you for your kindness the other day,' said Jane.

Bill waved it off, saying there was no need for that, and Jamie said 'Well, we wanted to, anyway, and thought there were some things you might like. We both felt it was nice to be doing something for other people for a change, rather than just surviving every day and fending for ourselves.'

'That's good of you; thanks,' replied Bill. The door to the house opened and Sally came bounding out: Max barked excitedly and jumped up at her and she gave him a big hug. Emma came out wiping her hands on her apron; she had evidently been baking. She hugged and kissed them both, saying how nice it was to see them, and invited them inside. Bill followed them in and they sat in the kitchen while Emma made tea. Jamie and Jane sat next to each other, with Bill and Emma on the other side of the table.

They sat chatting and Jamie told them about their encounter in Battle the day before, and how Jane had sent the young guys off with their tails between their legs at the barrel of a sawn-off. 'You should have seen her,' he said. 'She could have been in a Quentin Tarantino film!'

Jane blushed slightly while Bill smiled and nodded his head, and Emma reached across and patted her hand. 'Good for you, my dear! Well done.'

Emma got up and served them tea, along with a slice of apple pie that she had baked using last season's apples, served with thick fresh cream. They tucked into it with enthusiasm, licking their lips and complimenting Emma on the pie. They told them how they were having some success with the rabbit snares and had moved them around to different locations, and also about the pheasant they had shot on their way there the other day.

'When you leave,' Bill said, 'you want to stop off about a mile down the road. There's a big oak tree on the left with a field behind it and there's always pheasant out in the open there. I know you see them on the road often, but that's a good spot for them.' They thanked him and said they would stop there on the way back. Peter came in through the back door, said hello and asked how they were. He made himself a drink, saying he couldn't stay as he had to get back to work and said goodbye before going back out.

After they'd eaten Jamie went out to the car with Jane to bring in the things for Bill and Emma, while they cleared the plates and cups away. Emma nudged Bill then smiled and winked at him.

'What?' said Bill.

'Jane and Jamie… You know…'

'What?' he repeated, looking baffled.

Emma rolled her eyes and shook her head. 'They've become lovers since they were last here, you idiot! It's obvious.'

'Is it? How d'you know?' Bill looked bemused.

'Because I'm a woman and women notice these things, whereas men are hopeless at it! It's obvious; their whole body language is different- the way they look at each other and interact has changed.'

Bill smiled. 'Well, I'll take your word for it, love; but good for them.'

Jane came back in carrying a few boxes and asked if Bill could go out to help Jamie. Bill said 'Yes, of course' and went out. Jane unpacked the boxes and showed Emma what she'd got for her. Emma was touched and very appreciative; she gave Jane a hug and thanked her.

'Also,' Jane said, 'I got these for Sally; I hope you don't mind.' She unpacked the other sanitary products aimed at younger women. 'I didn't know if she was old enough yet to need them, but I thought it couldn't hurt.'

Emma brushed back a tear. 'Oh, bless you, Jane; that was thoughtful of you. Well, she's not there yet, but I'm sure it won't be long.'

Bill and Jamie came back in with the last of the boxes and Bill was appreciative of the things for him and the kids, thanking them both. He showed Emma what they'd been given and she thanked them both again. Jamie had saved the

136

shotgun until last as a surprise for Bill and took him back out to the car. He reached behind the seat, pulled out the shotgun and held it out to Bill.

'Wow! Nice gun, Jamie. That'll do you a treat, that will.'

'No, it's for you, Bill!'

'For me?' he said, surprised.

'Yes. I knew you only had the one gun, so I thought this would be good for you to have as a second gun... or as a first gun, come to that!'

Bill turned it over in his hands and hefted it, a big grin on his face. He was delighted and thanked Jamie. 'Nice balance,' he said, putting it up to his shoulder.

'It's got auto-ejectors and you can select which barrel fires first, so you can have a different load in each barrel if you want,' said Jamie. Bill commented that it might be a bit complicated for him to maintain, but Jamie smiled and said 'I thought of that, too.' He reached inside again and handed Bill the service manual for the gun, along with a carrying bag and ten boxes of cartridges in varying shot sizes. Bill grinned, thanking him again, and they went back inside, where he showed it to Emma.

Sally was sitting at the table with a can of soda and a packet of crisps; she thanked them both politely and they said she was very welcome. Max was lying in a warm spot by the range, gnawing on a bone that Emma had given him and then Phil and Sophie came in from working on the farm. They greeted Jane and Jamie then sat down at the table, while Emma made a huge pot of tea for them all and put out a plate of homemade biscuits and some cake. They all sat chatting for an hour or so and then Bill had a thought and asked them what guns they'd brought with them. Jamie said they had a sawn-off and an over/under.

'Well, I was just thinking,' Bill said, 'if you stop off at the field down the road for some pheasant you'll want a long gun. The sawn-off won't be any good at distance. Trouble is; with just one gun you might only get one bird before the others scatter. If I come down with you we stand a good chance of getting at least two, maybe three birds for you to take back. It'll be a good opportunity for me to try out the new gun, too. We could go now before it gets late.'

They thought it was a great idea and thanked him. Bill said they could drop him at the bottom of the drive afterwards to save them coming back up to the house, so they said their goodbyes in the kitchen. Emma hugged them both and thanked them again for the gifts and they promised to come back again soon. Bill swapped the two AAA cartridges in his gun for a smaller shot size and put more into his pockets.

Jamie put the back seats up again and Bill got in, with Max on his blanket beside him as the rear load area was full, then they waved to everyone and drove off down the track. They turned left onto the road and Bill directed them to the spot by the oak tree.

'Who's the better shot between you?' asked Bill.

Jamie admitted that Jane was and he just nodded. They got out, closing the doors quietly, and climbed up the bank. Max was quivering with excitement but completely silent and Jane patted him and whispered *Good boy!* Bill held up his hand for them to wait while he went forward a couple of yards through the bushes and peered round the tree trunk.

He came back shortly and spoke quietly. 'There are four birds about forty yards out, roughly in a line. Jane, you take the left two and I'll take the right. We want to fire the first shots together so we get them on the ground. The others will take off and scatter; be prepared to shift your aim straight away and we can try for them next. Aim just slightly ahead of the ones in flight. Jamie, you count us down so we shoot together.' They both nodded.

They crept forward to the edge of the bushes by the tree, just far enough clear of the foliage so they wouldn't snag. They knelt down, raised the guns to their shoulders and took aim, and then both said 'Ready'. Jamie counted them down from three and they both fired together. The first two pheasants went straight down and the other two took to the air in panic. Bill's two shots- him being an experienced shooter- were under two seconds apart and his second bird went down before it had gone a couple of yards. Jane's second shot took a couple

138

of seconds longer while she shifted aim and she narrowly missed the bird, but they did see a couple of tail feathers fly off and float down.

'Go Max!' said Jamie and Max shot off like a sprinter from the starting blocks. He raced out, picked up the first bird and brought it back then went back for the other two. He dropped the last one at Jamie's feet then sat there wagging his tail as if to say *Can we play some more?* They both patted him, saying *Good boy Max! Good boy!* Jamie gave him a couple of dog-treats from his pocket.

'Bloody good shooting, Jane!' said Bill. 'You were unlucky with your second shot.' She looked disappointed that she hadn't got both, but Bill said 'It's not easy taking a bird in flight, especially as this is your first time. If it's any consolation; at this range and with the spread of shot your barrel was probably less than half an inch off target. That's pretty good for a newbie!' Jane smiled and thanked him, feeling somewhat consoled.

They picked up the birds and climbed back down the bank to the car. Jamie opened the door and Max jumped in then he put the three pheasants in a bag on the floor. Bill was admiring his shotgun and reloading it.

'Excellent gun, Jamie! Thanks again, mate; I love it. I'm going to enjoy using this.' Jamie smiled and said 'No problem, Bill.'

They turned round at the next available spot then drove Bill back to the bottom of his drive. He kissed Jane and shook Jamie warmly by the hand, thanking them again and hoping to see them soon. He put the barrier back in place and waved goodbye as they drove off. They took a slow drive back and Jamie rested his hand on her leg; she looked across at him and smiled.

'You did really well back there,' he said. 'I don't mind admitting I might not even have got the first one. You're a natural, and I need to practise more!'

Jane smiled. 'Well, you know, some of us women have just *got it!*' They looked at each other and laughed and Max barked loudly from the back.

They arrived home after stopping off to check the snares and picking up one rabbit, parked the BMW in Jane's garage then carried the remaining boxes of things into the bungalow. They could sort out what was going into each house later. They usually cooked and ate in Jamie's kitchen, but tonight they decided to cook on the range in Jane's kitchen for a change. They prepared a rabbit casserole between them, with sea beet and sea kale along with other tinned vegetables, lentils and some herbs. Jamie lit a fire in the lounge and they sat on the sofa with a glass of brandy each, with Max sprawled on the carpet in front of the fire. While the food cooked they chatted about the day and how nice it had been to surprise Bill and Emma with their visit and the things they'd taken for them.

After they'd eaten and washed up Jamie went outside for a smoke and sat down on a patio chair after wiping it dry. He sipped his brandy and listened to the waves breaking on the beach. The night sky was clear and full of stars after the rain had passed and he leaned back, looking up at the inky blackness. There was no longer any light pollution from human habitation and he was seeing it just as people would have done three hundred or three hundred thousand years before. Jane came out and stood behind him, placing her hands on his shoulders. He reached up and touched her hand.

'You know something, Jane? Only a short time ago I was feeling pretty ambivalent about whether I lived or died, after everything that's happened. For a long time I thought *what's the point?* But something made me carry on regardless and I just kept on surviving and doing stuff... And now, since meeting you, I feel differently. It's so much better now there are two of us to share everything. There seems to be a reason to carry on; to live, to love, to help and support each other... I guess it's just human nature. And now there are Bill and Emma and the kids, too.'

'I know what you mean. I felt similar things, too, though I don't think I ever felt any ambivalence towards staying alive. For me, it was always a case of I *must* survive, though I don't really know why. I just felt that I had to. I think maybe I still had some small hope that, despite the odds, I might meet someone to share things with that would make life easier and more pleasurable under the circumstances.'

'And you have!' he said, looking up at her with a smile. 'Well, I think I'm going to turn in and get an early night.'

'Will you stay here tonight? I'd like to just lie there and hold each other.' Jamie said he'd like that, too, so they closed the place up and left Max in the lounge by the fire. They left the kitchen door open so he had access to his water bowl and went upstairs.

They lay there holding each other for over an hour before eventually falling asleep; occasionally talking quietly but mostly silent. After months of seeing nothing but death and rotting corpses the pleasure of lying next to another warm body was immeasurable. They took comfort in the physical contact and felt a sense of healing from their grief and their worries.

Seventeen

The weeks flew past for them as spring moved into summer. As the weather improved and the temperature increased, their crops started to shoot up and they were busier than ever in the garden. By early summer they were eating fresh mixed-leaf salads every day. Their beans, peas and spring onions had done well generally and they were already harvesting them, too. They had to experiment a bit with different preserving techniques; not without their share of failures. Their first attempt at lacto-fermentation with some young beans didn't work out and they had to throw away the first few jars after they went mouldy. They realised what they had done wrong and the second batch was good, though they had to wait a few weeks to find that out.

Once they knew what they were doing with the process they set to work with the peas and the beans. They also cooked up vegetable dishes with sugar, vinegar and spices, much as they had been doing with the meat dishes, and heat-treated them in the preserving jars so they would keep for long periods. They ate as much fresh produce as they could, picking things as and when they needed them; any surplus they might not get through in time was preserved for the winter.

They got into a routine of working in the garden, going out fishing when conditions allowed, and checking and relocating the rabbit snares on a regular basis. They found new locations to lay them with Max's invaluable help and rotated the snares between them all. Max had put on weight and was back to his normal size and fitness level. They tended not to do much hunting using the guns as they wanted to preserve their ammunition, but whenever they were out and saw a pheasant they would shoot it for the pot or to preserve.

Another regular, but time-consuming and tiresome task was the washing of clothes and bed-linen. They had tried washing things in the sea but everything dried salty and sticky and made things uncomfortable. Instead, they had to drive just over two miles to the rivers and streams along Sluice Lane, near the golf course. It wasn't ideal because of debris and weeds, but after the second time Jane had the bright idea of breaking into the leisure centre at the retail park and using the swimming pool to do their washing, which was far easier and also cleaner. The water was chlorinated and still fresh, and they bathed themselves at the same time.

As it got warmer more fish moved into the shallower coastal waters and they had better success fishing, eating fresh fish on the day it was caught and preserving any surplus. They usually smoked or pickled the oily fish like mackerel, while the white fish were either salted and dried or cooked and sealed in preserving jars. They visited the other smaller supermarkets and food shops near them, where they broke into the warehouses or storerooms behind the stores and found further stocks of food and drink, along with other useful items. They collected large amounts of salt, vinegar, sugar and oil for preserving food, which would last them a long time. They also put out various containers of sea water to evaporate so they could collect the salt and bag it for future use. The empty areas of both gardens were full of different-coloured plastic bowls and dishes containing evaporating seawater.

As the herbs in their gardens grew bigger they harvested them on a daily basis for extra flavouring in their cooking and preserving. Now that fresh salads and vegetables were becoming available they didn't need to use tinned produce as much, and their diet became better and far more pleasurable. Nettles had shot up in most gardens near them, which they picked sometimes and added to soups and casseroles for extra vitamins and minerals.

It was by no means an easy time for them, though, and for every few successes there was a failure or setback of some sort. They sometimes went for several days without getting any rabbits: either of them would come back empty-handed from checking the snares and shake their head, looking despondent. On the days when it was calm enough to take the boat out Jamie sometimes would sit there fishing for several hours without catching anything. At these times they had to make do with tinned produce as they were reluctant to use the preserved food that they were storing for winter. Sometimes, if they'd had a few days without catching any fish or rabbits, they had to go out hunting for pheasant with the guns, which was time-consuming and sometimes unsuccessful. Occasionally they got ducks from Egerton Park, though the birds there were becoming scarcer and more wary. They also lost some salads and vegetables in the gardens to pests, and not everything grew as well as they'd hoped. Covering things with fine mesh netting helped in the fight against pests, and they wished they had done it sooner.

It was frustrating for them frequently: they tried to stay optimistic but the failures, losses and setbacks often got them down and they would snap at each other, then apologise and make up. They had been aware that survival and self-sufficiency would be difficult, but the reality was far harder than they had imagined and it was a full-time occupation. Before the plague, if you tried growing food and it didn't work out you could always go to the supermarket and buy fresh produce; it was very different, though, when what you grew was all you had.

Between May and the middle of June they made a few more visits to Bill and Emma. They would have liked to have gone more often, but had lots of things to do on a regular basis. Bill and Emma were delighted to see them and on each occasion they would stay for lunch and chat for a few hours, always coming away with a small gift of eggs, cheese or milk. Bill loved his new shotgun and it had become his first gun.

On the morning of one of their intended visits, Jamie had

a fantastic couple of hours fishing, bringing home four bass, two pouting and sixteen mackerel. He always took out two or three rods with different rigs set up, one usually being for mackerel; he hit a shoal and was pulling them out two or three at a time before the shoal moved on. They took one of the larger bass and four mackerel for their friends, who were very grateful as they didn't have fish these days. Bill and Emma noticed the change in them as they grew closer, and also that they looked generally happier and more confident due to successes in their endeavours. They also saw when things weren't going so well due to setbacks and failures, when the couple would appear tired and not their usual selves.

By the middle of June, though, their cupboards and shelves were slowly filling up with preserved food for the coming winter and they realised they were going to need more preserving jars. They visited the retail park and found some in three stores there, but they needed more, and Jamie remembered that there was a kitchen shop in Battle. They were a bit reluctant to go back there after their last encounter, but they reasoned that they had weapons, and if they were quick and careful there shouldn't be a problem. It was a case of having to go, as they needed as many preserving jars as they could get. They agreed that if they got there and things looked dodgy they'd turn round and come back.

They took two shotguns- a sawn-off and an over/under- plus a hunting rifle, and Jamie had the Smith and Wesson in a homemade holster on his belt, made from an old leather bag he'd found in a charity shop. They had practiced more with the rifles and Jamie had become far more proficient, while Jane had become an excellent shot. They drove to Battle in the Toyota pickup and stopped by the Abbey, waiting there for a couple of minutes and looking up the high street with binoculars. Max could sense some tension in them; he whined quietly and Jamie stroked him. There was a red pickup parked in the road further up the hill, but no sign of anyone around. They drove slowly up the high street, then turned the truck around in the road and parked outside the kitchen shop, facing downhill. Jamie went inside while Jane stood on guard with the rifle in her hands and the shotguns within easy reach in the cab. Just in case anything happened, she put a lead on Max and tied it to the grab-handle above the passenger door as she didn't want him running off. He could sense something was wrong as his hackles were up and he was whining again; Jane stroked him and he licked her hand.

Jamie had taken two plastic crates in with him and made two trips to collect all the jars that were on the shelves. 'There's a door at the back up to the store-room. I'm just going to pop up there and see what else there is.'

'Okay, but be quick. I don't like hanging around here any longer than we have to.' He agreed and went back inside. He'd been gone a few minutes when Jane noticed movement further up the street by the pickup. She picked up the binoculars, focussed them, and saw two figures about a hundred and fifty yards away. They were coming out of a building or a shop carrying boxes. She recognised them as two of the guys they had encountered before, but now one had a shotgun over his shoulder. *Bugger!*

She thought about going into the shop to warn Jamie, but didn't want to take her eyes off them. Instead, she moved behind the truck's open door after reaching in to pick up a cushion they had in there for Max. She held it in the open window frame and rested the rifle barrel on it, watching them through the telescopic sight. The two guys put the boxes down next to the truck in the road and stretched their backs. One of them looked her way, saw their truck and spoke to the other. The one with the shotgun took it off his shoulder and the other reached into the back of the pickup and pulled out a baseball bat, then they started walking towards Jane. *Oh shit!* Max was up on his back legs looking out of the rear window and growling.

She didn't want to just shoot them on the spot without challenging them, so she shouted 'Stop there! I've got a rifle aimed at you and if you come any closer I'll shoot.'

They stopped for a few seconds and spoke together. They were now around a hundred and forty yards away and she made a slight adjustment for range on the scope. Maybe they didn't believe that a woman with a rifle could hit them from there, or maybe they were just stupid, but they carried on coming. Jane took careful aim and pulled the trigger. The .308 Winchester round was the commercial equivalent of the 7.62mm NATO round and its muzzle velocity was around 2,800 feet per second: the thick end of the baseball bat in the guy's hand shattered and wood shards exploded into his leg. The shot echoed up the High Street. He staggered but stayed upright and Jane worked the bolt, ejecting the spent casing and loading another round into the breach. The guy with the shotgun started raising it to his shoulder so Jane put another well-aimed round barely a foot past his left ear. He ducked and cringed and Jane shouted '…And no, I didn't miss! That was another warning shot. Now fuck off- again!' Max was barking furiously in the cab.

At that moment Jamie came bursting out of the door with the Smith and Wesson in his hand. He saw that Jane was alright and she said 'It's okay, hon, I think they might've had enough.' The two guys hesitated for a second, so Jamie raised the revolver and fired a shot off to their right. They turned and ran off back up the road, the one with the shotgun helping his injured mate.

'Time to leave, maybe?' said Jane. He gave her a wry smile then ran back into the shop and picked up the three boxes he'd been carrying. There was the sound of broken glass from two boxes, but he put them in the truck and dashed back in, coming out with another three. They got in the Toyota and drove off, whooping and hollering, with Max barking excitedly.

Jamie leaned over and kissed her on the cheek. 'Jane, I never expected to ever say this in real-life, but you're a bad-ass!'

She grinned and sniggered. 'I've never thought of myself as a bad-ass before! Mind you; you haven't done too badly yourself so far. Six months ago neither of us had fired a gun before: how times change!'

In the last two weeks of June they went out for walks every evening to locate fruit trees to harvest when the time came, marking the locations on a street map. The fruit was growing well on most trees due to the good weather they'd had predominantly so far. The cherries would be ready for picking within a few weeks, but the apples and pears would take considerably longer before they were ready. They would have to keep a close watch on the cherry trees in the area and harvest them as soon as was possible, before the birds ate them all.

One evening, in the last week of June, they diverted on the way home and stopped at The Colonnade, on the seafront behind the De La Warr Pavilion. It was a beautiful semi-circular structure supported by pillars, with turrets and balustrades above, built in 1911 to mark the coronation of King George V. In happier times before the plague there had been a popular café there, where locals and tourists would sit and enjoy the view. They had a flask of coffee with them and sat down outside at a table.

'I often used to come here for coffee and a snack,' said Jane. 'I'd sit here reading for an hour when the weather was good… such a shame.'

'I know: I often used to come here, too, and do the same.'

She gave him a nostalgic smile. 'You know, it's possible that at some point we were both sitting here at the same time, oblivious of each other!'

'And wouldn't that have been bizarre?' he replied, smiling. 'Both of us sitting here at the same time, maybe, not knowing how our lives would become entwined or what would happen in the near future…'

Max was stretched out on the ground beside them, enjoying the early evening sun. They looked at each other wistfully and Jamie poured more coffee.

'Hello there!' said a voice from above. Max jumped up and barked. They both jumped in shock and stood up, reaching for their guns. Looking up to the balustrade they saw two women's faces looking down at them. The one who had spoken smiled nervously.

'Whoops! Sorry to startle you. Hi; do you mind if we come down and join you?'

Jane recovered first and smiled in response. 'Yes of course; please do.' She and Jamie looked at each other in amazement. The two women walked round and down the steps to the promenade then along to The Colonnade. They were in their late forties probably and both had shotguns slung on their shoulders.

Max was tense at first, ready to jump to the defence of his family, but soon relaxed when no threat was detected. The two women introduced themselves as Sarah and Georgie; it was obvious they were sisters and they shook hands all round. Sarah was around five years older than Georgie and maybe into her fifties: both were dressed in classic country clothing and they had an air of elegance and robust good health about them. They had strong faces that in earlier times might have been called handsome, rather than pretty, and both bore a passing resemblance to Katharine Hepburn, especially Sarah.

'Goodness me!' said Sarah, 'You're almost the first people we've seen in months. It's nice to meet you, and to see there are some other people left!'

'Likewise,' said Jamie. 'Until fairly recently we'd seen only six people in several months- and two of those encounters were bad ones. We met a nice family near Hooe six or seven weeks ago, and also we've seen four more in Battle, and that was a bad encounter as well.'

'I know what you mean.' said Georgie. 'The two people we saw some time ago gave us trouble- a man and a woman. They raided our place and killed two chickens, then came into our house and started ransacking the place. I came downstairs with my gun and the woman cut me with a knife and knocked me down. I was lying on the floor when Sarah came back in from the farm and shot them both. We burned the bodies and buried the remains. The sad and ironic thing is that if they'd been decent people and had knocked on the door asking for help, we would gladly have helped them.'

'A nasty business and not something I'm proud of, but I won't dwell on it,' said Sarah. 'We drove down here this evening for a look around. We parked the Land Rover in the car park, wandered over and were amazed to see you two sitting here drinking coffee! You looked decent so we thought we'd say hello.'

Jamie and Jane had been sharing a cup and he had a spare one, so offered them some coffee. They accepted gladly and sat down with them to talk. The two sisters lived along Watermill Lane, a mile or two north of Sidley, which was on the northern edge of Bexhill. They kept chickens and bees and grew vegetables that they used to sell from the farm shop. They had several hives, and before the plague they had run courses on beekeeping and looking after poultry. They had run the place with their father until he'd become sick with the plague and died.

'It was horrible,' Georgie said. 'He came back one day from a visit into town and went straight into one of the outbuildings and locked himself in. When we went out to see what was going on he spoke to us through the door and said that a man had sneezed on him in town and he didn't want to take any chances, so he quarantined himself. Within two days he had all the symptoms and by the fourth day he was dead. There was nothing we could do. He refused to let us bring food in for him, but we poked a hosepipe through a gap in the wall so he had water.'

'After he died,' continued Sarah, 'we had to drag him out with a rake in case he was still contaminated and burn his body; it was awful.' Jamie and Jane said how sorry they were.

They had been surviving pretty well on their own so far. They had chickens and, therefore, eggs, a pair of goats for milk, and had stores of preserved fruit and veg' from the previous season, along with lots of other food they had stockpiled when it all started. They had planted vegetables the previous autumn and early this year and were harvesting some now, and there were many fruit trees on their property.

Jane and Jamie took turns in telling them about their own deeds and adventures since it had begun, and how they had met and joined together. Sarah and Georgie were interested in all they had to say and listened attentively. Both were amazed at Jane's account of how Jamie had saved her and then removed the pellets from her leg, and congratulated him. They were especially interested in the different preserving techniques they were using, including the making of jerky.

The light started to fade and the sisters said they should be heading back home. They gave each other their addresses and directions, and both couples told each other they were welcome to visit any time they wanted. Jamie and Jane accompanied them back to their truck in front of the De La Warr Pavilion and they all shook hands. Sarah and Georgie stroked Max and then started the truck and drove off, waving. They walked home discussing the encounter and feeling happy. It looked like there might be more survivors out there that they would meet in time, but they knew from experience that they weren't all going to be as friendly as Sarah and Georgie. They now had another two friends in the wilderness that Bexhill had become and didn't feel quite so alone.

Eighteen

The first two weeks of July were very busy for them, harvesting and preserving the cherries from the area. Most were a little under-ripe and rather tart, but they thought that if they left them to fully ripen on the trees they might lose most of them to the birds. Some trees were easily accessible from the road or from the front gardens of houses, while others were located in back gardens and involved climbing over walls and gates to gain access to them. They used leaf-collecting rakes sometimes for the fruits that were out of reach. On two occasions Jane was reduced to laughter watching Jamie struggle to climb the trees and shake the branches, while cherries rained down on her. After the second time he came down with his face covered in scratches from branches, looking rather annoyed.

She stifled a laugh behind her hand and said 'Oh, look at my poor baby's face!' then proceeded to kiss it better, trying not to smirk.

'Okay, clever-clogs, you can go up the next one and see how you get on!'

She proved a much more nimble climber than him and came down afterwards without a scratch on her. He said 'Hmph! Beginner's luck!' She just smiled smugly and stuck her tongue out at him.

Processing the cherries for preserving was extremely labour-intensive and took them ages. The ones that were to be dried had to be pitted and halved. They lowered the drying racks in the conservatory by their ropes and spread the fruit out over the mesh, before raising them again. The racks were completely full of cherries for two weeks. Once dried, which took around five days, they resembled large raisins. They had lost some of their tartness in the drying process and became nicer to eat, and were packed away in airtight containers and stored for future use. They preserved others in alcohol, using the cheap vodka they'd got from the warehouse, and some were made into compotes and sealed in preserving jars. Those cherries destined for alcohol preserving only needed pitting and went in whole, which saved a lot of time.

On top of the cherry harvesting and processing they also had to make regular trips to check the rabbit snares they had in various locations, which then involved cooking and preserving any they caught and making jerky also. They found they could speed up the jerky-making process by drying the meat in the Rayburn's warming oven with the door left open a crack. Another regular task was to collect the salt from the containers in the garden as the sea water evaporated and then refill them. All-in-all it was a pretty hectic time for them, involving long days.

There hadn't been much heavy rainfall during June, so they took water from the pond in the garden and also had to make regular trips to the lake at Egerton Park to fill water containers. Although the duck population there had diminished and those that were left were more wary, they managed sometimes to get one or two with the shotguns. On Friday of the second week, in late afternoon, they had a visit from Sarah and Georgie. They were washing-up in the kitchen and heard a truck pull up in the road: Jamie picked up his sawn-off and went to look, but put it down when he saw who it was. He called out to Jane and they welcomed them into the house, with Max jumping up at both women, barking and wagging his tail. They came bearing gifts; a plump pheasant they'd shot that morning, along with some eggs, onions, young carrots and some honey from their hives. Jamie and Jane were delighted and thanked them both.

'We thought we'd be presumptuous and see if we could

come for an evening meal!' said Georgie.

Jane said that would be great and put some water on to heat for tea. They showed the sisters around the house and the two gardens, explaining the modifications they'd made and the things they'd built, along with the planting they had done between them. Sarah and Georgie were impressed and said they were doing a great job, especially as it was, predominantly, all new to them. Jane admitted, though, that it definitely wasn't all plain sailing and they were having plenty of failures as well. At the bottom of the garden they opened the gate, showing them their access to the beach and the boat tied up to the railings.

'Well,' said Sarah, 'you've got a good setup here and I'm really pleased you're doing okay. Good for you!'

They went back inside and sat at the table talking about themselves. Both sisters had divorced many years before and had started the business together at their dad's farm: well, they called it "The Farm", but it was more a smallholding, really. Only Sarah had had children; a daughter who had been away at university in London when the plague had hit, and had died there. Sarah had been informed by phone as there hadn't been the manpower for a personal visit by the authorities due to the huge number of deaths occurring everywhere. Sarah cried as she related the story to them and her sister hugged her. Georgie had remained friendly with her ex and her step-daughter, both of whom had died. Jane and Jamie told them about the loss of their own families, too: all four had their own stories of loss and tragedy, as was to be expected. Jamie opened a bottle of wine and they toasted those no longer with them.

'I don't mind admitting,' said Georgie, 'that there have been several occasions over the last four months when we've been terrified and worried about the future…'

'… But what can you do except to just carry on, deal with it as best you can and survive?' added Sarah, and the others agreed with her.

To lighten the mood Jane told them how they had found Max on the beach at death's-door and had nursed him back to health, and what a great companion and working dog he had become to them. She told them how great he was at locating rabbit burrows for them to lay snares. Max stirred and looked up from his bed on hearing his name, but was far too comfortable to bother getting up.

They decided it was time to cook, so Jane went outside to pluck the pheasant while Jamie picked some beans and peas. After the pheasant was prepared and the lead shot removed she put it in the oven to roast with some herbs, while Jamie prepared a vegetable casserole to accompany it. While the food cooked he showed them the cellar that was filling up nicely with dried fish, jerky and other preserved food, then Jane took the sisters next door to show them her home. Georgie asked why they had two places and Jane explained how things had begun. She grinned, though, and admitted that since she and Jamie had fallen in love she spent most of her time at his place.

'We have disagreements on things sometimes, of course, but nothing that could be called an argument so far. It's just nice, sometimes, to come back here to sleep on my own and have my own space for a night. Besides,' she added with an impish grin, 'Jamie farts a lot in bed,' and all three of them giggled.

As it was a lovely evening they ate outside on the patio; the kitchen was often too warm now once the range or the stove was lit for cooking on. Jamie brought his MP3 player outside and put on some Spanish guitar music by John Williams. It was a relaxed occasion and they drank two bottles of wine between them. Sarah and Georgie were great company and, for a short while at least, they almost forgot the terrible situation they were all living in.

It came time for the sisters to leave and they hugged each other warmly. As they had no means of communicating with each other they arranged a date in two weeks' time for Jane and Jamie to go over to their place for lunch. They had told the sisters about Bill and Emma and said how nice it would be for them to meet each other if they could arrange it. Both women agreed that would be lovely then got in their truck, waved and drove off. They cleared up for the night and went to bed with a nice warm glow from the company that evening.

After the mad two weeks with the cherries they had a slight hiatus, as the apples and pears wouldn't be ready for some time yet, though they still had plenty to do in the gardens as more vegetables became ready for harvesting. On one day Jamie made some gun racks for the back of the cab in both trucks to store the rifles and shotguns when they went out, but they used the vehicles only when necessary, to conserve fuel. Whenever they went out locally to check the snares they either walked or took Jamie's bike. It proved to be too big for Jane, though, so they went to Halfords on the retail park and picked a nice bike for her, along with a rack and some paniers. When they got back Jamie made another wooden carrying platform for it from plywood, as he had done with his own bike.

While they were there, though, they heard a vehicle drive up and stop nearby- in fact Max heard it well before them and barked softly. They went outside cautiously with their shotguns, to see Phil and Sophie in their old Mondeo so they waved and went over to them.

'We thought that was your truck when we pulled up,' said Phil, smiling. 'We were only saying yesterday that we hadn't seen you in a while. Bill and Emma have been worried that you were okay.'

It had been over a month since their last visit as they had been so busy working and with all the harvesting they had done. They asked Phil and Sophie to apologise to Bill and Emma for them and explain why, and to say that they would come over tomorrow at noon, which the young couple said they would do. Phil said they had come to stock up on some things from Tesco's and asked if they had seen the warehouse there, but Jamie said they hadn't got around to it yet.

'Oh, man, you've got to see it! There's loads of food and drink in there.' As Jamie had done at Sainsbury's, Phil had recently broken into the warehouse at the back to find it well-stocked with all manner of food, drinks, clothes and other useful things. Phil walked through the store to open a door in the loading area while the others drove the vehicles round the service road behind the retail park and pulled up outside, where Phil was waiting for them.

'I keep telling Bill he should get his old van fixed and come down here and load it up. He could easily fix it himself, but he hasn't got around to it yet!'

They walked into the warehouse and found shelves loaded with all manner of produce. There were trolleys there so they all went along the aisles and loaded up with dried goods, tinned foods, cured meats such as whole salamis and chorizos, cases of wines and spirits and packs of bottled water. It was a huge warehouse- far bigger than Sainsbury's- and it took them a good while to find everything and load it into the vehicles. When they couldn't fit any more into the truck they said goodbye to Phil and Sophie, saying they'd see them at noon the next day. They drove home feeling pleased with their haul and unloaded everything between both houses.

Their reunion with Bill and Emma the following day was a happy one. It seemed far longer than the month or so since they had seen them and Jamie even got a big bear-hug from Bill. Sally was delighted to see Max again and played in the yard with him while the adults went inside. Emma took Jane to one side and told her that Sally had had her first period the week before; she had tears in her eyes.

'Thanks so much for the things you brought for her weeks ago. I'd told her long ago what to expect and explained everything to her, but she was still a bit scared when it happened, bless her.' Jane had tears in her eyes also and hugged Emma. When Sally came in shortly from playing with Max, Jane thought she detected a hint of new maturity about her in the way she acted and held herself. *The end of innocence,* she thought.

They sat around the kitchen table and had a good talk while the food cooked. Having been forewarned of their visit by Phil and Sophie, Emma had defrosted some meat and was cooking a big pork roast, which smelled great. Jamie and Jane apologised again for not coming sooner, but Bill and Emma understood perfectly. They were pleased things were going well for them generally and that they'd managed to harvest and store so much fruit, and commiserated with them when they heard how they were struggling sometimes to get enough meat. They had been busy themselves with harvesting in previous weeks and had had their own share of disappointments, too.

Jamie told them what they'd been up to, including their second visit to Battle, the run-in with the lads there and Jane's shooting skills.

'You should have seen him flinch and duck when I put a bullet a few inches past his left ear,' said Jane. 'I bet he had to go home and change his trousers!' They all laughed.

She told them about meeting Sarah and Georgie at The Colonnade and then the sisters coming round to see them for a meal. When Jane said where they lived and what they used to do, Bill realised that he knew them.

'Well,' he said, 'I don't really know them as such, but I met them once, briefly. I sent Phil and Sophie over to their place early last year for a weekend poultry-keeping course. They both said the sisters were lovely and it was a good course. I'm pleased they've survived and are doing okay. Phil and Sophie will be, too, I'm sure.'

'We were thinking,' said Jane, 'that it would be nice for us all to get together one day for a meal.' Bill and Emma said they'd like that.

'Well, we're going over to theirs for lunch next week, so why don't we arrange it now, so we can tell them when we go over there? You could all come over to ours, as you haven't seen our place yet.' They all agreed it was a great idea and arranged a date for two weeks' time.

Bill smiled. 'That gives me an excuse for getting the old van fixed and back on the road! I've been meaning to do it for ages, but kept putting it off.'

When Phil and Sophie came in from working out on the farm Bill told them the news about Sarah and Georgie and they were both happy to hear it. Jamie and Jane stayed for a couple of hours and had a lovely meal with them, then said that they'd better be heading back as there was work to do. Jamie returned Bill's jerrycan and thanked him, but Bill went over to the diesel tank, refilled it then gave it back to him. 'Keep it in the truck for emergencies, mate.'

Jamie thanked him and then they all said goodbye and hugged each other before driving away. They stopped off on the way back to check the snares, but there were no rabbits caught in them.

'Oh, bloody hell, Jane!' exclaimed Jamie angrily. 'What is it? Are we doing something wrong?'

'I don't know, hon. I mean, I don't think so. I'm no expert, but as far as I'm concerned we're doing everything right. It's how I remember my dad doing it and we're laying them like it says in the books. I suspect it's just not a foolproof method of hunting and has a low success rate. The snares can be knocked over; the hoop has to be at just the right height to catch whatever size of rabbit is running through it; and if the rabbit doesn't go through cleanly the snare can miss it, etc., etc. I don't think we're doing too badly really, Jamie. It's just a bit hit-and-miss: sometimes we get a few and sometimes we don't. We just have to persevere and to look at it like anything we get is a bonus.'

Jamie sighed. 'I suppose so. I'm sure you're right, darlin', and sorry I snapped.' He kissed her and she smiled and waved her hand to brush it away.

They left for home and went back to work in the garden. After finishing their work for the day they cooked a meal and then went for a walk along the beach with Max to watch the sun set behind Beachy Head.

Over the next week they had two days with some heavy rainfall, which was good news as the water-butts got topped-up, but it made working in the garden a muddy affair. Jane seemed down and rather withdrawn all week, and spent the nights at her place on her own. When Jamie asked her if everything was okay she gave him a weak smile and said it had been both her mum's and her sister Kate's birthdays that week. He held her tight, stroking her hair and comforting her as she cried into his chest for a long time.

On the night before their visit to Sarah and Georgie's he was lying alone in bed when he heard the back door open and close; Max didn't bark so he knew it was Jane. She came in and got undressed, slipped into bed beside him and held him close.

'Mum and Kate's birthdays aren't the only reason I've been withdrawn recently,' she said softly to him. 'Jamie... I'm pregnant.'

Nineteen

'Oh my God!' said Jamie, spinning in her arms to face her in the dark. 'How… I mean… Are you sure?'

'I'm pretty sure,' she replied. 'I'm over two weeks late. The only time in my life I've *ever* been that late before was when I fell pregnant with my ex, about seven years ago, but I miscarried after a few weeks. Also, I was sick this morning.'

'Bloody hell!' said Jamie, and then fumbled in the dark to light a candle by the bedside. They sat up and he held her hand. 'I thought we'd been careful,' he said.

'So did I;' she replied, 'but obviously not careful enough! I've calculated in my mind and it must have been near the end of June; around when we met Sarah and Georgie.'

'Wow! How do you feel about it?'

'I don't know… torn in two, I guess... And confused and terrified! That's why I've been so down and withdrawn recently; as well as Mum and Kate, of course. I mean… I've always wanted kids. It didn't happen with my ex, which was probably a good thing because he turned out to be not very nice. After we split up I threw myself into work for several years and never really met anyone else, so I thought I'd probably missed the boat as far as children were concerned. I don't know… If I'd met you a few years ago and this had happened, I would have been over the moon; but now? I mean, what sort of a world is this to be bringing a child into?'

'Well, on that argument, I've met couples over the years

who were saying the same thing *before* we had the plague! And if you went back to the fourteenth century and the original Black Death you'd probably have found people having the same conversation back then.'

'Maybe; but still... And the way things are now, there's almost no one left alive; there are no hospitals or doctors, or anything. How do you feel about it?'

'I'm not sure, but I think I need a drink!' He got up and put on his dressing-gown to go to the kitchen. 'Pour me a small one, too, please,' said Jane and he nodded.

The kitchen was still warm from the stove's heat and he poured two glasses of cognac then sat on the sofa in the conservatory. Max could sense that something wasn't right and he came up and rested his head on Jamie's thigh, whining softly. Jamie stroked his head and then Jane came in wearing her bath robe, sat next to him and cuddled up. Max nuzzled her leg and she stroked him, too. Jamie passed her a cognac and they clinked glasses.

'I'm scared, Jamie... really scared.'

'So am I, hon. I mean...' He struggled to find what to say. 'I feel pretty much the same as you do, I suppose: if this had happened a few years ago... etc. When I was married there came a time when my wife wanted kids and I didn't. Years after we'd split up I realised I did want kids, but just hadn't wanted them with her... Hindsight's a wonderful thing! For years I've thought that I'd love to have a little girl, but I've never met anyone since that I would have had kids with until meeting you. So now, here we are; faced with the reality of what we've both wanted for a long time...'

'But the timing couldn't be much worse, could it? There are no doctors or hospitals... what if there are complications?'

'I don't know, Jane, I really don't. Part of me would love to have a child with you, but I know what you mean. I'd much rather lose the baby than lose you; I couldn't bear that.' He had tears in his eyes and held her tight against him, and they kissed tenderly.

'I suppose we've also got Emma and Sarah for advice and help, as they've both had kids,' he said, and Jane nodded. 'I mean, we only have two options, really, don't we? We can either let nature take its course, or we can try to abort it... and if we tried that God knows what might happen! That could be even more dangerous than actually having the baby, couldn't it?'

'Yes, I think it could be,' she replied.

Jamie sighed. 'Well, then... I guess we're having a baby!' Jane wiped tears from her eyes, smiled at him and they kissed again. They raised their glasses and Jamie said 'Here's to us, and to new life in a world turned to hell!'

'To us, and to new life!' Jane repeated and they clinked glasses again. Max didn't know what was happening, but he barked and wagged his tail anyway. They finished their drinks and went back to bed, with Jane feeling so much better now that she'd got things off her chest and it was out in the open. She was also relieved and overjoyed at Jamie's reaction to the news.

In the morning they went down to the sea together to bathe and then made coffee and breakfast. Sarah and Georgie were expecting them at midday, so they spent a few hours harvesting and preserving some vegetables. They still had some time to kill and it wasn't worth getting dirty in the garden, so they took Max down to the beach for some exercise with a ball and gave him a good run around.

They left at about 11.40 and took the BMW, with Max in the load area and their shotguns on the back seat. They decided to drive through the Old Town to Sidley as neither had been up that way since the plague had hit the area. They drove along West Parade and Marina, turning left up Sea Road towards the Old Town and then down Holliers Hill to Bexhill Hospital.

What they saw there made them gasp and stop the car. The grassy slope by the middle hospital building was maybe thirty yards by fifty and it was full of body bags. There were hundreds lined up on the grass. Some had been ripped open, maybe by foxes or seagulls, and human remains were scattered around. Huge clouds of flies hovered in the air above them.

They looked on aghast. Obviously, they knew what the

death-toll had been because Bexhill had become a ghost-town, but if they'd needed any reminder then this was it. Their experience of the devastation had been limited to individual bodies or family groups in the houses they'd been into, and occasionally in the streets, but this was far different. It brought it home to them in a different way, somehow. The hospital and local authorities just hadn't had the time, the means or the manpower to dispose of all the bodies because of how quickly people were dying, before it was too late. Screens had been erected around the area to hide the sight from the road, but most had collapsed or been blown over by storms.

'And just imagine,' Jamie said, 'what it must look like in Hastings and Eastbourne, which are well over twice the size of Bexhill... or in London.'

'I don't even want to think of that! Come on, Jamie, let's get away from here.'

Jamie put the car in gear and drove off slowly. They crested the hill and down the other side to the bottom of Sidley, turned right and on into the high street. As they drove up it they saw that many shop windows were smashed, or doors standing open. Half-empty rubbish bags littered the pavements and road, having fallen out of wheelie-bins that lay on their sides and been torn open by seagulls. They carried on to the top of the high street then turned right just after the mini-roundabout into Watermill Lane and down the hill. Jamie pulled over at the bottom and started crying.

'My brother's house is down there,' he said between tears, pointing off to the right. He hadn't been there since it all began. Jane leaned over and hugged him with tears in her eyes also.

'Oh, honey, I'm sorry. Do you want to go in, while we're here?'

Jamie shook his head emphatically. 'No, I couldn't bear to see him like that. I'd rather remember him the way he was.'

'D'you want me to drive the rest of the way?' Jamie shook his head and wiped his eyes. 'No, it's okay; it's not much further.'

They carried on and the road soon became a narrow and

twisty country lane. The sisters had given them accurate directions and after a mile or two they found the entrance to the place. The gate had been left open for them and they stopped inside, closing it behind them, then drove up the lane to the house. There was a parking area to one side and they stopped the car and got out. Georgie and Sarah came out to meet them and when Jane opened the door for Max he jumped out and ran over to the women, who made a fuss of him. The sisters greeted them warmly and they hugged each other then went into the house to sit around the kitchen table. It was hot in there as the Aga was running, but the windows were open. Jane gave the sisters two bottles of wine and they both thanked them. It was obvious that some cloud was hanging over Jamie and Jane, and that he had been crying.

'Is everything okay?' asked Georgie. 'You both look troubled.'

'Well, we've just driven past Jamie's brother's house; it's the first time he's been up here since it happened,' replied Jane.

'Oh, you poor thing,' said Sarah, reaching over to put her hand on his. Georgie said how sorry she was, too.

'Thanks,' said Jamie. 'I'll be okay; it just brought it all back to me. Plus, we'd also just driven past the hospital and seen all the bodies for the first time.'

'I know;' said Georgie, 'we've been past there ourselves. It's a hell of a sight, isn't it?'

'It's odd, you know;' said Jane, 'we knew the extent of the deaths because there's no one around any more... but we'd only seen single people or families in the houses we went in. Suddenly seeing hundreds lined up like that was a real shock to us.'

'I'm sure it was,' said Sarah. 'Our father knew people in authority and he was told early on that they were digging mass graves in a secret location somewhere, but most of them either didn't get finished or didn't get filled before it was too late. The hospitals at Eastbourne, Hastings and Bexhill were swamped and they were turning people away as there weren't enough beds, facilities or staff to cope with them all. Most people just went home to die as there was nothing that could

165

be done.' She shook her head then got up and came back with a bottle of whisky and four glasses, but Jane declined.

'Well, cheers!' Georgie toasted. 'Here's to the living.' They all repeated the toast and took a drink.

'… And to the not yet born…' Jane added, quietly. Both women looked at her in amazement.

'Yes, I'm pregnant,' she said and gave them a weak smile.

'Wow!' said Sarah.

'Bloody hell!' added Georgie.

'Well, congratulations to you both… if that's appropriate to how you're feeling,' said Sarah, raising her eyebrows questioningly.

'Well, to be honest,' said Jane, 'it was a complete shock as it *certainly* wasn't planned. We thought we'd been careful.'

'How far gone are you?' asked Sarah.

'I'm well over two weeks late, which is unheard of for me. It must have happened around the time we met you; so that's, what, about five weeks? I've been down all week and struggling with it. I only told Jamie last night.' She was silent for a few seconds and then added 'I'm terrified!' and burst into tears.

Georgie moved next to Jane and put her arms around her. 'It's okay, my love, you'll be fine.'

'But will I?' said Jane through her tears. 'How? I don't know anything about pregnancy or childbirth, and there are no doctors or hospitals any more, or medical supplies…'

'Well, it probably won't be of any consolation to you at the moment,' said Sarah, 'but you must bear in mind, my dear, that women were having babies for hundreds of thousands of years before doctors or hospitals existed… and the human race survived and prospered! I completely understand your fear, though; I was terrified, too, when I fell pregnant with Lisa- and that was when we *did* have hospitals and doctors!'

Jane gave a snort and a small laugh, wiped her eyes and smiled at her. 'Thank you, Sarah, that does make me feel a little better!'

'And remember,' Sarah added, 'that I've had a child and your friend Emma has had two, also, so you won't be entirely alone and without support or knowledge.'

Jane got up, went round the table to give Sarah a hug and thanked her. Georgie jumped up and said 'Right- this calls for a celebration!' She disappeared down into the cellar and came back up with a dusty bottle of expensive champagne.

'We've had this for a few years,' she said, 'and were waiting for a suitable occasion to open it. To be honest, we'd sort of given up hope in there being one again, but this seems as good a time as any!'

She fetched four champagne flutes, corked the bottle and poured them all a glass, then raised a toast; 'To the baby!'

'*To the baby!*' they repeated and drank a mouthful.

'That's lovely,' said Jamie.

'It could do with being rather colder,' said Sarah, smiling, 'but beggars can't be choosers!'

'Have you had a chance to think of any names yet?' asked Georgie.

Jamie smiled and shook his head, but Jane said 'Well, actually... During some of my long nights lying awake worrying about it all, I did think of a couple of names for if it ever happened! If it's a boy I'd like Robbie, as my surname is Roberts- though he'd have Jamie's surname, which is Parker. If it's a girl I'd like Annie.'

She looked enquiringly at Jamie, who nodded and said 'Fine with me.' He then had a thought and smiled. 'I hope it is a girl, as I always wanted a daughter. Also, when she's older I'll be able to say to her "Annie, get your gun!"' They all burst into laughter and Georgie raised another toast to Robbie or Annie.

While the food cooked the sisters showed them around their property. It was a lovely place and a good size, without being unmanageable for them. Max followed them, sniffing at everything, but was well-behaved and didn't bark or make a fuss when they came to the chickens and goats. They showed them the beehives, chicken coops and outbuildings, and pointed out the stream nearby where they got their water from. The vegetable field was well laid out and the small orchard was well-tended; all the trees had been trained to a small size to make harvesting easier.

Since the plague they had reduced the vegetable-growing

to suit just their needs. Without the workers to tend the crops or the public to sell them to, there was no point growing more than they needed or could use. On a patch of lawn near the house was a raised mound of earth with a wooden cross on it, where they'd buried their father.

'We plan to get some horses soon,' said Georgie. 'There are quite a few in the area, running wild in the fields now, with no one to ride them. They've got plenty to eat and seem to be looking after themselves. We can easily make a couple of stables in the outbuildings. We're going to need them in the near-future, as the petrol and diesel that's left becomes unusable.'

This was something that Jamie hadn't given any thought to, and had no knowledge about, so he enquired further.

'Well,' answered Sarah, 'Dad did some research early on while he was still able to, and found that there wasn't really any hard data on the subject. Estimates varied hugely, but the general consensus seemed to be that fuel would become unusable within a year or so, probably. It's something to do with the complex hydrocarbons breaking down, and air and water being mixed with the fuel also. Any fuel left unused in vehicles will go off quicker because the tanks are vented, which will let air in. The best way to prolong its life is in sealed containers, apparently, but even that won't make it last forever.'

Jamie scratched his head, lost in thought. This was news to him- and rather worrying news, at that- and he mentally kicked himself for not thinking of it before. They went back to the house and the sisters got the meal ready. He forgot about fuel problems for a while, though, as Sarah and Georgie had prepared a fantastic rabbit and pheasant pie, with lots of vegetables to go with it and gravy. They finished with some homemade goat's yoghurt and dried fruit with honey.

After eating they retired to the lounge with coffee and sat talking for a couple of hours, looking out at the garden and the fields beyond as the sun moved westward. Max lay stretched out in front of the fire, having eaten the rabbit remains. Jane was feeling slightly easier in her mind after talking to Sarah, though she was still very nervous. She felt relieved, however, that she would have the help and support of the two sisters in the future. It was now late afternoon and they made ready to take leave of their friends. Sarah and Georgie came out to the car with them and they hugged each other.

'Remember,' said Sarah, 'we're always here for you if you need any help or advice. Come round whenever you like.' Jane was grateful and thanked them both.

'I almost forgot,' said Jamie, 'Bill and Emma are coming to ours next Friday for lunch, and we were hoping you'd come, too. It would be great for you to meet each other. In fact,' he added, 'you've already met Bill before.' He explained about Phil and Sophie going to their place for a course the previous year and both women remembered them, and Bill vaguely, as they'd only met him briefly. They said that would be great and promised to come.

Jane drove off down the track, stopping at the bottom for Jamie to open the gate and close it behind them, then turned left and drove back towards Sidley. They chatted as they went, but Jamie fell silent as they passed the turning to his brother's house and hung his head; Jane took his hand and gripped it. They came back to the main road and turned left, over the roundabout and into the high street. Just as they passed Lidl they caught movement to their right and saw a figure come out of a small supermarket. They couldn't believe their eyes and Jane braked to a halt immediately. Standing on the pavement was a young girl waving at them; she had a dirty face and matted, long blonde hair, but was wearing a pristine green dress.

Twenty

They got out of the car and, as a precaution, Jamie reached into the back seat, picked up the sawn-off and slung it over his shoulder by its strap. They crossed the road to where the girl was standing and Jane knelt down in front of her. She looked about ten or eleven, and was rather thin and under-nourished. Jamie stood a couple of feet away, looking around and listening.

'Hello, honey, my name's Jane and this is my partner, Jamie. Are you okay?'

The girl nodded. 'Kind of... but not really; I'm scared. Is it okay to be scared? Mummy and Daddy said I mustn't be, but that was a long time ago.'

'Oh, honey, of course it's okay to be scared- I'm scared and so is Jamie. What's your name?'

'My name's Megan.'

'And how old are you, Megan?'

'I'm twelve now. It was my birthday yesterday. I know because I've been looking at my diary every day. That's why I'm wearing this dress. All my clothes were dirty and I wanted something nice to wear for my birthday. I found this dress in the charity shop down the road.' Jane wanted to cry but she managed to remain composed.

'Well, happy birthday for yesterday, Megan. Are you on your own, or do you have any family?'

Megan shook her head. 'Mummy and Daddy died in

170

February from the sickness. They're in their bedroom. It started to smell bad a long time ago and there were lots of flies, so I had to put tape over the bottom of the door.'

'Oh, Megan, I'm so sorry.' Jane looked up at Jamie; his jaw was set and she could see that he was struggling to keep it together. 'How did you manage to survive, Megan?' she asked.

'Mummy shut me in the cellar when they thought they might get sick. Daddy had filled it with lots of food and drink, and with candles, buckets and blankets. They said I mustn't be afraid and I mustn't come out until help came, but no one came. They got very sick and one day it went quiet. I waited for ages, but no one came. Is everyone dead?'

'Nearly everyone, my love. How long were you down in the cellar?'

'Three weeks and six days. I checked my diary, wondering when it would be safe to come out. When no one came after all that time I thought I should come out as it smelled really bad in the cellar because of the toilet buckets.'

'You're a very brave girl, Megan, and your mum and dad would be proud of you. What have you been doing since then?'

'Well, I carried all the food and drink that was left up to the house and I've been sleeping on the sofa in the lounge. It was really cold and I had to put lots of blankets on it. I didn't want to go upstairs because Mummy and Daddy were up there, but I had to. All my clothes were in my bedroom, so I took them all downstairs. The electricity and the water worked for a while and then it stopped and there was no television. I put lots of bowls and pans and plastic boxes out in the garden to collect rainwater.'

'That was very good thinking, Megan; good for you! You're a clever girl.'

'But all my food ran out, so I've been going to the supermarkets and I've managed to find some food. Also, I've been getting food from the houses in the streets nearby where the doors were open, or climbing through windows. There are dead people in all of them and it's been awful. Have you seen many dead people?'

171

'Yes, my love, I'm afraid we've seen lots of dead people. It's been awful for us, too, and we've been just as scared as you have.' She looked up at Jamie with a silent question and he nodded without hesitation. She turned back to the girl.

'Megan, would you like to come home and stay with us? We live a couple of miles away, by the sea. We could look after you now; would you like that?'

She gave Jane a big smile and said 'Yes please, I'd love to,' then burst into tears. Jane hugged her, fighting back tears herself. 'Do you need to get anything first from your home?'

'Well, I'd like to get a photo of Mummy and Daddy if that's alright, and my grandma, too. And I'd like to get my teddy. I know I'm twelve now, but I still like my teddy; is that okay?'

'Of course it is, Megan; you just show us where to go.'

They got back in the car and Jamie took the other shotgun off the back seat and put it in the front so Megan could sit down. They introduced her to Max, who promptly licked her face, making one clean patch on her left cheek, and she laughed for the first time in five months. Jane and Jamie looked at each other with heartbroken expressions on their faces. The girl's laughter amidst the ruin that lay about them was something they had never expected to hear, and this felt like the best thing they'd done since the plague had begun. They drove up a side street under Megan's direction and stopped outside her house. Jane asked her if she would like them to go in with her, but she declined.

'It's okay, thanks; I only need a few things and I won't be long. What will I do about clothes? Only, all of mine are ruined and filthy and I don't think I want to wear them any more.'

Jane smiled. 'Don't worry about that, honey; we'll go shopping tomorrow and get you some new clothes.' Megan thought for a second then nodded and went inside.

She came back out two minutes later clutching a couple of framed photos, her teddy bear, a diary and her favourite blanket. She put them on the back seat, climbed in and they drove off. They had to stop off on the way home at the latest locations where they had snares set, and picked up two rabbits, which was great news.

Jane looked at Jamie and winked, saying 'Swings and roundabouts!' He just smiled at her in return. Megan was amazed to see them and said how clever they were, then asked if they were going to eat them.

'Yes, honey,' said Jane, 'we're going to cook you a lovely rabbit casserole tonight and you can eat as much as you like.'

'Oh, good,' Megan declared, 'because I've been starving lately and I'm sick of cold, tinned food! Mummy cooked us rabbit once last year and I thought it tasted like chicken.' Then she went quiet, looked down and picked up her teddy to cuddle it.

They arrived home and Jane parked the BMW in her garage then they went into the bungalow and through to the kitchen. The range was still warm from their cooking that morning and there were plenty of hot embers left, so Jamie raked them up and added more fuel to get it going again. Max curled up on his bed and Megan sat down on the floor and stroked him. Jane went over to her and ruffled her hair.

'Well, missy, I think the first thing we should do is take you down to the sea for a good wash. Would you like that?'

'Yes I would!' she replied. 'I haven't been in the sea since last summer and it'll be nice to be clean again.'

Jane fetched a couple of towels and the bottle of travel wash then they headed off down the garden holding hands. As they went she showed Megan all the vegetables they were growing. She said 'Cool!' and then said again how clever they were. She also thought it was cool that they had their own private steps to the beach and she ran off down to the sea. Jane went after her, a tearful smile on her face. Megan undressed quickly before Jane caught up and dashed in, shrieking and laughing. Jane followed and they were soon splashing each other: she was grateful for all the water in her eyes as it hid her tears. She couldn't imagine what this poor girl had been through in all those months on her own and it made her feel so good to see her laughing and having fun.

Jane fetched the travel wash and Megan hesitated for a second but let her soap her hair and help to untangle the matted curls. Jane then handed her the bottle and moved away a few yards to let her wash herself. Megan smiled shyly in gratitude, then turned her back and washed the rest of her body.

After they'd washed, Jane said 'Wow! It's hard to believe there's a pretty girl underneath all that dirt,' and Megan smiled. Jane went back to the beach to get Megan's underwear and socks and washed them.

'Don't worry about putting these back on,' she told Megan, 'we'll dry them by the stove for tonight. Tomorrow we'll go to the shops and get you some new things.'

'Okay,' she replied.

Jane got out first, dried herself and got dressed, then told Megan to follow when she was ready and walked back up the beach. Megan came out and dried herself, then got dressed and followed Jane back to the steps, where Max was waiting for them at the top, wagging his tail. When they got back to the kitchen they found it warming up nicely and Jamie was busy preparing the evening meal. Jane hung the towels and Megan's clothing up to dry by the range then showed her the third bedroom, where she would be sleeping.

'It will be *so* nice to sleep in a proper bed again,' she said to Jane. 'That camp-bed in the cellar was really uncomfortable and the sofa wasn't much better. I won't miss them at all!' Her face clouded over for a few seconds and she looked down, but Jane stroked her hair and smiled, then showed her where she and Jamie would be sleeping.

'We'll be nearby, so if you need anything or you're scared at night you just have to come and knock on our door.'

She then showed Megan the toilet and gave her a tour of the house before going back to the kitchen. Jamie had the meal underway and had just put a casserole in the oven. They all went to sit in the conservatory while the food cooked and they let Megan have the sofa, telling Max to jump up with her to keep her company. She sat there stroking him while they sat on the chairs opposite and they chatted until the meal was ready.

They kept the conversation away from Megan's time on her own and her parents' deaths; instead telling her about the

174

things they had done, and about fishing, growing vegetables and trapping rabbits. They told her about meeting their new friends Bill and Emma, and Sarah and Georgie, and how Bill and Emma had a daughter of about her age. Megan said she would like to meet her and Jane said that she would do in a week's time when they came for lunch, which pleased her.

Megan, inevitably, asked them about the plague and why everyone had died. They answered her questions as best they could, but were honest with her and said that they didn't know what had happened and didn't have any answers.

'But the Prime Minister and the Government will sort things out and put everything back to normal, won't they?' she asked. Jane glanced at Jamie as if to say *what the hell do we tell her?*

'Well, honey,' said Jamie, 'we don't know for sure, but we don't think there is a government any more. We think everyone died. We've seen almost no one in the last four or five months. We don't know what's going to happen in the future, but we can't rely on anyone coming to help us, ever. That's why we're growing our own vegetables and catching rabbits and fish to eat, because there won't be any supermarkets or shops any more. We've got to look after ourselves from now on. There won't be any more electricity, or TV, or running water in the taps, or schools, or anything else that we used to have. Everything has gone now, Megan-everything.'

Megan sat in silence for nearly a minute, digesting it all, but it was almost beyond her comprehension. She began to speak but then started crying instead. Jane went over and put her arms around her. 'It's okay, Megan, Jamie and I are going to look after you. You don't have to worry about anything.' Megan stopped crying and Jane pushed Max to one side and sat down next to her.

'Did you answer my wish?' she asked Jane after a while.

'How do you mean, honey?'

'Well, as it was my birthday yesterday I wanted a birthday cake, but all the cakes I found in the shops were mouldy. I found some tins of rice pudding, so I opened one and put a candle in it, then I lit it and blew it out and made a wish; because that's what you're supposed to do when you blow out the candles.'

'And what did you wish for?' Jane asked.

'I wished for someone to come and save me and to not be on my own, and then today you came.' Jane hugged her. 'Then yes, Megan, we've answered your wish.'

By then the food was ready so they went back into the kitchen and served up the meal. Megan ate like there was no tomorrow and put away a big plateful, then asked if she could have seconds. They smiled at her and said of course she could. After eating they cleared the things away and washed up, and within about half an hour Megan was asleep in her chair. Jamie picked her up, carried her to the bedroom and laid her on the bed. It was a warm night so he didn't bother with all the covers, but he put her favourite blanket on top of her and tucked her teddy bear in next to her. She stirred and rolled over to clutch her teddy then murmured 'Night-night, Daddy.'

Jamie bit his lip to keep from crying then went over to the chest of drawers opposite the bed and lit a candle he'd made from vegetable fat that would burn through the night. He put a glass cover over the candle and went back to the kitchen, where Jane was making some bread for the next day. After pouring himself a whisky he sat down on the sofa in the conservatory, where she joined him shortly and snuggled up next to him.

'… And then there were three,' said Jane.

They sat there for some time talking about Megan, amazed that she had looked after herself for all those months. They also discussed how it might impact on them and the way they were living, but they didn't have any answers to that yet and would just have to play it by ear. They closed up the house and went to bed. Jane awoke in the night and went to check on Megan, but she was sleeping soundly, still clutching her teddy.

When they got up in the morning Megan was still asleep, but she came into the kitchen after about twenty minutes, rubbing her eyes.

'Well, good morning, sleepy-head!' said Jane. 'You've slept

for over ten hours; you must have needed it.'

'Good morning,' she replied. 'That was the best sleep I've had since... well, for months and months. Thank you for putting the candle in my room. I woke up in the night and couldn't remember where I was and got a bit scared, but then I saw the candle and remembered. It was still burning just now so I blew it out.'

'That's okay, sweetie,' said Jamie. 'I thought you might need it last night. Good girl for blowing it out.'

They sat at the table and ate a breakfast of bread with cured meats, dried fruit and some of the honey that Sarah and Georgie had given them on their last visit. There was only tea or coffee to drink, so Megan just had water. Jane made a note to see if she could find some other drinks that Megan might like when they went out. After they'd eaten Jane asked if she'd like to come with her to take Max for his morning walk and she said she'd love to.

It had clouded over in the night and the sky was now overcast and dreary. Megan only had her green dress to wear, so Jane went next door and came back with one of her comfortable baggy jumpers. She put it on over the top of Megan's dress; it came down to her knees and she rolled the sleeves up for her. Max was already waiting by the back door, wagging his tail in anticipation.

Jane put on her coat, checking that there were spare cartridges in the pockets, and picked up her sawn-off, slinging it over her shoulder. They walked through the garden and down the steps to the promenade, then walked along to the next steps down onto the beach and headed east, walking just above the water line. Megan chased Max around and threw a piece of driftwood for him to fetch, which he ran after eagerly; Jane watched her with a smile on her face. After a while Megan came back and walked beside her.

'Jane?'

'Yes, honey?'

'Do you and Jamie always carry a gun when you go out?'

'Yes we do, sweetie; we have to, for protection. These are dangerous times now, Megan. There are no police any more,

177

so there's no one to maintain law and order. I know there aren't many people left, but some of them might be bad people. And because there's no law any more some people think that they can do anything they like.'

'I know there are bad people out there because I used to see it on the news sometimes and hear Mummy and Daddy talking about it. My mum told me long ago that I must never go off with strangers. You and Jamie were different, though, because you rescued me, and I had a good feeling about you. I always know when I don't trust someone. Have you met any bad people yet?'

Jane sat down on the pebbles and Megan sat beside her; she thought for a while about how much to tell her. She didn't want to scare the girl, but on the other hand she had to make her aware of the dangers and the times they were now living in.

'Yes, honey, Jamie and I have met bad people- very bad people. About three months ago three men attacked me. They shot me and they were going to do horrible things to me.'

'Were they going to rape you?' Megan asked, surprising Jane. 'Only, I heard about it early last year and wasn't too sure what it meant, so I asked my mum. She explained it to me, and I know there are some bad men out there who hurt women and girls.'

Jane hesitated for a second. 'Yes, Megan, they were going to rape me, but Jamie saved me. That's how we met.'

'What happened to the bad men?'

'Well… I hit one with a hammer to protect myself and he died, then Jamie had to shoot the other two to protect me and to protect himself. The men would have killed us otherwise.'

Megan thought for a second. 'Good! I'm glad Jamie shot them because I don't want anyone to hurt you,' and she threw her arms around Jane. Jane hugged her and said 'Megan, I don't want you to think that every man- or woman- we might meet is going to be bad. They probably won't be; but because of what's happened to the country some people might be desperate and do bad things because of that.'

Megan thought about this for a second and then nodded. 'Okay; I think I understand.'

They stood up, called to Max and made their way back, with Megan holding Jane's hand the whole way. When they got home Jamie had cleared away the breakfast things and was busy cleaning the porch roof. Jane pointed it out to Megan, telling her that Jamie had built it, and showed her how it collected rainwater in the barrel for them to drink. Megan told Jamie he was very clever and then gave him a hug. He was really touched; he thanked her and bent down to kiss her forehead.

Jane left again shortly after with Megan to get her some new clothes. She packed a few tools into the boot of her Golf in case she needed to break into any shops and drove to Devonshire Road in town. There were several clothes shops nearby and she managed to find what Megan needed. She was pleased that Megan wasn't particularly fussed about what she wore and proved to be very practical in her choice of clothes.

They found all the essentials like socks, underwear, tops, shirts and trousers, and got her several coats and fleeces for when it got colder. They loaded everything into the car and then Jane took her into the Co-op, where they walked along the aisles looking for some drinks that Megan might like. The place, like all the other food shops and supermarkets, had been ransacked by people panic-buying or looting, and rubbish littered the floor. There wasn't much left in there, but they managed to find two tins of drinking chocolate and some cocoa powder, along with some tins of powdered fruit drink and a few bottles of fruit squash. On top of one shelf Jane was pleased to find a few tins of condensed milk that had rolled to the back. From there she drove round to Sackville Road where there was a good shoe shop; she wanted Megan to have good quality footwear and they found several pairs of shoes and boots to fit her.

They went home pleased with their shopping trip and Megan said she was looking forward to wearing her new things. Back home, they found Jamie working in the garden and they went out to help him. Megan got changed into some new clothes and a pair of Wellington boots they'd found to fit her and she showed Jamie, who said how lovely she looked.

They showed her how to harvest some of the vegetables and salads and picked enough for their lunch and evening meal. They spent the rest of the day out in the garden, with Megan asking them lots of questions about the food they were growing. She found it all fascinating and wanted to know everything.

Jamie went out on his bike in the evening to check the snares and came back with a rabbit, which they cooked that night. After their evening meal they sat and played cards, but by nine o'clock Megan was falling asleep, so she went to bed wearing her new pyjamas. Jane went to sit on the sofa with Jamie and they talked for a while. She told him about her conversation with Megan on the beach that morning, and Jamie thought she had done the right thing in being honest with her.

'She's got to know how things are now. From now on she's going to be growing up in a completely different world from the one she knew six months or a year ago. She realises that now, I think, but there are probably still some things that she can't fully comprehend yet.'

'I know, but that will happen in time; she's a smart kid. I'm just so pleased that we found her in time; I don't think she would have lasted much longer otherwise. She needs to put on at least another stone, probably more.'

'Well, we'll soon fatten her up! And just think; if we'd been a minute earlier or later we might have missed her.' Jane smiled at him, stroked his face and kissed him then they went off to bed.

Twenty-one

During the next week they noticed a change in Megan as she got to know them better and became used to her new surroundings and her new situation. For the first few days her mood was prone to change suddenly and she would go from being happy and laughing to sudden bouts of crying or sadness. It was hardly surprising, given the trauma that she had suffered: for five months she had struggled to survive on her own and to find enough food and water to live on, and hadn't spoken to anyone during that time. On one occasion Jane found her curled up on her bed in tears, clutching the photo of her mum and dad.

As the week progressed, though, the crying and the mood swings became less frequent. Jamie and Jane discussed it when they were on their own in the evenings and they knew it would probably take several months for Megan to put everything behind her and move on. It wasn't just losing her parents that she had to contend with, or the months spent on her own; there was also the whole new order of things in the country for her to understand and come to terms with.

During the days spent working in the garden with them, or when out and about checking snares with either of them, she talked constantly and asked sensible and pertinent questions. She always thought carefully about what they told her, trying to get her head around it all. She began to understand better that this wasn't a temporary situation that would be resolved, and that this now was their way of life. Max's company was a constant tonic to her and she spent a lot of time playing with him, which they were pleased to see.

She was keen to learn about cooking and preparing food, and watched them both in the kitchen, always asking if she could help with something. Jane showed her how to make bread: they still had some packets of dried yeast left, which would be usable for a while yet, and Jamie demonstrated how to prepare a rabbit and she wasn't at all squeamish. They showed her how to prepare different vegetables and explained the importance of preserving the food they gathered or caught for the winter when things would be scarce, now that there weren't fridges or freezers, and she was intrigued by it all. She also started to show some independence, asking Jane if she minded if she went down to the sea to wash on her own, and Jane said of course not.

Towards the end of the week Megan opened up a bit about her parents and her time on her own, and although sad she was able to talk about it without crying every time. On one such occasion Jane asked her if she had seen any other survivors in all that time.

'Well, I didn't see any people in the streets,' she answered, 'but I saw three cars go past. I think the first two were in March or April and the third one was in May. I saw the first two through shop windows while I was out looking for food. The first one had two men in it and was going up the road to Ninfield. The second one had a man and a woman in it. I ran outside and saw it go up to the roundabout and turn down Turkey Road.' She explained that the third one had been going down the road into town, but she had only seen the back of it. From her description it sounded like it might have been a Land Rover. It was just possible that she had seen Sarah and Georgie on a trip into town, but then again a Land Rover was a fairly common vehicle in the surrounding areas.

The weather improved as the week progressed, becoming warm and sunny. On the Thursday Jamie offered to take Megan out fishing on the boat and she jumped at the opportunity. Bill and Emma and Sarah and Georgie were coming for lunch the following day and he hoped to catch something to cook for them. He put a life jacket on her and tightened the straps to their maximum; it was still a bit loose but she certainly couldn't fall out of it. She whooped and yelled with a mixture of fear and delight as he rowed out over the breaking waves until they got further out and it became calmer. He pointed out to her that they needed to fix a point of reference on the shore to see how far they drifted and he used the blue tarp tied to the railing again.

He showed her the different fishing rigs set up on the three rods and explained the differences and the reasons for them. He used one with lures and another baited with strips of rabbit flesh. They were out for over an hour without any bites, but then he caught four decent mackerel and a good-sized bass. He let Megan hold the rod and reel it in and she was beside herself with excitement. After that, though, she began feeling a bit sea-sick so he rowed back to shore. They drew the boat up the beach and tied it up, secured the tarp over the top and then went back to the house. He showed Megan how to gut the fish and then put them in the cellar in a bucket of seawater to keep cool until the next day.

Later in the afternoon, while Jane was busy in the kitchen with Megan, he set out walking to the railway at Westcourt Drive to check the snares they'd put back there. He had a canvas bag with him for rabbits and his sawn-off over his shoulder. It was a nice walk in the late-afternoon sun and he noticed that several apple trees were nearly ready for harvesting; *they must be an early-ripening variety* he thought to himself. He climbed up the siding by the bridge and onto the track and checked the snares. He was relieved to find one rabbit, which he put into his bag, but was disappointed that there weren't more. Some snares had been knocked over and he had just finished resetting them when he heard a vehicle coming from the direction of the sea; it sounded like a lorry or a truck with a big diesel engine.

He went to the bridge's south side and looked out, hidden behind a bush. Round the bend from West Parade into Richmond Avenue, directly in front of him, came a large truck,

183

moving slowly. To his amazement it was an army vehicle, bearing Red Cross insignia, and he could see three men in the cab in army uniform as it drew closer. He rushed down the siding to the road, back under the bridge and waited on the pavement. The truck stopped twenty feet from him; three soldiers jumped out of the back and stood on the pavement with rifles at the ready.

The cab door opened and two officers climbed down and stood to one side, careful not to impede the soldiers' fire, if necessary. Both had pistols in holsters on their belts.

'Good afternoon, sir. Would you please remove the shotgun from your shoulder and place it on the ground in front of you,' one of them asked. Jamie didn't have any option, so he took the shotgun off his shoulder and laid it down as requested, along with his bag.

'Thank you, sir; just a precaution, you understand? May we have your name, please?'

'It's Jamie; James Parker. Boy, am I surprised to see you!'

'Mr. Parker, may we ask what your state of health is? Do you have any sickness of any kind, or have you been ill?'

'No, I'm in perfect health; rather ironic, given the circumstances,' he said with a slight smile. 'I caught the plague about five or six months ago; I was in some sort of coma for six days and then woke up. It took me over a month to recover, but since then I've been tip-top.'

The two officers looked at each other and then back at Jamie. 'Well, then you're a very lucky man, Mr. Parker, and you're in a tiny minority,' said the other officer. 'We've only encountered twenty-two other people so far in the south-east who contracted the plague and survived.'

'Make that twenty-three;' Jamie replied, 'my partner, Jane, also caught it and survived. We met about three months ago and hooked up.' The officers looked at each other again with surprise and then came forward to stand in front of him. Both saluted, introduced themselves and shook his hand.

'Major Harry Miller, British Army,' said the first man. He was in his early forties and well-built, with short dark hair and a moustache. He couldn't have looked more like the archetypal

British Army officer.

'Major Thomas Cunningham; I'm a doctor with the Royal Army Medical Corps,' said the second. He was of a similar age to Miller, but shorter and slighter. He had sandy-coloured hair, with a friendly, studious-looking face and round glasses. Miller looked back at the soldiers and waved his hand and they stood easy, but kept an eye on proceedings.

'Pleased to meet you,' Jamie said. 'Well, I never expected to see you, I must admit. What are you doing here?'

'Over the last six weeks we've been making a tour of the southern towns and the coastal areas,' said Miller, 'to establish what the situation is and to see how many survivors there are. We've just come from Hastings.'

'How is it there?' asked Jamie.

'Terrible, just like everywhere else,' replied Miller. 'Very few survivors it seems; the few we did meet were in poor health, and we saw many more corpses on the streets than we've seen in Bexhill. We don't have transportation facilities, but we're directing anyone we meet who needs help to make their way to Tunbridge Wells. We've established a refugee camp there, a mile north of the town on the A21. It has pretty good medical facilities and a quarantine area.'

Cunningham then spoke. 'London is probably rife with cholera, typhoid and all manner of other diseases. The army hasn't been in on the ground, but another Company has done several fly-overs by helicopter. The streets are littered with corpses. We have road blocks on the major routes out of London, but we don't have enough personnel to man them all, obviously. Those few survivors who have escaped London to the south we've escorted to the refugee camp for treatment.

We're also worried about the possibility of a further outbreak of plague in London, but we don't know enough about it yet to understand how it survives or multiplies. It's also possible that there aren't enough survivors there for it to spread. We've got a team of scientists working on it at a secret research facility. I'd recommend you be careful about contact with anyone you meet from now on. Make sure you ask them about their health, where they've come from, whether they've had any contact with other people and when that was. If they have had contact with other people but it's been over seven days and they look healthy, the chances are they're okay. If it's less than seven days, then be wary. '

'I'll do that, thanks. How is the army holding up?'

'Not too well, Mr. Parker, to put it mildly!' replied Miller. 'We've lost well over ninety-five percent of our forces, which leaves us with fewer than two thousand personnel, spread around the country. There are also around two thousand mixed personnel from the navy and the air force, again spread all around the country.'

'Really? I'm surprised there are so many left.'

'Well, our troops had better training and discipline than the general public, Mr. Parker. Added to that was the fact that most troops were on military bases, ships or airfields, and not mingling with the public as much, as well as having Noddy suits.'

'Noddy suits?' Jamie enquired, looking baffled.

'Sorry- common army jargon!' Miller said with a quick smile. 'CBRN suits, to give them their official name: Chemical, Biological, Radiological and Nuclear suits. Used to be called NBC, but the boffins changed the name to confuse us all. Frankly, though, if everyone had worn them when they should have we might have lost far fewer people.'

'And the government?' asked Jamie.

Miller hesitated for a second. 'There is no government, sir; not as such. They all perished in London as far as we can tell. The Queen and most of the Royal family survived, as did the Prime Minister and a couple from his Cabinet, and they're in a safe place, but there's nothing they can do. It's a bit difficult to have a government when there's no one left to govern, and no taxes to collect,' he added with a dry smile.

Cunningham then took over. 'Can I ask you, Mr. Parker, how you're coping, how many of you there are and what the situation is here in Bexhill?'

'Well, we're just about coping okay, so far, but it's been tough. Jane and I met around three months ago and we moved into a couple of houses by the sea whose occupants had died.

We're working towards becoming self-sufficient and we've planted vegetables and are harvesting fruit and preserving it. We also fish, trap rabbits and make our own jerky, amongst other things.'

'Well done, Mr. Parker, and good for you,' said Miller.

'We've also now got a young girl with us, called Megan,' said Jamie. 'She's twelve and an orphan. We found her last week; she'd been surviving on her own for nearly five months since her parents died, bless her, so we took her in. I don't think she would have lasted much longer if we hadn't found her. We've hardly seen anyone else in Bexhill in all this time. We met a family and two others on a farm near Hooe and have become good friends, and also two sisters a few miles away on a smallholding north of Bexhill.'

They stood and talked for another ten minutes, with the two officers asking him more questions and writing things down in a notebook, and Jamie asking several in return.

'Could I ask you what the prospects are, please?' Jamie said.

'Well, I won't lie to you, Mr. Parker;' said Cunningham, 'we don't know what the prospects are, but they're not looking good; that's for certain. The country seems to have lost close to a hundred percent of its population, from what we've seen. There's almost no one left anywhere in the south-east so far. We don't have any hard figures, obviously, but based on what we've seen in recent months we might estimate that over 99.9 percent of the UK population has died. There is a possibility that in some more rural and isolated areas like Scotland, Wales or Cornwall there are many more survivors, but even that can't be guaranteed. During the 1918 to 1920 flu pandemic people were dying in all corners of the world; even on remote Pacific islands. That pandemic showed that there aren't really any safe havens in the modern world. There are around a hundred-and-fifty survivors at the refugee camp so far, which is a drop in the ocean considering what the area's population was, but we don't expect all of them to survive.

There's no infrastructure or services and there won't be any for the foreseeable future. Fuel reserves will probably become unusable within a year or so, we think. The country is more or less going to revert back to the Middle Ages- or worse. There are a few thousand armed forces personnel dotted around the country, but there's very little we can do, in reality. We can't produce food, for instance, and we can't produce electricity, or fuel, or medical supplies. All we can do is assist people where we can, and attempt to distribute the food and supplies that are left to those who need it, while we can. But fuel will run out, generators will fail and communications will fail. We in the modern world have become so reliant on technology and the service industries that we've lost the basic skills that even people in the Middle Ages possessed. People will have to start learning things again that it's taken mankind thousands of years to develop... Need I go on?'

'No;' replied Jamie, 'we'd kind of worked these things out for ourselves over the last six months. That's why Jane and I have been growing food and learning preserving techniques.'

'I take it you haven't been checking for radio broadcasts, then, Mr. Parker,' asked Miller. Jamie felt a little foolish for not having done so.

'No. To be honest, Major, all our time has been taken up with just surviving and we hadn't given any thought to it.'

'Well,' Miller answered, 'we've been broadcasting several times a day for around three months on 93.5FM to let anyone listening know about the refugee camp at Tunbridge Wells. We announced this by loudspeaker on our flights over London, too. We'll be broadcasting any news on that frequency from now on, so it might pay for you to listen in.' Jamie said that he would do so.

'By the fact that you're on foot, I'm guessing that you live nearby; is that correct?' asked Cunningham.

'Yes, just five minutes away,' replied Jamie.

Cunningham looked at his watch. 'Well, we have to get back to the camp, but as we're so close... Would you like us to come back with you so I could have a look at the girl- Megan- and give her a quick examination?' Jamie said that would be great, so Miller instructed him to climb aboard. It was a bit of a squeeze with four in the cab, but it wasn't for long. The driver turned the truck around and Jamie directed them to the bungalow. When they pulled up outside, the door opened and Jane stood there in amazement as Jamie climbed from the cab followed by the two officers. He walked up to her, smiling, and kissed her.

'Look who I found on my travels! Major Miller and Major Cunningham, this is my partner, Jane Roberts.' The two officers saluted and shook hands with her and she greeted them warmly.

'Well, I'm sure Mr. Parker will fill you in later, Miss Roberts, and we can't stay long,' said Cunningham, 'but I'm a doctor with the Royal Army Medical Corps. I offered to come back and give Megan a quick examination while we were in the area. I believe she's been on her own for a long time and I'd like to check her out, if that's okay?'

Jane welcomed them inside: the officers removed their caps and they went through to the kitchen, where Megan had been told to wait. She introduced them to Megan and they all said hello.

'Honey, these men are from the army. This is Major Cunningham; he's a doctor and he'd like to examine you to check that you're healthy. Would that be okay?'

'Are you just like a normal doctor?' Megan asked.

Cunningham smiled. 'Yes, Megan, I'm just a normal doctor, but I'm in the army so I have to wear a uniform like a soldier.'

'Okay then, I guess,' she said. Jamie directed him to Megan's bedroom and he picked up his medical kit and followed her inside. He asked Miller if he would like some coffee, or something stronger.

Miller saw a bottle of Scotch on a shelf and nodded to it. 'A small one would be great, thanks.'

Jamie poured them both a good measure and they raised their glasses and drank. Jane was busy preparing the evening meal and while they waited Jamie showed him the gardens and the vegetables they were growing, along with the improvements they'd made. Miller was impressed and said they were doing a grand job. Jamie told him that Jane was pregnant, but still had nearly eight months to go and that they were both worried.

'Well, bear in mind,' Miller said, 'that the camp isn't too far away from you, and we have doctors and nurses there if you need help or advice.' Jamie thanked him and they went back inside.

Cunningham came back with Megan and smiled. 'She's doing okay under the circumstances. Some borderline malnutrition, but nothing too serious, and a fair bit of weight loss, but she'll soon put that back on if you feed her well. I've given her some multi-vitamins to take; one a day for a month, and I'm sure she'll be fine.' They both thanked him.

'There's one other thing;' Cunningham said, 'would you object to me taking a blood sample from you? You've both survived the plague, which is extremely rare: it's possible that it might help our scientists to learn more about the bacterium, and why you survived when most others didn't.' They had no objections so he took samples from them both.

The two officers said they had to leave, so Jane and Megan said goodbye and Jamie went outside with them to their truck. They stood on the pavement and shook hands; Jamie thanked them both and they wished him good luck, saluted and got into the truck. The driver turned around in the road then they waved from the window and drove off. Jamie went back inside and the kitchen was filled with the smell of baking bread and rabbit casserole.

He kissed Jane and ruffled Megan's hair. 'Well, missy, it looks like you're doing okay.' Megan gave him a big grin.

Twenty-two

Jamie told them about his meeting with the officers and he repeated Cunningham's warning to be wary of contact with strangers without questioning them first. He explained that the army were concerned about survivors from London, who might be carrying new diseases, slipping past their road-blocks because they were so thinly-stretched. He also explained to Megan that things weren't going to change in the country just because there were now some army people to help out where they could.

'I understand that now,' she replied. 'I mean, we learned some basic stuff about supply and farming at school, and it's not like the army people can become farmers and grow wheat and potatoes, is it? And they can't, like, open Tesco's again and fill the shelves with food, can they?'

'No, honey, you're absolutely right,' Jane answered.

Later on, after Megan had gone to bed, he and Jane sat up talking further about his conversation with the officers and what he'd been told.

'Well, it's great that the refugee camp has been set up at Tunbridge Wells,' said Jane, 'and reassuring to know there are doctors and nurses there.'

'I agree, but… Well, I don't want to be pessimistic, but you're not due for another eight months or so yet and that's a long time. Anything could happen between now and then. Will the camp even still be there in eight months?' He shrugged.

191

'Oh, well, there's nothing we can do on that score and no point thinking about it.'

'It's very worrying, though, what he told you about the prospects for the country, but I'm glad he was honest with you about it. I suppose it's no different to what we'd thought anyway, is it?'

'No, it's not. All he's done is to confirm our suspicions that, basically, we're on our own from now on. As he said, even though there are a few thousand armed forces personnel left, there's actually not much they can do. They can't man pumping stations and sewerage plants to get water flowing again, or power stations, and they can't farm the land to produce food for people.'

'What on earth is going to happen in a year's time, Jamie? Or less, even! When the fuel either runs out or becomes unusable they won't have any transport; generators and batteries will fail, along with their communications. What will they do then?'

He thought for a few seconds. 'Well, I wouldn't be at all surprised if that will be the end of the army. Without transport or communications they won't be a structured force any more. And when medical supplies and food run out what will be left for them to do?'

'Who knows? Maybe they'll just disband and settle wherever they happen to be; I don't suppose many will have homes to go back to any more. Maybe they'll become local peace-keeping forces, to replace the police, or form small communities. Anyway, this is all academic, really, and just supposition. I can't see how it will affect us, though, or change what we're doing; until today we didn't even know they still existed.'

'Yes, I suppose you're right,' he admitted. 'Come on, let's go to bed.'

In the morning Megan was up before them. They'd sat up late talking the night before and as a result were later than normal to rise. When they came into the kitchen they found that she had got a fire going in the range, made some breakfast rolls that were ready to go in the oven when it was hot enough, and had also made them coffee!

She put her hands on her hips, looked at them with a mock-stern expression and, in imitation of her mum, said 'And just *what* sort of time do you call this? Must I do *everything* in this house?'

Jane and Jamie looked at each other and burst out laughing, with Megan joining in. Jane leaned forward to hug her, then immediately let go and dashed to the toilet to throw up. Megan got worried and panicked.

'Oh my God! Jane hasn't got the plague, has she?' Jamie rushed over and put his arms around her. 'No, honey, she's okay, honestly. Don't worry, nothing's wrong.'

Jane came out and drank some coffee, then gave Megan a hug. 'Honey, I'm sorry to scare you and there's nothing wrong with me. Megan... I'm pregnant. This is called morning sickness and it's what most pregnant women get early on. I'm sorry we hadn't told you yet. I only really knew just before we met you and we didn't want to bother you with it this week while you were settling in with us, as things have been hard enough for you as it is. We were going to tell you soon.'

Megan threw her arms around her. 'Oh Jane, I'm so glad you're not sick! I couldn't bear that to happen.' Jane started crying and hugged her back. After they had recovered they sat at the table and talked about it with her.

'But there aren't any hospitals or doctors now, are there?' she said. 'So what will you do?'

'Well,' Jane answered, 'there is the refugee camp run by the army now at Tunbridge Wells, and they have doctors and nurses there who can help me,' which seemed to satisfy Megan. She omitted any other misgivings that she and Jamie might have so as to not worry the girl.

While Jane and Megan got breakfast underway Jamie took Max out for his morning walk along the promenade. After breakfast they tidied the place up a bit and got ready for their friends' visit. Jane made some olive bread, which Megan helped her with, while Jamie prepared the fish they'd caught the previous day. They made a Mediterranean-style fish stew with onions and tinned tomatoes, as theirs wouldn't be ready for a while yet, and herbs from the garden.

They heard a vehicle pull up earlier than expected and when Jamie went to look he saw Bill's old Renault van outside, so he opened the door and went out to welcome them.

'I see you finally got the old van fixed!'

Bill grinned as he shook his hand. 'Well, it was about time, I suppose! Didn't take much, in the end. Glad to have it back on the road.'

Sally came up and gave him a hug, followed by Emma. 'Where's Pete?' asked Jamie. 'Oh, he's busy working on a small project with Phil,' replied Emma, 'and he wanted to get it finished today. He sends his regards, as do Phil and Sophie.'

They went through to the kitchen and Jane greeted them warmly with smiles and hugs, while Max barked and jumped up at them all. Megan was standing by the back door, looking both excited and a little shy.

'Hello- who's this, then?' asked Emma.

'This is Megan,' said Jane. 'We met her last week in Sidley. She'd been surviving on her own for about five months so we brought her back to live with us. Megan, this is Emma and her husband, Bill, and their daughter, Sally.'

They said hello and Megan came forward and shook their hands, smiling, saying how pleased she was to meet them. Sally said hi and gave her a big smile.

'Is it okay if Sally and I take Max down to the beach?' asked Megan. Sally was keen and the adults said yes, of course. Megan grabbed Max's ball and the three of them ran off down the garden while the adults looked on, smiling.

'It'll do Megan a power of good having Sally to play with,' said Jane, with tears starting in her eyes.

Emma put her arm around her. 'And Sally, too, I think. She's missed having girls her own age to hang out with. So, tell us all about her.'

Jane told them how they'd met on the way back from Sarah and Georgie's the week before, and how she had spent a month in a cellar and another four months scavenging for food on her own after her parents had died. Bill shook his head and Emma had tears in her eyes.

194

'The poor thing,' she said. 'What an awful thing to go through! She's all skin and bone.'

'You should have seen her a week ago,' said Jamie. 'She's put on a fair bit of weight already since then, hasn't she, Jane?'

'Yes, she has, and she already seems like a different person to the scared little girl we met, bless her.'

Bill gave them a bag containing some eggs, milk and fresh cheese and they both thanked them. Jamie made them all coffee and they sat at the table talking about Megan.

'That was a really good thing you did,' said Bill, 'bringing her back with you like that and taking her in.'

'To be honest, mate,' said Jamie, 'we didn't even need to think about it. There was no way we could have left her on her own.' Jane agreed with him.

After their coffee they gave Bill and Emma a tour of the two houses and gardens. They were both impressed with all the things the couple had done there, and with all the food they had managed to preserve for the winter. They stood at the bottom of the garden looking out the gate at the two girls playing with Max on the beach, shrieking and laughing. Bill looked pensive.

'Well, you've got a pretty good setup here,' he said, 'and a nice spot. Have you given any thought to how long you might stay here?'

Jamie smiled. 'Blimey! No, we hadn't even thought that far ahead, to be honest. And just recently we've had other things on our mind, too, apart from Megan…'

'You're pregnant, aren't you?' said Emma; Jane gave her a small smile and nodded.

'Bloody hell!' said Bill. 'I mean… Well, congratulations!'

'I knew straight away,' said Emma.

'Not much escapes you, does it?' said Jane, smiling fondly at her.

'No; not a lot!' she answered, smiling. They all hugged each other and Bill shook Jamie's hand warmly.

'Well, it wasn't planned, as you might imagine;' said Jamie, 'but now that it's happened…'

'Well, this calls for a celebration,' said Bill. They went back into the house and Bill produced a bottle of home-made wine that he'd brought.

'One of the last bottles from last year's vintage: parsnip and apricot wine, from my old Dad's recipe,' he explained. Jane got some glasses and he poured them all a glass, though Jane diluted hers with some water. Bill thought it was sacrilege, but he understood.

'Any names yet?' asked Emma.

Jane smiled. 'Yes- surprisingly! Either Robbie or Annie.'

'To Robbie or Annie- whichever comes first!' said Bill. They repeated the toast and drank. Jamie coughed slightly. It was thick, sweet and powerful stuff, more like a strong sherry.

'Wow!' he said. 'That'll put hairs on your chest!' Bill smiled and nodded, then looked serious again.

'Well, I was going to say something before, out in the garden, but your little curve-ball put me off my stroke with your news!' He looked at Emma, who nodded. 'The thing is; me and Emma have been talking recently- and this might be even more relevant now, what with Megan and the pregnancy. Well, we wondered if you'd be interested in coming to live with us at the farm? We're very fond of you both. We've got plenty of space there; there's a wing in the house that's unused, or we could convert one of the buildings in the top yard. What used to be the chicken shed, back in my dad's day, even has its own water supply and a hand-pump. Dad diverted the supply to the house about thirty years ago and it still works.

We'd be glad of your company and we could all look out for each other out in times to come, which aren't going to be easy, as you know. There are acres of land we haven't used yet and we could grow a lot more crops and breed more animals. We're going to need to get horses for transport soon as well, I imagine, and we can make stabling for them in the top yard. Also, Megan would be great company for Sally now and we could make a lot of improvements between us. You're good with your hands, Jamie- and you, Jane- and we could get a lot done to make things better for all our futures.'

Jamie and Jane were surprised and touched by the offer, and told them so. Jane put her hand on top of Emma's. 'Thank you so much for that. It's a lovely offer and we'll give it serious thought. At the moment, though, we're keen to reap the rewards of our labours in the garden this year. But, certainly at the end of the year, it could be something for us to do. We'll think about it and keep you posted.'

Just then, they heard a vehicle pull up at the front and Jamie went out to welcome Sarah and Georgie. They hugged and he ushered them inside and through to the kitchen. They had brought more eggs, along with honey and a pheasant. Jane hugged them both and introduced them to Bill and Emma and they all shook hands. Bill and the sisters remembered each other and said how nice it was to see each other again.

Jamie went out to call the girls back, while Jane told Sarah and Georgie about Megan. They were shocked and saddened to hear her story and both said what a great thing she and Jamie had done in bringing her back with them. Shortly after, Max came in panting and flopped down on his bed, closely followed by Megan and Sally, smiling and laughing. Jane introduced them both to the sisters, who hugged them warmly and fussed over them, saying how pretty they both were and how pleased they were to meet them.

They ate outside on the patio as the weather was good and everyone agreed that the fish stew was delicious. Jane said that Jamie should take most of the credit for it, especially as he'd gone out to catch the fish.

'And don't forget Megan,' Jamie added, 'she was the one who reeled in that whopper of a bass!'

Megan gave them a big grin. 'It was great fun… but I did start feeling a bit sea-sick after an hour. I didn't puke, though!' she added, and everyone laughed.

Megan asked Sally if she wanted to play Scrabble and she said yes, so they disappeared into the kitchen to sit at the table. Jamie found his dictionary for them in case of disputes, then opened a bottle of wine and went back outside.

'They seem to be getting on well,' Georgie commented, and all agreed that it was lovely to see them having fun together.

They sat in the sun and talked for several hours. Jamie told them of his meeting with the army the day before and the others were surprised and listened with great interest to all he had to say. He told them of the radio broadcasts and what frequency they were on, and also repeated Major Cunningham's warning to question anyone they might meet about where they'd come from, their state of health and whether they'd had contact with other people recently.

'It's a good thing they've got the refugee camp set up,' said Bill, 'but it's also a bit worrying about survivors from The Smoke possibly coming down here and bringing new diseases with them. I hadn't given any thought to stuff like that and we'll all have to be careful about anyone we meet from now on. Let's hope they meet the army road-blocks first and get taken to the camp for quarantine and treatment,' and they all agreed with him.

They discussed transport and fuel lifespan, too. What the Major had told Jamie reinforced the research that Sarah and Georgie's father had done before his death: that the remaining fuel would possibly become unusable within a year or so.

'Well, it's now been well over six months since that fuel was produced,' said Jane, 'and possibly as much as eight or nine, which means that we may only have the use of vehicles for another six months, and maybe a lot less... which is worrying. It means that anything we might need for the future that can't be carried, or that we need to source from any distance, needs to be gathered and stored in the next few months.'

'You're right, Jane,' said Bill, 'and it looks like I repaired the van just in time!'

'How much red diesel do you have left in your tank, Bill?' she asked.

'Ooh, probably around forty gallons, maybe more. Why?'

'Well, I was just wondering; is that tank vented?'

'Yes; it has to be for the pump to work.'

'Well, that means that the diesel will degrade quicker because of air and moisture ingress; isn't that right, Sarah?'

'Yes,' she replied, 'at least that's what Dad told me.'

'I think you should empty the tank, Bill,' said Jane, 'and

198

decant it all into sealed containers. That will stop any more contact with air and moisture and, hopefully, prolong its life. You can then just use a can at a time, when you need it.'

Bill scratched his head and nodded. 'I think that's a good idea, Jane; well done. I hadn't thought about that before. I know where I can get a load of jerrycans from, so I'll get onto that straight away.'

It came time for the guests to leave as they all had things to do at home. Sarah and Georgie left first, after kissing the girls and hugging everyone. Jane went out to see them off and they waved as they drove off. When she came back the girls were packing away the Scrabble board.

'Who won?' she asked them.

'Well, it was pretty neck-and-neck all the way,' said Sally, 'but Megan just beat me at the end with a couple of good scores, and I had a bloomin' X and a J that I couldn't get rid of!' Megan grinned.

They all went out the front and said their goodbyes, saying they'd see each other soon. Jamie said that it might be a couple of weeks, as some of the apples were ready for harvesting and they would be busy. Bill reminded them to think about their offer and they said they would. The two girls hugged each other hard then Sally climbed into the van after her parents and they drove off, waving.

Soon afterwards Jane drove off with Megan to check the snares at another location, coming back later with a rabbit, which was good news. Jane said there had actually been two in the snares, but one had looked sickly so she'd discarded it. While they were gone, though, Jamie sat outside at the patio table, thinking about the future and all they'd talked about that afternoon, writing things in his notebook as he thought of them. There were lots of things for him and Jane to discuss that night, after Megan had gone to bed.

Twenty-three

That night, with Megan in bed asleep, they sat in the conservatory talking and both felt really happy that Sally and Megan had got on so well during the day. Megan had told them earlier that she and Sally had sat on the beach talking and that Sally had held her hand when she told her about losing her parents and her time surviving on her own. She thought they could become good friends, which had made them smile and give her a hug, saying how pleased they were. After talking generally about how nice the day had been they turned the conversation to important matters.

'So,' Jamie said, 'what d'you think of Bill and Emma's offer?'

'Oh, God, Jamie, it's so bloody hard! I don't know what to think; I love this place and I love being next to the sea. We've worked so hard over the last three months to make this place our home and putting things in place for the future. It seems such a shame to abandon it now, after all we've done.'

'I know what you mean and I feel exactly the same; I love this place and what we've done here. However: I did some thinking earlier, after you and Megan went out, and I think we have some hard realities to confront. I've tried to think about things logically and dispassionately, but it's not easy. It might be a bit jumbled, but let me just run through it with you.

Yes, we have a good spot here; we're close to the town and lots of facilities, such as the Sainsbury's warehouse, clothes shops and DIY supplies, etc. But for how much longer will that be relevant? The food in the warehouse might last another six months or so before it's unfit for consumption or runs out. I know the tinned produce will last longer, but is it worth staying here just for that when we could take it all with us to the farm? Then there are the builders' merchants and the materials there: it's great while we have vehicles, but what about when they've gone? I can't see us carrying timber, cement and other materials two miles or more when we need to make repairs or improvements, etc.

We also have to think about where we are now, as a location. Bexhill's a ghost-town- there's no one left here. We've got Megan and our baby to think about now, as well as ourselves: do we really want to be living here on our own for the next thirty years? Bill and Emma are about four miles away, which is no problem while we have transport, but what about after that? It means walking or cycling there every time we want to see them or even just ask them something. And what if one of us becomes ill? It's going to be tough for the other to cope with everything. At their place we'd have company as well as support, for us and for the kids. On our own here Megan's got no one her age to interact with and it'll be hard on her.

And then there's the issue of transport: we don't know for sure, but we have to plan for the possibility that in six months or less we won't have any. What are we going to do then, when we need to make trips to collect things? How are we going to harvest all the fruit in the area and bring it back for preserving? We could carry a couple of bags each at a time, but look how long it took us to harvest the cherries and preserve them: if we had to do it on foot we'd probably lose most to the birds. If we want to get around any distance in the future, or to transport anything, it's going to have to be with horses and a cart, and we can't possibly keep them here in town. We could probably get by without them, but our living radius, so to speak, would only be a couple of miles, and it would be difficult.

And last- but by no means least- there's the baby, when it

comes. You're due in the middle of March, according to your calculations, and by then it's possible that we won't have the vehicles. If we're here on our own what will we do when you go into labour, especially if you're early? We'll have no means of getting over to Bill and Emma's, or of letting them know so they can come here, and they won't have any transport anyway. And the same applies to Sarah and Georgie.' He paused and blew out his cheeks. 'Well, those are my initial thoughts: what do you think?'

Jane was silent for a while, thinking about what he'd said. 'Well... wow! You've given this a lot more thought than I had yet... as usual!' and she smiled. 'That's one of the things I love about you, Jamie; that you're so practical. For me, it was initially going to be more of an emotional reason why we might stay here, though I think I would have reached similar conclusions to you in time. I think you're probably right. I had hoped to have the baby here, but all the things you say make sense, really. I was hoping we would have a long time living here and enjoying it, but it seems that won't be the case. Are you dead-set on moving to Bill and Emma's?'

'Well, emotionally, no I'm not, hon. I think a lot of Bill and Emma, obviously, but I love being here with you and I love being next to the sea, both for living here and for fishing. But it's not just you and me now, is it? And then there are all the other points that I raised. My view, regardless of what I feel, is that we *have* to move to Bill and Emma's. They're a lovely couple and we get on great with them, so it's not as if it will be difficult living there. I'll miss this location terribly, but I think it's for the best. Furthermore, I think we need to start making tracks *now*. Like you, I want to see out most of this year here and harvest all of our crops, but I think we need to make preparations to move to Bill and Emma's straight away.'

'Really? So soon?'

'Yes. We don't know for sure, but we may only have another three or four months left of the vehicles being usable, and we're going to have to make use of that time to transport a lot of our stuff over there, prior to actually moving in.'

'Well, if we're moving there, then I'd like to be in our own place, rather than in the house with Bill and Emma, so they can have their privacy and family time together, and we can have a bit more independence as well.'

'I agree,' said Jamie, 'and you beat me to it! That will mean converting one of the buildings in the top yard; probably the old chicken shed, as Bill suggested. We'll have to transport timber and building materials there and do the conversion soon, while it's still summer and while we still have the vehicles. Also, we'll need to take the wood-burner from the lounge over there and install it in the new place.'

'Wouldn't we be better off with the smaller range from my kitchen, so we have better cooking facilities and an oven as well?'

'Yes, we would,' Jamie replied. 'Only trouble is, it probably weighs a third of a ton and I don't know how we'd move it! Maybe I'll have a chat with Bill about it to see if he has any ideas. As you said earlier, we'll need to gather everything that we can for the future and store it at Bill and Emma's farm, while we have transport. My idea is to more or less empty Screwfix, B&Q and the other builders' merchants near us of anything that could be needed for future repairs, maintenance or projects. We're going to need nuts, bolts, washers, screws, nails, brackets, gaskets, materials for plumbing repairs, cement, sand, ballast, timber, sheet materials, tools, etc, etc.'

'Wow, again! You *have* had your thinking hat on, haven't you? Did you come up with all of this in the hour that Megan and I were gone?'

'Pretty much, yes, but it's been on my mind constantly since they asked us today.'

Jane leaned over and kissed him. 'Well done, clever-clogs! I think I have to agree with you, so it looks like we're moving in a few months, then.'

'I'm glad you agree, hon, as I'd hate for you to be against it or feel upset by it. We'll still be here until the end of September or maybe October, I reckon. That will give us a chance to harvest everything we've planted. We'll break the news to Megan in the morning. How d'you think she'll take it?'

Jane smiled. 'Well, to be honest, I think she'll be over the moon! Living on a farm in the country, being close to Sally and having farm animals to feed… Need I say more?'

Jamie laughed and hugged her. 'I think we should go over to their place after breakfast tomorrow and let them know the news. It's only fair that we tell them straight away and I'll need to discuss lots of things with Bill. We'll also have to look at the old chicken shed to see what work needs doing to it to make it habitable and make a list of things we'll need to get.'

'Okay, that's a good idea. Well, I'm off to bed- are you coming?'

'I'll be in shortly. I'm going to have a small whisky and a smoke and see if anything else comes to me that we'll need to do.'

She kissed him and then stroked Max and said goodnight. Jamie went into the kitchen, poured himself a drink and went outside for a smoke. He wandered down the garden path and Max followed silently to look after him. He opened the gate and sat on the top step, looking out at the full moon in the sky directly above; the white surf shone brightly as the waves broke on the beach. Max sat down and nuzzled his arm: Jamie put his arm round him, pulled him close and stroked him.

He thought of the day he'd found the bungalow and moved into it, remembering how things had been then. It seemed far longer than just three months because it had been so intense and they'd been fully occupied the whole time. It had become his home and he would be sad to leave it, but Bexhill was no place to live any more, isolated as they were, and it would be worse when they had no vehicles. Their future lay with Bill and Emma at the farm and he knew they were doing the right thing. And it wasn't as if they would be moving completely out of the area: the farm was only a couple of miles or so from the outskirts of Bexhill. He got up and went back to the house, with Max walking beside him. He brushed his teeth then looked in on Megan, who was sleeping peacefully. He went to his room, got into bed and Jane rolled over to snuggle up to him.

When he awoke in the morning Jane had already risen. He remembered snatches of a dream he'd had before waking. In it he'd seen what was either a young man or woman- he couldn't tell which because of the distance- on horseback in a marshy area with stunted trees dotted around. Then they were looking through a pair of binoculars and he could see a hunting rifle slung over their shoulder. It had all gone fuzzy after that, but for some reason he had the feeling that it was linked to him somehow.

When Megan got up and they were all sitting around the table they told her of Bill and Emma's offer to go and live at their farm, and that they had decided it was the best thing to do for them all. She gave a little shriek of excitement.

'Oh, wow, that's brill! I can see Sally all the time then, and Max will love being in the country, too.' Then she turned more thoughtful. 'I mean, I like this house and being by the sea and all that, and I know how hard you've worked here, but I find Bexhill creepy now with no one around. I don't believe in ghosts… or zombies; like that rubbish Mum and Dad used to watch on TV when they thought I was asleep; but I just find it creepy. D'you know what I mean?'

Jane and Jamie both smiled; they looked at each other and she winked at him.

'Yes, honey, we know exactly what you mean,' said Jamie, 'and that's one of the reasons why we've decided to go; not because it's creepy, of course, but because there's no one here any more. We need to be around more people, with friends who can help and support each other in the future.'

After breakfast they got the BMW out of the garage and put two shotguns inside, then Max jumped into the load area. Megan sat in the back, leaning over the seat to stroke him. As they went they could see apple trees along the way full of fruit, some almost ready for picking.

'I was just thinking;' said Jane, 'as we're not staying in the bungalow we won't need to go mad harvesting and preserving all the apples to see us through the winter like we did with the cherries. There's a whole orchard at the farm, isn't there? And Bill and Emma will be picking and either storing or preserving all that they can. We can help them with it when we move there.'

'Well, thank goodness for that!' Jamie exclaimed, laughing. 'That was rather a mad two weeks. We'll probably just need to pick enough for a few months and store them for our use until we move to the farm.'

They got to the farm in about ten minutes with there being nothing else on the road, and when they pulled into the yard Jamie beeped the horn and stopped outside the house. Emma opened the door, smiled and came out to welcome them. They got out of the car and Emma hugged them all, then Bill came out, too, grinning.

'I'm guessing you've got an answer for us already, as you're back so soon!'

Jamie and Jane both nodded, grinning back at them both. Bill and Emma didn't need to ask what the answer was; they could see it in their faces.

'That's great news!' said Bill. 'We're really pleased, aren't we Emma?'

'We certainly are! You've made my day,' she said and hugged them all again. Bill took Jamie's hand in both of his and shook it warmly, then kissed and hugged Jane and Megan. Sally came to the door, saw what was going on and yelled with delight, running over to them.

'You're coming to live with us, aren't you?' she said excitedly. They all smiled at her, nodding, and she hugged them. Megan was just as excited as she was and Max was barking and jumping up at them all, almost wagging his tail off.

'Come on, Megan,' said Sally, 'bring Max and I'll show you around the farm.' The two girls ran off down the yard with Max running along beside them. The adults all smiled at the girls and then went inside to the kitchen. They sat at the table while Emma put the kettle on to make tea.

'Well,' Bill said, 'we didn't expect to hear back from you so soon, but I'm glad. I guess you did a lot of talking last night?'

'Yes, we did,' Jane replied. 'Well, to be honest, Jamie did most of the talking and I did most of the listening, although I would have arrived at the same decision if I'd had time to think about it! He had it all thought out, pretty much, while Megan and I were out checking the snares. We both love the house and where we are, and we've put a lot of work into it, but your offer makes perfect sense to us for many reasons.'

Jamie then took over and told Bill and Emma everything he'd said to Jane the night before. They listened attentively, nodding and agreeing at various points with what he said.

'That all makes sense,' said Emma, 'and it's good that you thought it all through properly. We thought it would be a good idea to convert the chicken shed, which was why Bill suggested it. And we understand that you'd want to stay there until the end of the season, after all the work you've done there- we'd do the same in your position.'

'I agree,' said Bill, 'and I like the idea of bringing as much stuff as we can here from the DIY stores and builders' merchants. There's going to be a lot of "make-do-and-mend" in years to come and the more materials we've got here, the better. If something goes wrong and needs repairing, the chances of getting an exact spare will be tiny, so we'll have to improvise with whatever is to hand; even down to having the ability to make rubber gaskets or washers for water pumps and stuff. We can turn one of the outbuildings in the top yard into a materials store. Somewhere like Screwfix will be ideal for getting all that stuff, and we can put up racks and shelving in there for it all.'

'Good idea, Bill.' said Jamie. 'I think that once we've converted the chicken shed you and I should sit down and make lists of all the things we might need: tools, materials, fixings, etc. Obviously, you know this place better than me and can say if there are any specific things we'll want for here.'

Bill nodded. 'I also think we should start on the conversion now, while the weather's good and we have the vehicles, as you both said. Once it's done we can begin moving your things over. We can bring most of it here, just leaving you with enough stuff at the bungalow that you'll need, until you're ready to move in.'

They all agreed and smiled at each other, and after finishing their tea they went for a walk to look at the old chicken shed. The top yard was another large concrete apron, about forty yards long by twenty wide. Along the left-hand side were adjoining buildings for maybe ninety feet; two lower buildings nearest the house first and then three large barn-type buildings with high pitched roofs and sliding doors. At the far end was a gap and then one long, lower building ran perpendicular to them along the yard's top edge, divided into four separate units. Beyond them were fields and farmland. It was to these that they headed. Along the yard's right-hand side, marking the farm's boundary, were a drainage ditch and thick hedge.

The furthest building on the right was the old chicken shed and Bill showed them inside through a door on the building's end. The main area was a good size, with a space partitioned off at the back to make a small room. In the wall to the left was a door to another room, with an open loft or mezzanine area above it, accessed by steps against the wall opposite the main door. The room on the left had been turned into a sort of kitchen area many years before and had a large ceramic butler sink, with a hand-pump above it to supply water, and wooden worktops on two sides.

Jane and Jamie looked round the place and both agreed that it would make a great living area with some basic improvements. They would have to get used to having a lot less space than they had at the bungalow, but that was to be expected. They discussed it for a while and decided on a few things: maybe a new partition wall upstairs to make a bedroom, some better insulation and basic décor, and lots of shelving or racking for storage in the kitchen and living areas, and the wood-burner, of course.

'If you wanted to,' said Bill, 'you could even make a porch area, or a sort of conservatory, over the entrance. It faces east so gets the morning sun, which might be nice: just a thought.'

Having made some decisions, the women then went back to the house for a chat, leaving Bill and Jamie to draw up a list of materials they would need for the job. They looked at each other and grinned; both men loved a project to get stuck into and they were looking forward to it. It would be the first step towards their future life together at the farm and they had a busy couple of months ahead of them.

Twenty-four

During the next week Jamie drove to the farm each morning to work with Bill on converting the old chicken shed into their new home, while Jane and Megan stayed at home to work in the gardens. He used his car to save the fuel in the trucks, and took all his cordless power tools and tool kit to leave at the farm. Bill met him at one of the builders' merchants in Beeching Road in his van on the Sunday and they loaded up with timber, sheets of plywood and various other materials and fixings. The weather had turned during the night and became overcast and drizzly for two days, which made it awkward as they couldn't cut the materials outside. Having to cut things inside slowed them down a little due to the space, but they made do.

Back at the house, Jane and Megan were getting wet and muddy while working in the gardens. Megan didn't seem to mind the weather and was happy stomping about in her new wellies and waterproof coat, while Max watched them from the shelter of the porch. Jane did some exploratory digging to see how the carrots and potatoes were doing in her garden and was dismayed to find that the ones she looked at were rotten. She did some more digging to find that a large number had suffered the same fate. This was a real blow to her as they were relying on this crop to see them through the next two months, and she didn't know whether it was through disease or some sort of pest. She went further down the garden and checked the parsnips, but they were unaffected, thankfully.

She went next door to the bungalow's garden and checked the vegetables there: all the potatoes, carrots and parsnips that she checked were okay and she breathed a sigh of relief. It meant they would be a bit short on vegetables, but most of the salads were still okay, though they had lost a fair number to slugs. They had brought some of the salad pots into the conservatory to protect them from slugs in previous weeks, but it was too hot in there and they found the plants were bolting too quickly, so they'd moved them back outside into some shade and covered them with netting, which helped.

Jane was pleased at her decision to double-up on the planting of everything in both gardens. Jamie had wanted to use the space to plant a bigger variety of vegetables between the two gardens, but Jane had been insistent that they shouldn't do that. She'd thought it was better to have the same things spread over two different areas for just such an occurrence, and had been proved right. She gave Jamie the news that evening and he was as disappointed as she had been, but said well done for her decision and kissed her. He told them that the work was going well despite the weather, and they had nearly finished building the partition wall in the loft area for their bedroom.

On the Tuesday Bill came to the bungalow in his van with Phil to help Jamie take out the stove from his lounge and the range from Jane's kitchen. Jamie had told Bill about Jane's idea to take the range so they would have a proper oven and cooker in the new place, which they both thought was a good idea- if only they could get it out and transport it! Bill had a hydraulic lift that he used for shifting logs, which he said would do the job as it was rated for over a ton, but it would still be difficult. He also brought some sturdy steel ramps that might be useful.

It proved to be a rather long and cumbersome job as it was so heavy. After disconnecting the flue they managed to get the hydraulic lift's platform underneath the range and raise it, but negotiating the doorways and getting it out to the front garden was a bit of a nightmare. Once outside the three men stood there scratching their heads, thinking of ways to get it into the back of the van. The problem was that the lift's platform didn't go up quite high enough to be able to slide it into the van and none of them wanted to risk injury lifting it in. They stood there for a while, each coming up with ideas that were debated and dismissed. Jane stood silently next to them, listening to what they said and thinking, before chiming in with a suggestion.

'Why don't you use the Toyota instead of the van? If you park the Land Rover in front of it you could run the winch cable over the cab's roof, wrap it around the range and drag it up the ramps into the back.'

The three men all looked at each other for a few seconds and then Jamie, grinning, said 'I'll tell you what, guys, why don't we use the Toyota instead of the van, then we can use the winch…' He ducked just in time as Jane's right hand came up to clout him. They all laughed and then congratulated her on the idea.

Jane grinned. 'What would you lot do without us women? Sometimes it just takes a bit of lateral thinking!' Megan clapped and cheered, giving Jane a high five with a big grin on her face.

They moved the vehicles around accordingly and set to work, and in a short while the range was sitting securely tied down in the back of the Toyota. Jane asked what they would do at the other end to unload it, but Bill said that was no problem as he had a big hoist with block-and-tackle to drop it down onto the hydraulic lift again. After that, the stove from the lounge was a piece of cake, relatively speaking. There were some extra pieces of flue and various fittings left over from the installation in the garage, so Jamie took these along with the flues they had removed. As an afterthought he put the welding gear into the truck as well, in case they had any problems.

They said goodbye to Jane and Megan then headed off in the two vehicles, stopping off in Beeching Road to visit Screwfix and the two builders' merchants to pick up extra fittings that might be needed. Back at the farm they unloaded the range using the block-and-tackle and managed, with a lot of sweating, to get it into place in the kitchen area. They then did the same with the stove in what would be the main living area, on the same wall as the door.

Bill and Jamie thanked Phil for his help and he went back to his work on the farm, saying 'No problem, guys; give me a shout if you need me again.'

They knocked a couple of holes in the wall near the top to take the flues outside for the range in the kitchen and the stove in the lounge, but had problems with the angles and the fittings they had. Jamie had to use the welding gear to cut some of the tubing to fit and weld it in place. It was the first time he'd done any welding in nearly twenty years and the results were a bit rough-and-ready, but functional. He looked at Bill and shrugged.

Bill grinned at him. 'Well, I suppose a blind man on a galloping horse would like to see it!' and they both laughed. Emma brought them some big slices of pheasant pie with a couple of beers and Jamie said it was just what the doctor ordered and kissed her. They sealed up the holes in the wall around the flues with fire cement and by late afternoon both jobs were finished. They stood back to admire their work and clinked their beer bottles together.

'We'll fire them up tomorrow after the cement has set, to test them,' said Bill, and Jamie agreed.

For the remaining afternoon they installed studwork inside the lounge, which would be lined with plywood panels, giving a cavity for extra insulation in the winters. They finished up for the evening, saying they'd see each other in the morning, then Jamie drove home. He stopped at their two snare locations, but again there were no rabbits in them. He shook his head, sighing, and then carried on home.

Megan rushed to greet him when he arrived, saying 'Hi Jamie' and gave him a hug. He bent down and kissed her, then Max jumped up at him, barking and wagging his tail, and he patted and stroked him.

'Well, that was a nice welcome! Thank you.'

Megan grinned at him, took his hand and led him through to the kitchen, where Jane was busy working. On the kitchen worktop were the freshly-prepared carcasses of four pheasants and three good-sized rabbits. Jane grinned at him and he kissed her.

'Jamie,' Megan said excitedly, 'Jane and I went out hunting this afternoon! We walked all the way to the golf course at Cooden Beach and we hid in the bushes for ages and Jane shot *four* pheasants and then three rabbits later on. It was so cool! And Max was just brilliant; he didn't make a sound. He sat there watching, all tensed-up, and then ran out as soon as Jane had shot the pheasants and brought them back.'

Jamie smiled. 'That's fantastic Megan, and just what we needed. Well done to all of you!' He kissed Jane again and then Megan.

Jane said 'Well, we haven't done too well recently with meat, so I thought I'd go out for the afternoon to see what I could get. It turned out well, and Megan and Max enjoyed themselves!'

They sat down with a drink and he told them about the work he and Bill had done, and that the range and stove were installed and would be tested the following day. Jane and Megan were pleased and congratulated him. Not long after their evening meal Megan was nodding off, so she went to bed while they sat up and talked. Jamie said he thought it would be a good idea if they went back to the gun store sometime soon to collect the rest of the ammunition for their guns, along with several other weapons, maybe. There was, after all, no point in leaving it all there; extra weapons and ammunition would be useful for the future and they could take everything to the farm. Jane agreed it would be a good thing to do and they went to bed soon after.

On Wednesday morning Jamie and Bill fired up the range and the stove to see if the flues drew well enough and to check for any internal smoke leaks. All seemed fine, though, and they slapped each other on the back for a job well-done. With the range lit the kitchen heated up in no time and they had to open all the windows. The last job on that front was to fit two cowls over the tops of the flues to stop rain coming down them. By Thursday afternoon they had finished building the stud walls and lining them with sheets of plywood. They also made some repairs to the units in the kitchen and added extra shelves for storage.

As the place was a lot smaller than the bungalow and they would be short on storage space, Bill said they could use the unit next door and either put in some cupboards or extra shelving. He told Jamie that it was full of old junk mainly, but hadn't got around to sorting it out for years. They wouldn't be able to store clothes or furnishings in there as it was unheated and such things would get damp in cold weather, but they could certainly use it to store preserved food and all of Jamie's tools could go in there, along with their bikes. Jamie thanked him and said that would be great. They arranged to meet at the retail park the next morning to pick up some more materials. Also, he had promised to take Megan to Halfords to get a bike for her and then take her on to the farm to spend the day with Sally while he was there working. Back at the bungalow he gave Jane and Megan an update on the work progress and they were looking forward to seeing the improvements.

The following morning he and Megan left earlier than they had arranged to meet Bill, to give them time to choose a bike for her. They pulled up outside Halfords and everything looked normal. Jamie had the sawn-off slung over his shoulder and, as usual, he stood in the entrance for a minute listening, just to be sure. It was all quiet, though, so they went in and climbed the stairs to the bike section. Megan looked at all of the bikes suitable for her age and size, and Jamie said she should get the biggest one that she could ride comfortably with the saddle lowered a bit, to give her time to grow into it and be able to use it for a few years. She tried a few and then picked a nice mountain bike in green.

'This is great; can I have this one, please?'

Jamie looked at the price tag and made a face. 'Blimey! I'm glad we haven't got to buy this!' Megan laughed and smiled up at him. While they were there he picked up a couple of spare inner tubes, a stirrup pump and some puncture repair kits then carried the bike out to put in the back of the BMW.

'I need to go to Wickes to look at some things now, honey, and that's where we're going to meet Bill.'

'Okay,' she replied cheerily.

They walked off round the corner, chatting about her new bike. She was excited and couldn't wait to ride it. 'It'll be great- I'll be able to ride along the promenade and take Max for runs.'

They reached the corner of the warehouse when Megan said she needed to pee. Jamie pointed her to some bushes by the fence, set back a little between the buildings, while he wandered away a few yards and turned his back.

Forty yards away to his left, out of his line of sight, two figures came out of Wickes and saw him. It was two of the guys they had encountered at Battle and they recognised him straight away. One had a shotgun over his shoulder and he was the one who'd been injured when Jane shot his baseball bat on their last visit. He scowled angrily then swore, swung the shotgun down and started to raise it to his shoulder.

At that moment Megan came out and saw them. She screamed 'Jamieee!' and he span round. She ran into him, knocking him over just as the shotgun went off. The blast caught her instead of him, knocking her off her feet and flinging her backwards like a rag-doll. She hit the ground hard and lay there unmoving. Jamie scrambled to his feet, looking in horror at Megan's crumpled body.

'Nooooo!' he screamed. He heard an engine start and rev loudly. Neither of them had seen the red pickup parked behind an abandoned van outside the store. The truck took off, heading for the exit opposite him.

Jamie had always been a fairly calm and even-tempered man. He'd never been in trouble in his youth and hadn't been the kind to get into fights, but now blind rage erupted in him like never before and completely overtook him. He bent down, picked up the sawn-off and ran to intercept the truck as it neared the exit, screaming and swearing like a madman. It swerved by him just feet away; he raised the shotgun and fired both barrels through the open window, hitting the driver full in the head and face. The out-of-control vehicle smashed into a lamp-post with steam coming from the shattered radiator.

The other guy climbed from the wreckage, his face a mess and covered in both his own blood and that of his mate. He stumbled, trying to bring the shotgun to bear on Jamie, but couldn't see properly because of the blood in his eyes. Jamie broke open the sawn-off, ejected the spent cartridges, then scrambled frantically in his pocket to get two more and loaded them into the gun. He raised it to his shoulder and fired both barrels again, barely feeling the huge recoil. The blast took the guy in the centre of his chest and he flew backwards and hit the ground. He didn't bother checking if they were dead- it was obvious.

He ran back to where Megan's lifeless body lay and looked down at her in despair. The shotgun fell from his hand and clattered on the ground. The left side of her body, from the neck downwards, was covered in blood. He sank to the ground, lifted her frail, still body and cradled her to his chest, howling and sobbing for this beautiful young girl who had come into their lives and given them such joy.

Twenty-five

He sat there on the ground clutching Megan to his chest for several minutes, rocking her body with tears streaming down his face and oblivious to everything. He was barely aware of Bill's van screeching to a stop nearby, or of him jumping out, swearing and cursing as he ran over to him. He knelt down next to him, his face full of grief. Jamie was covered in Megan's blood and Bill thought it was his.

'Oh, fucking hell! Jamie, are you okay? Are you injured?'

Jamie didn't respond but just sat there in a daze, sobbing. Bill shook his shoulder and then lifted his face so it was level with his own.

'Jamie!' he said loudly. 'Come on, snap out of it! Are you hurt?' Jamie's eyes slowly came into focus and he stared at him.

'The fuckers killed her, Bill,' he sobbed. 'It was meant for me and she saved my life.'

'Are you hurt, too, Jamie?' he asked again and Jamie shook his head.

Bill looked down at Megan's body with tears in his eyes as Jamie held her and he noticed a small movement in her chest. He reached his hand across and felt at Megan's neck for several seconds.

'Jamie, she's not dead! She's got a pulse! I can feel it. It's a bit slow and erratic, but she's alive!'

Jamie shook his head to clear it and felt for himself. Bill hadn't been mistaken; he could feel a pulse and Megan was alive.

'Jesus, Jesus! Oh, thank God!'

'Jamie, where's your car? You've got to take her to the army camp at Tunbridge Wells right now. They've got doctors and medics there. They're the only ones who can help her now.'

Jamie shook his head again, trying to remember. 'It's round by Halfords.' He fumbled in his pocket and gave Bill the keys to the BMW and he ran off, returning a minute later with the car. They lifted Megan carefully between them and placed her on the back seats, then covered her with Max's blanket from the boot. Jamie had recovered from his initial shock and grief and was now thinking more clearly again. He got into the driver's seat.

'Jamie, whatever you do, don't go mad! Take it steady- you don't want to come off the road and kill both of you! And keep talking to her and reassuring her.'

Jamie nodded. 'Bill, can you go to the bungalow and tell Jane?'

'Course I will, mate. You take it easy; drive carefully and I'll see you soon. Best of luck, mate.'

Jamie thanked him and then drove out of the retail park, his mind racing as he thought of the best way to go. The quickest way was the new road to the top of Hastings to pick up the A21, so he headed up Wrestwood Road to join the Combe Valley Way from the new roundabout near Sidley.

That journey was probably the best piece of driving he'd ever done in his life. He drove as fast as was practicable, slowing carefully for the bends and speeding up on the straights. Never before had he been so focussed or concentrated so hard; all his thoughts bent on Megan's survival. He spoke to her constantly, reassuring her that she would be okay. He didn't know if she could hear him, but he kept it up nonetheless.

It was just over thirty miles to the army camp and it went by in a blur. On some of the straight stretches he was doing well over a hundred miles-per-hour. He got there in just over forty minutes. Signs had been placed at intervals along the road, announcing the camp's presence, and he found it easily. He pulled off the road into a gated entrance to a large field, full of huge tents and various army vehicles. A soldier stood guard at the gate, his rifle at the ready, as Jamie jumped from the car and approached him. The soldier looked at him warily; Jamie's face, hands and clothes were covered in Megan's blood, which he had forgotten about, and the soldier held his rifle on him.

'Please, you've got to help me. I've got a wounded girl in the car- she's been shot and needs help immediately.'

'Sir, please stand to one side,' the soldier said, his rifle still covering Jamie as he went to look in the car.

'Is Major Miller or Major Cunningham here?' Jamie asked urgently. 'I met them in Bexhill a week ago. They know me and the girl- her name's Megan and I'm Jamie Parker. Major Cunningham examined her at our house.'

'Major Miller is out today, but Major Cunningham is here. Please wait here, sir, while I try to contact him.' He walked off a few yards and spoke into his radio.

Jamie opened the rear door, knelt down and stroked Megan's hair, kissing her forehead and telling her that everything was going to be okay. The soldier came back after a minute, telling him that Major Cunningham had been informed and asking for him to wait, and Jamie thanked him. After several tense minutes Cunningham came running up with two orderlies carrying a stretcher.

The soldier opened the gate for them and they approached the car. Cunningham was a professional and he didn't waste time with greetings. He merely nodded to Jamie and bent down to look at Megan for a short while. He nodded to the orderlies and they lifted Megan carefully from the car and onto the stretcher. Cunningham instructed them to take Megan to the medical tent immediately and they set off across the field.

'Private Baker; direct Mr. Parker to the vehicle parking area and have him wait there. I'll come when we have news.' Baker saluted and Cunningham nodded to Jamie again and ran off after the stretcher.

'Thank you, Major...' Jamie called after him and Cunningham raised his hand in response.

The soldier gave Jamie directions and he thanked him, got back in the car and drove across the field to where he'd been instructed to park. He passed a number of tents and army trucks, one of which looked like a command vehicle with lots of antennas on the roof. He parked the car and turned the engine off, then sat there for a few minutes as his heart rate came back to normal. He picked up his rucksack from the footwell, rummaged inside and pulled out his hip flask. He took a couple of mouthfuls of whisky, put it back in his pack and then sat back in the seat. The adrenaline was starting to wear off and he felt like he was sinking.

He opened the door for some fresh air and got out. He looked around him at the camp and further down the field he could see other civilians; probably other survivors who had either made their way there or been brought there by the army. The first half of the camp was all army and medical operations and quarters. He took the blanket from the back seat and put it on the grass to sit on, but saw the bloodstains on it and tears came into his eyes again as he wondered how she was. He picked the blanket back up and threw it angrily into the back of the car, then sat back down in the passenger seat, where there was more legroom.

He'd been there nearly half an hour when Jane pulled up next to him in his Seat. He got out of the car and she looked in horror at Megan's blood on his clothes and face, then burst into tears and threw her arms around him. She looked up at him desperately.

'How is she?'

'I don't know, my love. Major Cunningham took her away to a medical tent half an hour ago. All I know is that she was breathing, but unconscious. All we can do is wait.

Jane... Megan saved my life: I'd be dead now if it wasn't for her. She threw herself into me and pushed me out of the way and took most of the shotgun blast...' He started crying again and Jane hugged him.

'Who were they?'

'It was two of the guys from Battle. I think the one who shot at me was the bloke you injured when you shot his

221

baseball bat, but I can't be sure.'

'Did you get them?' she asked, with fury in her eyes.

'Yes- they're dead.'

'Good! I hope the fuckers rot in hell!'

They sat in the BMW and Jamie related the whole thing for her. She said she hadn't been able to get her Golf started as the battery was too low, so had taken his Ibiza. Bill had driven off after hugging her and telling her not to drive madly, and she'd said they would tell them when they had some news. Bill had offered to take Max to look after so they didn't have to worry about him or leave him on his own, and Jane had said thanks, that would be great.

After that they both went quiet for some time. They sat there for another three hours or more, talking occasionally but mainly just lost in their own thoughts, before seeing Major Cunningham walking towards them. They got out of the car, both holding their breath, but then Cunningham smiled as he got nearer to indicate good news. He dispensed with the formality of a salute and shook their hands instead.

'Well, Megan's out of danger. She's heavily sedated but stable, and she's going to be okay.' They let out a huge sigh and breathed again, then thanked him.

Cunningham smiled. 'Her injuries actually looked worse than they were and it was misleading due to the amount of blood on her. It was small shot that their gun was loaded with, so the pellets didn't do as much damage as larger shot might have. She only caught part of the shot pattern, because if she'd taken the whole load then she wouldn't be alive. We removed dozens of pellets from her left arm, side and neck and have put her arm in a sling, which she'll need to keep on for at least a week or two, probably. The arm will be very painful for a while and she'll have only limited use of it, but it will heal in time.

Ironically, the worst injury was from her head hitting the ground when she fell. That's mainly why she was unconscious and she has bad concussion, but we think she'll be fine. We'd like to keep her here for observation for another two days after this, to monitor her progress. You can come late Sunday afternoon to collect her as long as we're happy with her progress. Would you like to see her? She's sedated and sleeping now, but you can have a look at her.'

They said they'd like to, so Cunningham led them to the recovery tent and showed them Megan's bed. They thanked him again and shook his hand before he walked off, saying he'd see them on Sunday. They looked down at her lying there and Jane started crying again and hugged Jamie. Her head was bandaged and so was her left arm, which lay outside the sheets in a sling. Her chest rose and fell rhythmically and she was sleeping soundly. Jane knelt down beside her and put her hand gently on Megan's right shoulder.

'Hello Megan, my love; it's Jane,' she said softly. 'Jamie's here, too. You get well soon and we'll see you in a couple of days. We love you very much.' She leaned over and kissed her cheek carefully. Megan stirred and murmured in her sleep. Jamie bent down to kiss her, too, then they got up, left the tent and walked back to the cars.

The soldier on the gate let them out and they drove home at a much slower pace than on the way there. They dropped off Jamie's Seat at the bungalow first and he went in to wash the blood off himself. He changed his clothes and then they carried on to Bill and Emma's in the BMW. It was after three in the afternoon when they pulled into the yard and stopped by the house; the door opened almost immediately. Bill, Emma, Sally and Peter came out, followed by Phil, Sophie and Max, barking and wagging his tail. Jane and Jamie got out of the car and went over to them.

'She's going to be okay!' said Jane with a relieved smile and they all hugged each other, crying tears of relief. Sally was overjoyed and hugged Jane and Jamie several times.

They went into the kitchen and sat at the table, where Jane told them everything that had happened at the camp and what Major Cunningham had told them about Megan's condition, and that they could pick her up on Sunday afternoon; all things being well. Jamie then took over and filled in the blanks for them about what had happened at the retail park.

Neither of them had eaten anything since breakfast so Emma rustled up some ham and eggs for them, which they appreciated greatly. Afterwards, they sat in the conservatory chatting for a while and Bill poured them a brandy, which Jane diluted heavily with water. They raised a toast to Megan and drank her health, sending up a silent prayer for her recovery.

They decided, under the circumstances, to take the weekend off from work on their new place and to resume on the Monday, as long as Megan was okay and back home. After that they took their leave and headed off home. They stopped off on the way to check the snares and collected one rabbit, which they cooked that night.

The place seemed empty and quiet without Megan and they were in a sombre mood all evening. Jamie opened a bottle of wine, but Jane only had a small glass and he drank the rest himself. It had been an emotionally exhausting day so they retired early and were pleased to get into bed, where they lay for a long time holding each other, talking quietly occasionally. Megan had found a real place in their hearts in the short time she had been with them and they already loved her like she was their own. They missed her terribly and couldn't wait to collect her on Sunday.

Twenty-six

They awoke early the next morning and decided to drive over to Sarah and Georgie's to tell them the news about Megan and also about their decision to move to the farm with Bill and Emma. First of all, though, they had regular chores to attend to, including collecting salt from their containers in the gardens and refilling them with fresh seawater. They already had many bags of sea salt that they used on their food and in their cooking. The tomatoes in the conservatory were coming along well and they would soon be able to harvest some, which they were looking forward to. By ten o'clock they were ready to leave so they jump-started Jane's Golf to give it a run and charge up the battery. Max jumped in the back and they headed off.

Sarah and Georgie were delighted to see them and asked where Megan was. They told them the news inside and the sisters were horrified to hear what had happened. They hugged them both again, saying how sorry they were and hoping Megan would make a full recovery. Jamie recounted the whole saga for them and they were shocked.

'I'm glad you got the bastards!' said Georgie, feeling no remorse for them. They congratulated him on thinking to take Megan to the army camp.

'Well, to be honest, it's a good job Bill was there to think fast, because I'd completely lost it and was fit for nothing!' Jamie said with a grim smile.

It was too early for lunch and Jane said they wouldn't stay long as they had things to do, but Georgie made them tea and gave them a slice of apple pie each. Things were going well for the sisters and they had harvested, stored and preserved lots of produce for the winter. They had also begun converting one of their sheds into stables. They had been busy in recent weeks scouting the area for several miles around.

'We didn't get around to telling you on our last visit when we were all together at yours,' said Sarah, 'but we've located four places to get horses from. We've also thought of you two and Bill and Emma, too. We've collected two horse boxes, one of which is for you; we've got them here, round the back.'

Jamie and Jane said that was great and thanked them. They then told the sisters about Bill and Emma's offer and that they were going to move to the farm, and had started converting the chicken shed that week. Sarah and Georgie were delighted and agreed that it made perfect sense, as they now had Megan and would also have the baby when it arrived.

'We've also seen a horse-drawn cart, but haven't collected it yet,' said Georgie. 'It will need a fair bit of repair work, which I'm sure you'll be able to do. You might as well have it and take it to the farm as we won't really need it, I don't suppose.'

This was great news as a horse and cart would be needed for taking the kids out and for collecting stores and materials, and they both thanked the sisters again.

'I know it's not our place to offer,' said Jane, 'but we wondered if you might entertain moving to the farm also, if Bill and Emma were in agreement?'

'Well, it's a nice thought,' said Sarah, 'but no: we were born in this house and we'll die here, as Dad did. We've got everything we need here and we'll only be about four miles from you by road, and probably a bit less across country by horse!'

They chatted for a while longer and then Jamie said they would head off. Sarah asked Jane when she was due and she said mid-March, by her calculations.

'Well, I'll come over to stay sometime in February, then, to help with the birth, but we'll talk more about that at a later date.'

Jane was grateful and also relieved. She thanked her and gave them both a hug then they departed, saying they would see them soon. When they got home Jamie said he supposed he should take the boat out fishing while the weather was good, even though his heart wasn't in it with Megan on his mind.

'You should go;' she replied, 'it might do you good and take your mind off things.' Jamie agreed, so he got the rods and set off down the garden. He was out for around two hours and although it didn't take his mind off Megan, he came back with three fish, one of which was a decent size.

The next day, Sunday, they were on tenterhooks all day with thoughts of going to the camp and collecting Megan. They wondered how she was and whether she would be well enough to come home. The day dragged; they couldn't focus on anything and got very little done around the place. They didn't know what time Major Cunningham had meant exactly by "late afternoon", but by two-thirty they could stand it no longer so they set off in the BMW, with Max in the back.

When they arrived at the camp an hour later the soldier on guard was different from before, but he'd been warned of their arrival and directed them to the parking area as before, where Major Cunningham would meet them once he had been contacted. They waited for around fifteen minutes before the Major arrived and he greeted them, shaking their hands with a smile.

'Well, you'll be relieved to know that Megan's doing okay and you can take her home today.' They gave big sighs of relief and smiled, thanking him.

'She's out of bed and waiting for you. She's going to have to take it easy for at least a month; maybe two. The wounds will heal okay and we've started a course of antibiotics for ten days, to combat any infection. She'll need to keep the bandages on her head for a few days more at least. Because of the concussion she'll probably experience dizzy spells, blurred vision or nausea for at least another month or more, so be aware of that. It's best if she does nothing strenuous and just rests, basically.'

They shook his hand again and thanked him. As they walked to the medical tent where Megan was, the Major asked what had happened, saying he hadn't had a chance before as he'd been too busy. Jamie gave him a brief account of the events and of their two run-ins with the guys at Battle. He also spoke of Jane's attack on the day they'd met. Cunningham shook his head, saying what a shame it was that the few survivors who were left couldn't work together for their own good. He didn't pass any judgement on Jamie's actions following Megan's shooting. Just before they got to the tent Jamie told him they would be moving in a couple of months to their friend's farm near Hooe as it seemed the best thing to do, what with having Megan now and Jane's pregnancy. Cunningham said it seemed like a good opportunity for them and wished them well with it. Jamie gave him the farm's address written on a piece of paper and said it was marked on Ordnance Survey maps.

'Major Cunningham…' Jane began.

'It's Tom… at least while there are no troops around!' he said, and they smiled.

'Tom,' Jane continued, 'we don't know what's going to happen in the future- I suppose none of us does- but if ever you're in the area, or if there's anything we can do for you, please feel free to stop by; you'll always have a warm welcome from us.' She shook his hand again and kissed his cheek. He was touched and thanked her, then shook Jamie's hand. He wished them well, gave them a sharp salute and departed for other duties.

They entered the tent and saw Megan sitting in a chair beside her bed; she saw them and beamed, though it was tinged with pain. She struggled out of the chair weakly and they hurried over to her. Mindful of her injuries, they hugged her gently with tears in their eyes. She looked pale and fragile and clung to them for a long time.

'Come on, honey, let's take you home,' said Jamie.

An army nurse standing nearby smiled at them and gave

them Megan's antibiotics, wishing her a speedy recovery. Megan hugged the nurse and said 'Thank you for looking after me, Karen.' She also gave them some strong painkillers, but said to use Paracetamol and Ibuprofen first, only using the strong ones if she really needed them, and not to mix them with others. They thanked her and left to return to the car.

Jane went in the back with Megan and Max gave her a warm welcome, barking and licking her face, which made her smile. Jamie drove home sedately and Megan slept for most of the journey with Jane's arm around her. He parked in the garage and Jane took her into the bungalow. Jamie was just closing the garage door and saw Megan's new bike against the wall where he'd put it on Friday evening. He sighed and shook his head, closed the door and went into the bungalow.

Over the next two weeks Megan's recovery was slow but steady. They removed the dressings regularly and washed the wounds with saltwater, which seemed to help. She had dozens of small scars forming from the pellet wounds, from her neck down to her waist and covering most of her left arm. She avoided the strong painkillers after taking them a couple of times, as she said they made her woozy and constipated. Instead, she took only Paracetamol and Ibuprofen and gritted her teeth when it was very painful. She kept the arm in the sling and gradually was able to use it more as time went on. She had to be careful of making any sudden movements otherwise she got dizzy and felt sick.

They noticed a change in Megan during that time: it wasn't just the wounds, the pain and the recovery, but something else. There seemed to be a new maturity to her because of what had happened. It was like she now had first-hand experience of what the world- and people- could be like, which was different from the five months she had spent surviving on her own. She was still quick to laugh and smile, but there was an underlying level of seriousness developing within her, or of sadness maybe. They spoke about it when on their own in the evenings and wondered if it was also the beginning of her transition into adulthood, which the attack maybe had hastened.

During those two weeks Jamie went to the farm every day to continue with their new home. On the Monday morning after collecting Megan he went there and gave everyone the good news about her return. He updated them on her condition and they were over the moon at the news.

He and Bill realised they needed to dispose of the two bodies outside Wickes, so they took care of it that afternoon when going back for more supplies. After getting what they needed from the store they went over to the pickup truck. Looking at it now, without the rage he had felt at the time and its associated adrenaline rush, it was a sickening sight. The driver had part of his skull missing and his face was an unrecognisable mess, while the guy on the ground had a huge hole in his chest and was covered in blood. Seagulls or crows had been picking at the bodies.

'Well,' said Bill, 'you certainly took care of them, mate! Remind me not to get into an argument with you in the future!' and they both smiled grimly.

Bill picked up the shotgun and looked in the cab, finding a half-full box of cartridges. He said it would do for Phil and put it in the van. They lifted the other guy's body into the passenger seat between them and closed the door. Jamie went back into Wickes and came out with two bottles of paint thinners, which he sloshed around the truck's interior and over the bodies. Bill got in the van and started it while Jamie lit a piece of rag and threw it through the window. The flames built quickly and by the time they were back on the main road the truck was engulfed in flames. They continued with their work at the farm and got the place finished by the end of August.

On its completion Jamie, Jane and Megan went there for a celebratory lunch and a small opening ceremony. Jane and Megan were excited to see the result and they weren't disappointed. Bill had tacked a length of ribbon across the doorway and they let Megan cut it before they all went in. Unbeknown to them all, Phil and Sophie had got hold of some party poppers and set them off when Megan cut the ribbon, and they all jumped and laughed.

It wasn't yet filled with their furniture, but the structure and décor were finished. The living area was painted in white silk emulsion to maximise the light. Megan's bedroom in the partitioned-off area at the back was painted in a pale green, which she loved, and there was a surprise in there from Sophie. Jamie hadn't known until fairly recently that she was an accomplished artist, but when she had told him of her intention he was delighted. Hanging on the wall was a beautiful framed pencil sketch of Max that she had done for Megan. She loved it and hugged Sophie while thanking her. There were some ornate candle holders attached to the wall for lighting, and several bookshelves.

Jamie had measured the living room carefully to determine which furniture from the bungalow would fit and had marked spaces for them. In the gaps between they had installed shelf units and bookcases they had collected from stores in the area, and there was a space against one wall for the dresser from their kitchen. The stove in the lounge sat on ceramic tiles, with space next to it for storing logs and there were more candle holders on the walls. The concrete floor throughout had been swept and scrubbed and Jamie had sealed it with several layers of acrylic varnish. To brighten the place up and to make the floor warmer underfoot there were lots of thick rugs in various ethnic designs that went well together. On the wall opposite the door hung three framed photos: Jane with her mum and sisters outside the De La Warr Pavilion; Megan with her parents, and Jamie with his mum, brother and sister. Jane and Megan were touched and hugged him.

In the kitchen the old units had all been repaired and painted in white gloss and there were new cupboards on the walls and various storage shelves in every available space. The range cooker had a storage area for logs next to it and the hand pump above the sink had been repaired and painted in white enamel metal paint.

The thing Jamie was proudest of, though, was the lighting he had installed. He had collected several solar-powered LED floodlights and installed them throughout the place. As the building faced south and would get maximum sunlight he had installed the solar panels on the roof there and extended the cables inside to wall switches. The solar panels charged up the lead-acid batteries and would give them plenty of light when fully charged.

Upstairs in the loft space above the kitchen they had partitioned off an area for Jane and Jamie's bedroom, with its own door. Jamie had decided they wouldn't need the whole space as their bedroom so there was an open area at the top of the stairs like a landing. It had a small table and two chairs next to a dormer window, with a view out across the yard, and a cupboard for storing linen and bedding. Jane and Megan were thrilled with everything and they thanked Bill and Jamie for their hard work, telling them it was fantastic and giving them both hugs again. Bill and Jamie had big grins on their faces and nodded to each other.

They then took them all outside to show them the other thing they were rather proud of. Behind the building, a few yards to one side, they had built a composting toilet. It was raised on stilts, with four steps up to it, and was enclosed on all sides, with its own door. It had a corrugated steel roof and there was another solar-powered light in there with a sensor, which would come on as soon as they went inside; it even had a proper toilet seat fitted. Jane and Megan had both been wondering what they would do for a toilet, but hadn't said anything, and they were surprised and delighted with it.

'Well,' Jamie said, 'I can't take credit for that, apart from helping to build it. The design was all Bill's idea. They've got one like it on the other side of the farm, but we thought we'd need one a bit closer to home. The underside is open to the air all round. Waste breaks down naturally and you'll be surprised how little smell there is, really. We haven't worked out what we'll do when all the toilet paper stocks are used up, but we'll think of something.'

They went back to the farmhouse, where Emma opened a couple of bottles of Prosecco that Phil and Sophie had got from Tesco's warehouse. They raised a toast to their friends' new home and looked forward to them coming to live at the farm with them. After that they sat down to eat a lovely meal that Emma and Sophie had prepared for them, and it was a happy and relaxed occasion. Jane and Jamie were now looking forward to moving into their new home in less than two months, and to be living with these people who had become such good friends.

By mid-afternoon, though, Megan's arm was hurting and she'd suffered a couple of dizzy spells, so they left after hugging everyone and thanking them for lunch. Back home, they gave Megan some painkillers and she went off to her room for a sleep. Jane made some coffee and they sat in the conservatory with the sun coming in through the tomato plants, talking about their new home.

'I can hardly believe it's the same place I saw three weeks ago. You two have done a fantastic job and I'm really proud of you,' said Jane, kissing him.

'Thanks, hon. I'm pleased with it, too, and I'm looking forward to moving in and making it our home. I know we'll have a lot less space than here, but we'll get used to it.'

'I'm glad about the composting toilet! I was wondering for a while what we were going to do. I had visions of having to tramp off across a windswept field to some bushes every time I needed the loo!' she added, and they both laughed.

'Moving away from the sea will be my biggest regret, though,' said Jamie. 'I'm going to miss the sound of the waves breaking on the beach in the evening.'

Twenty-seven

As they moved into September, summer started giving way gracefully to autumn. Megan's condition continued to improve and the spells of dizziness and nausea grew less frequent. Her arm improved greatly, too, and she was able to manage without the sling, though it was still rather stiff and painful.

Many apples and pears in the area were now ready for harvesting and they made several trips in the first two weeks to pick them.

'How do we know if they're ready for picking?' Jamie had asked Jane beforehand.

'We cut one open and look at the pips; if they're dark brown then they're ripe and if not then we leave them.'

They didn't go mad like they had with the cherries, but collected several large bags. They stored some for use over the next few months, ensuring only perfect ones were kept, as any blemishes or bruises would cause them to rot and spoil the others. These ones were wrapped in newspaper or straw and placed in boxes in the cellar. The remainder were preserved for future use: half were made into purees and bottled and the rest they cored, sliced and dried in a low oven, which was a long and laborious process. Now that the weather had turned cooler it wasn't practicable to dry them on the racks as they had with the cherries. Back at the farm the whole household there was also busy with their own orchard as fruit became ready.

Megan helped with the fruit preparation but had to take

regular breaks when her arm became painful. Having been inactive due to her injuries, by mid-September she had put on several pounds and was getting back to a more normal weight for her age and size. One day, they were all in the kitchen working when Jane asked Megan to do something for her.

'Okay, Mum,' she replied. Jane and Jamie looked at each other.

Megan caught the look and said 'What?'

'You called me Mum, honey.'

'I know I did. Do you mind?'

Jane was moved and looked at her lovingly. 'Oh, Megan, of course I don't mind, if you're happy calling me that. I'm touched that you think of me that way and it's lovely. Jamie and I love you like you're our own daughter, and that's how we think of you now.'

'Well, it's the same for me, too. I still miss my parents and I think of them often, but I love you both and think of you as Mum and Dad now... You're my family.'

She hugged them both tightly and they got a bit tearful. Jamie held her for a long time, remembering their ordeal at the retail park and how she had saved his life.

In the middle of the month there was a bit of an Indian summer for well over a week, when it grew hot again and the sun shone from almost clear blue skies. They ate outside every evening during that time and on one occasion Jamie was looking up at the sky with a glass of wine in his hand, looking pensive.

'Look at the sky,' he said to them. They looked up and both said it was a beautiful, clear blue sky.

Jamie nodded. 'Yes, but what's missing? Apart from clouds, I mean.'

They both looked stumped for a few seconds and then Megan smiled. 'Planes! There aren't any planes!'

Jane tutted and shook her head. 'Of course! Well done, honey; you're right.'

'Yes,' said Jamie, 'and I can't remember the last time I saw one, or any vapour trails. It's been that way for as long as I can remember. When was the last time you saw any?' Neither of them could remember.

'Well, I'm guessing it must have been back near the start of the year, or thereabouts. That means the plague was global for that to happen; it's not just the UK that was affected, but everywhere.' It was a sombre thought and they went quiet for a while thinking about it, then Jamie shrugged. 'Sorry! I didn't mean to put a dampener on things… it just suddenly occurred to me.'

In the coming weeks they made several trips to the farm to move their furniture and possessions into their new home. Between the Toyota and the Land Rover they managed to fit everything in and didn't need to use Bill's van. They took their favourite sofa, one of the armchairs, the double bed from their room and Megan's single bed. Jamie and Jane slept afterwards in the spare bed in the other bedroom until they were ready to move in, and Megan said she was happy to sleep on the other sofa in the lounge until then.

By this time Jane was about three months gone, and even though she barely had a bump Jamie was still a bit concerned about her lifting heavy things. She waved him away and told him not to fuss. 'I bet no woman in Neolithic times ever said "Can you lift this for me, darling, as it's a bit heavy and I'm pregnant."!' Jamie laughed; he still looked a bit concerned, though he left her alone.

They also took the coffee table from the conservatory that they all liked and the dresser from the kitchen, but left the kitchen table and chairs until they were finally leaving. They took most of the crockery and kitchen equipment, too, leaving just enough for them to get by with in the interim. They decided to leave a few things there for when they came back for a fishing trip or to spend a day by the sea sometime. Jamie would leave the fishing tackle in the garage and they picked out some older kitchen utensils and pans that could stay there, along with some tinned food, matches for lighting the stove and a few other bits.

On one morning Megan knocked on their door after she'd heard them stirring. 'Mum, can I talk to you, please?'

'Of course, honey; just let me get dressed and I'll be right with you.'

She went into the lounge to sit on the sofa with her and Megan told her that she'd had her first period. She was a bit shy and embarrassed about it, but Jane put her arm around her and reassured her, saying there was nothing to feel any embarrassment about and that she could talk with either her or Jamie about anything. She got some sanitary towels for her and they sat and talked for a while, then Megan smiled in gratitude and hugged her.

They still had a lot of vegetables to harvest and preserve before they left, along with the remaining tomatoes. Not all had grown as well as they'd hoped but they'd still had a good crop. They had been eating them in salads or making tomato sauces and the flavour was wonderful.

They'd not long returned from a trip to the farm one afternoon when Sarah and Georgie turned up for another visit to see how Megan was doing. Jane welcomed them inside and the sisters made a fuss of Megan, saying how pleased they were to see her looking so much better. They went out to the patio and sat down while Jamie made them all tea.

The sisters asked how the move was going and Jane said it was almost done, apart from the things they'd left at the bungalow until they were ready to move in. Sarah and Georgie were delighted and said they would come over soon to see the place. They then took turns telling them what they'd been doing in the last few weeks. They had finished the stables at their place and now had four horses and a pony that they had collected from the surrounding area. They had been around horses most of their lives, so it was nothing new to them. Jane and Jamie were pleased to hear it and congratulated them.

'Two of the horses and the pony are for you to take to the farm when you're ready, and we know where we can get more. We thought the pony would be good for Megan and Sally when they're ready. We've got saddles, bridles all the kit that'll be needed for them,' said Sarah. 'Have either of you ridden before?'

Jane said she had done a fair bit in her youth but not for

many years, while Jamie had never ridden before. They knew that Bill and Emma had been around horses for years, though they hadn't kept any at the farm before. They would need to convert a building in the top yard into stables, which they planned to do after they had moved there in mid-October.

'Well, once you're settled in and the stables are ready we can bring the horses over between us all and we'll give you some instruction on riding and looking after them,' said Sarah.

'That's brilliant, thank you,' said Jane, smiling, and Jamie agreed. Although the vehicles were still running fine they were aware that it might only be a few more months before they started having problems with the fuel. None of them knew for sure, of course, but it was better to be prepared beforehand. They suspected that the petrol vehicles would be the first to suffer, but that the diesels might go on for a lot longer; at least that was what they hoped.

Megan went into the house and came out with her bike. Now that her concussion and the associated dizzy spells had almost gone she had been out a few times on it, being careful to take it slowly at first.

'Dad?' she said, after waiting for a break in the conversation, 'Would you mind carrying my bike down the steps for me, please? I want to take Max out for a run along the promenade.'

'Of course not, honey, but don't forget your helmet,' Jamie replied.

Megan nodded and went back inside, coming out wearing her cycling helmet and fixing the strap. They walked off down the garden with Max and the sisters looked at Jane, who beamed at them.

'I know... She calls us Mum and Dad now, which is really touching. She's changed an awful lot recently and is growing up quickly. We don't know if it's because of the shooting or just her hormones.'

'Maybe it's both. I could see a change in her as we came in,' said Sarah. 'It's lovely to see her doing so well and I'm so pleased for you.'

Georgie agreed and Jane told them that Megan had also

recently started her periods. Both women said '*Ah, bless her!*' in unison.

In the third week of September, on a trip to the farm, Bill and Jamie decided they should sit down together and make a list of all the materials and tools they would need to get and bring to the farm for the future, while they still had use of the vehicles. They agreed, jokingly, that as this was "man-stuff" it needed to be done in a pub! After lunch, Jamie, Bill, Phil and Peter walked to the village pub three-quarters of a mile away and broke in. Bill hadn't been there since before the plague, but he knew the owners had died early on. It felt strange at first sitting there in an empty pub, but it didn't last for long.

The beer on tap was undrinkable, of course, but there were still plenty of bottles left on the shelves, along with various spirits. They all got drinks and sat at a table by a window, and pretty soon it almost felt like old times. They spent a couple of hours going over things and making a list of everything they might want, and talking about the machinery at the farm and what spares might be needed. They also discussed things they would need for converting one of the barns in the top yard into stables.

After nearly three hours they were all rather drunk; Peter was only seventeen and was the first to flag, followed by Phil. By the end the writing on their list wasn't very legible. They staggered off home with Bill and Jamie singing *Bohemian Rhapsody*, which Phil and Peter thought was a bit old-school, but they joined in anyway. Back at the farm the women tut-tutted at their condition, but Emma and Jane glanced at each other and smiled, knowing it had been good for all the men to get out together for once and let off steam.

During those last two weeks of September Jamie, Bill, Phil and Peter made several trips to all the DIY stores and builders' merchants in Bexhill, bringing back huge stocks of everything they thought might be needed in years to come. They also visited the gun store on the outskirts of Hastings and picked up several more shotguns and rifles, along with most of the ammunition left there. There were some smaller twenty-bore shotguns that they picked up, too, which had become more popular in recent years as they were lighter and had less recoil, and they would also be good for the girls to practise with as they got older.

They collected many racks and shelving units and erected them in two buildings in the top yard to use as storerooms, after clearing them of junk that had been in them for years. All the timber and sheet materials they collected were put into the big barn in the main yard. There was a lot more timber that they wanted to pick up from several places in town, but they would continue to make trips over the next couple of months. They stored screws, nails, washers, brackets, gaskets, nuts, bolts, tools, and all manner of other useful things in plastic storage boxes on the shelves, along with glues, sealants, chemicals and plumbing supplies. They also collected materials like sand, cement and ballast for making concrete, for any future projects or repairs. Another place they visited was a garden centre, where Jamie picked up two flat-packed greenhouses and other supplies, as he and Jane wanted to create a garden in the field behind their place where they could grow herbs, tomatoes and other plants.

They erected the greenhouses far enough back from their building that they wouldn't be in its shadow and would get full sun. The tomato plants from the conservatory that were still producing fruit were transported to the farm and put into the greenhouses, and Jane dug up the perennial herbs from their garden and put them into containers temporarily, to be planted in the new garden when they were ready. She also thought it would be a good idea to dig up a few sea beet plants from the beach behind the bungalow to transplant into the new garden.

It had been a rather hectic six weeks for them, but by the middle of October it was all done. Their preserved food was now spread between their new kitchen and the unit next door, which was now filled with the converted wine racks from their cellar and several other shelf units for storage. Jamie had also fixed hooks high up around the edges and across the ceiling and there were many string bags hanging there containing onions, root vegetables and fruit. There was a space set aside for all his tools and their bikes were against the wall near the door. Outside, near the hedge, was a covered storage area for logs for the stove and the range.

They had brought the Toyota pickup, the BMW and Jamie's Seat to the farm, along with the Land Rover, but Jane decided to leave her Golf in the bungalow's garage as they didn't need it. The dining table and chairs from the bungalow's kitchen were brought over and now sat in the space allocated for them in the living area. They'd also found a small round high table and two bar stools that fitted in the kitchen, and the patio table and chairs were in the yard in front of the building. Through the gap between their row of buildings and the ones on the yard's adjacent side they would be able to see the sun going down at certain times of the year. Max hadn't been forgotten about: he had a lovely rattan dog-basket filled with thick fleecy cushions and blankets to snuggle-up in.

Finally, there was just one more trip left to make to pick up the last few bits and pieces before it got dark. Jane asked Megan if she was coming but she smiled and declined, saying she was happy pottering about the place with Max, unpacking and getting her bedroom sorted. Max was lounging in his new bed and looked like he wouldn't be doing much pottering for a while. She kissed them both and they drove off in the Toyota. Secretly, she had wanted them to have time on their own together to say goodbye to their old home. As soon as they had driven off she put on her coat and walked off across the yard to the farmhouse.

It didn't take them long to load the last few things into the truck then they went back into the bungalow. They walked from room to room holding hands, remembering things that had happened in the five months or more that it had been their home. It felt like they had lived in the place for years with all the things they'd done and achieved there, as it had been their first step on the road to survival and self-sufficiency. They had tears in their eyes and held each other as they remembered the day they'd met, when Jamie had come running down the road with the shotgun and saved her life.

They went outside and walked around the gardens,

commenting on things they'd made or done and remembering successes and failures with growing food.

'God! D'you remember the evening you came running back in your dressing gown after finding Max half-dead on the beach?' said Jamie, shaking his head.

'How could I forget it? We were so lucky to find him, and that he survived. He's been a fantastic companion.' Jamie smiled and agreed with her.

She sniggered. 'And what about our mad drive along the seafront to Galley Hill in the RS2000?'

'… Singing *Summer of '69* at the tops of our voices!' he added, and they both laughed.

They kissed and then walked back through the house to the truck and drove back to the farm. They parked in the yard, walked to the door and went inside. Megan had lit the stove and also the range in the kitchen and the place was warm and cosy, with candles burning on the walls. She was standing there smiling in the green dress she'd been wearing when they met her. Behind her on the wall was a banner she'd made with Sally's help, which said *Welcome to our new home, Mum and Dad!* Jamie and Jane smiled and then got tearful, as Megan came over and held them both tightly.

Twenty-eight

When they got up in the morning, having been woken early by the crowing of cocks and cockerels, they weren't sure what to do with themselves at first. After the sustained activity of recent months they seemed to have come to a sudden stop. Over the last five months at the bungalow they had got into a routine, with regular work and tasks that needed doing every day. Now that all the vegetables had been harvested they had no garden work to attend to, there were no containers to collect salt from and refill every day, and no rabbit snares to check or move around.

Over breakfast they realised they'd forgotten to check the snares the previous day because of the move. They also needed to remove them all from where they had them set as they wouldn't be visiting that area on a daily basis from now on, so it wouldn't be right to leave them there.

Obviously, they would soon start helping around the farm with the regular tasks there, such as tending to the animals, maintaining the infrastructure and preparing the land for the planting of new crops when the time came, but nothing had been discussed between them yet. They decided they should keep up their production of sea salt at the bungalow. Although they currently had large stocks of salt, it was still a finite resource that would need to be replenished, so they agreed to go to the bungalow on a two-weekly basis over winter, as time and other jobs allowed.

'I'll take Megan and Max to remove the snares,' said Jane, 'and then go on to the bungalow to refill the containers in the conservatory with seawater.'

'Okay; and I'll go and have a chat with Bill about the stable conversion.'

He put on his coat and boots, kissed them both and then walked off across the yard to see Bill, stopping halfway to stroke the three farm cats that were lounging by one of the barns. They were semi-feral creatures that lived on the farm, sleeping in various places depending on the weather. Although they liked attention and being stroked they wouldn't be picked up like a domestic cat might, and they helped keep the mice and rat population under control.

Jane put a few things in a bag then put on her Barbour and a woolly hat as it was a bit chilly, and Megan did the same. She took her sawn-off from the gun rack by the door and put extra cartridges in her pockets and in the bag. As an afterthought she also took a long shotgun in case they saw anything worth shooting. Max was already waiting eagerly by the door, wagging his tail.

They drove off in the BMW and on the way Jane changed her mind, deciding to go to the bungalow first and then pick up the snares on the way back. They parked on the drive and went into the rather empty-looking house. Megan got two buckets and they walked down to the beach to fill them, with Max trailing behind. They carried the water back and laid out as many containers as would fit in the conservatory before pouring some water into each. They had found that a typical three-gallon bucket of seawater yielded around twelve ounces of salt and they had gathered a good stock over the last five months.

'Well, missy,' said Jane, 'hopefully when we come back in two weeks it will have evaporated and we'll have another bag of salt for our store.'

Megan smiled. 'I think the salt we collect tastes much nicer than the salt we used to get from the supermarket.'

'Yes, honey, I agree; that's because it's rich in iodine and has other trace elements that commercially-produced salt often doesn't have.'

Megan nodded. 'Dad said something similar to me when we were down on the beach a while back.'

They called Max in from the garden then left the house and drove away, stopping first at the railway bridge on Westcourt Drive. Jane smiled to herself as she remembered going there with Max to lay their first snares, while he'd still been recovering. They walked along the railway line removing all the snares, but there were no rabbits caught in them. Jane was disappointed but Megan said maybe they'd have better luck at the next place.

They climbed down the embankment to the pavement and were standing by the car when Max barked and then they heard a vehicle, but because of echoes from under the bridge they couldn't tell where it was coming from. Jane was on her guard instantly; all the more so because she had Megan to protect. She took the sawn-off from her shoulder, cocked both hammers and held it down by her side in her right hand, turning her head each way to listen and watch. She could feel her heart beating faster as adrenaline kicked-in.

At that moment a motorhome turned left into the road from Cooden Drive behind them. It pulled up about twenty feet away and then a man and woman got out of the cab. They waved and said hi then started coming towards them. Max came forward and stood in front of Megan; his hackles were up and he was growling low in his throat.

Jane held her left hand up, palm outwards. 'Would you mind staying where you are, please, and not coming any closer yet?'

The couple stopped about five yards from them, looking hesitant and glancing at the sawn-off shotgun in her hand.

'Please;' said Jane, 'I don't mean to be unfriendly or hostile, but could I ask you a few questions first?'

'Okay,' said the man. 'What do you want to know?'

'Can I ask you about your state of health; are either of you ill or have you had any sickness of any sort?'

The man gave a little smile and relaxed slightly. 'Well, I can understand your concern, but we're all fit and healthy. Our two kids are in the back and none of us have been ill.'

'Thank you,' said Jane. 'And could I ask where you've come from and when was the last time you had any contact with other people? I'm sorry to ask, but I need to know.'

'That's quite alright,' said the woman. 'In fact, we should have done the same, I suppose. We left our home near Potters Bar in Hertfordshire nearly two weeks ago to come to live in Bexhill. My cousin lived here, but he and his family died in hospital from the plague. We got stopped at an army checkpoint near Sevenoaks and escorted to a refugee camp near Tunbridge Wells for screening and registration. We were there for ten days and got the all-clear yesterday morning, then arrived here at lunchtime and have moved into my cousin's house nearby.'

Jane smiled, thanking them, and relaxed somewhat. She patted Max, saying 'Okay, Max. Good boy!' Max stopped growling but still looked alert; ready to move at the slightest threat to his family.

'Great dog you have there,' said the man. 'This might be a long-shot, but your name wouldn't be Jane Roberts, would it?'

Jane was taken aback. 'Yes it is: how did you know that?'

The man smiled. 'Well, we met Major Cunningham several times during our stay at the refugee camp. When we told him we were heading for Bexhill he said there was a possibility that we might bump into you and your partner, Jamie. If we did, he asked us to pass on his regards and to say he hopes Megan is doing well. We also met Major Miller a few times, whom I understand you met.'

Jane relaxed further and smiled, thanking them for passing on Cunningham's message and apologising for the questions. She lifted the sawn-off and un-cocked the hammers then slung it back over her shoulder. The couple relaxed at that and took it as a sign to come forward.

'I'm Matt Turner and this is my wife, Zoe.'

'Hello; pleased to meet you. I'm Jane- obviously- and this is our daughter, Megan.'

They all shook hands and smiled as the tension started to drain away. The man was tall and lanky with long dark hair, a high forehead and greying beard. His wife was only a few inches shorter and willowy, with long blonde hair parted in the middle. Both were in their mid-forties and Jane's first thought was of New Age hippies. Matt turned round and waved to the vehicle; the door opened and a boy and girl got out and walked over to them. They were obviously twins and were around Megan's age. Zoe introduced them as Amber and Luke and they all said hello.

'I have a feeling that you have good reason to be wary and to carry a sawn-off shotgun?' said Zoe.

'Yes;' Jane replied, 'several reasons, actually! I may tell you about them sometime, but now probably isn't the right time.'

'Oh, God!' said Matt, 'I hope we haven't jumped out of the frying pan and into the fire by coming here! Are things really bad in Bexhill?'

Jane smiled grimly but shook her head. 'Well, I'd guess things are probably no worse than where you've come from. The state the country's in brings out the best and the worst in people everywhere. There's no one left here, pretty much; it's a ghost-town. If there are still other survivors here in town then we haven't seen them in six months, but we've had trouble with people from other areas- and I mean big trouble. It sounds, though, as if you've run away from trouble of your own back in Potters Bar.'

'Yes;' Zoe replied, 'there was a bunch of thugs who were lording-it over the few survivors left in our area. They acted like they were now controlling the town, causing lots of problems for people and being threatening whenever they went to get anything. I mean, we'd planned on coming to Bexhill anyway as we wanted to live next to the sea in my cousin's house. He'd lived here most of his life and I know the area well because of that. We'd planned on moving down in early spring to start planting crops, but things got so bad that we felt we needed to leave right away.'

Zoe hesitated and then started crying. Matt put his arm around her, saying everything would be okay.

'We had the same sort of thing happen here,' said Jane. 'It was in Battle, actually, but it migrated to here.'

Megan looked uncomfortable, moving close to Jane and putting her arm around her. Jane held her and kissed her head.

'Do you have any weapons?' Jane asked them, and they shook their heads.

'Well, I'd suggest you get some fairly soon, just to be on the safe side. We never go anywhere unarmed any more. I can tell you where there's a gun store on the outskirts of Hastings and give you directions. We've taken a lot of weapons from there, but there are still some shotguns left.'

'I suppose that would make sense,' said Matt, 'and they would also be good to have for hunting.'

'What are you doing for food at the moment?' Jane asked.

'The army gave us some tinned and dried food when we left;' replied Matt, 'enough for a few days. And we have a fair stock in the van, too. We were just going out to look now, actually. We've also seen apple and pear trees around here that still have some fruit on and were going to collect some.'

Jane told them about the warehouse at the back of Sainsbury's that still had a lot of food in it, as it wouldn't be fair to keep that knowledge from others who needed food. She also mentioned the other smaller supermarkets nearby where they had broken into the storerooms or warehouses and found more food and drink, as well as Tesco's. They were both very grateful and thanked her.

They carried on talking for a while: Matt had been an electrical and mechanical engineer most of his life and Zoe was a herbalist and had run her own business. They were looking forward to fishing and growing their own vegetables in their new home. Zoe's cousin's house was only half a mile away from the bungalow, in Hartfield Road; the next road along the coast. It had an Aga and a wood-burning stove, a conservatory, and backed onto the beach, as the bungalow did.

Jane said they'd better be going and that it would be nice to meet again soon, once they were settled in. They seemed like a nice couple and their kids were friendly and polite. Jane gave them directions to the gun store and they gave her their address, asking her to come round sometime with Jamie, which she agreed to do. As an afterthought Jane told them that they'd been snaring rabbits on the railway line on-and-off for the last five months and offered them the snares she and Megan had just collected.

'It's a bit hit-and-miss, but we've had a fair number of rabbits from here in that time. You'll need to check them every evening and move them to different locations occasionally. The positions are still marked so you'll know where to set them.'

They were touched and thanked her several times after taking the snares from her. They all shook hands and then Jane and Megan got into the car and drove off. They stopped at the other two locations, removing all the snares and collecting one rabbit from each place. Megan and Jane grinned at each other then headed back to the farm.

When they parked in the yard the left-hand barn's doors had been removed and they could see Jamie and Bill in there working. They got out of the car and Max ran into the barn to see the two men and to be nosey.

'Coffee?' Jane shouted to them and they smiled and nodded.

She and Megan went inside to make drinks. They had decided they would keep the range in the kitchen ticking over during the day for background warmth, and stoke it up in the evenings for cooking and more heat. For small cooking tasks or just for boiling water for drinks they used the wood-gas camping stove and the Kelly Kettle, keeping a supply of small twigs and bits of wood in the kitchen for them. Something Jamie had incorporated into the kitchen was a small canopy, under which these items could be used, so the kitchen didn't fill with smoke. He had taken a small section of flue out through the wall, to which the canopy was attached. There was a baffle in the top that could be slid over to stop draughts when it wasn't in use. It worked well unless it was very windy, when sometimes a bit of smoke blew back into the kitchen.

Jane got the kettle going and when it had boiled she made coffee and took mugs out to the men. They were busy cutting both doors in half to make stable doors, where the top half could be opened independently of the bottom. They stopped working and thanked her for the coffee.

'How did you get on?' Jamie asked.

'Okay,' said Jane, 'we removed all the snares and picked up two rabbits, which was great. We also refilled all the containers at the bungalow- as many as we could fit in the conservatory.'

Jamie told Bill of their intention to keep up the salt production every few weeks over the winter.

'Well, it's a good idea,' said Bill. 'We've all got a good supply but it will run out sometime, and we're always going to need it for preserving and cooking.'

Jane then told them about meeting the Turner family and Major Cunningham sending his regards. 'I couldn't believe it when he said "*Your name wouldn't be Jane Roberts, would it?*"!'

Bill and Jamie laughed and she related the whole meeting to them, which they found interesting, especially that he was an electrical and mechanical engineer and she was a herbalist.

'The more people we know with different skills, the better,' said Jamie, and they both agreed.

Megan came out to join them with a cup of tea and they sat talking for a while before Jamie and Bill got on with their work. Jane said she and Megan would plant the herbs and salads they'd brought with them from the bungalow in what would be their garden behind the house.

First, though, she took the two rabbits over to Emma for the meal that evening. Sarah and Georgie were coming to visit to see their new home and to catch up with them all. Phil and Sophie had been out that morning and shot three pheasants between them, which were prepared and lying on the worktop. Sophie had been practising in recent weeks with one of the smaller 20-bore shotguns they'd picked up from the gun store and was getting on well with it. Jane said she would come over later to help Emma with the meal then she and Megan went back to work in the garden. Sally came round to help and to talk with Megan while they worked.

They hadn't been able to bring the bay tree from the bungalow as it was too big to dig up, but Jane had found two replacements growing in large pots in the garden of a house in their road, which she was pleased about. They removed one from its pot and planted it behind the greenhouses. The other she decided to keep in its pot outside the kitchen, next to their patio table. The five sea beet plants she had brought were planted out, along with the other herbs. The sea beet would be great to have as they produced a large crop of leaves and were perennial.

Sarah and Georgie arrived two hours before sundown, towing the horse cart behind the Land Rover. Bill and Jamie went down to meet them and the women came out of the farmhouse to welcome them. They all exchanged hugs and said how great it was to see each other, then looked at the cart. It was a one-horse model and looked a bit rickety at the moment.

'We had to take it easy on the way here,' said Georgie, laughing, 'as we thought one of the wheels might fall off!'

Bill had a quick look. 'Me and Jamie will soon have it fixed-up like new.'

'Yes,' said Emma, 'and meanwhile I'm still waiting for you to fix the chest of drawers and the wardrobe in our bedroom!'

'Ah,' replied Bill, grinning 'but they're not essential for survival in the post-apocalypse world we're now living in!' He winked at Jamie, who tried not to laugh.

Emma looked at Jane and rolled her eyes, saying 'Men!' and they all laughed.

Sarah and Georgie went to see their newly-converted home and were very impressed, saying what a great job they'd all done and how cosy it was. They then went back to the farmhouse and chatted before the meal. The two sisters had been out on the horses in recent weeks, getting them used to being ridden again and being around people. They had also taken their trailer out on several trips and collected large amounts of hay and straw from the farms they'd visited. They said it would be good if Bill could bring his van over so they could collect more and Bill agreed.

They had to bring in another table to seat all eleven of them for the meal, but they managed to squeeze round. It was a great evening, catching up on everything they'd all been doing and discussing plans for the coming weeks and months. Bill said the stable should be finished in a week or so, and then they could bring the first two horses over from Sarah and Georgie's place.

The next chapter in their lives would soon begin: having horses for transport instead of vehicles. They didn't know for sure when the fuel would start deteriorating, but they were prepared for it. It would be probably the most significant thing to affect every survivor in the country since the plague. Without transport there would be greatly reduced movement and communication of people between regions; to join other groups, meet new people, or to trade goods and skills. Most people's operating circle would be limited to within a few miles of where they lived.

Twenty-nine

The weather started to change as autumn took hold: the temperature dropped, the wind increased and the leaves on the trees turned to beautiful hues of gold and bronze before starting to fall. The area surrounding the farm was dotted with small woods and copses and looked very picturesque. They would all take a day off from their work now and then, and Jamie, Jane and Megan began exploring the countryside around the farm to get to know the area. Megan's wounds and head injury were fully healed by then and her dizzy spells and nausea had stopped. Max always accompanied them and they found new places to lay snares for rabbits.

They always took an Ordnance Survey map with them and Jamie started teaching Megan map-reading skills. He showed her how to use a compass to navigate and how to read the land's topography from the map. Jane, while admitting to be no expert, had a fair knowledge of herbs and plants and would stop now and then to show them a particular plant when they came across one that she knew. It wasn't the best time of year for it, though, as most things were now dying back for the winter. On one such walk they came across a small copse that hadn't been managed for decades at least. Jamie had done some conservation work years before and had learned a bit about woodland management.

'Do you see here, Megan, where the trees all have multiple trunks coming out from the base?' Megan nodded. 'Well, this

253

is called coppicing. It's a way of managing the woodland, both to keep it under control and to provide wood for different uses. It's been done in Britain for thousands of years, but not so much in recent times.' She asked how it was spelled and wrote it in the notebook she carried with her.

'Several deciduous trees were coppiced, such as hazel, ash, sweet chestnut, birch and willow. The tree is cut back to its base at regular intervals, causing lots of new shoots to grow. Those new shoots grow up straight and when the time is right they are cut down and harvested to make fencing, firewood, stakes, tools and many other things. And then the shoots grow again and the whole process is repeated.'

'How long does it take for them to grow back?' Megan asked.

'That depends on the type of tree, and the uses people had for the wood,' he answered. 'It could be a three, five or seven year rotation for some trees, or longer for slower-growing varieties. They would coppice one area per year and then move on to the next place the following year. Eventually they'd develop a cycle where there was wood to be harvested every year. A tree that's coppiced regularly will never die of old age because it's continually regenerating.'

Megan found this interesting and said she would read up on it from the books they had at home. Jamie wondered aloud if it was something they should start doing to provide wood in years to come and Jane agreed.

The work back at the farm had continued and within two weeks of them moving in the stable was finished. They hadn't known how many horses they should cater for, but they had built six stalls in the barn, each with its own gate and water trough. They made several trips to Sarah and Georgie's place to help them gather more hay and straw from the farms near them, which would be shared out between them. There were other farms in the area around Hooe where they found more stocks as well. In early November they made further trips into Bexhill to collect more timber and materials for storing at the farm, visiting all the DIY stores and builders' merchants in the town.

In addition to the equipment the sisters had already got for them, they also visited an equestrian centre not far from the farm, where they picked up other equipment and sundry supplies. There were carcases of several dead horses in the stables there; whether they had died of the plague or of dehydration from being trapped they didn't know. From damage to some of the stalls, though, it looked like some horses had managed to escape, and they found six roaming in the surrounding fields. They went home and returned with a bag of apples and carrots and the horses came to feed from them. Even though they didn't plan to take any back to the farm just yet they wanted the horses to get to know them and get used to being around people again.

In the second week of November they made two trips to Sarah and Georgie's and brought back the two horses and the pony that the sisters had got for them. Once the horses had settled into their new surroundings they took them out for short rides in the fields around the farm. Bill and Emma had ridden often in recent years, and it didn't take long for Jane to get back into the swing of it. Jamie was unsure at first, though, and felt uncomfortable.

'I think I prefer my horsepower to be under the bonnet of a vehicle!' he said one day, and they smiled at him and chuckled.

'Don't worry, mate, you'll soon get the hang of it,' Bill replied.

Jane had to resist laughing at the sight of him sitting there on the horse looking terrified, but was understanding with him. At night, though, when they were alone together, she would tease him playfully about it. The cart was repaired by Bill and Jamie and they trained both horses to pull it, in the yard at first and then on short road trips nearby. Sarah and Georgie came over on several occasions to help out and to check they were doing things correctly.

Jamie, Jane and Megan also became involved in the daily running of the farm and helping to tend to the animals, although that was primarily Phil and Sophie's role. They got to know them a lot better during this time and the young couple would come over in the evenings for a drink and a chat. On their numerous visits during the year, prior to moving there, Phil and Sophie had usually been busy around the farm and they hadn't had the chance to get to know them as well as they would have liked.

In mid-November they drove into Bexhill to collect salt from the bungalow and refill the containers, and then went to visit Matt and Zoe to see how they were settling in. They had made one trip back two weeks before to collect the salt, but hadn't had time to visit them then. The couple were delighted to see them and invited them inside. Jane introduced Jamie to them and they all shook hands.

'I'm sorry we haven't come sooner,' said Jane, 'but we've been really busy with things back at the farm.'

'That's okay,' said Zoe, smiling, 'we understand. We've been pretty busy ourselves as well.'

They went through to the large kitchen, which was lovely and warm from the Aga. Matt made coffee for them while Zoe showed them around and then they sat at the kitchen table chatting. Matt asked them how they were settling in at the farm and they told them what they had been up to, with building the stables and getting the horses. It turned out Matt and Zoe hadn't known about fuel deterioration, and that vehicles might be unusable within a few months.

'Bloody hell!' said Matt. 'I had no idea. That's a real shock to us. How long have you known?'

'We found out at the end of June or early July, I think,' Jamie replied, glancing at Jane for confirmation and she nodded. 'Our friends Sarah and Georgie told us about it, from research their father had done before he died. To be honest, we hadn't thought about it before that, either. We've been planning for it ever since. I must add, though, that this isn't set in stone; there wasn't much in the way of hard data on it, apparently. It's possible that the remaining fuel might last much longer and we may have use of vehicles for another year, but we didn't want to take any chances.'

They told the couple they had been making trips to gather anything they might need for the future while they still had usable vehicles. Matt and Zoe said they should do the same thing as soon as possible, in case they did lose the vehicles. As their motorhome was rather uneconomical, Jane suggested they break into some houses nearby to get the keys to other vehicles they could use, to which they agreed.

The couple had been using the snares Jane had given them, but it had taken several attempts before catching any rabbits. They'd been to Sainsbury's warehouse and some smaller supermarkets and stocked up on provisions, for which they thanked Jane again, and had also visited the gun store near Hastings. They now had three of the smaller 20-bore shotguns and had shot some rabbits, ducks and pigeons with them. They had prepared the garden for planting vegetables and had sown seeds in pots in the conservatory for planting out when they were big enough. They had a water butt outside that collected run-off from the roof, which they were filtering and boiling, much as Jane and Jamie had done. Jamie asked them if they had bikes and they said they did, so he told them about the rack and paniers he had made to carry water for his own bike, but had never got to use.

Matt smiled. 'Great minds think alike! I've built a trailer that fits onto the bike and it can hold a couple of large water containers. I've taken it to Egerton Park to test and it works fine.'

He took Jamie out to the garage to show him and Jamie was impressed and said what a great job he'd made of it. When they got back to the kitchen Luke and Amber came in from walking on the beach. They said hello to the visitors and Luke said they had found a boat on the beach, going back towards town.

'Yes,' said Jamie, 'that's ours. I converted it to a rowing-boat earlier in the year and have been using it for fishing when the weather was good. You're welcome to borrow it when it's calm enough, but it's not the right weather for it now. All we ask is that you put it back in the same place and tie it up securely, with the tarp over the top. We plan to come back to the bungalow for fishing trips in the spring when it's warmer.'

They both thanked them and Matt said he would go to the

fishing tackle shop in Sackville Road soon to stock up on gear. He planned on getting beach-casting rods as well to be able to fish from the beach until the weather became good enough to take the boat out. Megan had brought Max's ball so she and the twins took him outside to play with him.

When they had gone Zoe turned to Jane. 'Would you mind expanding on the troubles you hinted at when we met by the railway, please? I feel the need to know.'

Jane told them everything: being shot and nearly gang-raped by the three thugs, then being saved by Jamie; the two incidents in Battle and Megan's shooting three months earlier. The couple were shocked and horrified by what they heard. Matt said how glad they were to have shotguns now, and both said how pleased they were that Megan was okay.

'Well, I don't think you should get hooked-up on it,' said Jane, 'but just be aware when you're out and about, that's all. You can't take anything for granted now, and make sure you check stores and warehouses before going inside; we always stand outside listening for a minute first. I know we haven't seen any more survivors in Bexhill, but they could come in from other areas. I mean, for all we know, there might still be other people left in the surrounding countryside who could make their way here. I'm not saying they're going to be hostile or dangerous, but they're likely to be wary and on edge, like I was when we met. And… I know it's horrible to think about, but you've got to be prepared to use those guns on people if it comes to it, to protect yourselves.' Zoe and Matt looked mortified at the prospect.

'Jane's right,' said Jamie. 'You mustn't dwell on it, but you've got to be aware of the possibility. Hope for the best, but prepare for the worst. If someone had told me a year ago that I was going to kill four people in the space of five months this year, I'd have said they were crazy! But you do what you have to do when the time comes.'

Jamie looked down and Jane reached over and put her hand on his. It went quiet for a while as the couple thought about what they'd been told. Matt looked at Jamie with fresh eyes; it was hard to imagine this nice, unassuming man having killed four people. Zoe broke the silence and asked them if they would stay for lunch. Knowing the couple weren't set up properly yet and were still living from tinned produce, they thanked them but declined the offer, saying they had things to do, but secretly not wanting to use up their supplies.

They sat and talked for half an hour longer and then called Megan back from the garden. Jane gave them directions to the farm and said they were welcome to visit, or if they needed help with anything. They were appreciative and thanked them both warmly for the visit and for the advice. Jane and Zoe hugged and Matt and Jamie shook hands, saying they hoped to see each other again soon. On the way home they agreed that Zoe and Matt were very nice and they could see the friendship developing over time. They also thought the couple needed to wise-up a bit more about surviving in the world they were now living in!

By the end of November they had collected two more horses from the fields by the equestrian centre and had them settled at the farm. Jamie was getting more confident in the saddle and didn't look terrified every time he mounted a horse, which Jane was pleased about. Megan and Sally were learning to ride the pony and, like most young people, seemed to have no fear about such things and approached it with excitement and enthusiasm. Peter was the same, though he was four years older than Sally and had done some riding before. Phil and Sophie were somewhere in between; they still had some of the exuberance of youth, but also the wariness of slightly older people.

Between the three households at the farm they had been working on the land over the past month, preparing it and sowing winter vegetable crops for the following spring. Jamie, Jane and Megan had settled well into their new home and had got used to having much less space. It seemed cosy to them now and needed far less wood to heat than the bungalow had done.

In the evenings since moving in they had continued with Megan's education, as they thought it was important to do so.

It was a relaxed learning environment and without the constraints of school Megan loved it and became enthusiastic about subjects that she had previously shown little interest in.

Along with the essential subjects of reading, writing and arithmetic, they taught her history, geography and domestic skills such as cooking and sewing, as she would need to be able to repair clothes in future years. As it was relevant to them they told Megan about the original Black Death: a combination of bubonic and pneumonic plagues that had devastated Europe for over four hundred years, on and off. They also told her of the 1918 - 1920 flu pandemic, which had been cited as possibly the most deadly pandemic in recorded human history; killing between fifty and a hundred million people around the world in less than three years. Megan was astonished by this; she was so used to hearing that someone had had "the flu" that she had trouble equating the two things. However, the new variant or mutation of the plague that had happened nearly a year ago made that pandemic seem small by comparison.

There were also lessons, some practical, on subjects that had never appeared on any school curriculum before, to do with survival in the new world. These included setting traps for animals, map-reading, making fire, making water safe to drink, identifying edible plants, how to strip down a shotgun or rifle, and other useful things that she was going to need to know in the years ahead. She seemed to absorb it all like a sponge and they made it a fun process. Once a week they had a quiz night to test her on things she had learned that week, with different treats on offer as prizes. Sometimes they would be food or drink prizes and other times they would be things she wanted to do.

One morning in the last days of November, Jamie, Bill and Jane were in the top yard by the stable when they heard a vehicle approaching in low gear on the rough track up to the farm. From their slightly elevated position they could see almost to the road, apart from the last fifty yards that were beyond a bend in the treeline. An army Land Rover appeared round the bend, bumping through the pot-holes. As a precaution Jamie went back to the house, coming out with his sawn-off over his shoulder and a handful of cartridges, which he put in his pocket, then the three of them walked down to the main yard to meet it. They stood by the small lawn in front of the mobile home waiting, and as the truck entered the yard Jamie and Jane recognised the occupants.

'It's Major Cunningham; he's the doctor who treated Megan,' said Jane for Bill's benefit. 'And that's the nurse we met when we picked her up on the Sunday.'

The vehicle stopped and Cunningham and the woman got out and walked over to them, smiling. 'Hello Jane, hello Jamie. Nice to see you again. This is Lieutenant Karen Chambers.'

The Lieutenant was in her late thirties and pretty, with short blonde hair and dimples in her cheeks when she smiled.

'Hello, Major,' said Jane, 'and hello Lieutenant; nice to see you, too. This is Bill Anderson, who owns the farm.'

They all exchanged greetings and shook hands.

'How is Megan doing?' Cunningham asked.

'She's doing very well, thank you, Major,' said Jamie, 'and she's fully recovered- thanks to you!'

Cunningham smiled, as did the Lieutenant. 'I'm very pleased to hear it; that's great news.'

He removed his glasses, ran his hand through his hair and then put the glasses back on. 'Well, the reason we're here is to have a chat with you, if we may. I'll explain more in detail if you have time, but to cut a long story short the camp at Tunbridge Wells is closing in two weeks' time and the unit is disbanding. We'll no longer be army and Karen and I are looking for a place to settle in this area. When it happens we wondered if we might stay with you for a short while until we can sort something out.'

Thirty

'Well,' said Bill, 'why don't we all go into the house and sit down, rather than standing out here in the cold?' They all agreed and crossed the yard to the house. Emma was in the kitchen and introductions were made.

'Hello Major, Lieutenant; it's nice to meet you,' said Emma.

'Please, just call us Tom and Karen,' said Cunningham.

Emma offered to make tea for everyone and then Megan came in with Sally, followed by Phil, Peter and Sophie.

'Well, hello Megan!' said Karen. Megan smiled, went over and hugged her.

'Hi Karen, hi Doctor Cunningham. It's nice to see you again.'

'Hello Megan,' said Tom. 'Wow! You look well, and much better than the last time we saw you. You've filled out, too.'

Megan smiled. 'Mum and Dad said I needed fattening up!' She turned to Jane. 'Mum; Karen was the first person I saw when I woke up and she was really lovely.' Karen smiled and Jane nodded her appreciation to her.

Bill introduced them to Sally, Peter, Phil and Sophie, who all smiled and said hello. Tom asked how they were getting on and they chatted for a while about their accomplishments before Jamie asked what they all wanted to know.

'So, Tom, you say the camp's closing down?'

'Yes. We've given it a lot of thought, but basically we've

done all we can under the circumstances and there's not much left we can do. Food, fuel and medical supplies are almost gone and we've used up the resources from the surrounding area. We've treated and fed around three hundred people since May and got them back to a decent state of health. Obviously, they weren't all there at the same time as we couldn't have coped, with only around sixty personnel. But people have come and gone as they got better and then drifted off to make new lives for themselves- or try to, at least. If I'm honest, I don't hold out much hope for some of them, but hope I'm proved wrong.

No one has ever been faced with these circumstances before, but that's out of our hands. We're army and medical staff; we can't teach them how to grow food or to become self-sufficient, though we gave lectures on a few basic things like making water safe to drink. Many people have made their way down to the coastal areas in Kent and Sussex and we've transported some, as we could. Some of them were from those areas anyway and have gone back to their homes as they recovered their health. My biggest hope is that survivors will form communities to help each other.

There are only a couple of dozen people left at the camp now and they've all been informed about what's happening. The number of survivors on the roads south-east of London has dwindled almost to nothing in recent months. People just don't seem to be moving around any more, especially as we're going into winter. We've got people on checkpoints standing around all day doing nothing and personnel are getting restless to start making new lives for themselves.

The army is finished, really, and there's certainly no future in it for anyone. I mean, it was a career for most people and a way of life. There's no hierarchy or infrastructure left and no one's been in charge overall since the plague happened. What was left of companies like ours have been operating pretty much autonomously since then, making their own decisions and just doing what they could to help people and what they thought was right; sometimes under the command of Majors like Miller and myself, but often under lower-ranking officers, or even NCOs. Once the fuel is gone or becomes unusable we'll have no generators, and therefore no communications or other equipment. As equipment breaks down we haven't the spares or the personnel to fix it, and no chance of being re-supplied. An army can't function without re-supply of essentials like water, food, fuel and spares, whether it's performing an offensive or a humanitarian role.'

Tom paused and sighed. He took off his glasses and wiped them on his shirt before putting them back on. 'All the troops and personnel have done fantastic work since the plague. We couldn't have asked more of them, but we all knew there was no future for us, long-term.'

He gave a wry laugh. 'Possibly for the first time in military history we had a democratic vote about what to do! Usually, soldiers are given orders and they just follow them, but these are dire circumstances that have never happened before. People voted overwhelmingly for us to disband, so that's what we're doing. Everyone wants a chance to start a new life. I daresay most of them will team up to form groups and find places to live together; camaraderie has always been a big part of army life. Some are talking about going back to live at the barracks in Kent. Ultimately, though, it all comes down to food; everyone is going to have to start growing things, or they won't survive.

Karen and I have no family left since the plague and our home has been the army for many years, serving either here or abroad. My immediate family were all up in the Midlands and Karen's were in Cumbria. We both had large savings in the bank to buy a property in later years, but that's irrelevant now. We want to settle in this area and we'd like to be fairly close to you folks, if possible. I liked you two from the outset, when I came to your place to examine Megan. You've got guts and determination and you seem to have your heads screwed on right. We both did basic survival courses, but that was years ago and neither of us really know anything about growing food, farming or trapping, so we were hoping to learn from you folks if you'd be willing. We wondered if you knew of any properties that might be suitable nearby that we could take over?'

'Well, there's the Simpson's place, isn't there, Bill?' said Emma.

'Yes, that would be probably the most suitable place around here that's close to us. It's about half a mile away, on the edge of the village. It's a decent house with a good plot of land and it backs onto fields. It's got a couple of out-buildings, a covered storage area out back that's useful and it has log-burners and open fires for heating and cooking. Water will be your main problem. There may be water butts that collect run-off from the roof; I can't remember. If not, you'll have to install some. Other than that there are a few lakes within half a mile. The other option would be to dig a well, which would be difficult but not impossible. The Simpsons died in there, so you'd have to clear their remains and clean the place, but I'm sure that wouldn't be a problem for you.'

'And we'd be more than willing to help you out with things,' said Jamie, and Jane agreed. 'I mean, it's not like we're experts, or anything,' he added, 'but we've done okay so far, for the most part. Bill and Emma have far more knowledge and experience in self-sufficiency and farming than we do.'

Karen and Tom thanked them and said how grateful they were. Emma asked Jane to help her and they served slices of cake and pie for everyone to have with their drinks.

'You're welcome to stay here for a few days when the time comes,' said Bill, 'until you can move into the place, if you think it's suitable.'

'That's very good of you, Bill, thank you,' said Karen. 'We've got a tent we can pitch in a field somewhere.'

'Nonsense!' said Emma. 'You'll stay here in the house. We've got a spare bedroom you can use. It's the least we can do after what you did for our Megan.'

She put her arm around Megan, who looked up at her and smiled. Karen and Tom were moved by their hospitality and thanked them again.

'By the way,' said Jane, 'we met the Turners after they left the camp and came to Bexhill last month, and they passed on your message, thank you. We went round to see them a couple of weeks ago and they're getting organised. I think they'll do okay.' Tom said he was pleased to hear it.

After they'd finished their drinks and cake Tom said they'd better be getting back to the camp as there was much to do. Bill asked if they wanted to see the Simpson's house before they went.

'No, that's okay thanks, Bill,' said Tom. 'We'll take your word for it and I'm sure it will be okay. We'll have a look in a couple of weeks when we leave the camp and come here.'

They all went outside to see the visitors off. Everyone shook hands and Tom and Karen thanked them again. Just before driving off Tom said 'It's funny, you know; over the last eighteen years I've served in many war-zones around the world, and I never had to worry about where my next meal was coming from. But now...?' He smiled and drove off, waving.

They went back into the house and chatted for a while about the implications of the camp closing and of Tom and Karen coming to live nearby.

'Well it will certainly be handy having a doctor and a nurse in the neighbourhood, especially with your impending birth' said Bill.

'Yes it will,' said Jane, 'but I'm not sure how much they'll be able to do in the future without drugs and medical supplies, apart from diagnosing or advising on the treatment of some injuries and suchlike. I wonder if, when they come here, we should visit all the pharmacies in the area, and maybe the hospital, to see what we can find. Tom and Karen will be able to determine which things might still be usable for another year or more.'

'Good idea,' said Emma. 'It's also possible, though, that with most of the population gone a lot of common ailments like colds, coughs and other viruses will stop because there aren't the people to breed the germs and pass them around.'

'That's a good point, Emma, and quite possible,' said Jamie.

'I think it will pay us to get to know Matt and Zoe much better,' said Jane. 'I mean, I'd like to anyway as they're a nice

266

couple, but Zoe's a herbalist and we're going to need to know about such things in years to come. Humans all around the world have been using medicinal herbs and plants to treat common ailments and illnesses for thousands of years.'

'That's true,' said Bill. 'Why don't you go to see them and invite them here for a meal one day soon? I'd like to meet them and I'm sure there will be skills and knowledge we can share in the future that will benefit all of us.' Jamie said they would do that.

'Maybe in the spring or summer, when everything's growing, she can come out with us to help identify herbs and plants in the area that will be useful,' said Jane. 'We can harvest them when they're ready and take them to her for turning into remedies or tinctures, or whatever it is she does with them, and in time maybe we can learn to make our own as well.'

They all agreed that would be a good thing to do. Jamie told Bill about his idea to start coppicing the area again. 'We're certainly going to need wood in the future for fencing, hedge repairs and fuel, etc., and the sooner we begin managing the surrounding woodland, the better.'

'I agree, mate' said Bill. 'The same thing occurred to me earlier in the year, but that was before we met you and I kind of forgot about it. We'll need to repair the hedges bordering our fields fairly soon as they haven't been tended to for a few years now. The woods around here haven't been coppiced for at least thirty years, since my dad's day. I've got three of his old billhooks in the tool shed, though they'll want cleaning up and sharpening before they're usable, I suppose.'

Peter said 'Let me know when you're going to make a start, will you? I'd like to come, too.'

'Of course, Pete,' said Jamie, 'we're going to need a few of us, anyway.'

'That's great. It's something I've wanted to do for a couple of years. I was looking into doing some courses on countryside management before the plague came and ruined everything! I'll look forward to it, cheers.'

'I'll tell you what you could do in preparation, Pete;' said Bill, 'you could clean the rust off your granddad's billhooks and sharpen them up.'

'Okay, Dad, I'll get onto it,' replied Peter, smiling.

Jamie, Megan and Jane left, saying they'd see them later. Megan called to Max, who got up from his warm spot in front of the range, stretched, and followed them back to their place. Jane went into the kitchen to make lunch, while Jamie and Megan sat on the sofa and Max curled up in his new bed by the stove.

'What's a billhook, Dad?' asked Megan.

'It's a tool used in hedge-laying and forestry work, honey, and for making hurdles; like a heavy curved knife. They've been used for hundreds of years and there are several different types from different counties around the country. After lunch I'll get mine to show you- it's probably easier than describing it to you.'

'When you say hurdles, do you mean like in athletics?'

'No, sweetheart, though I think that's where the name and the sport originated. A hurdle is a fence panel, made from interwoven young branches that have been got from coppicing, as they're long, straight and pliable. A billhook is used to split the branches down the middle to make them easier to weave through the uprights horizontally.'

He picked up a pencil and paper and drew a diagram to explain it to her. It made a lot more sense to her after seeing the picture he'd drawn. 'It's been a bit of a dying craft for many generations now, sadly. I've never made hurdles, though I've done some hedge-laying and coppicing.'

After lunch Jamie went next door to find his billhook and took it back to show Megan, along with the cigar-shaped sharpening stone used with it. It had a wooden handle with a heavy steel curved blade like a hook and was around twelve inches long. Jamie showed her how to sharpen it outside with the cigar-stone and she tried it for herself.

'I used to love going out for walks in the woods with my parents,' said Megan, 'though neither of them really had an interest in it the way you and Mum do.'

She looked down and fell silent as she thought of them, and Jamie put his arm around her and kissed her head. She looked up at him with a wistful smile and hugged him. When they went back inside Jane was sitting on the sofa with her hands on her belly.

She smiled at Megan. 'Honey, come and feel this; the baby's started moving around and kicking.' Megan sat next to Jane and put her hand on her stomach, concentrating. After a minute the baby kicked and Megan jumped slightly, looking at Jane and smiling. 'Oh wow, Mum! That's amazing. It must feel so weird! I can't imagine what it must feel like to have something growing inside you and to feel it move like that.'

Jane smiled at her. 'Well, hopefully you'll experience it someday as well.' Megan gave a little smile and blushed, mumbling something that Jane couldn't catch, and then she hugged her and went quiet. Jane grinned and stroked her hair.

They needed to check the new rabbit snares and Jamie said he'd go out with Max. Megan jumped up, saying she'd go with him, so Jamie got a bag and took a shotgun from the rack on the wall, along with extra cartridges. Max got up, wagging his tail and eager as ever. They kissed Jane and left, heading out across the field to the rear. They walked along the hedgerow to their right, staying to the edge of the field and keeping their eyes out for pheasant as they walked.

'Dad?'

'Yes, honey?'

'When did you first realise you loved Mum, and how did you know?'

'Ooh, blimey! I don't know, sweetheart; it just kind of happened as we were, sort of, thrown together by circumstances. We were both scared and lonely and realised we needed each other. I mean, we got on well from the start, but I don't recall there being a definite moment when I suddenly felt I loved her. We kind of just grew into it and our feelings got stronger over time.

If we'd met before all this had happened I don't even know if we would have got together, if I'm honest; maybe, maybe not. But we saw things in each other- qualities, I mean- that we probably wouldn't have seen in normal life before the plague. Most people never got the chance to show their true colours: who they really were and what they were capable of. I don't think I ever did. Since the plague, we've had to do things that we'd never have done before. Relationships of all kinds have been magnified because of our circumstances, and because we realise how precious life is and how important people are in our lives. D'you know what I mean?'

'Yes; I get what you're saying and it makes sense, I guess.

It's just that...' She got slightly embarrassed and mumbled a bit. 'Well... Mum, like, got me thinking with what she said about me hopefully having a baby one day... and I wondered if I'll ever meet someone and fall in love...'

Jamie smiled and looked lovingly at her. 'Well, I certainly hope so, honey.'

Twenty feet ahead, Max stopped suddenly at a gap in the hedge and went stiff as a board, looking into the next field. Megan pointed to him and Jamie took the shotgun off his shoulder. They both crouched and moved quietly up to where Max was standing. Jamie peered through the gap and saw two pheasants within a couple of feet of each other, about thirty yards out. Megan stroked Max and whispered 'Good boy, Max!' Jamie kneeled down and brought the gun to his shoulder.

'If I'm lucky I should get them both with one barrel.'

He took careful aim and fired. Both birds dropped together and Max raced off to fetch them. Jamie and Megan looked at each other, smiling, and then gave each other a high five. When Max brought the second bird back Megan gave him a couple of treats and patted him. They carried on to where the new snares were and found one rabbit, which pleased them, and then turned round and headed for home.

Later that night, when Megan was asleep, they were sitting on the sofa talking quietly. Jane was stretched out, leaning back against him and he was stroking her hair.

'Megan asked me something when we were out this afternoon that made me think,' said Jamie.

'What was that, hon?'

'Well, she asked me when I first realised that I loved you, and how I knew.'

Jane smiled. 'And what did you tell her?'

'I said I didn't know; that there wasn't really a definite moment as far as I could remember. We didn't date over a period of months, or have time apart to miss each other's company, like people used to before the plague; we've just always been together... I just came to love you the more I got to know you and saw what great qualities you had; your strength, determination and resourcefulness. The thing I thought of this afternoon, though, was that I don't know if I've ever actually told you I love you in those words. Everything's happened so quickly and it's been so full-on this year...'

'Oh, Jamie, that doesn't matter, honey! I know you love me and I've always known. It shows in everything you do and say.'

'But I do love you, Jane; more than anything. I just wanted to tell you that.'

Jane turned round and kissed him, stroking his face and thick beard.

'And I love you, too. I think I was already falling in love with you the first week we met. You treated me like an equal and there was never any macho bullshit about you.'

She smiled at him. 'Come on, Mr Romantic, let's go to bed.'

Thirty-one

By early December they were feeling quite settled living at the farm. A routine had been established, of sorts, and there was always work to be done on a daily basis. Self-sufficiency- and, therefore, survival- was pretty much a full-time practice. When they'd left the bungalow to live at the farm they hadn't been sure how it was going to work, but things had soon sorted themselves out. There were now new rabbit snares to check every day, horses to be looked after, other farm animals to tend to, work to be done on the land, maintenance of the infrastructure, and work on the ground behind their building to make a garden.

Since they had been working daily around the farm and contributing to its upkeep they had received a regular share of eggs, milk, butter and cheese that Emma produced, and sometimes a chicken. The eggs and dairy products were welcome additions to their diet, which they'd really missed when they'd been at the bungalow.

Their overall happiness increased greatly: they had been isolated in Bexhill, but now felt part of a small community, working together towards something. As a family unit their mutual love and respect deepened every day. The change in Megan was astonishing and so heart-warming for them to see. When they'd met her she had been a scared and somewhat introverted girl who had suffered greatly from what she had been through, but now she was maturing quickly and blossoming into a young woman. Her confidence had increased dramatically since her recovery from the shooting and she seemed to look at the world through new eyes. She was keen to learn everything they could teach her, whether it was practical things around the farm or her schooling in the evenings. She and Sally had become firm friends and spent a lot of time together.

During the first week of December they began coppicing; Jamie, Peter, Phil and Sophie went out several times to the nearest copse to work on it. Bill said he had too much work to do at the farm, but Jamie suspected that he didn't like the idea of leaving the women and girls on their own and unguarded, though he didn't say anything to him.

Jamie gave them a short talk on tool safety first and how to use them properly. Their main tools were a bow saw, a pair of loppers and a billhook and, like any tools, there was a right and a wrong way to use them. He showed them how to cut the trunks down to the stool, how to minimise the chance of infection to the tree by angling the cuts to shed water, and then how to sned the branches with the billhook or loppers. Snedding was a very old word, meaning to trim the smaller outer branches and leaves from the main trunk, leaving it smooth.

They made piles of all the brash- the discarded small branches and leaves- which would become home to numerous different creatures in time, and at the end of each day they brought a horse with the cart to take the logs back for storage and seasoning. The younger folks enjoyed it and easily out-paced Jamie, sometimes teasing him playfully by saying things like "You're getting old, Jamie!", or "Come on Jamie- no time for slacking!" Jamie just laughed and smiled with them. Peter, in particular, had a great time. He was as tall as his dad, but much leaner and looked quite studious, though he proved adept with the tools and made the work look easy. They didn't coppice every tree but thinned them out a lot, which would let in more sunlight and encourage wild flowers to grow as a result.

Back at the farm, Jane and Megan worked on the garden

area behind their place, digging over the soil and making beds for planting. They sowed onions, garlic, potatoes and several other vegetables in preparation for spring, and as they worked they chatted constantly about various things. One day near the end of the week, they stopped for a coffee in mid-morning and Jane noticed that Megan was looking thoughtful.

'Mum?' she said after a while.

'Yes, honey?'

'Would you mind telling me about your sisters? I was wondering what it was like for you as I always wanted a sister, but my mum and dad couldn't have any more children after I was born, for some reason. I think they explained it to me when I was younger, but I can't remember why now. I had some cousins that we saw often, but they were all spoilt brats and I never got on with them!'

'Of course I don't mind, sweetheart- you know you can always ask me anything.'

Jane told her about Debs and Kate; about their relationship, how close they had been and the fun they'd had together, both as children and as adults. Jane had been the middle sister and had loved them both dearly, and after a while she got upset and started crying.

Megan looked distraught and hugged her. 'Oh, Mum, I'm so sorry. I didn't mean to upset you.'

Jane smiled at her through the tears. 'Megan, honey, don't be silly; you didn't upset me. It's only natural for you to ask and it's nice for me to talk about them, even though it hurts. It's all part of the grieving process and we mustn't bottle these things up inside us. I think of them every day, but I haven't talked about them for a while and it's nice to do so.'

Megan felt better at that and when they went back outside to continue working she spoke in depth about her parents for the first time, which pleased Jane. 'I know they loved each other,' she said at one point, 'but they were always bickering about things. I never see you and Dad bickering.'

'Well, maybe they had some money problems, sweetheart, or troubles at work. You must understand, Megan, that before the plague everyone had to go to work- often in jobs they

274

didn't like- to earn enough money to live on, and to pay the mortgage or rent and all the bills. That could be very stressful for lots of people, Dad and I included. It's different for us now, compared to how things were back then. Since the plague we've been free of all that; we haven't had to earn money just to be able to live. We live now by our own devices. You're never going to experience having to get a job to earn enough money to live- and thank God for that! If Jamie and I had been together before the plague, you may well have seen us bickering about things, too!

I know we've had plenty of stresses and problems since the plague: learning what to do to survive, and when our vegetables haven't grown properly or have been lost due to disease or pests, and when we've gone a bit hungry because we didn't get any rabbits or fish, or had to make special trips just to get water, etc., but it's a different sort of stress. Before, we were at the mercy of money, employers, the government, taxes, insurance, and all manner of other stressful things that dictated our lives. Now, we're just at the mercy of nature and our own resourcefulness, and that makes a big difference. Do you see what I'm saying?'

Megan thought for a while before answering. 'I think so, yes. It's kind of hard because I'm only twelve and I've never had to earn money- apart from doing chores for my pocket-money- but I see the difference and think I understand what you mean.'

'You know, in many ways- apart from all the deaths and losing loved-ones, I mean- I've never felt so alive or so fulfilled before, and Jamie said something similar to me before we met you.'

The following Monday they had a visit from Sarah and Georgie, who rode into the yard on their horses. They hadn't seen them for three weeks so it was a lovely surprise. After taking the horses up to the stable they all went into the farmhouse.

'We had a lovely ride over,' said Georgie. 'We came partly by road, but mainly across country as we wanted to see what it was like. I took a bearing on the map from our place to here and just followed the compass; it's almost due west and wasn't difficult. There were a few awkward places with hedges and ditches, but it wasn't too bad and we enjoyed it. I think the horses did, too!'

They sat at the kitchen table and had a good talk about what they'd all been up to since they last saw each other. The sisters were pleased that Jamie, Jane and Megan had settled well into their place and that they were all getting on okay with the horses.

'Oh, we bumped into your friends Matt and Zoe and the twins last week,' said Sarah. 'We'd gone to the retail park for some things and they were there, too. We said hello and got talking and then found out that you knew each other.' She chuckled; 'I nearly said "small world", but then, of course, it *is* a small world now! We invited them back to our place for a drink and a snack and had a lovely talk for a couple of hours. They're a nice couple and they seem to be getting things organised for themselves. We said we'd be coming to see you today; they send their regards and said they'll come over on Wednesday for a visit. Matt said he had a surprise for you, but he didn't elaborate on what it was.'

Emma asked them to stay for lunch, which they accepted gratefully, and they sat talking for a few hours. They were surprised to hear about the refugee camp closing and the army disbanding, but said they could understand it under the circumstances and were pleased that Tom and Karen would be coming to live close by.

'It must be a bit of a relief to you, Jane, that there'll be a doctor and a nurse nearby for when you give birth!' said Georgie.

'Oh, blimey, you're right, there!' she replied, and everyone laughed.

'Something else that Georgie and I were talking about recently:' said Sarah, 'how would you like to keep bees and have your own honey? We've still got a few hives left in the barn that never got sold and we can set everything up for you in the spring.' The others looked at each other and, without needing to confer, they all nodded enthusiastically and said thank you. Having their own honey in the future when all the stocks of sugar had been used up would be a real boon.

It came time for the sisters to leave so Jamie went up to the stable and brought their horses down to the yard for them. They all kissed and hugged, saying they would see each other soon, and as the sisters rode off down the track in their Barbours, shotguns slung over their shoulders, Jane grinned and turned to Jamie.

'The Sussex hunting set!' she said, and Jamie laughed out loud. The others, of course, didn't get the joke and Jamie had to explain.

'Earlier in the year, before we met Sarah and Georgie, we went to get some new clothes from a shop in Battle. Jane was posing with her shotgun in a Barbour jacket and hat and asked me if she'd fit in with the Sussex hunting set. I said something like "Right now, we probably *are* the Sussex hunting set!"' Everyone laughed and then they dispersed to get on with their work around the farm.

On the Wednesday, as promised, Matt and Zoe arrived in mid-morning. Jane heard the vehicle on the track from the top yard and got the binoculars to see who it was as she didn't recognise the car. She saw it was them and went to tell Jamie then they walked down to the bottom yard to meet them. They pulled up in the yard in an ancient Mercedes estate that must have been forty years old. They all exchanged greetings and said how nice it was to see each other.

Jamie looked at the car and smiled at Matt. 'I see you got yourself another vehicle, then? Couldn't you find anything newer than that?'

Matt smiled. 'I'll tell you what, Jamie; when the fuel does deteriorate, I bet this old thing will still be going long after that BMW of yours has kicked the bucket! These Merc' diesel engines can run on really poor quality fuel- they were designed that way for use in all sorts of environments. After you told us about the fuel situation I kept my eyes open as we were driving around the town and spotted this on someone's drive.' He gave a wry smile; 'Of course, I knocked on the door to see if the owner wanted to sell it, but there was no answer! As it was on the drive and in such good condition I knew the owner must have used it regularly, so I broke in, found the keys and then jump-started it from the motorhome.'

Jamie smiled. 'Good for you, and good luck with it!'

They all went over to the farmhouse and Jane introduced them to Bill, Emma and Sally, who greeted them warmly.

'Our son, Peter, and Phil and Sophie who live here, are around somewhere,' said Bill. 'You'll meet them soon, too.'

They went into the kitchen and Zoe gave Emma a couple of bags, containing two good-sized fish, a pheasant and a bottle of wine. Emma smiled and thanked her.

'We haven't had fish for a while, so these will be most welcome.'

'You haven't been out in the boat in this weather, have you?' asked Jamie.

Matt laughed. 'No chance, mate! I got some beach-casting gear from the tackle shop in Sackville a few weeks back. I went down yesterday and caught these using some worms I dug up from the beach.'

'Ah, well done. I'd intended to try that myself but didn't get around to it before we left.'

They sat down at the table while Emma and Jane got drinks for everyone. Max was moving amongst the newcomers, wagging his tail and getting lots of attention. Megan and Sally said they would take Luke and Amber for a look around the farm so they went off, with Max in hot pursuit.

'It was nice that you met Sarah and Georgie,' said Jane. 'They came round on Monday and told us about it.'

'Yes,' said Zoe, 'that was a nice surprise. They're a great couple, aren't they? And their place is really cool. Sarah, in particular, reminds me of Katharine Hepburn.'

'Yes!' said Jamie. 'That's who it is! She- well, both of them, actually- always looked familiar, but I could never pin down who it was they reminded me of. Ha ha!'

They all laughed and agreed with Zoe and Jamie, then talked about what they'd been up to in recent weeks. Zoe said she'd identified the sea beet growing on and near the beach, and that they'd been eating it regularly. 'It's great, isn't it?' said Jane. 'We brought several plants with us and have planted them out the back. Apparently, they'll grow well in normal soil or in pots, too, and not just by the sea. They're obviously a tough plant.'

Zoe agreed with her and the conversation turned to other plants and herbs. She liked Jane's idea of going out with them in the spring and summer to identify medicinal herbs and became very animated.

'I love it down here; it's fab! This area is so abundant with different varieties of herbs and other plants that we can use, both for medicinal and culinary purposes. It's a herbalist's dream, really. There are lots more things we can eat than you might know about. Sussex was well-populated by Neolithic Man for good reason! There are several different habitats within a relatively small geographical area; from deciduous woodland, to chalk downs, to marshland like the Pevensey Levels, and down to the coastal areas. I've already been out a few times on my bike, out past the golf club, and identified many species that we didn't have around Potters Bar. Between us we can identify and gather lots of beneficial plants that will help us in the years to come.'

It was nice to see Zoe so enthusiastic and they all agreed it would be great to learn more from her about the plants around them. Peter, Phil and Sophie came in for lunch, followed by Megan, Sally and the twins, and were introduced to Matt and Zoe before they sat down to eat. After lunch Matt said he had a surprise for them. He went out to the car and came back with a large cardboard box, which he put on the table and then removed a few items of equipment.

'CB radios: I've had them since about February, but haven't had a use for them until now. I brought them down with us as I knew they'd be useful. When the plague really began spreading I thought we'd need some form of communication system to keep in touch with people if the utilities went down. I went to several places and picked up lots of equipment, and I've been working on them over the last few weeks. I've got five sets and I've rigged them up to operate with a car battery and a solar panel to trickle-charge the batteries.'

'Bloody hell, Matt, that's brilliant!' said Jamie.

'Thanks,' Matt replied, 'but they will have their limitations, of course. I mean, we won't be able to just leave them turned on all day and speak when we want to, as the solar panels won't supply enough current. But, if we put the solar panels in a south-facing position to constantly trickle-charge the batteries then we can arrange pre-set times to turn on the sets so we can talk. They'll be great for arranging visits and trips or exchanging news, but they won't be any good for emergencies as we won't be able to leave them on permanently.'

'We'll be able to leave ours on permanently,' said Bill, 'as we have mains power. The barn roof's covered in solar panels, which charge up the batteries and supply mains through an inverter. Emma's in the house most of the time, so she'll be able to hear any messages.'

'Well, that's great,' said Matt. 'You can leave yours on all the time, then. It won't create much drain on your system and it means that we'll be able to contact you any time we need to. If you need to contact us, though, we'll have to have pre-arranged times. Sarah and Georgie can have a set, too, so we can all keep in touch. I can set the rig and antenna up this afternoon.'

This was great news and they all thanked Matt. It would add a whole new dimension to their lives from now on: being able to talk, exchange news and arrange visits between them all would be a real blessing.

'Blimey!' said Jane. 'Who'd have thought that in the twenty-first century, in the age of GPS, smart phones and the internet, we'd be communicating by CB radio again!'

Thirty-two

The following Thursday, just after lunch, Jamie heard two vehicles coming up the track and went to look. Two army Land Rovers were bouncing through the pot-holes, the second of which was towing a large water bowser. He called to Jane in the garden and they walked down to the main yard to meet them. Megan had gone over the fields with Sally to check the rabbit snares. Bill also heard the vehicles and met them in the yard.

Tom and Karen got out of the first Land Rover and came over to shake hands with them, smiling. As the second vehicle pulled up they saw it was Major Miller and a woman they hadn't seen before, and they climbed from the truck and walked over to them. The woman, like the others, was in uniform: she was in her mid-to-late thirties, with olive skin and high cheek-bones, and was strikingly attractive but very tough-looking, with short cropped hair.

'Hello, Major Miller,' said Jamie, extending his hand. 'Nice to see you again.' Jane said the same and they all shook hands.

'Hello Jamie, hello Jane. Nice to see you, too. And please, call me Harry. This is former Warrant Officer Maria Vasquez.'

She smiled, shaking their hands, and her face softened, completely changing her appearance. 'Hi; I've heard a lot about you from Tom and Harry and it's nice to meet you.' There was a slight trace of a Spanish accent in her voice.

'This is Bill Anderson, who owns the farm,' said Jane, and

they exchanged greetings and shook hands.

'Shall we go into the house?' said Bill. They all agreed and followed him into the farmhouse. Emma smiled at them as they entered and introductions were made, and Bill invited them to sit at the table while Emma put on a large kettle for drinks.

'Tom told me the awful news months ago about what happened to Megan,' said Harry, 'and I'm so pleased to hear she's made a full recovery.' Jamie and Jane smiled and thanked him

'So, how did it go with the closing of the camp?' asked Bill.

'Oh, it went fairly smoothly, under the circumstances,' said Harry. 'The remaining survivors left over the last week. Some of them had developed close bonds and a group of four families said they were going to settle together by the countryside on the edge of Bexhill, near Cooden. Two of the families were from that area anyway and the other two were refugees from London. We got their vehicles going for them and gave them what fuel and food we could spare to get them on their way.'

'What about the other troops and medical staff?' asked Jane.

'Well, some wanted to see if any of their families had survived in various parts of the country so they headed off in all directions. The majority, though, knew their families were gone. A large contingent has gone to take over Scotney Castle; the National Trust place near Lamberhurst. There's a big manor house there with extensive grounds and a moat, with plenty of room for them to farm the land. Some of the troops are coming down to this neck of the woods: when they heard that we were coming down here they decided they would, too. They're going to look for suitable places close to each other where they can help each other out, or maybe form a small commune.'

'Oh, so you're coming to live here, too?' asked Bill.

'Yes,' Harry replied. 'Tom and I have served together for many years and we thought we'd stay together.'

'The four of us are going to live together in the house

down the road,' said Tom. 'Obviously, we can't all impose on you, so we're going to get the house cleared and cleaned this afternoon and move straight in. We've got plenty of stuff with us in the vehicles for disposing of the remains- tarps, body-bags, strong disinfectant, etc. Mindful of what you said about water, we brought one of the water bowsers with us and filled it up from a lake on the way here, so we've got 220 gallons to keep us going for now. We thought we'd dig a well somewhere out the back over the next few weeks.'

'I shot a couple of pheasant on the way down so we'd have fresh food for tonight,' said Maria, 'and we also raided Tesco's warehouse at the retail park and stocked up on provisions for quite a while.'

'Well, why don't you bring the pheasant here and have a meal with us after you've finished at the house?' said Emma, which they said would be great and thanked her.

'As the Commanding Officer,' said Harry, smiling, 'I had first dibs on what we took with us from the camp. We've got an L85A2 rifle each, two shotguns and our service pistols, plus a good stock of ammunition. We've got some medical supplies, a comprehensive tool kit and also two VHF radios with solar panel chargers, along with various other useful bits of kit.'

'Can the radios operate on CB frequencies?' asked Jamie.

'Yes, they can. You can set whatever frequency you like.'

'That's handy,' said Bill, 'as we now have a CB radio here, so we'll be able to talk on them. Matt Turner set it up for us last week, and also for our friends Sarah and Georgie a few miles away, so we can all keep in touch.'

They all agreed that this was great and would be very useful in the future. They talked for a while more, before Harry said they'd better make a move and get the house cleaned. Bill said he would go with them to show them where it was. They said goodbye and that they would see them later when they'd finished.

Bill got into the Land Rover with Tom and Karen and, back on the road, directed them towards the village and pointed out the house. They pulled into the gated entrance and parked by the side of the house, then got out and walked around the property, ending up at the back. They saw that there were, indeed, two large water butts at the rear corners of the house, collecting run-off from the roof.

'Well, that's good news,' said Karen, 'and one less job for us to do!' The others agreed with her. They all commented that the house and grounds looked good from the outside, and that the out-buildings would be useful. Maria tried the back door and it was open.

'If you don't mind,' said Bill, 'I won't come in with you. I've seen my share of bodies this year, but they were friends and I'd rather not see them like that. I'll walk back to the farm and you can come over when you're ready. If there's anything you need give us a shout.'

They thanked him, saying they would see him later. Karen gave Bill the bag with the pheasants to cook for them later and he headed back to the farm.

It was dark by around four p.m. and the four of them arrived at the farm just after six, having walked there with torches. Bill invited them inside and ushered them through to the kitchen, where introductions were made to those who hadn't yet met. The younger folks went and sat in the conservatory.

Maria had a British Army combat shotgun slung over her shoulder and Harry had his Glock 17 pistol on his hip. They removed them and asked Bill where to put them, so he said in the hall up by the door. Jamie asked Maria about the shotgun so she handed it to him.

'It's an auto-loader; twelve-gauge with seven-shot capacity. It fires 9mm buckshot or solid slugs- great for combat but not very good for pheasant, really! There's only nine pellets per cartridge, so you've got to get pretty close to guarantee a hit.'

Jamie smiled and said 'Nice!' before handing it back, then she took the two weapons and put them in the hall. Karen handed Emma two bottles of wine and she thanked her and got them all a glass. They stayed in the kitchen so they could talk while preparing the meal and Jamie went back to chopping vegetables with Jane while they chatted. Tom said they'd cleared the bodies and burned them out back and would bury

284

the remains the next day. Between them they'd cleaned and disinfected the relevant areas and the place was liveable now. There were four bedrooms, so they didn't need to use the ones where the bodies had been yet.

'Everything's a bit musty at the moment,' said Karen, 'but we're used to that and we've all slept in far worse places! There's a good supply of logs out the back and also inside, so we'll be okay for heating and cooking for a while.'

'The first thing we're going to do tomorrow,' said Harry, 'is to go shopping for some new clothes. None of us has any civvies and we've been living in three sets of musty uniforms for nearly a year! We noticed an M&S and a Next at the retail park in Bexhill, so we'll go there in the morning.'

'Amen to that!' said Maria.

It was a relaxed evening; the guests were great company and interesting to talk with, and they discussed many plans for the future. Later on, Jamie went out for a smoke and Maria said she'd join him. They stood in the cold air and chatted, the only other sounds being the calling of a tawny owl in the trees nearby and the horses in the stables. The sky was clear and filled with stars.

'I guess this is going to be a huge lifestyle change for you after the army,' said Jamie.

'Oh, man, tell me about it!' said Maria, laughing. 'But I'm looking at it as a new challenge; we all are. We've got a lot to learn in the years ahead about growing stuff and we're looking forward to learning from you guys.'

She hesitated for a second. 'I've heard from Harry and Tom that you and Jane have had some difficult moments and seen action. I just wanted to say good for you for looking after yourselves and doing what needed to be done. It's not easy for civilians with no training to do those sorts of things.'

Receiving praise and respect from this tough army career-woman was unexpected and Jamie felt a bit self-conscious. He smiled and mumbled slightly with his reply, looking down. 'Thank you, Maria. Well, you just have to do what's necessary sometimes.' They smiled at each other and went back inside.

The radios were proving extremely useful for exchanging news and arranging visits between them all, as they had imagined. They had agreed between them three times in the day when they would turn on the radios for thirty minutes in case anyone needed to get in contact, but said that they should keep the talking to a minimum to conserve the batteries. When the days lengthened and there was more daylight for the solar panels they would be able to talk for longer periods.

In the lead-up to Christmas they were able to make arrangements and discuss what they would all bring. Bill and Emma had decided to have everyone over to the farm; Matt and Zoe and their army friends had no fresh produce yet and it would have been a bit dismal for them to have Christmas dinner from tinned food. Megan and Sally scoured the area around the farm, collecting holly and fir-tree branches to make wreathes to hang in their houses. Bill, Peter and Jamie took the van to Tesco's warehouse and loaded it up with plenty of drinks and food. There were many sweet and savoury products that were still within their use-by date, which was good.

Maria said that she and Harry would provide Christmas dinner and asked Jane if she could borrow one of their hunting rifles; the L85A2 rifle they had was a decent weapon but it was no match for a proper hunting rifle over long distances. Two days before Christmas they came back with a fallow deer, which they butchered and hung in an outbuilding at the farm, and Max was happy to get the off-cuts they didn't need.

Christmas day was a joyous occasion, with Bill and Emma having a full house of nineteen people. Sarah and Georgie came, and Matt and Zoe with the twins, along with the four army folk. Emma and Jane split the cooking between them as they needed both ranges for all the food. Karen prepared various dishes at their place and brought them over, as did Zoe, Sarah and Georgie. They only got presents for the kids, which were mostly books and board games. Jamie and Jane found pocket identification books on trees, plants, wildlife and fish for Megan to carry when she went out, plus her first knife, which she would need for the future: it had a fixed four inch blade and a nice leather sheath. Jamie said he'd give her instruction on its safe use and she grinned and thanked them both.

After their Christmas dinner Bill got up to say a few words. 'Emma and I are so pleased to have you all here; Merry Christmas, everyone!' They all cheered, raised their glasses and said *Merry Christmas!* He went quiet for a few seconds and his face changed as he became serious. 'Well, it's been a very difficult year for everyone, to say the least. We've all lost family and friends to the plague and experienced hard times. Some of us have seen and done things that... Well, you know what I mean. No one in their wildest dreams could've imagined this happening eighteen months ago.'

He looked on the verge of tears and paused to compose himself. 'I'm not a religious person, but my mother was. If she were here now she'd probably be quoting from the Book of Revelation about The Four Horsemen of the Apocalypse, with Death riding out on his pale horse to kill with sword, famine and plague, and how it's come true. I don't know about that, but an apocalypse has certainly happened.

None of us knows what the future will bring, but I'm really happy that we've met all of you lovely people. We're going to have hard times ahead- I think we all know that- but it's going to be a lot better now that we've got each other to rely on for help. We all bring something different to the table in terms of skills, knowledge and experience and we're going to need all of it if we're to survive the difficult times ahead. Here's to us!' He raised his glass.

They all raised their glasses. '*To us!*' they repeated.

Over the next month winter tightened its grip and the temperature dropped below freezing regularly at night, with thick frosts covering the ground in the mornings, although there was no snow. Bill said it was the coldest they'd had at the farm for several years. Jamie and Jane were thankful for the smaller size of their new home as it was much easier to heat than the bungalow would have been in that weather. They still went there to collect salt, but less frequently now because of the temperature.

On trips into town they began seeing a few people here and there; the first they'd seen in Bexhill in over eight months. They stopped to talk when they could- or when people allowed them; some were wary of strangers and hurried on their way. Most were friendly, though, and they spent time talking with them: some were former refugees from the army camp, but others were folk returning to their homes after nearly a year away. These people had fled the town at the start of the plague to live with family or friends in rural areas: some said they would stay but others were returning just to collect things left behind in the panic.

Their four army friends had been busy with improvements at the house and they saw them regularly as they were just down the road. Harry and Maria dug a well in the garden, lining it with bricks, and built a covered structure around it with a bucket and winch. Maria had let her hair grow since arriving and without the severe crew-cut and army battle-dress she looked stunning, especially in the tight jeans and sweater that she often wore. Jane caught Jamie looking at her behind on one occasion and nudged him playfully in the ribs; he looked at her and just shrugged and they grinned at each other.

By the end of January Jane was looking rather big and had a distinct waddle to her stride. She was getting tired more frequently and finding it harder to do some things now, which she hated. Tom and Karen turned up at the farm one afternoon with a surprise for her. Knowing that Bill and Emma had mains power, they had driven to the Conquest hospital at Hastings and brought back an ultrasound machine so they could give her a scan. Jane was very moved by this and hugged them both, saying how grateful she was. She could imagine what horrors they must have seen at the hospital. They went into the spare bedroom at the farmhouse to conduct the scan and Karen told her that the baby looked healthy and everything seemed normal. Jane was relieved beyond words to hear that as she had been so worried in recent months.

'Do you want to know the sex?' asked Karen.

She thought for a second. 'Yes, please.'

'You're going to have a daughter,' she said, smiling.

Jane smiled and then burst into tears, hugging them both. She walked back across the yard with a little smile on her face. When she got inside Jamie and Megan were sitting expectantly on the sofa, holding hands.

'Well,' she said, grinning, 'everything looks normal and healthy. We're going to have a baby girl!'

'Oh, wow!' said Megan. 'I'm going to have a sister!'

Jamie just sat there speechless, with tears rolling down his cheeks.

Thirty-three

In the first week of February the weather worsened and they had a few days of heavy snow. It settled to around two inches deep on the ground, but in places had been blown into drifts over two feet deep. It looked like Max had never seen snow before as he was running around madly in his excitement, while Megan and Sally made a snowman in the top yard, complete with an old hat and scarf.

Jane's back and neck had been giving her pain for a while and Jamie gave her regular massages using some ointment Zoe had made, which helped ease the pain somewhat. Tom told her he had painkillers that would be safe for her to take if the pain got too bad, which she thanked him for but declined. Karen also spent time with them on several occasions, going through breathing exercises and procedure for when she went into labour. They told Megan over dinner one evening that the baby would have her name as a middle name, which made her smile and feel proud.

'Annie Megan Parker,' she repeated a few times, liking the sound of it.

By the following week the temperature had risen a few degrees and the snow started to thaw, turning the yard to slush. One morning, Jane came out of the kitchen and paused to look at Megan sitting at the table, surrounded by books and writing in her notebook. Her wavy blonde hair cascaded over her shoulders and she reached up with her left hand to tuck it behind her ear, as she often did. Jane smiled to herself, thinking once again how lucky they were to have found her and that she had survived the shooting and recovered fully.

Megan sensed her watching and looked up. 'What?' she asked, a curious smile on her face.

'Oh… Nothing, honey. I was just… I don't know; feeling grateful, I suppose, for having you in our lives.'

'You're not going to get all slushy on me and cry, are you?' she asked teasingly.

'I might,' Jane smiled. Megan grinned and tutted, rolling her eyes theatrically.

Jane went up to her and kissed the top of her head. 'How'd you like to come and help me choose some clothes for the baby and get some other supplies?'

'I'd love to, Mum. I've nearly finished my writing- won't be long.'

Jamie drove them into town in the Land Rover, leaving Max with Sally and Peter. They visited the pharmacies in the town centre first, picking up all the nappies they could find, along with other supplies they would need. They took everything that was left on the shelves and Jamie also broke into the store-rooms, where there was more stock.

Snow-drifts had piled in the shop doorways on Devonshire Road, which, along with the broken glass in some stores, made it look even more like an abandoned ghost-town. There wasn't a great choice for baby clothes there, though they found some. After that they drove to the retail park, where there was a better choice. It was the first time Megan had been there since the shooting and they were both a bit concerned about her, but she showed no signs of distress.

They went into M&S, where Jamie left the girls to look at baby clothes while he got some new things for himself, including some nice woollen jumpers, then it was onto Next and Boots for more of the same. Before entering each store Jamie stood outside listening for a while with the sawn-off on his shoulder, but there were no sounds of anyone else there. When they'd finished and were loading the bags into the truck they heard vehicles approaching.

Two vans appeared, drove into the car park and pulled up by Tesco's. Jamie took the sawn-off from his shoulder and held it down by his side, while Jane did the same with hers and cocked both barrels in readiness. Megan looked worried and moved close to Jane, putting her arm around her.

Three tough-looking guys climbed out, followed by two women. Two of them had L85A2 rifles over their shoulders and Jamie realised they must be ex-army, so he waved and said hi. Two of the men approached them and as they got nearer he recognised one as having been the guard on the gate the day he'd taken Megan to the army camp, so he relaxed somewhat. He in turn recognised Jamie, remembering that he knew Miller and Cunningham, and his demeanour changed as he also relaxed. They re-introduced themselves and shook hands. The guy- Baker- whistled to the other three and waved for them to come over.

Introductions were made, they all shook hands and stood chatting for a while. One of the women had been a nurse at the camp and she recognised Megan from her stay there, saying how well she looked. Jamie told them that the two Majors, Maria and Karen were just down the road from them and that they saw them all the time. The army guys said to pass on their regards and tell them where they were living, saying they should come and visit.

There were eight of them altogether- four couples who had paired up during the year since the plague- and they had found places close together in Cooden, near the golf course, as they'd all agreed that they wanted to be near the sea. They gave Jamie the location and he said he'd pass it on. The other woman asked them if they knew anywhere where they could get seeds for vegetables and salads. Jane grinned, pointing behind them to B&Q, saying there were plenty in the garden section there. She also told them of the pet and garden supplies shop by Sainsbury's and the garden centre at Bulverhythe, on the road to Hastings. The woman thanked them and said they would go there next. They said goodbye shortly afterwards and drove back to the farm.

By the third week of February the temperature had risen

further. The morning frosts had almost stopped and the ground became a bit more workable. Bill and Jamie gave a few of their seed potatoes and other vegetables to their army friends down the road to get them started with planting their own crops, for which they were grateful. They repaid the kindness with a couple of pheasant that Maria had shot.

One thing that had irked Jamie about their new home since moving in was the lack of a bathroom. So far they had made do with heating water and washing in the sink, and he had installed a bathroom lock on the door for privacy when they were washing, which would have to continue as there was no room for a separate bathroom. He was thinking of Jane now, though, and thought it would be nice for her to be able to have a bath of sorts, so she could soak in hot water to ease her aches. He thought of several possibilities, like a horse trough or similar, but discounted them as being a bit too ugly to have in the kitchen! He knew the sort of thing he wanted, but not where to find one. He spoke to Bill, who told him of a reclamation yard outside of Bexhill, on the Ninfield Road, where he might find something. He told Megan of his intention and she thought it was a great idea, saying she would come with him to help him look.

They set out one morning, telling Jane they were going to the bungalow to check the salt evaporation and leaving her resting on the sofa. Jamie took the Land Rover and drove into the village, then turned right onto the road to Ninfield.

'Dad, do you think Mum's going to be okay with the birth, now that there aren't any hospitals? I've been worried about it recently as we get nearer.'

He was worried, too, but he didn't want to pass that on to Megan. 'Of course she will, sweetheart. We've got Tom and Karen now, and both of them have experience of births from their time in the army. You mustn't worry, honey- everything will be okay.' Megan seemed a little happier by the fact that Jamie didn't seem worried and was confident.

At Ninfield they cut across back onto the Bexhill road and found the place after a mile or so, pulling into the yard and parking the truck. They got out, Jamie with the sawn-off over his shoulder, and stood listening for a while, but it was as quiet as a graveyard.

They walked around the yard looking at all the pieces of architectural salvage there: flagstones, cast-iron roll-top baths, doors, old log-burning stoves and numerous other interesting pieces. They couldn't see anything suitable outside so went into a large building where there was more stock. Jamie was just thinking it was a wasted trip when Megan called to him from the other side of the building. 'Dad, look at this!'

He went over to her. She had lifted a tarp and underneath was an old copper bathtub. It was dirty and full of cobwebs, but was just the sort of thing he had been hoping to find. He smiled at Megan. 'Perfect! I wasn't expecting a lovely copper one, though.' She grinned back at him. He found a broom and brushed out most of the cobwebs and other debris. It was about two-thirds the size of a normal bath and much thinner and lighter, with high sides. You certainly couldn't stretch out in it, but once filled you could have a good soak with your knees up. It was heavy but he was able to pick it up on his own so he carried it outside and put it in the truck.

He drove to the hardware store in Bexhill next and got some tins of Brasso metal polish, before heading back to the farm. Megan looked through the window and could see Jane sleeping on the sofa, so she gave a thumbs-up to Jamie and he carried the bathtub from the truck into the barn. He spent a couple of hours cleaning and polishing it to a high shine before going back to the house.

Later in the afternoon, as it was getting dark, Jane said she was going over to the farmhouse for a natter with Emma, which she often did at around that time. They knew she would be at least half an hour, and as soon as she had gone Jamie brought the now-gleaming tub from the barn and put it in the kitchen. They put more fuel in the range and stove to stoke them up and heated kettles and pans of water. As it neared the time when Jane would return they filled the tub and Megan added some bubble-bath then lit candles around the kitchen. They sat down on the sofa to wait and Jane came back shortly. She walked in and looked at them sitting there, knowing instantly that something was up.

'Okay you two scoundrels, what have you been up to?' she asked with a smile on her face.

'Well… You know how you've been wanting a bath for ages?' said Jamie. 'Have a look in the kitchen.'

Jane opened the door and gasped. 'Oh my God! Where did you get that?'

'Oh, we just found it somewhere,' said Megan, grinning.

Jane got all weepy, then hugged and kissed them both, saying how beautiful it looked. Jamie went upstairs and got her bath robe for her. She closed the door, got undressed and sank into the tub, laying her head back and revelling in the luxurious feeling of hot water covering her body for the first time in over a year.

Jamie wondered if it was time for Megan to learn how to shoot so he broached the subject with Jane one night.

'I don't see why not,' she said, 'but why not ask her what she thinks? She'll soon tell you if she's not ready or doesn't want to.'

He spoke to Megan over breakfast the following day, making it clear that it was her choice, but she thought it was a good idea and was optimistic.

'I mean, I've got to learn sometime and I already know how to strip the guns down, anyway.'

The next day, Jamie took her out with one of the lighter 20-bore shotguns. They walked two hundred yards from the farm and set up some pieces of plywood as targets. He gave her a good talk on gun safety and showed her how to tuck the stock tightly into her shoulder to prevent any bruising, and the first time she fired she gave a little squeal and grinned at him. He showed how the shot pattern spread with distance and the size of shot being used, and she could see the effects on the sheets of plywood, teaching her the effectiveness of the gun at different distances.

At one point she looked thoughtful and turned to him. 'I understand now how I survived the shooting, Dad. If they'd been closer, or if I hadn't been moving, I would have died, wouldn't I?'

'Probably, honey- or we both might have. It was a very brave thing you did and you almost certainly saved my life.' She hugged him and he kissed the top of her head.

'What happened to them, Dad? Did you kill them?'

Jamie looked down and closed his eyes tight, nodding. 'I thought you were dead, honey. I thought I'd lost you. I've never felt such rage and it all happened in a blur…'

Megan held him tighter. 'It's okay, Dad, I understand. I love you.'

'I love you, too, sweetheart.'

She got her first pheasant two days later when they went out with Max. She came back pleased as punch and showed Jane, who smiled and congratulated her.

By early March the first signs of spring were beginning to appear. Buds were swelling on the trees and the first shoots from some of their perennial herbs were emerging from the soil in the garden. Jane was pleased to see them as she walked around looking at everything. As their thoughts turned to warmer weather ahead and the prospect of al fresco dining, Jamie realised he'd left the chimenea at his flat and hadn't got around to collecting it and taking it to the bungalow. It would be a nice addition to their patio table and chairs for barbeques and also as a heat source on chillier evenings when they wanted to sit out. One morning at the end of the first week, when Jane and Megan were busy preparing rabbits in the kitchen, he found the keys to his flat and told them he was going to pick it up.

He drove the Toyota into town, parked outside the house and walked down the steps to his flat. It felt weird stepping into the place; he hadn't been back there since leaving for the bungalow in April and it seemed like an age ago, rather than just eleven months. The flat was cold and musty and he walked into each room in turn, remembering things from over the years.

He went into the lounge and sat on the sofa, looking at the CDs in the racks covered in dust. He remembered his brother coming over one night a couple of years before, and them getting drunk while listening to old music until the early hours. He smiled at first and then the pain of the memory hit him. He started crying as he thought of his family, looking at some of their photos on the walls and shelves.

The flat represented to him not just *his* old life, but the old world before the plague had come: society, films, TV, music, mortgages, bills, work, and many other things. So much had happened since that he felt like a different person. He had a partner and an adopted daughter now, both of whom he loved deeply, and very soon would have his own daughter; born into the ruins of a decimated country. He, Jane and Megan had had to fight for survival over the last year- literally, on several occasions- and it had changed him. He was tougher and more resilient now, but also far more grateful and appreciative of everything around him and of everything he had. Between them, and with Bill and Emma, Sarah and Georgie and the rest of their friends, they had laid the foundations for their survival in the bleak times that lay ahead.

Back at the farm, Jane was at the kitchen sink when she felt a spasm in her abdomen. She clutched the sink and bent over it, wincing. 'Ooh, blimey! Are you trying to tell me something, Annie?' She walked into the lounge clutching her belly and sat down on the sofa.

Megan looked at her. 'Are you okay, Mum?'

'Yes, honey, but I think it's started! I think she's decided to come earlier than I thought.'

'Oh my God! And Dad's not here!'

Jane smiled at her. 'Don't worry, sweetheart, I've probably got at least seven or eight hours more of this before anything happens!'

Megan didn't look particularly relieved by that and sat there fretting. She went and sat beside Jane, putting her arm around her and asking if there was anything she wanted.

'Well, I'd love a large whisky, but I'd better not have one! A cup of tea would be nice, though, please.' Megan went into the kitchen to put the kettle on and made them tea when the water had boiled.

Half an hour later Jane had another contraction. 'Ooh! I'll tell you what, honey; would you go over to the farmhouse, please, just to let them know that it's begun?'

Megan nodded and ran off as fast as she could, which made Jane smile, then she lay back on the sofa. Presently, Emma arrived with Megan.

Emma looked at her and smiled. 'And so it begins…' she said, sitting down next to Jane and holding her hand. 'Don't worry, my love, it'll be okay. I've sent Phil and Sophie to tell Tom and Karen that you've gone into labour.'

At his flat, oblivious to things happening back home, Jamie sighed and got up from the sofa, wiping his eyes on his sleeve. He went out to the courtyard and carried the chimenea through to the truck, securing it with pieces of wood and old blankets. He went back inside and took down the remaining family photos and also picked up an old family photo album that had got left behind, so he could show Jane and Megan. He took a last look around and then climbed into the truck and drove home. When he got back and parked in the yard, Megan came running out to greet him and tell him the news. He went inside and rushed over to Jane, kissing her and asking if she was okay.

'Yes, honey, everything's okay! Don't worry; we've got a long time yet.'

Shortly afterwards, Tom and Karen turned up and Karen took her upstairs for an examination, to see how far dilated she was. They came back down and said everything was going okay. To save her having to climb the stairs again they decided to use Megan's room behind the lounge and put a waterproof sheet on the bed. Jamie kicked himself for not having thought of that sooner.

Tom said 'Well, we might as well stay for the duration now we're here,' so they started preparing some food for everyone.

Bill went outside with Jamie and passed him a hip flask filled with brandy. 'Thought you might need this, mate!'

Jamie smiled and took a couple of mouthfuls, thanking

him. 'Bloody Hell, Bill, it's actually happening!'

'Don't worry, mate, everything will be okay.'

Harry and Maria arrived shortly to wish them luck. 'We won't stay,' said Maria, smiling. 'I'm sure you don't want a big audience! We'll come back later, after the birth. *Buena suerte!*' She kissed and hugged Jane, Megan and Jamie, and Harry kissed them and shook Jamie's hand warmly, then they departed. Over the next few hours Jane's contractions became stronger and more regular and she walked around as much as possible, puffing and breathing deeply as the pain increased. Phil, Sophie, Peter and Sally came over to give her their love and wish her luck, then departed so as not to crowd her.

Jamie supported her as she walked around the garden over several hours and he massaged her back and neck when they went back inside. They stoked up the stove in the lounge and left the door to Megan's room open to let the heat in and warm the room more. At one of their scheduled radio communication slots Emma went on air back at the farmhouse to tell their friends the news. Matt and Zoe must have been out as there was no response from them, but she spoke to Sarah and Georgie, who said they'd come over. They turned up half an hour later in the Land Rover and both women hugged Jane and kissed her. They sat with her talking while she gasped and clutched her belly at regular intervals, breathing deeply and sometimes getting up to walk around.

Eventually, at around seven in the evening, things began happening in earnest. Jane's waters broke and her contractions became much more frequent and stronger, so they went into the bedroom. The others left to go back to the farmhouse, leaving just Jamie, Megan and Emma. Megan's room was only small, but there was space beside the bed where Jamie could sit and hold Jane's hand, while Emma sat on the sofa holding Megan's hand in the lounge. Tom gave Jane a pethidine injection to help with the pain, which she was grateful for.

Jamie hated seeing her in pain and felt helpless, but he held her hand throughout, wiping her forehead with a damp cloth regularly and encouraging her to breathe and push as Tom advised. Finally, after another hour, with one final push and a scream from Jane the baby emerged. Tom and Karen checked it over and declared her healthy and everything normal. The baby gave its first howl and Jamie and Jane burst into tears: on the sofa in the lounge Emma and Megan heard the sound and they started crying, too. Karen wrapped her up and passed her to Jane, who looked down at this miraculous creation in her arms, tears streaming down her face. Jamie mopped her sweat-covered forehead and she looked up at him with a pain-tinged but incredibly happy smile.

'Look, Jamie; look what we've made! We've got a beautiful daughter. I love you so much, honey.'

Jamie was almost speechless, but he mumbled 'I love you, too, Jane. I'm so proud of you,' then bent down and kissed her. Jane passed the baby to him and he cradled her in his arms, gazing in wonder at his daughter and bending down to kiss her forehead.

'Hello, my darling Annie,' he said. 'Welcome to the New World.'

The End

About the author.

Tony Littlejohns was born in north London in the early sixties, the youngest of three siblings. He worked in engineering for twenty-one years after leaving school, but left after his divorce in 2001 to pursue other endeavours. From his voluntary work with Raleigh International between 2001 and 2006 he developed an interest in survival and bushcraft, having spent months living in the jungle while working on projects in Belize, and later work in Chile.

After fourteen rather itinerant years, moving around the UK for a variety of jobs, he settled in Bexhill-on-Sea, East Sussex, in 2015, where he now lives. He has had a love of writing and poetry for thirty years and always dreamed of writing a novel one day. One morning in late 2016, while walking on the beach after watching an apocalyptic film the night before, the first lines of a story came to him. The Hoffmann Plague is his first novel.

Printed in Great Britain
by Amazon